MEN OF THE NORTH
#6
NORTH
THE GENIUS

Books in this series

For the best reading experience and to avoid spoilers this is the recommended order to read the books.

To be alerted for new book releases sign up to my list at **www.elinpeer.com** and receive a free e-book as a welcome gift.

PLEASE NOTE

This book is intended for mature readers only, as it contains a few graphic scenes and some inappropriate language.
All characters are fictional and any likeness to a living person or organization is coincidental

DEDICATION

I dedicate this book to the quirky ones.
You're my tribe of people.

Elin

CHAPTER 1
Testing Sex-bots

Shelly

It was fascinating to watch Nmen have sex.

Even after two weeks of being at the research and development facility in the Northlands, I was still intrigued by how many different ways the men could have sex with the robots.

Sometimes I found myself looking at the replay of the test session with my head angled and brows furrowed. It blew my mind how creative some of the men were in finding new positions and how different sex was from one test person to the other.

Some of the men were in the room for less than five minutes, others played with the robots for close to an hour.

My job was to analyze the data we received from the sex-bots to help us perfect our product line. With sensors installed in the test robots some of the many things we could measure was which area of the robot was touched the most, how much pressure was applied, depth and speed of penetration, and of course how long each hole on the robot was in use.

Sitting in my office I was going over the reports from yesterday's five sessions. There was neither need nor time for me to watch all the sexual encounters, so I had preprogrammed the system to look for anything related to fetishes and a long list of keywords. In general, I relied on the statistics from the robots, as well as the men's commentary, which was recorded while they used the robot. The system was pretty good at ignoring grunting sounds that came out non-verbal, but today the report was full of incoherent nonsense that made it harder to read.

The system alerted me that a session had involved a fetish and I had just opened up to see for myself when a call came from Charlie, the man I worked for at Advanced Technologies. His hologram popped up in front of the video that was playing of test subject 44 and the sex-bot.

"May peace surround you," Charlie said and smiled at me. I almost laughed at his reaction when he turned his head and saw the video playing. It all happened so fast that most people would have missed it, but my eyes were trained to look for body language and I saw the micro-expression of contempt when Charlie lifted the corner of his mouth.

"May peace surround you too," I replied in a calm voice.

"What in the world is he doing?" Charlie nodded toward the Nman in the video. By now his expression had settled into wrinkling his nose up. "Is he smelling her feet?"

"He's a podophile."

"A what?"

"A foot fetishist."

The older man shook his head, and mumbled, "I don't know how you do it, Shelly, or why you chose *this* project."

"I'm a biologist; procreation is interesting to me."

"Yes, well, in this case it's more like an imitation of procreation, isn't it?"

I didn't answer the question since it was rhetorical. We both knew that these robots didn't collect semen like others of our models did.

"If all men were like that guy," I pointed with my chin to test subject number 44, who was currently licking the sex-bot's toes, "we would all be extinct. He prefers to use

2

her feet to jerk off and so far, he hasn't shown much interest in her reproductive parts."

Charlie stared at the sexual encounter without responding.

"How are things in the Motherlands?" I asked.

"Good." He cleared his throat. "Very good. But we miss you of course." Shaking his head as to clear his thoughts, he turned from the video to me. "Would you mind turning it off while we speak? I'm finding it rather distracting, not to mention disturbing."

Mindy, our newest sex-bot model, not yet released to market, was smiling and encouraging the Nman with a velvety-soft voice, whispering, "Don't stop, your tongue feels amazing." He complied just as I paused the video, leaving the naked Nman in a rather unflattering position with his eyes closed and his tongue far out of his mouth.

"Mindy looks beautiful. How are the men liking her?" Charlie asked.

I shrugged. "Number 44 looks like he's enjoying himself, don't you think?"

"You don't sound too excited."

"I just believe we could do better if we developed a new generation of models. Mindy is nice, but no real women look like her in real life. Her dimensions are obscure. Her eyes and lips are too big, breasts the size of hers would be too heavy to stand out as perkily as that in real life, and no woman has skin that flawless, legs that long, or a waistline that small."

"Shelly, Shelly, Shelly..." Charlie said in a sing-song voice. "We discussed this already. Sex-bots aren't supposed to look like real women. They are sexual fantasies of the perfect woman."

I gave him a pointed stare. "Nature has already perfected women over thousands of years. There's no need to make an artificial-looking sex-bot when Nmen are longing for the real thing. We should always design with biomimicry in mind. And besides, male sex-bots in the Motherlands look like real men, so why can't the female versions be the same?"

A line formed between Charlie's brows. "I agree that innovation should be inspired by nature, but in this case our previous research has shown that Nmen prefer the enhanced version of women. That's a fact."

"Hmm." I fiddled with my sleeve. "I would still like to put that to the test."

"Yes, you said that the last time we spoke. Did you interview some of the testers like you said you would?"

"Uh-huh. Seven so far."

"And did you follow my safety instructions?"

"Yes, the test subjects never saw me. I used the hostess-bot to ask the questions I wanted answers to."

"Good. I don't like the idea of you being alone up there in the Northlands. You could have done the same work from here with a remote connection."

"I told you it makes it easier for me to be on-site."

Charlie sighed. "Maybe, but if you saw the cost for your bodyguard you'd agree with me that it's excessive."

"You think any expense is excessive, but I hardly ever go anywhere, so it can't be that bad. Feel free to deduct from my personal points; I have plenty."

"Look, I don't want you to stay in the office because you're afraid of the expense for the bodyguard. We hired him to keep you safe when you go out and it's important to have balance in your life. So, go out, Shelly, I mean it."

"Women can go out without an escort now."

"It's too risky, Shelly, and my sources tell me that it's rare to see a woman by herself."

"As long as I use common sense and don't go down a dark alley or stay out after dark, it's fine."

"Shelly, you won't leave your office without security. It was part of the deal we made when you insisted on going to the Northlands and I expect you to honor it."

I gave a small sigh. "Of course."

"Good. Now tell me how your interview subjects responded to your idea."

"They were all positive about the idea of a natural version, but the problem is that when they were shown pictures of potential models for the robot, each chose a different woman."

"Well, that just goes to show that tastes differ, and what's ideal for one man isn't ideal for another."

"Which is why we should find a way to develop affordable robots for each person according to their preferences, tastes, and fetishes."

Charlie jerked his head back. "I can't believe you just said that. What an enormous waste of resources that would be. A personalized sex-bot for each man..." He shook his head. "That's not the Motlander way."

I sighed. "I know, but Nmen aren't like us. They don't like to share and since most of the men will never be with a real woman, a robot might be a good alternative to a life companion."

Charlie was dressed in a blue sweater with a large pink butterfly printed on the front. It looked soft and comfortable, which were the two main objectives for Motlander fashion. That, and the fabric's being produced without harming the environment in any way. With a thoughtful expression he pointed out, "You speak as if it's a must for a man to be paired with a woman to live a fulfilled life. Look around the Motherlands and tell me: how many men do you see that have that desire?"

"You can't compare Nmen and Motlander men," I pointed out. "You Motlander men are surrounded by women and grow up with mothers. Most Nmen never speak to a woman in their lifetime. To them the embrace of a woman is something they can only dream of."

Charlie shifted his balance. "That might have been true ten years ago, but today many are in a relationship."

I was so tired of hearing that myth. Crossing my arms, I drummed my fingers on my arms. "Five hundred thousand men in relationships might sound like many, but with a population of ten million, that's only five percent. The Northlands still have nine-and-a-half million single men and that, Charles, makes for a huge market. If we could find a way to produce the robots at an affordable price, it would improve the men's life quality. I know it would."

"Is that the psychologist in you speaking?" Charlie asked, referring to the fact that I had three different degrees. With the highest measured IQ in the Motherlands, learning had always been easy for me. I'd finished my psychology degree at the age of seventeen, my engineering degree at twenty, and my biology degree at twenty-two. After that I'd worked three years for Advanced Technologies, where I was now Charlie's head of design and engineering.

"Maybe it's not the psychologist in me, but the fact that I'm a caring person," I said in a flat tone.

Charlie looked at me like he didn't know if I was being serious.

"Of course you are," he said, a bit too slow, and underlined the lack of conviction by looking away. It hurt a little because all my years growing up in the Motherlands, I'd been told I was lacking empathy and social filters. Some joked that it came with being a genius, and there were days when it suited me fine. People mostly left me alone. Or at least they didn't come to me for advice on personal matters. It was for the best, since I tended to be logical about things and unwillingly upset people with my direct answers.

Still, there were days when I felt alone and wished I could swap my brain for a better social awareness that would make people like me. Maybe it would help if I learned how to stop myself from breaking into random lectures about things no one but me found interesting. Or if I stopped pointing out the inconvenient truths that normal people in the Motherlands would know not to say out loud. But why wouldn't people like to know that they had something stuck in their teeth, dandruff on their shoulders, or that they were bad cooks? And why should it be socially acceptable for people to fart and the rest of us to pretend we'd lost our sense of smell and not call them out on it?

"By the way," Charlie continued. "Congratulations on the design award for the CBC. Not that it wasn't expected, but still."

"Thank you."

"It seems prestigious design awards are raining down on us ever since we got you aboard the team." Charlie smiled and softened his voice. "I know you don't like it when I praise you too much, Shelly, but I'm proud of you. You should be proud too."

He was right. I didn't like attention or praise for my inventions and designs. Maybe because everyone, not least my mom, the famous and beloved councilwoman, Sheana Rene, had always expected me to grow up and do something remarkable with my genius – like find a cure for all disease or add an extra hundred years to the lifespan of humans. The pressure in my chest just from thinking about it made me close my eyes.

"You deserved that award," Charlie said with a nod.

"Not sure about that." I breathed and opened my eyes again. "It feels like I was cheating a little."

"Because you're a genius?"

"I don't like that word."

"It's not your fault the other nominees didn't have the luck of being born with a brain as brilliant as yours."

His words made me feel uncomfortable. It wasn't like I'd done anything to be this smart. Other nominees had worked for years on their products while I'd spent less than three months developing my ideas for the CBC product line before I began testing it on myself and others. CBC was short for Convenient Beauty Care and was developed for busy women like me who didn't prioritize going to a beauty salon. With my product, much of the work on my skin and nails was done while I slept. In the beginning it had taken some getting used to, but now it had become relaxing to fall asleep while my CBC device massaged my scalp and face. Often, I was fast asleep while my skin was being cleaned and treated.

I hadn't invented the device because I was a vain person. The truth was that as a teenager, I'd had terrible acne, not to mention a bushy unibrow. Plenty of well-meaning people had given me uninvited tips on fashion and beauty care for as long as I could remember. I'd never paid much attention since there were about a million other things more important to me. The idea for the CBC device had come to me when my sister, Rochelle, made a comment about a year ago. We had been at our mother's place when Rochelle pointed out that I was once again wearing a mismatched outfit, and that my nails were cracked and unmanicured.

"When are you going to take some pride in how you look? A weekly visit to the beauty parlor shouldn't be too hard," she complained.

"Don't have time," I responded.

"It's a priority, Shelly."

"Not to me."

That day Rochelle had turned to my mother with exasperation, "I swear, someday I'm going to sneak in and do Shelly's nails while she sleeps."

Those words had stayed with me for days and become my inspiration to design what had become the biggest must-have item this summer. Beauty had always been for other people, but waking up to see my skin glowing with health, and my nails shining with a new fun color, had become a highlight of my day, and I was amused when people from my past didn't recognize me with my new fancy haircut and new looks.

"Rumor has it you're up for the 2448 Designer of the Year Award," Charlie teased.

I shook my head. "You don't know that. They won't give nominations until December."

"Shelly, honey." He gave me that parental look of *I-know-what-I'm-talking-about*. "It will happen. If not next year then soon. You're amazing at what you do."

"Which is why you should trust me when it comes to the natural sex-bot," I said and raised an eyebrow. "I would also like to add some more fetishes to the programming of Mindy."

"Fetishes. What kind of fetishes?" He turned back to the frozen image of the Nman licking Mindy's toes. "Looks to me like Mindy already has that covered."

"Like her predecessors, Mindy only accommodates the most common and basic fetishes; why not expand that to include more? Who are we to judge? And the robots don't care."

Charlie rubbed his chin and chewed on his lips, making them disappear. My mind was analyzing as always and concluding that talking about sex made him feel uncomfortable. In a melodic voice inside my head, I used a rule to remember. *A thing you don't like to hear – will make your lips disappear.*

"You're not talking about the freaky stuff, are you?" he asked and again his nose wrinkled up a bit.

I lifted my shoulders in a shrug. "These past two weeks I've encountered fourteen different fetishes including voyeurism, sadism, masochism, nasolingus, pygophilia, titillagnia, urophilia, katoptronophilia, knismolagnia, podophilia, and a few others."

Charlie's eyes were wide and he blinked a few times. "Could you say it in English?"

9

Since he'd invited it, I began a small lecture. "Voyeurism means people who achieve arousal from watching others in sexual situations. Sadists like to inflict pain on others, while masochists like to receive pain. Nasolingus describes people who enjoy sucking on a person's nose. Pygophilia is one of the most common fetishes. It describes people who like to see, touch, and play with buttocks. I can't tell you how many of the Nmen touch, knead, and slap Mindy's butt." I continued explaining the fascinating kinds of fetishes. "Knismolagnia is for people who enjoy being tickled, while titillagnia is for the people who enjoy tickling others. Urophilia has to do with urination."

"Eww." Charlie scrunched up his face in shock.

"Katoptronophilia is for people who enjoy sex in front of mirrors, and we already talked about podophilia." When Charlie looked lost, I added. "Foot fetish, remember."

Charlie's chest rose in a slow inhalation before he exhaled audibly. "And you find this *interesting*?"

"You don't?"

"No." He shook his head vehemently. "I find it bizarre."

"It's no different from the Motherlands. Our test groups show similar findings."

"Hmm, I wasn't aware of that." Charlie rubbed his forehead.

"How about you? Do you have any fetishes yourself?" I asked out of curiosity.

His hand flew to his chest and he protested, "Shelly, that's a very inappropriate question to ask."

My eyes fell to his collarbone, avoiding his disapproving eyes. "My apologies."

I'd done it again. Crossed a social boundary without wanting to. An awkward silence stretched between us.

"Ehm, all right then." Charlie cleared his throat. "I'll check in with you in a few days again."

"Okay."

"Keep up the, ehm…" He looked to the film of Mindy and test subject 44. "Keep up the good work, Shelly."

"Thank you, Charlie, I'll do that, and say hi to the others."

With a wave of his hand he was gone and that was when I noticed the red light blinking an alert.

CHAPTER 2
A Fucking Favor

Marco

Two steps into my apartment, my low growl was growing to a shout. "Storm, where the fuck are you?"

I slammed the door behind me with my foot and stalked straight for Storm's bedroom banging on his door.

The deep bass from the music grew in volume when the door swung open and Storm raised his chin in a silent greeting.

"What did you do to my kitchen?"

Leaning his head out of the door, Storm looked at the gigantic mess in the open kitchen and shrugged. "Don't worry, I'll clean it up in a minute."

"How many times have I told you to clean up after yourself? I didn't agree that you could live here and trash my place."

"No one cleans anymore; it's so old-fashioned. Why don't you get a Home-Bot?"

"Do you have any idea how much those things cost? If you want to get one, be my guest, but until you do, clean up your shit." I didn't stay around to argue the point further.

Storm had needed a place to stay after his wife, Gennie, filed for a divorce five months ago. The two of them had been a mismatch from the beginning and after meeting her a few times, I agreed with him that the woman was crazy. The first month he lived here, I'd been sympathetic to his grief, but now my patience had run dry.

If Storm had been such a messy pig when he lived with Gennie, it was no wonder she had been arguing with him all the time.

With bare feet and only a pair of pants on, Storm began to clean up the kitchen while I made myself a cup of coffee.

"Gennie called today," he said.

"And?"

"And she wants me to sign the papers so she can remarry."

"Wow. Is she seeing someone?"

Storm brushed the crumbs from the table down onto the floor and let my old vacuum cleaner take care of it, while he moved over to do the dishes. "From what I hear, she's been seeing more than one." His voice was low.

"What are you going to do about it?"

He turned to look at me. "My gut tells me to fight for the marriage, but I think that ship has sailed. To be honest, I kinda wanna sign the papers and move on with my life. You know, let her be someone else's problem."

"And your pride?"

"I'm not the first Nman to regret marrying a Motlander. Those women are lunatics. Did I tell you Gennie wouldn't allow me to burp or fart in my own house?"

"Yes, you told me."

"And did I tell you she wanted me to call her every day while I was at work, and give up meat, beer, and swearing?" Storm shook his head. "I'm not saying all Motlanders are crazy because I've met some great ones at the school. But Gennie was an uncompromising and mean bitch."

"If it makes you feel better, those issues are normal among the mixed couples," I pointed out. "I've heard some of the same complaints from my friends."

"Doesn't it make you wonder why women like Gennie come here in the first place? For ten years couples have

13

been clashing over issues like these, and by now Motlanders who sign up for the Couples Matching Program should know what to expect from us Nmen.

"And vice versa," I said and protested when he put a crystal glass with the other glasses. "That thing is antique. It was a present from Boulder and Christina."

"You want to wash it yourself?" Storm asked.

"No, I want you to stop using it and I want you to wash it in your hands, carefully."

Closing the dishwasher, Storm started it and turned to me. "You're smart not to take part in the Matching Program. For every amazing woman, there's five crazy ones, if you ask me.

"At least Gennie and I had good sex while it lasted. My friend Henrik's wife won't touch his cock. She says it's ugly."

I laughed. "Maybe it is. Did you see it?"

"No."

Sipping my hot coffee, I joked. "I bet it's crooked as hell."

"Maybe, but she won't suck him or let him have anal sex with her either. I'm telling you, many of the Motlander wives are prudes."

I shrugged. "Sex is new to them. Maybe it's a matter of building trust."

"What are you now, a fucking sex therapist?"

"I wish. With all the problems mixed couples are having, I'll bet I could make a lot more money being a sex therapist than a mentor." I returned to drinking my coffee and after a few minutes of silence, I spoke again. "To be honest, all your pain does make me happy with my decision that I'll marry a Northlander."

Storm rolled his eyes. "Yeah, because that's working out great for you, right?"

He was referring to the fact that I'd already been in three tournaments and made it as one of five champions

14

twice. Both times, the brides had chosen someone else, which I blamed on the fact that the men chosen had both been wealthy.

"I have a good shot in the next tournament. I've been training hard."

Storm was kicking at a pair of shoes, moving them to the hallway. "Too bad the bride is ugly."

"Louisa isn't ugly."

"She's no beauty queen either, but I guess with a million dollars as your prize money, you can afford to give her some cosmetic surgery."

I smacked my tongue. "Some people are beautiful on the inside."

"Right. And you can always turn off the light when you have sex with her." Storm's tone was sarcastic.

"Shut the fuck up." I gave him a pointed stare over the rim of my coffee cup. "I'd take nice and ugly any day over crazy and beautiful."

"Fair enough, but what if Louisa is ugly *and* crazy? You've never spoken to her, so how would you know?"

"She's a Northlander, that's a good start."

"And if you don't win her?"

"Then I guess I'll have to wait for the next tournament."

"Just remember that you're getting older. The brides are only twenty-one and you're already thirty. Chances are they'll pick someone young and good-looking like me."

"Hey, I'm fucking handsome."

"Yeah, now, but soon you're going to grow fat and have a double chin," Storm teased. "This is your last chance to be picked and you know it."

Part of me knew that he was right. The age difference would be too significant if I had to wait a few more years. It was already something that concerned me now.

"Don't worry, man, there's always the Matching Program if you're desperate to get a wife. Maybe you'll have more luck with a Motlander bride than I did."

"I'm not desperate and I told you, I'm not interested in the Matching Program."

"In that case, have fun with the sex-bots." Storm stretched his arms and gave me a smile. "Speaking of which, I'm running late for a test run of the newest model. I heard she's phenomenal."

"Wait a minute. You got invited to try out a new model?"

"Uh-huh. I have to be there in forty minutes."

I scratched my beard. "That's odd. Why didn't I get an invitation? I fucking helped start the test group."

Storm threw up his hands. "I don't know, man. Maybe you're just not good at sex."

"Fuck you." I flipped him my finger.

"Then it's probably the age thing. You turned thirty and they need young virile men to test their bots." He grinned. "I'm sorry, but you're a senior now."

He ducked when I threw a spoon in his direction. "It's too bad that they didn't pick you," he continued. "You've got a lot of spunk left for an old guy."

Storm was twenty-three and had been my student for almost a year when he was thirteen. Back then we'd both been thrown into the first experimental school that mixed Northlander boys with Motlander children. He had stayed at the school until he was fifteen, while I'd gone on to start the second experimental school in the Northlands.

It was only two years ago that we'd reconnected.

"Tell you what," Storm said and looked at the time again. "You can take my spot and test the bot."

"No thanks."

"Come on, I know you want to and I've got a bunch of things that I need to get sorted anyway. You'd be doing me a favor."

"I said no."

Storm tilted his head. "Marco, I mean it. You'd be doing me a big fucking favor." His face split in a grin. "Get it? A *fucking* favor." He looked proud of his pun and couldn't stop grinning. "If they call you in later, I can go for you. They'll never know that we swapped, and honestly, it's all run by robots anyway. They don't give a fuck as long as you're an Nman."

My fingers drummed on the table. I had been tense for a few days and could use the release. "Okay, I'll do it."

"Great." Storm clapped his hands together. "Just give them my name and if the robots have facial recognition and call you out for not being me, tell them it's their fault for not sending you a VIP invitation. Remind them that you helped start the testing program up here."

I moved when the automatic vacuum cleaner came toward me. "That's right. I deserve to test that model."

When I passed Storm, he patted me on my shoulder. "Have fun, my friend. Test that bot to the limits."

"Will do," I said and opened the front door. The last thing I heard Storm say before I closed the door was "At least sex-bots aren't prudes."

CHAPTER 3
Awkward

Shelly

The red alert indicated that the Nman currently in session had asked for help. As protocol described, the alert automatically dispatched a service bot.

Researchers like myself only visited this facility on occasion and it was rare for us to interact with the test people.

I switched over to see images from the cameras in the test room and saw a man standing bent over Mindy, who wasn't moving.

The same service-bot who acted as the hostess, and who would have welcomed the man when he arrived, entered the room. "What's wrong?" she asked with a polite smile and moved toward Mindy.

"You tell me." The man raised himself up to his full height. From the way he stood with his back to me, I couldn't see his face but his brown curls and deep voice reminded me of someone from my past, and that alone made my pulse speed up.

It can't be him.

"We didn't even get started before she shut down. Guess you can call that a flaw in the design." He crossed his arms and leaned back on his heels. Like Mindy, the man was naked. He looked fit and strong like most Nmen, with defined muscles and broad shoulders.

It can't be Marco. I specifically made sure he wasn't included in the test group.

"If you give me a second, I'll run a quick reboot of Mindy." The service-bot didn't move while it attempted to

18

reboot the sex-bot. On my control panel I could see the system that was linked to all robots in this facility run a reboot on Mindy, but nothing happened.

"Let me try one more time," the service-bot said in a friendly tone.

Again, nothing happened and I sighed. This was the third time this week that Mindy had suffered a breakdown. I wasn't impressed with the engineers who had designed her, and I already had a long list of improvements I wanted to make before Mindy went into production.

After three attempts at rebooting Mindy, the service-bot apologized to the Nman. "I'm terribly sorry, but I'm afraid we'll have to reschedule your visit for some other time. Mindy is currently unresponsive and will need to have service done."

"Don't you have a spare that I can test?"

"Not at this time. I'm very sorry."

"Can I at least play with one of the older prototypes – you have some of those here, don't you?"

I tilted my head and narrowed my eyes. *That voice.*

"For you to play with a different prototype would serve no purpose. The testing of older robots has no relevance since they are already in production."

"I know, but now that I'm here, it's kinda disappointing to leave without..." He trailed off.

"Without what?" the service-bot asked and picked up Mindy from the floor like she weighed nothing.

"It would be disappointing to leave here without a release." The man sat down on the bed and I gasped when I saw his face.

It had been ten years but there was no doubt that it *was* Marco.

Taking a step back I stared at him. He looked even more handsome than I remembered, with his long curly brown hair and those eyes that had been full of mischief and challenge when we used to banter ten years ago. The Marco I remembered had been twenty years old and had brought out strange desires in me. This Marco was thirty and had me sweating from the sight of his naked body. With the way he sat leaned forward, I couldn't see his most private parts, but it still felt wrong watching him like this.

Don't be silly. What is visible you've already seen when the school visited that beach in the Motherlands. Marco was only wearing shorts then.

Except it wasn't the same, since the knowledge that he was bare excited me. Holy Mother Nature, he had packed on weight and muscle these past ten years. I couldn't take my eyes off him.

"We could reschedule you for tomorrow morning if you'd like," the service-bot offered.

Marco looked frustrated when he ran a hand through his hair. "I can't, I'll be working tomorrow morning."

The two of them talked about availability while my brain was running in circles. I was tempted to do the one thing I'd promised myself not to do which was reconnect to see if he remembered me.

It's been ten years; of course he doesn't remember. You were just a kid in his eyes and you only knew him for a few months.

I'd had such a crush on Marco back then, and he'd seen me as nothing but an annoying kid who was too smart for her own good.

For years after my time at the school, I'd casually asked about Marco when I spoke to Kya, the teacher at the school where Marco and I had both taught as assistant teachers. But six years ago, someone had shared with me that Marco had married and after that, I never asked again.

I watched in a haze as Marco pulled on a pair of pants with harsh movements that revealed how annoyed he was to have wasted his time.

Why is he here?

20

His name wasn't on the list, and even if it were, it wasn't normal for Nmen to have sex with others once married, but maybe sex-bots didn't count.

At the same time as Marco closed his pants and bent down to pick up his shoes, I stood in a room not far from him, frozen in an inner battle between desire and reason.

Let him walk away. He thought you were a nuisance when you knew him. You had nothing in common back then and you have even less in common now, the rational part of me argued.

But then Marco looked up and I got a full view of the face that I'd spend hours studying in secret when I was younger. Back then he'd had stubble; now his beard was full, dark, short and trimmed. His nose was just wide enough to be perfect, and then there were those incredible golden eyes framed by thick black lashes. My stomach did a somersault and all impulse control momentarily left the building.

I had to see if he remembered me.

With my heart hammering I released my ponytail and let my fingers comb through my thick dark hair. I didn't have a mirror, but the white camisole, long soft blue skirt, and sandals that I was wearing would have to do.

Stepping out into the hallway, I felt detached from my body when the crazy impulsive part of me walked to the test room and knocked on the door.

What are you doing? the rational part of me screamed. *This is going to be so awkward for both of you. What are you even going to say to him? You were never good with people. Hurry back to the office before he sees you.*

"Yeah?" Marco called from inside the room and looked up when I opened the door.

"Hey." His smile grew when he saw me.

"Hey." I smiled back, expecting Marco to say my name in recognition, but he didn't.

21

"Did management take pity on me after all?" he asked with his shirt in his hand and waved me closer. "You're not an old prototype though; I've never tested you before."

He thinks I'm a robot.

It was so awkward that I didn't know what to say.

Told you this was a mistake. He doesn't have fond memories of you, because he doesn't remember you at all. If he did, he'd recall that he used to call you Brainy and make fun of you.

While I stood hiding my disappointment behind a smile, Marco moved into my personal space and let his finger run down my bare shoulder. It sent shock waves down my spine.

Please remember me, I willed him, although logically, I knew it had been ten years and that as a late bloomer, my transformation into becoming a woman had happened after we had last met. I looked nothing like the child he had once known.

Say something, tell him you're Shelly... come on, don't just stand here with a stiff smile on your face.

"You want to have some fun with me?" he asked with a charming smile that left even the rational part of me in a puddle on the floor. I should have resisted when he pulled the strap of my camisole down over my shoulder. I should definitely have objected when he cupped my breast. *Come on, Shelly, say your name*, I urged with my inner voice, but when I opened my mouth to speak it was something else that came out.

"Does your wife know that you're here?"

He looked up. "My wife? That's an odd question."

I kept my face passive, waiting for an answer.

"No. I'm not married."

"You're not?"

Marco looked like he just remembered something. "Wait, what I meant to say is that Gennie will soon be my ex-wife."

He was a bad liar and rubbed his nose before muttering, "Anyway, I don't want to discuss her."

"Understood."

Understood? Really? With that kind of robotic answer it was no wonder he didn't think I was human.

"Good, then why don't we focus on some more pleasurable things?" Marco took my hand and the craziest thought entered my head. *I could have sex with Marco, right here and right now.*

This might be my only chance.

It would just be an experiment.

No one would find out.

I rubbed my temple to clear my head from the craziness, but it didn't help.

I wasn't interested in a relationship with a man, but I was curious about sex, and the only man I'd ever felt physically attracted to was standing right here in front of me asking me to have sex with him.

With a racing heart I ignored all the alerts in my head.

Sure, this wasn't how I'd imagined making love to Marco in my teenage fantasies, but in a way pretending to be a sex-bot had advantages, and my brain ran a quick analysis.

1: We could keep all emotions out of the sex and avoid any awkward conversations about the past.

2: This would be excellent research in terms of my natural woman sex-bot idea.

3: Marco would never have to know my real identity.

4: He came here for sex, and I would give him what he wanted as well as fulfilling one of my own desires. It would be a win-win situation and no one would get hurt.

After justifying it to myself, my decision was made. Smiling at him, I said, "We're sorry about Mindy's meltdown. On behalf of the management I'm here to offer you an upgrade."

Marco gave me a quizzical smile. "Upgrade?" The way his eyes roamed down my body made me aware that I did not have the impossible measurements of a sex-bot.

"My name is Natura and I'm the next generation of sex-bots," I lied. Natura was a very common name in the Motherlands and one that I had jotted down on my notes weeks ago.

"Pretty name," Marco said and with a playful smile he walked over to the bed and stripped back out if his clothes before he threw himself on top of the blue sheets. "I'm intrigued," he said and lifted himself to his elbows to study me.

Move seductively toward him, I ordered myself but my brain was currently busy just breathing and keeping that stupid smile plastered on my face. This was incredibly awkward.

"Tell me about your upgrades. What's so special about you?" With a curious smile, he waved me closer.

I licked my lips and finally managed to walk slowly toward the bed. My impression of a sexy swagger became a clumsy hand on my hip and some stiff steps that would hardly impress any man.

"I'm... I'm the closest thing to a real female that has ever been created. For now I'm just a prototype and the testing of my functions wasn't supposed to happen yet, but with Mindy's breaking down, management decided to let you test me."

"Lucky me." Marco reached out to me. "Come here, I want to touch you."

My heart was thumping full speed and my smile was a grimace when I stopped by the bed and took his outstretched hand.

"Sit," he ordered and I quickly complied.

Up close Marco's eyes were even more breathtaking, with those green specks mixed with the brown colors that I liked so much. He had a faded scar under his eye and one

24

larger scar by his temple that hadn't been there ten years ago, but one thing that hadn't changed was his full lips that I had imagined kissing so often. When he smiled, one of his lower front teeth was a bit crooked – a detail I'd forgotten about him.

To me, Marco was still the most attractive man in the world.

"What was your name again?" he asked.

"Natu… Natura," I stammered when he got up on his knees and started investigating me. With him naked and on his knees, a certain part of him came so close to my face that I had to close my eyes to avoid hyperventilating.

"You're different," he muttered. "You even flush red. Why would they make a sex-bot shy?"

Thinking fast, I came up with an answer. "That's because of the virgin program that I come with."

"The virgin program?" Marco lifted my long brown hair and sniffed the skin on my neck. "You smell good."

"Thank you."

His strong hands were searching my scalp and I knew he was looking for uneven surfaces. He was an experienced tester and knew weak spots were often hidden underneath the hair. With me he found none.

"Your hair looks and feels very natural, and your scalp is smooth."

"That's because I'm an upgrade. It's real hair," I assured him.

"Impressive." He leaned closer and looked deeply into my eyes. "Wow, your pupils even dilate and contract. Someone has really done a good job making you."

I smiled and this time it was more genuine.

"The virgin program," he muttered again and started undressing me. "Is that why you aren't dressed in sexy lingerie? I've never seen a sex-bot with this many clothes on."

"Yes. It's part of the authentic experience of being with a real woman and getting to undress her."

"What is the virgin program exactly?"

My design ideas helped me answer his question. "Ehm, I will learn as I partake in sexual activity, but since you're my first... sex partner, I have no experience and will need you to teach me."

"Fascinating." Marco brushed his thumb over my fingernails. "Am I really the first to test you?"

"Yes."

"What about the engineers? Haven't they at least taken you for a spin?"

"A spin?" I tilted my head. "The engineers that created me are female, and none of them have spun me around. Would you like me to spin for you?" I'd never observed any of the Nmen asking Mindy to spin for them, but if it turned Marco on, I was willing to do it.

He chuckled. "Never mind. You might not be the typical sex-bot, but your shyness is definitely a novelty and you're cute."

"Thank you. Also, management would appreciate if you kept this experience to yourself since my model isn't supposed to be tested yet. Mindy is being fixed as we speak and she'll return soon."

"I can be discreet and I'm honored to be given this opportunity. Now lift your arms," Marco instructed and removed my white camisole. "Huh!" he said and studied my breasts. "How odd."

I felt humiliated and hurt by his reaction and instinctively covered myself with my hands, looking away. It was such a stupid plan. How could I have thought he would be interested in me when just down the street he had access to unlimited sex-bots with perfect dimensions, not to mention a variety of programs designed for his pleasure. Charlie had been right; Nmen preferred artificially improved sex-bots.

"Don't do that," Marco said and pulled at my hands. "Let me see you."

"You don't like what you see."

"I do, I'm just surprised they made your tits this small."

My breasts weren't small. They were a normal handful but compared to sex-bots most women would seem small-breasted.

"Do they expand?" He cupped them as to feel their weight and squeezed my nipples, probably looking to see if there was a size regulator in them.

"No, they don't expand. I told you, I'm meant to be like a real woman and real women come with breasts of all sizes."

In his explorative state of mind, Marco leaned in and suckled on one of my nipples. The tingle that ran from my breast and down south made me jerk and give a small sound of surprise.

"You feel incredibly soft and I swear I felt…" He leaned in with his ear to my chest and stayed like that for a few seconds until he looked up again. "Shit, they even gave you a heartbeat."

"Yes, and it speeds up and down depending on what I'm doing," I explained.

"Kudos to the engineer who made you." Marco's eyes shone with excitement. "I'm really happy Mindy broke down today."

"You are?"

"Open your mouth," Marco instructed. When I did, he examined my mouth like a curious boy inspecting his new toy. "It looks completely real."

"I know."

"Can you retract your teeth when you do oral?"

"No, a normal woman doesn't have retractable teeth."

"Huh. Come here, I want to try something." With excitement, he turned my head to his crotch. "Suck me."

I was staring at his huge instrument and it was terrifying.

"Come on, Natura, just open your mouth and blow me," he said and pressed his tip against my lips.

You wanted this, I reminded myself and opened my mouth a tiny bit.

"Open up wider," he coaxed and grinned when I looked up at him. "That's it, pretty girl, open your mouth and let me test how real you feel."

It felt like he forced my jaw open with his insistent pushing and my eyes watered when he started rocking back and forth.

"Son of the Devil, you feel good." He moaned and closed his eyes. "Good girl, take it all." With a hand behind my neck he pressed his cock down my throat and thrust a few times before I broke free, coughing and heaving for air.

"What's wrong?" he asked with deep frown lines on his face.

"You're suffocating me," I managed to say between two fits of coughing.

"You have to *breathe*?" Marco sat back on his haunches and ran a hand through his hair. "Look, it's impressive that you're so close to the real thing and all but giving you a gag reflex and the need to breathe, that's just stupid. Who the fuck would do that?"

"That's how real women are. They breathe, you know," I defended myself.

"Yeah, fair enough, but you should record this in your log. First tester isn't happy with gag reflex and your need to breathe. Those two functions should be suspended during oral. And adding teeth retraction would be great as well."

"Noted," I said dryly and drew a last deep breath through my nose before I felt all right again.

"Why don't you take off your panties and let me inspect your pussy? Marco used a matter-of-fact tone.

After his last comment that he wasn't happy, I didn't feel like exposing more of my imperfect body. "Would you like to end the session? Maybe I could go and see if Mindy is ready for use." I got up from the bed, grabbing my white camisole and walking toward the door.

"Hold it!" Marco called behind me. "I don't want to end the session and you'll come back here right now."

With my eyes closed and my shoulders low, I returned, just like a robot would.

"Take off your panties," he repeated and with mechanical movements, I tugged at them.

"Not like that," he stopped me with a hand. "Play some music and dance for me."

Shoot – all bots were connected to the sound system, but I wasn't and on top of that I couldn't dance.

"I'm sorry, but that's not part of the virgin program."

"Huh!" He scratched his short beard. "Then what is?"

"It's recommended to make a virgin feel safe and be gentle with her," I said, looking down.

"All right. So how do I do that?"

I hesitated before I answered. "Maybe stick to the basics and go from there."

Marco sat quietly on the bed, and for a second I thought he'd lost interest in me, but then he got up to stand in front of me and lifted my chin. "How about we start with a kiss then?"

CHAPTER 4
Virgin Sex-Bot

Marco

The sex-bot's eyes blew my mind. I'd always felt that eyes were the mirrors of people's souls, so it confused the hell out of me that I was gazing into artificial eyes and reading emotions.

Natura was shy and uncertain – and it was all there in her eyes. I'd seen lifelike artificial eyes before but someone had worked wonders with this sex-bot, because she made me *feel* shit. The way she flushed red, stammered when she got nervous, and couldn't look me in the eye when she was shy; I could fully imagine a young virgin would be just like that, and when she almost fled the room I had actually felt remorse for shoving my cock down her throat.

Over the last eight years, I had tested plenty of sex-bots, but to train one as I would train a woman spoke to my protective side. I indulged in the fantasy that she was real and smiled before I kissed her. At first she was tense but when I pulled back and gave her a smile, she relaxed a little.

"You said I'm your first tester. Will others get to test you later today?"

"No, it was only because you were already here. There were two other tests planned for Mindy today, and as protocol describes, they'll be rescheduled.

"Does that mean we have no time limit?" I asked. "Can I keep you all night?"

Natura looked surprised. "I can't confirm that. Your request has been directed to the management team."

"Good. Tell them that I'm very disappointed Mindy is down and that I want to spend the night with you in compensation."

"All right. Message sent." Natura sounded a bit too monotone, so I made a comment for the log.

"Note to designer. Voice became robotic just now."

Natura blinked and looked down.

"Hey." I kissed her again and backed her to the bed while letting my hands move down her back. "It's okay," I whispered. "We're going to take it slow and make love all night and I'll leave your designers all my notes."

She was quiet and let me push her gently down on the bed.

"Let me see how good a job they did with this part of you." I smiled and slid my hands down her hips and thighs. "What the fuck?" I touched again and leaned in to see closer. "Is that tiny hairs on your thigh?"

Natura stiffened and watched me examine her.

"How is that possible?" The hairs were so fine and blond that they weren't visible unless you looked closely. I blew on them and was fascinated with the way they lifted from her skin and how real it made her look. My eyes went to her arms and I saw it was the same thing. "Wait, I want to try something." Getting out of bed I grabbed the pitcher with water, fishing out an ice cube.

"What are you doing?" she asked.

"I want to test something." She didn't protest when I placed the ice cube on her thigh and watched in fascination as her skin reacted, creating little goosebumps. "Incredible," I breathed. "Your hair is real and your skin is real too, I don't understand.

"My skin was grown from human tissue," she clarified.

I narrowed my eyes. "Wow, I can't believe that's possible – is that even legal?"

"Of course; human skin is grown and used for transplants in case of traumas all the time. So far it's been

31

too costly to use on robots but I'm a prototype designed to test if the men of the Northlands are willing to pay a higher price for the experience of something close to human," Natura explained. "I'm meant to be more than a sex-bot."

"More?"

"A companion."

"Huh! How much higher a price are we talking about?" I asked.

"The price hasn't been determined yet."

"Huh!" I removed her panties, spread her legs, and touched the triangle of dark hair on her pussy. "Nice."

"You like it?" she asked with that adorable shyness.

"Uh-huh," I said distractedly because I was busy spreading her folds and checking the details. It confused me that I didn't see any of the normal signs of fabrication. There wasn't a line along the inner thighs and I wondered how they would take out the lower area for cleaning. "How does your hygiene program work?"

"I shower, like real women."

"No way!" I exclaimed. "You're serious?"

"Yes. I shower just like you do."

"No." I took a minute to look at her lying on the bed, ready for me with her legs spread and her eyes full of... what? I pulled back when I noticed her chest rising and sinking rapidly, her eyes fixed on me, and her pupils dilated. "Are you okay?" I asked.

"Yes, I'm just nervous. It's part of the virgin program."

"Then let's get that virginity taken care of so you can enjoy it." It sounded lame even to me. The thought that a sex-bot could enjoy sex was wishful thinking, of course, but Natura was so realistic that I indulged in the fantasy that she *was* real. "Do you have a lubrication function?"

"Yes, but it's activated by foreplay."

"Interesting." I lowered my head and let my tongue touch her soft folds, expecting a chemical taste. My eyes widened as it was anything but. "You taste different."

"Bad?"

"No, just different. I can't compare it to real women, but I like it."

Natura relaxed a bit as I kept licking her and massaging her with my fingers.

"Note to designer, the small moans are arousing and sounds very realistic, at least compared to the old porn I've seen from the past," I commented. "The temperature and softness of her insides are well done too, but she feels small."

Natura followed my movements with her eyes. She looked so pretty and innocent.

"Does your virgin program reset for every client or will you eventually become an experienced lover?"

"That part hasn't been decided yet. Management is still figuring out what functions to program me with."

"You're wet enough," I concluded out loud and spread her legs while lowering myself on top of her.

The sex-bot tensed up when I pressed the tip of my cock inside her. I creased my brows when I didn't just slide right in. "I think they made you too narrow," I said and pressed a little harder.

A sound of pain escaped Natura and it made me stop. Sure, I knew there were programs for men who enjoyed abusing sex-bots and the bots would pretend to be hurting, but we weren't playing that sort of game. Why was she closing her eyes and tensing up like that? I pressed even harder but it was like there was a wall of resistance.

"Fuck!" I breathed and let my head fall. "Note to designer, prototype has major flaw. Pussy too small for intercourse."

"It's because I'm a virgin," Natura said, her eyes almost teary. "And you're very large."

"Excuse me?" I stared at her, wondering why she was pretending to be so emotional. Why would anyone think that would be a turn-on for men?

"Females have a hymen that traditionally proved to the man that he was the first to be with her. This was important in the past because a man needed to be sure that he wasn't marrying an already pregnant woman and supporting another man's offspring."

"Say what?" I scrunched up my face.

"Since my model is designed to be sold to private consumers, the idea is to guarantee the buyer that he's the first to use the robot."

"Ah, that makes sense."

"You'll have to push through that wrapping," she instructed.

"Okay, but if you're wrong it's going to be painful for me too. I don't feel like banging my dick against a wall much."

"The hymen will break if you push through it," Natura insisted.

"Are you sure it's not a design flaw and you're just covering it up with a story?" I rocked back and forth slowly, enjoying the feel of the tip of my cock inside her. I had never heard of such a thing.

"Yes, I'm sure."

"But won't I break you if I push through?"

"No."

"Will it be restored for the next test person?"

"No, it doesn't work like that."

"Note to designer, sex-bot sounds a bit flat in her tone of voice some times. Try giving her a more amorous or flirtatious tone."

Placing her hands on my shoulders, she bit down on her lower lip with a determined expression on her pretty face.

On impulse, I kissed her and just kept rocking in and out with only the tip of my cock. She was a bit clumsy in her kissing, eager and inexperienced at the same time.

"Don't push your tongue down my throat. Do like this," I instructed and taught her how I liked to kiss. She was a quick study and imitated the way I nibbled on her lips and played with her tongue.

With my focus on our kissing, my cock grew impatient and my hip movements became harder and deeper. Natura arched and made sounds of discomfort, but I figured it was all part of the program and designed for men who were turned on by that sort of thing.

I pushed in and out with greater force now and our breathing grew heavier. She still felt incredibly tight, but I could feel her insides adjusting to my size.

"It feels good now, and I like the feature with her breathing matching mine."

Natura leaned her head back and lifted her arms, her mouth open and her eyes closed.

"She looks like she enjoys it." I noted to the designers, "That's good."

"I do enjoy it," Natura breathed and met my thrusts with a rocking movement of her pelvis.

"Can you do any dirty talking?" I asked before I suckled on her nipple.

"Dirty talk?"

"Just whisper something arousing in my ear."

"Right." She looked uncertain.

"Don't tell me I have to teach you that too."

"No..." She licked her lips and slid her hands into my hair. "You feel so big inside of me."

"That's right. Go on." It was my turn to close my eyes and pretend that Natura was a real woman who wanted me.

"I love your strong body and the way you fill me."

"With what, babe? Say the word."

"With your…" She trailed off.

"I fill you with my large what?" I pushed in deep and watched her eyebrows draw together.

"With your erection."

"Cock, babe, I want you to say cock."

"Okay…" She stopped talking when I picked up the pace and her moans grew deeper, her hands on my shoulders gripping firmer.

"Yes, yes," she breathed into my ear and this time her tone was anything but flat.

My balls tightened and I had to pull out to prevent myself from coming. Supporting my weight on my forearms, I kept close to her and whispered into her ears. "I wish this was real."

Her nails bore into my shoulders.

"I really wish that you were mine and that I'd won you in a tournament."

She didn't answer me, but then, how could she? Natura was a robot designed to satisfy men's sexual fantasies of a woman. She had no clue about the outside world and was only an imitation of my deepest desire.

I'd never taken a sex-bot missionary style, and I thought about turning her around and trying other positions. Yet, something kept me between her legs, face to face with her. Sex with Natura was somehow different and more intimate than with any of the other robots I'd been with. She felt so incredibly realistic to me.

"Don't stop," she whispered, and caressed my face.

I leaned in and kissed her deep, pouring all the longing for closeness and love that I felt in my heart into that kiss. Someday, I hoped to find the real thing and experience making love to my wife like this.

Natura responded with the same burning passion, and I had to catch my breath after our kiss.

"You're learning fast," I noted and smiled at her.

"Thank you."

"You sure you don't know how much pricier you'd be than the other models? I sure hope I can afford it."

Natura smiled back at me. "Management will be pleased to hear that you're satisfied."

"Not quite yet." I began moving again. Sliding in and out of her without a problem now. "First I'll come inside you."

Her eyes widened. "How about you come on my belly instead?"

"No, I want to come inside you."

"It's better if you come on my belly or breasts."

I kept rotating my hips, and pressed deeper, my right elbow supporting my weight while my left hand played with her tits. "How cute that you argue with me. What a clever way of making it seem authentic."

"I'm not trying to argue with you." Her low moans grew in volume. "I just really want to... ehm... see what it looks like when you come."

"Too bad, sweetie. This is *my* fantasy and I'm filling you up with my babies."

"I'm a sex-bot, you can't impregnate me, so why not come on..."

"Shhh..."

She didn't protest when I fucked her harder.

"Wrap your legs around my hips as if you want to hold on to me."

Natura complied and I imagined this was my wedding night and my wife was giving herself to me.

"You like it, don't you?"

"Yeeees."

Her body arched against me, her heels digging into my butt and her hands grabbing my shoulders like she was holding on for dear life. "Yeees."

The moment her inner pump started milking my cock and she exploded in a simulated orgasm was timed to perfection. I closed my eyes and let go of my own euphoria, focusing on my sexual fantasy of impregnating my future wife.

I was squeezing her with my large body and usually it didn't matter since the sex-bots were designed to withstand it, but Natura pushed at me complaining that she couldn't breathe.

I rolled to her side, catching my breath and looking her over. "Note to designer, the breathing function is annoying and limits how long the user can lie on top of her after sex. On a positive note, model looks gorgeous with flushed cheeks and dilated pupils."

Natura turned her face and in a soft voice she asked, "You think I look gorgeous?"

"Uh-huh. Oh, and note to designer, the part about her inner pump only activating when simulating an orgasm is new. All other models I've tried have been able to turn the function on and off depending on preference."

Natura looked at me. "Anything else you'd like to add?"

"Yes, I'm impressed with how authentic you look. Especially your eyes. I've seen lifelike eyes on robots before, but it's almost as if yours shine with intelligence and..."

"And what?"

I chuckled. "I was going to say emotions, but that just sounds stupid."

"New technology."

"Yeah, but it's like you have actual feelings."

"I've been programmed to read body language and tone of voice, and to decipher humor. If you feel I'm providing a natural response to your behavior, that's a sign that the design team behind my model have succeeded."

"How come you can talk about things like this?"

Natura looked up at the ceiling. "While my sexual program is limited to begin with, I'm equipped with programs for casual and stimulating conversation. I'm meant to be a companion, not just a sex-bot."

"No way!" I rubbed my nose and smiled.

"I can also do a bit of humor."

"With a robot like you, there's no need to marry a real woman," I joked. "Can I teach you to cook too?"

Natura looked away. "So far cooking isn't included in the prototype of my model."

Just when she said it her stomach growled.

"What was that?" I asked.

She looked flustered. "Just another authenticity feature imitating hunger to make me seem more human."

I narrowed my eyes. "Look, I get that somewhere in the Motherlands an engineer had a field day creating the closest thing to a real woman, but if you tell me that you fart and burp too, I have to draw the line. That's just not charming or attractive in a woman."

Natura gave me a small smile. "Some might disagree. There are people who get aroused by that sort of thing."

"Not me. Note to designer, I truly like this model, but maybe find a balance between real and practical." I turned her face from side to side, studying it. "And maybe make her a bit less polished. It's only real up-close that I can see her imperfections." I licked her skin. "You taste salty, like real sweat. That's a genius detail."

She raised an eyebrow.

"Do you know if they'll make your model in different variations?"

"You mean a model with bigger breasts?" she asked in the dry tone she had used before.

"I'm just curious if there's going to be different skin tones, hair colors, height, and all that."

"I don't know."

"Are you modeled after a real woman?"

"Yes."

"Not a living one, I hope?"

39

"Why?"

I thought it was self-explanatory, but still answered. "Because who would want to have a sex-bot made in your image? In case the poor woman ever came to the Northlands, every man here would associate her with a whore."

Her large brown eyes blinked before she got out of the bed. "On behalf of management, I thank you for taking the time to test me. Your input is valued."

"Hey, wait a minute. You said you didn't have any testers after me, so why can't I spend more time with you? I would love to go a few more rounds. Maybe you could pretend to be my wife or something. I would like that."

"I'm afraid your request to spend the night with me has been declined." Natura kept dressing herself, with her back to me.

"Note to designer. You've got to work on the post-sex behavior of the model. Her voice has gone back to flat and she seems dismissive, like she wants me gone. That's not going to entice clients at whorehouses to wanna come back."

Natura put on her clothes and sandals and walked to the door. Her long shiny brown hair flicked back when she gave me a last look over her shoulder and exited the door.

Why the hell did I feel like I'd hurt a dead thing? That shouldn't be possible. Sex-bots were flirtatious and fun. None of them expressed emotions except lust and joy.

Whatever the engineers had cooked up in their laboratory this time, it came with a scary side effect. That Natura machine was real enough to make you feel things, and it confused the hell out of me.

CHAPTER 5
Dumb Genius

Shelly

For someone with a sky-high IQ I was unbelievably stupid. For eight days now, I'd been trying to make sense of my crazy behavior.

I slept with Marco.

I actually slept with Marco.

Hundreds of times, I'd repeated the words in my head, but they still felt unreal to me.

I'd seen enough Nmen having sex to know that it reduced otherwise sensible people to nature-driven horny primates.

But the sounds I had made when I was with him. The way I had moaned and arched my body. I closed my eyes.

It was the most embarrassing thirty minutes of my life.

It was the most amazing thirty minutes of my life.

I was unable to connect the person I'd become in that room with Marco to how I saw myself.

Shameful over my behavior, and shocked that I'd allowed him to come inside me, I blamed myself again and again.

Regretting it.

Not regretting it.

Regretting it again.

Getting pregnant from one time of having sex was unlikely. But I wasn't a risk taker by nature, so why hadn't I stopped him?

Because a sex-bot didn't say no. It would have blown my cover, and I wouldn't have known how to handle that humiliation.

41

I ignored the little voice saying that I had found his words of shooting his babies inside of me arousing. I wasn't the kind of woman to dream about husband and kids, so why had it turned me on? Just thinking about it made me cringe, and the only explanation I could find was that the need to procreate was a predisposition from ancient times that had served to secure the survival of the human race.

Now that my hormone levels had returned to normal, I was determined to take what had happened in that room with me to my grave. No one could know about what I'd done. Especially not Marco.

It was close to six p.m. when the hostess-bot alerted me that someone was asking for entry to our office building.

We didn't have any test sessions planned for today, and my heart began thumping fast in my chest as I thought that maybe Marco had returned.

A look at the outside camera revealed that it wasn't Marco but my friend Tristan who wanted in.

I had the service-bot unlock the front door and let him in before I walked out in the hallway to greet him.

"Hi there, I'm looking for Shelly Summers," Tristan said and waved at me.

"Very funny." I grinned and opened my arms.

Tristan almost picked me up when he squeezed me in a tight hug. "I just haven't gotten used to seeing you so pretty, yet."

"Are you saying I wasn't pretty before?"

He laughed. "Your beauty has always shone from the inside."

"Aww, thank you." I tilted my head.

"It was just hard to see because of the imitation of a troll you had going on." Tristan winked at me and hurried to say, "I'm kidding, I'm kidding."

I shrugged. "It's okay. As long as I don't have to do any actual work for it, I'm keeping this look." I led him into my office, which was full of robot parts, boards with drawings and calculations, and Mindy, who stood in the corner looking like a sleeping beauty. "It would be different if I didn't have the CBC. Beauty is superficial and nice to have but not a top priority for me."

Tristan plunked down in my chair, lifting one leg to rest his ankle on the opposite knee. "It's not a priority for me either." With a casual movement he reached up to intertwine his fingers and somehow made them seem like a comfortable pillow behind his head. Giving me a charming smile, he added, "I was just fortunate enough to be born with both brains and good looks. Sorry that you weren't that lucky."

Others might find Tristan's humor mean, but my six months in the Northlands as a teenager had taught me about irony and sarcasm. It wasn't used much in the Motherlands, but I'd become fond of it. The Nmen didn't get offended when I said something harsh. Most times they thought I was being ironic and laughed it off.

Motlanders, however, found me too direct and insensitive.

"Thank you for your sympathy, but it's okay. We all bear our crosses. For instance, I see you still suffer from bad eyesight and a bit of narcissism." I gave him a sweet smile.

Tristan leaned his head back and laughed. "God, I missed you and your sharp tongue, Shelly."

"I missed you too." It was true. Tristan and I had first met at the experimental school on the west coast when we were both fifteen, and for years we'd been out of touch. It wasn't until a year ago, when Advanced Technologies had hired him to lead the department for aerodynamics, that we'd reconnected.

"Why are you here, Tristan?"

"I'm here to take you out."

"Out where?"

"You'll see. Just close down the systems and don't ask questions. It'll be fun."

I gave him a skeptical look. "Fun?"

"Yeah, tons of fun."

"Coming from you that word makes me nervous. Last time you said that, you took me to a fight club. I've never been so scared in my life."

"You were the one who said that you're curious to see more of the Northlands, yet you hide away in here."

"Will there be people brawling and fighting?"

"Nooo, don't worry, Shelly."

I inhaled deeply and gave him my sternest look. "Tristan, I'm not going with you unless you tell me where you're taking me."

His hands came down and he moved to the edge of the seat. "Fine! One of the drones I designed is competing tonight. I want to be there when it wins."

My forehead wrinkled. "Then you go. Drone races are too overwhelming for me. The noise and all those people."

"I'll keep you safe, I promise."

"It's not my safety that concerns me. I'm just not good with crowds of people."

Using his chin to point to my workstation, he ordered, "No more excuses. Shut it down. You're coming with me. Charlie's orders."

I put my hands on my hips. "Charlie sent you?"

"Yeah, he mentioned that you work too much and that he worries about you. I didn't even know you were in the Northlands until he told me."

"I see."

"Hey, don't give me that look. I wouldn't be here if I didn't want to spend time with you. And really, I'm the one who should be offended that you didn't tell me you were here to begin with."

I cleaned up my workspace. "Sorry, I meant to. I've just been busy."

"You're forgiven, but only if you come with me to the drone race."

With a sigh of resignation, I looked at him. "It's just going to be you and me, right?"

"That's the plan. Unless you have some cute girlfriends you want to invite."

My raised eyebrows said it all.

"No, that's what I thought." He laughed. "So just me and you then. With me there you won't even have to bring that protector along that Charlie hired for you."

"Thank god. To be honest, I don't like him much."

"Why? Is he coming on to you?"

"No, he's just very talkative and sometimes it's too much. I've tried giving him the cold shoulder, but you know how Nmen are – they don't get offended by Motlander rudeness."

Tristan laughed and came up with all sorts of ideas on how to offend an Nman.

An hour later we were sitting high up on bleachers overlooking a large area where drones were lining up to race.

"Sorry about the food. This place doesn't have many vegetarian options." Tristan held out his box to me. "The chicken sticks are good and spicy though, wanna try?"

"Tell me again, when did you begin eating meat?" I asked and took a bite of the large breadstick that had been my only choice of food.

"When I was enrolled in school here. They didn't always have vegan options so it was either starve or eat meat."

"I'm sorry to hear that."

Tristan swallowed a bite. "I don't eat a lot of meat, but I've learned to enjoy it when I do."

45

"How is your family doing?" I asked, knowing that Tristan had an enormous family since he grew up in a family unit in the Motherlands with his biological mom, and also had a family on his father's side.

"Do you mean my dad and Athena?"

"Yeah, how are they?"

Tristan smiled and looked at the action in front of us. Eight drones were hovering above the ground in the starting area, while the last two were slowly lifting up to get in position. "Sometimes, I envy my dad and Athena. What they have together is so rare." He turned his head to me and looked serious when he spoke. "Did you know they hold hands in public? Like they can't stand to not touch each other." Tristan shook his head. "It's weird, but at the same time, I fucking wish I could find that with someone."

"I'll hold your hand if you want me to," I offered and held it up for him to take.

Tristan took me up on my offer and smiled. "Thank you, Shelly. You're a good friend. Too bad that we don't have that chemistry thing between us."

"We wouldn't have been a good couple. You're as quirky as I am."

Tristan laughed. "No one is as quirky as you are."

"That bad, is it?" I wanted to release his hand, but he grabbed it more firmly.

"You're perfect the way you are, quirky and all."

While Tristan returned his attention to the race and watched the drones take off, I kept thinking about his words: *No one is as quirky as you are.*

"Fucking amateur." The man in front of us screamed as the crowd erupted in shouts and boos after a blue drone bumped into a red one that had a black line in the shape of a lightning bolt on it.

There had to be at least two thousand people spread out on the bleachers, and more viewers would be located along the route. Drone races were popular in the Northlands.

"Did you see that?" Tristan stood up, shielding his eyes from the sun with both hands and looking in the direction of the drones. "He blew it. I told the pilot to push to the max from the beginning. I fucking built that machine to take a beating, and then he goes easy." Grumbles of annoyance were followed by more complaints. "And why would he try to get on the right side of number eight? He could have been number one by now."

"The pilot can still catch up, can't he?" I asked to cheer him up.

"I doubt it." Keeping his eyes fixed on the large screen where we could follow the race, Tristan sat down again, grabbing for another chicken stick in the box.

"Sure you don't want one?" he asked.

"Yes, I'm sure." While he watched the race, I looked at the men around us, catching some of them staring at me with curiosity. These past ten years thousands of women had moved to the Northlands, but men still outnumbered women by a lot, and strict laws protected women from being approached or touched by strangers without the woman's consent. It wasn't illegal to look, though, and many of them had no manners when it came to ogling women. I ignored their staring eyes, finding none of them the least bit attractive. Again, memories of my time with Marco flooded back and I took a deep breath to steady my beating heart.

"Hey, Shelly…"

I turned my head to meet Tristan's eyes. "Yes?"

"Stop thinking about your work. I can hear your head spinning, and you need to relax for a few hours."

"I wasn't thinking about work."

"Good, because you need some balance in your life."

"I'm balanced," I lied, knowing full well that a seventy-to eighty-hour work week didn't leave room for much else.

"I was just looking at the spectators, wondering what is going on with the beads."

"Ahh." Tristan waved his hands in a dismissive way. "It's a fashion thing. Apparently, Magni wore a single dark blue bead in his beard, and you know how everyone wants to be like him."

I counted at least twenty or thirty men, each with a single bead braided into his beard.

"Magni would be the last person I would expect to wear a bead. That's something Motlander men would do."

"Maybe he lost a bet," Tristan guessed. "Either way, he looked pretty badass with it and now it's high fashion."

"Do you talk to him often?"

"Nah, sometimes. Mostly, I speak with Mila."

Mila had been a student at the experimental school, and she'd been adopted by Magni, the second in command in the Northlands, and his wife, Laura.

"I heard she's still kind and gentle," I said.

"Who, Mila?"

"Yeah, who else? You didn't think I would call Laura or Magni gentle, did you?" The two of them were stubborn Northlanders with a love for weapons and fight techniques.

He kept his eyes on the screen. "Mila is the best. She runs an animal shelter now, you know, helping sick and injured animals."

"How old is she? Twenty?"

"Sounds about right." Tristan said and waved over a service-bot selling ice-cold beer.

"Is it true that she's going to have a tournament?" I asked.

"I don't know. It's possible. Both her parents are traditionalists and want her to marry a strong warrior." He reached for the beer, asking me over his shoulder, "Do you want one?"

"No thank you. I don't drink beer."

Tristan got what he needed and the service-bot left. "It's inevitable that she's been influenced by Magni and Laura to think a tournament is a good idea."

I took another small bite of the breadstick and scratched my nose. "It's so old-fashioned. Men fighting for a bride…"

"At least the minimum age of the brides was raised to twenty-one. It used to be eighteen up until seven years ago. Mila still has time to make up her mind."

"Tournaments are barbaric," I exclaimed. "Mila is too good a person to be pressured into something that medieval."

"Hey, it worked out well for Laura and Magni. They seem happy together. Maybe it'll work out for Mila as well." Tristan gave me a small smile and looked back at the race.

My analysis of his body language told me that he didn't want to discuss it further, but he had triggered me and I began ranting. "Tristan, did you know that until June 2433, brides were only fifteen years old when they were dressed up and made to pick between five champions? The warriors were grown men, sometimes more than twice the age of the bride, and they held enormous power. Their child brides couldn't work, vote, or even walk freely. To say that it might work out for Mila is both ignorant and mean. If you consider yourself a friend, you should do everything in your power to stop her from marrying a stranger."

"But Mila isn't going to be a child bride, is she? She's an adult and capable of making her own choices. If she thinks a tournament is the way to find a husband, then I'm going to support her right to choose that for herself." Tristan patted my shoulder. "Let it go, Shelly, it's none of our business."

But letting go of things was hard for me, and I needed the last word on the matter. "It's just that I don't believe in tournaments. It's wrong."

"Then don't have one," Tristan said pragmatically.

"Mila shouldn't have one either," I insisted.

"And maybe she won't. It's probably just a rumor or wishful thinking on Magni's part."

I leaned forward in my seat, both my elbows on my knees and my chin resting in my palms. "I hope you're right about that."

Two minutes later Tristan jumped up from his seat. "That's it! Take him, take him, take him!" He raised his hand in a fist and screamed out with joy when his drone overtook a large green one on the large screen. "Son of the Devil, he's in third place now…" Tristan's eyes were wide open and he gave another scream of excitement when his drone overtook another competitor. Leaning forward, he pointed to the side. "They're going to be flying through here in a second – get ready."

I stood up too, infected with his excitement, and cheered with him when the small dots on the horizon quickly grew in size.

"Yes… come on. Push her. Push her to the max." Tristan was up on his toes when his drone sped past us in a flash. The crowd exploded in a rush of adrenaline with the speed and closeness of the drones. Men were roaring their excitement, and when Tristan's drone took the lead my friend celebrated with everyone around him.

"I fucking designed that drone. That's *my* drone," he told the men around us, who gave him words of admiration.

Technically, it wasn't *Tristan's* drone, but for once I understood that now wasn't the time to point that out.

When he flung his arm around my shoulder, I looked up at him and smiled. "Looks like you built a good drone, Tristan."

His face split in a wide grin. "Of course I did. Told you, I've got both looks and brains."

CHAPTER 6
Sex-Bot on a Field Trip

Marco

Storm handed me a beer and a turkey leg. "I wish we had better seats," he complained. "I bet Tristan could have gotten us backstage passes with his connections."

"Did you ask him?" Hunter, who was one of Storms best friends, asked.

"Yeah, but he never got back to me. I think he's still pissed about what happened when I married Gennie."

"What are you talking about?" I asked and ripped off a piece of the turkey meat with my teeth.

Storm swallowed a mouthful of beer and shook his head. "I was an ass to Tristan and my other friends. Completely forgot about them and just wanted to be with Gennie."

"Yeah, you were an ass," Hunter agreed. "I figured you were scared that she would like us better than you."

"It crossed my mind." Storm leaned back in his seat, his eyes hidden behind a pair of sunglasses. "I mean, she sure as hell never liked me much."

"Did you meet her?" I asked Hunter.

"Uh-huh."

"And what did you think?"

Hunter looked away, taking a long sip of his beer.

"I take it you're not a Gennie fan either?"

"Nope. Not a fan."

"You're not going to get any trash talk from Hunter," Storm said. "But I have no problem saying that Gennie is a bitch."

Hunter looked away.

"I know she came on to you." Storm was looking at Hunter. "Tristan told me what happened between you and Gennie."

Because of the bright sun, Hunter's pupils were small when he met Storm's eyes. It made the green color of his eyes stand out. "I didn't touch her." His tone was serious.

"I never said you did."

"Are you two even watching the race?" I asked to break the tension.

Storm patted Hunter's shoulder. "Don't worry about it. Tristan told me how you turned her down."

Hunter gave a solemn nod. "I would never touch a married woman."

"I know. Hey, why don't you call Tristan? He has to be here somewhere." Storm looked around the stands. "Do you see him?"

"No, why don't you call him yourself?"

"Told you – I did, several times, but he's ignoring me."

Hunter had updated his wristband to the newest model and judging by how long it took him to maneuver the thing and call Tristan, I figured he wasn't that familiar with it yet.

"Hey, where are you? What? Speak up, Tristan, I can't hear you." Hunter pushed at his small earbud. "Are you at the race?

I could only hear Storm's part of the conversation as he spoke.

"Yeah, we're here too. Storm got tickets although they aren't very good. Row twenty-four, in the yellow section. Where are you?" Hunter turned around. "Fuck it! I knew you had better tickets. I bet you can see the pilots when they fly by and all."

Storm pushed Hunter on the shoulder. "Ask Tristan if he can get us in backstage after the race. I want to see his drone up close."

Hunter delivered the request and nodded. "Got it. Okay, see you there."

"What did he say?" Storm asked, and because he was leaning over me, I pulled back, lifting my beer and turkey drumstick out of the way.

Hunter gave us a satisfied grin. "Tristan told us to meet him at the VIP entrance after the race."

"Yes." Storm lit up. "That's what I'm talking about. Not that it should be necessary if you would play your celebrity card."

Hunter was a star soccer player; we could never go anywhere without him being surrounded by fans. He'd already taken pictures with several people on our way to our seats. If he wanted to go backstage all he had to do was go down there and throw his name around, but that wasn't Hunter's style.

"Where is Tristan?" I asked and turned around in my seat.

"Four rows from the top, in the middle – do you see him?"

I squinted my eyes. "No. Is he the one wearing a drone hat?"

Hunter laughed and pointed but there were at least fifty rows between us and the top. "He's four... no, five seats to the right of that guy."

"In a yellow t-shirt. Yeah, I see him." I frowned. "Wait, is that a female next to him? Is he with her?"

"I don't know, I didn't ask him."

"Storm, give me your sunglasses for a second. They have zoom function, right?"

"Of course."

I pulled them off his face and he protested.

"Hey, be careful, don't break them."

"Where do you zoom on these things?" I felt for any buttons on the side."

"Here, let me do it." Storm showed me how to zoom in and I looked up at Tristan again, this time seeing him as clearly as if he were sitting right in front of me.

"What the fuck?" I kept staring at the sex-bot sitting next to him.

"What is it?" Hunter asked.

"Tristan is with... ehh... a woman." I took the glasses off and Storm was quick to snatch them.

Taking a look for himself, Storm whistled. "Damn, she's a pretty thing. Who is she?"

"Let me see," Hunter insisted and when he got the glasses on, he kept looking at Natura. "Nah, not my type."

Storm slapped Hunter's shoulder. "What do you mean she's not your type? She's hot."

"Nah, she looks a little masculine."

I gaped at him. "Masculine. Are you high or something?"

"Don't mind him." Storm rolled his eyes. "Hunter is screwed up when it comes to women. I hope she's one of Tristan's sisters and we can get him to introduce us to her."

My knees bobbed up and down with restless energy while my head was spinning to find answers. Tristan worked for Advanced Technologies, but not with sex-bots. At least not as far as I knew. Why was he with a prototype? Was this part of her training to interact with real people? Had he taken Natura out on a field trip of sorts? Was Tristan one of the engineers working on her, and if so had he seen me having sex with her?

My jaw tensed from the thought of being watched by someone I knew. That would be weird.

"Storm, remember I told you that I tried out that prototype last week?"

Storm's head was leaned back, his eyes on the large screen. "The natural sex-bot. Sure, why?"

"It's *her*."

55

He gave me a sideways glance. "What are you talking about?"

"Tristan is with the sex-bot that I tested out last week."

"Give me my glasses back." Storm turned in his seat to zoom in on Natura again. "The virgin bot?"

"Did you say virgin?" Hunter asked and Storm was quick to fill him in.

"Don't tell anyone. I promised that I wouldn't talk about it," I pointed out to both of them.

Storm gave a dismissive hand signal. "Telling your best friends doesn't count."

"You two aren't my best friends, I just tolerate you because you had a free ticket to the drone race."

Storm grinned. "Don't be an ass. We all know that you love to hang with us instead of all the oldies you call friends."

He had a point, since my two closest friends had married years ago and changed because of it.

"Do you think you could contact the test facility and ask if I could test her too?" Storm asked eagerly.

My first instinct was to say no. I didn't feel like sharing Natura, but that didn't make any sense, so I muttered, "I guess."

"What are you doing?" I asked when Hunter started fiddling with his wristband again.

"I'm calling Tristan to ask if he banged her too."

"Don't. She'll know I told about it and then Storm will be blacklisted from the test team."

"Me?" Storm jerked back. "I didn't tell anyone."

"I took your spot, remember? They think it was you testing her out that day."

"Riiight." He nodded. "Shit, I would have never given up my spot if I'd known I could be trying out an advanced sex-bot like her."

Hunter borrowed Storm's sunglasses again to get a second glance at her. "She doesn't look like a sex-bot. She looks like a real woman."

"That's the whole point," I said. "She's the closest thing to a real woman that has ever been produced."

"What if she *is* a real woman?"

Storm slammed the back of Hunter's neck. "Idiot. In what universe would a real woman walk in to offer herself as compensation for a broken sex-bot? Most women are fucking scared of us Nmen."

"She *was* a robot," I assured Hunter. "Well made, but definitely a robot. Women don't behave like she did. Not with strangers anyway."

"Okay, okay, I was just messing with you." Hunter gave a grin and returned to watch the race.

I kept thinking about what the hell Tristan was doing with the sex-bot and turned around one more time, squinting my eyes to see them.

No way!

What I saw blew my mind. Natura was taking a bite of a breadstick.

Fuck!

Robots didn't eat.

Either Natura was in fact a hybrid or... my eyes widened as a simpler and much more likely explanation hit me like a hammer.

"What's wrong?" Hunter elbowed me. "What did that drumstick ever do to you? You don't have to smash it."

My hand had squeezed the drumstick so tight that the meat was all mushy.

"I'll be right back," I muttered, making my way out to the center aisle. When a service-bot passed me, I threw away my drink and food, drying my hands on a napkin while taking two steps at a time up the stairs.

I was in good shape but was still breathing hard when I made it to the sixtieth row and could see Tristan and the woman only ten more rows up.

"Tristan," I called out but he didn't hear me over the noise from the crowd. Natura, however, did see me, and her whole face stiffened.

Maybe it scared her that I was running up, red in the face, and shouting his name.

She got up, saying a few words to Tristan and moving away from me toward the aisle on the other side. Tristan hadn't seen me yet but called after Natura, shaking his head, and telling her to wait for him. She continued to make her way out of the row, not taking any time to listen to him.

"Tristan," I called again and forced myself through an entire row of people who pulled their legs to the side to let me pass. I reached the aisle just in time to block Natura, who was coming down. She stopped abruptly when she saw me standing right in front of her.

"Marco." Tristan lit up behind her, not seeing her reaction. "What a coincidence. I didn't know you were here."

"I wasn't supposed to be." I looked from her to him. "Nero couldn't make it, so Storm gave me his ticket."

"Oh, you're with Storm?"

"And Hunter," I added.

"Oh, okay. Do you remember Shelly?" Tristan had a wide smile on his face and swung a hand toward Natura.

"Shelly?" I looked back at her and gave a shake of my head in response to his question. I had only ever known one Shelly and this woman wasn't her.

"She worked at the school for a short while in the beginning," he elaborated. "I thought you'd remember her." Tristan came closer, stopping a step above me. "Shelly had a sister named Rochelle at the school."

I heard what he was saying, but it made no sense. The Shelly I'd know had been petite, flat-chested, and far from pretty. This woman was much taller and drop-dead beautiful. There was no resemblance between them.

"I remember Shelly. I used to call her Brainy," I muttered in disbelief, studying her closely. Maybe her eyes did look a little familiar.

"That's right. Shelly and I both work for Advanced Technologies now."

"I didn't know that." My eyes were willing her to look at me, but Shelly's gaze darted around looking everywhere but at me.

"It's okay, it's been ten years since you last met and Shelly has changed a lot. I wouldn't have recognized her either."

"Ten years, huh?" I starred at her. "Funny, it feels like I just saw you the other day. Although I wouldn't have recognized you with the new look. What happened to you?"

"I grew up," she said and looked down at her shoes before she gave me a stiff smile. "Look, I'd love to catch up, but I have to go."

"What's the rush?" I asked, stepping in her way when she tried to get past me.

"She needs to use the rest room," Tristan explained behind her, his eyes looking up at the large screen.

"No problem. I can take Shelly. We're old friends, after all."

Before she could object, Tristan gave me a grateful smile. "You sure? I'd hate to miss the last rounds, but I promised our boss, Charlie, that I would act as Shelly's protector for tonight."

"Don't worry about it. I'll keep her safe."

"You don't mind, do you, Shelly?" Tristan asked her and with her shoulders tensed up, she gave a silent shake of her head.

59

"Great, let's meet by the VIP entrance in ten minutes," Tristan said and hurried back up the stairs while Shelly was running down the stairs. Either she had to pee badly, or she didn't want to talk to me.

"Shelly." I grabbed her by the arm and swung her around to face me when we were near the rest rooms. "Stop for a second. There's something I have to tell you. Something important."

She seemed nervous and couldn't look me in the eye.

"Are you aware that Advanced Technologies has created a prototype of a sex-bot that is an exact copy of you?"

She narrowed her eyes. "What did you say?"

"It's true. I've seen it."

Shelly blinked a few times.

"Did you know?" I repeated.

"No. I mean yes."

My face hardened. "You let them do it?"

She moved her feet, shifting her balance. "It's complicated."

"Is that a yes?"

"Marco, I'm sorry, but it's none of your business."

"None of my business." I jerked back, anger brewing inside me. "The hell it is."

"It's just a prototype. The final version won't be modeled after me." She turned to leave again, but I was quicker and blocked her.

"I don't care that I haven't seen you in ten years, Shelly. No one is going to make a whore out of you. Not even if it's for research. Does Tristan know?"

"No. You can't tell *anybody*."

I didn't tell her that Hunter and Storm already knew part of the story.

"Just tell me this. Did you authorize Advanced Technologies to make a sex-bot in your image?"

60

Shelly drew in a large inhalation of air and bit her lower lip, but she didn't answer.

"Did you?" I pressured her.

"Can we just drop it? I don't want to talk about it."

"No, we can't just drop it. I saw it... her... the sex-bot."

"And?"

"And I didn't know it was modeled after you. Otherwise I would have never..." I scratched my shoulder, not able to finish the sentence. If Shelly didn't know I'd tested the bot, I sure as hell wouldn't tell her.

Her eyebrow rose. "You would have never what?"

"Nothing. Just tell me what you know about the sex-bot."

Shelly looked down, her lips closed tightly.

"What the fuck, Shelly? You used to be outspoken and honest. What happened to you?"

"I told you, it's complicated."

"Did you swap your personality for beauty or something? Looks like you changed both inside and out." My words were nothing but a low mumble, but when she raised her gaze to meet mine, she looked like I'd shaken her to her core.

"You wouldn't understand," she whispered.

"Then explain it to me."

Shelly closed her eyes for a second, and when she opened them there was a pained expression on her face. My lungs felt like someone was squeezing them in a fist. Whatever she was about to tell me, it wasn't good news.

"Marco, I..."

I stopped breathing, afraid of her next words. Something was not right; I could see it in her eyes.

"The thing is..."

"Shelly... Marco, did you see it? My drone won." Tristan's voice sounded from somewhere behind me. More than a little frustrated, I turned around to meet the proud drone engineer. It was tempting to ask him to give us a few minutes, but he came jogging up with such an infectious smile that I couldn't help but congratulate him. The moment between Shelly and me had passed and she was looking right past me to Tristan now, with a smile on her face that looked a lot like relief.

"Did you find the rest room?" Tristan asked her.

"No, we got caught up in talking about our shared past," Shelly replied and hid her shaking hands behind her back. "I was just reminding Marco about the time he reminded me to stay out of other people's private affairs." She gave a small laugh. "You know how I always asked the most obscene questions back then."

"You still do." Tristan grinned.

"Of course, Marco was right. Privacy is important."

This was just like the old days when Shelly would talk to someone else and make sure I was close enough to get a message that was really for me. I smiled a little, intrigued by her unique way of communicating.

"And I was just reminding Shelly that she forgot an important detail in what I was teaching her back then. There are some situations where the concern of friends takes priority over privacy," I said in a casual tone, as if this was just a theoretical conversation.

With a happy bounce in his steps Tristan began to leave, waving for us to follow. "Come on, we're going backstage to celebrate."

Shelly didn't look at me when she took a few steps toward him and stopped. "I would love to go and celebrate with you, but I don't feel well."

I couldn't take my eyes off her. My brain was still trying to understand that this beautiful woman was the adult version of the quirky teenager I had once known. It made no sense that a person could transform this much. She was half a head taller, had filled out in the right places, and there was no trace of her bushy eyebrows or major scars from her acne.

62

This Shelly looked like she spent a lot of time on her looks, while the Shelly I'd known couldn't care less about that sort of thing.

Brushing her shiny shoulder-length brown hair back, she addressed Tristan again. "Would you mind walking me to your drone? I promise to send it back to you after I get home."

Tristan's face fell. "You're not staying?"

"Sorry, but I've got a major headache."

"But…" He turned his head toward the VIP area and back to her. "How about we stay for half an hour and then I'll take you home? I won't let you go home by yourself."

"That's nice of you, but I can manage. I'll be fine."

"Please, Shelly, give me ten minutes. Hunter is waiting for me by the VIP entrance. He's going to be disappointed if I don't get him in."

Shelly reached up on her toes and kissed Tristan on the cheek. It attracted attention from men passing by, and envious comments were heard from a few of them.

"You go meet Hunter and Storm. I'll make sure she gets home safely," I offered.

Tristan looked torn. "No, Marco, it's okay, I'll take Shelly home myself."

"Hey, I was going home anyway. You might as well stay and have fun."

Shelly had already begun walking, not waiting for us to decide. I had a strong feeling that she was hoping she could get away alone, so I clapped Tristan on the back. "Go! I've got Shelly." I didn't wait for him to agree but hurried to catch up to Shelly, who was speed walking away from us. I didn't care if she started to run, I'd fucking catch her and get my answers.

63

CHAPTER 7

Answers

Shelly

I was walking as fast as I could without running. Maybe the universe would take pity on me and let me get away before Marco caught up with me.

My pulse was in fight or flight mode and my eyes darted around looking for something to save me. A drone for hire would do it, but those weren't allowed this close to the race. My feet moved quicker as I headed for the arrival and departure area, my mind replaying the nightmarish moment when I'd seen Marco come running up the stairs, calling out Tristan's name.

Except for our encounter a week ago, I hadn't seen Marco in ten years. What were the odds of running into him at an event with thousands of people?

Wishing that I had wings and didn't need a drone to get away, I kept my head down, ignoring all the long looks from men that I passed.

"Hey, are you lost? Where's your protector?" someone called out to me.

"You want me to escort you home?" another offered.

Those were the nice comments. Other men were more aggressive and one spread out his arms as I came storming by. "Hey, beautiful, are you looking for me?"

I'd already passed him when I heard Marco's voice telling the man to drop dead.

When I looked over my shoulder, Marco was right there, and probably had been for the few minutes I'd been thinking I was getting away.

After our brief eye contact he fell into step beside me but didn't say a word until we were at the departure area.

"My drone will arrive in a second." He looked up to the line of drones waiting to pick up their owners.

"Which one is it?" I asked.

"The white one."

We waited for another five minutes, me feeling small in a crowd of large Nmen. A pregnant woman and her husband were standing not too far away. She was leaning against his chest and his arms were around her with both his hands on her belly. She smiled at me, probably assuming that Marco was my husband. I couldn't tell her that his hand on my shoulder weighed two tons on my conscience. To her and everyone else, it would seem that Marco was my protector. But as I saw it, it was the crowd keeping me safe from him. As long as they were there, he wouldn't demand answers.

When his white drone landed, a few made comments about it being a wreck. The small drone looked old and scratched-up, inside and out.

"I know Tristan's drone is much nicer," Marco said as we lifted up from the ground. "I wish teaching children paid as well as being an aerodynamic engineer."

"Your drone is fine," I said and looked out the window. We Motlanders didn't have private drones. It was considered an unnecessary luxury and a waste of resources. Our drones were public ones, and few of them were in better shape than this one.

"Where do you live?" Marco asked.

I'd rented a room with a Motlander and her husband, but I hated staying there and most days I slept on the couch in the office. I was torn about where I wanted to go, so I hesitated.

"Let me know when you're ready to talk," Marco said but I still didn't look at him.

"Shelly, at least tell me where to take you."

Slowly, I swung my head to meet his eyes. I'd always found them vibrant and expressive in comparison to mine. "How about we drop you off first and then you let the drone take me to my place?"

"Why?"

"Isn't it obvious?" My shield was up. Out of two evils I'd rather he thought me unpleasant than know the truth about what happened between us.

"You don't want me to know where you live?"

The incline of my head confirmed that.

Marco leaned forward resting his forearms on his legs. "What the hell did I ever do to you?"

"I don't know what you're talking about."

"The last time I saw you was ten years ago and you asked me for a hug. I don't recall us being enemies. What's with the ice queen attitude?"

I looked away.

"Look at me. We used to have fun together. Don't you remember?"

"I recall us bantering a lot."

"Sure, but it was friendly banter. You were my brainy sidekick and I was your..."

My eyes widened. "My what?" Did he know I'd had a huge crush on him?

"Your entertainment. You always commented on the stupid shit I did and we made people laugh." Marco shook his head. "You used to have a wicked sense of humor, and now you're cold and treat me like I'm a no one. I wouldn't have taken you for a snob."

"A snob?"

"Yeah, you know, too good to hang with a simple guy like me. So what if I'm still a mentor and you're some big deal in the Motherlands?"

"I still have a wicked sense of humor. It's just temporarily gone."

"Why?"

Scratching my collarbone and avoiding his eyes, I searched for a plausible reason. "There's been a lot of stress at work."

"You work for Advanced Technologies, right?"

"Yes."

"What do you do exactly."

"I design products. One of my latest inventions was a beauty-bot."

"Why am I not surprised?" Marco pointed to my hands. "I like the colors and the message."

Holding up my hand, I spread my fingers. Each one had a small letter written in white on top of a marine blue background.

"Live & Learn," he read.

"It's a reminder."

Marco lowered his brow and gave me a serious glance. "Shelly, the sex-bot I saw had something similar but not the same colors or message." Marco's attention was fixed on my face as if to read my expression.

I tried looking him in the eye to signal confidence, but the questions emanating from him made me nervous and I looked down and mumbled, "I told you that I don't want to discuss it."

"And I told you I want answers. I'm not going to let this go so you might as well tell me," he pressured in a firm voice. "What do you know about the sex-bot? If they did this against your will, I'll help you fight it."

"I don't need your help. I want you to forget about it."

"Not happening," he said and pushed out his jaw with a determined expression. "Why are you here? In the Northlands, I mean. I thought you lived in the Motherlands."

"I've been here for some weeks now. I'm doing some research for Advanced Technologies."

"What kind of research?"

I was never good at lying, so I sighed and stuck with the truth. "All I can tell you is that at the moment I work at the test and research facility on Mayor Street. Most of the ti..."

I was cut off when Marco interjected, "Mayor Street. That's the place they test sex-bots."

"As I was saying," I continued. "Most of the time I analyze statistics to improve the experience for the end user."

"On sex-bots?" Marco's tone was full of disbelief.

I sunk lower in the seat, rubbing the bridge of my nose as if I could hide my face when I muttered, "Yes."

"You work with sex-bots?"

"Correct."

For long seconds neither of us spoke.

"Tell me the truth," Marco said and moved closer to me, his face hard. "Do you know I was in your facility last week?"

I licked my lips, my eyes blinking a few times. "I'm aware."

"Did you *see* me test the bot?"

My eyes focused on a spot on the floor.

"Shelly, look at me." Marco's voice rose a bit.

When I did, he read the answer on my face.

"Fuck... you did, didn't you?"

"I'm sorry." My cheeks felt hot and I fiddled with a ring on my finger, turning it around and around.

"Who invented that bot? Did you?" This time his question sounded accusatory.

"Marco, maybe it's better if we don't discuss this. No one ever has to know about it. We could just forget it ever happened."

His hands covered his face for a moment, and he swore, low. "Tell me the truth, Shelly. Why me?"

"What do you mean?"

"Why did you pick me to test the bot? Or maybe the whole thing was a set-up. Was I even the first one to test it?"

"Yes. No one else ever saw it," I insisted.

"Then why me?"

"I don't know. You weren't even supposed to be there. I made sure you weren't included in the testing rounds."

"Why?"

"Because I didn't want you there." It was the truth.

"I took Storm's place," Marco explained and there was a long break when we just watched each other before he spoke in a low, incredulous tone. "You watched me have sex with a copy of you."

I didn't know how to respond to that, so I didn't.

"Were you repulsed or excited?" Marco challenged me, his nostrils flaring with a brewing anger.

"You always knew that scientists were watching the test sessions. You're told about it every time you come in," I reminded him.

"True, but I had no idea I was being watched by someone I knew."

"That should teach you not to lie," I said without thinking and right away my face flashed cherry red from my embarrassment. *Who am I to talk?*

"If you want to talk about truth, then how about you share a few details with me?" We had reached the city and the drone was flying toward the opposite end of where I wanted to go.

"Can you take me to the test facility?" I asked.

"As long as you start talking."

"There's nothing to tell. You were there, you experienced it yourself, and it's best to just move on."

Marco instructed the drone to fly north as I'd requested and turned to me. "Do you know how strange it is for me to look at you and know that I had sex with you… or rather with Natura."

I fiddled with my hands. "It's strange for me too, but it was just an experiment. There's no need to think about it ever again."

Marco scoffed and laughed at the same time. "Yeah, right. That sounds like a solid plan."

"I mean it; you don't have to see me again."

"But don't you understand that I'll be wondering?"

"About what?"

He threw up his hands in the air. "Where do you want me to start?"

I said nothing, my eyes taking in the city beneath us and my thoughts spilling over. "The buildings look so different here. In the Motherlands most have plants and herbs growing from top to bottom."

"This isn't the Motherlands, and you're changing the subject."

"Did you know that underwater farming is becoming a big thing in the southern part of the Motherlands? We're using large airtight growth houses anchored about seven to nine meters under the surface." I began ranting. "It's an effective way to eradicate threats from vermin, storms, droughts, and frost that could harm the crops on land."

"Shelly."

"Most people don't know this but the pressure under water makes the plants grow faster."

"Shelly." Marco was staring at me. "Stop lecturing me about plants. I want to know if you sent in that sex-bot to fuck me."

I jerked my head back, my eyes wide in shock. "What?"

"Did you?"

"I don't know."

He tilted his head, his lips pressed together in a flat line. "It's a yes-or-no question."

"It's complicated."

"All right, if it's so fucking complicated, then let's take it one question at a time so even a non-genius like me can understand. Did you know it was me in that room?"

"Yes," I admitted. "I saw your alert that Mindy had broken down."

"Did you send in the bot to have sex with me?"

"You asked for a different model."

70

Marco raised an eyebrow. "So you sent in a prototype modeled after you?"

I tucked a lock of my hair behind my ear. "Kind of."

"Kind of?"

For someone who spoke without filters on any normal day, I was being very careful about not revealing too much.

"Did you authorize having the sex-bot modeled after you?"

I swallowed hard and thought about my answer when the drone began descending. "Oh, look, we're here." Never had I been so happy to see the test facility.

"You didn't answer my question." Marco looked anything but happy that we had arrived.

I counted the seventeen seconds in my head until the drone was on the ground and the door slid open.

"Thank you for taking me back," I said and hurried out.

Marco followed and when I entered the facility, he didn't ask to be invited inside. "I'm not leaving until you tell me everything," he said and crossed his arms with a stance that told me he wasn't going anywhere.

If you want him gone, all you have to do is tell him the truth. He'll be furious and storm out of here.

"Shelly, before Tristan interrupted us at the drone race, you were about to tell me; I could see it in your eyes."

Turning around, I walked down the hallway to my office, leaving the door open for him. Mindy stood in the corner with her scalp open. I was waiting for a new part for her to arrive from headquarters.

"She broke down again?" Marco asked.

"Yes, second time since you were here."

"And Natura. Where is she? Can I see her?"

"Why?"

"Just curious."

"Sorry." I took a seat on my swivel chair, my elbows resting on the sides and my fingers weaved together.

Marco chose to lean back against the table in front of me. "What aren't you telling me?"

I laughed a little, the tension getting to me. "We haven't seen each other for ten years, and after thirty minutes in my company you expect me to tell you *everything*?"

"No, of course not, I just want to know about Natura. Did you create her?"

I shrugged, trying to come across as relaxed. "What if I did?"

Marco inhaled deeply. "I'm not sure whether to compliment you or be disgusted with you. Natura is incredible, but to make her a copy of yourself is wrong on so many levels, Shelly. Most men here use sex-bots and everyone would recognize you on the streets. Can you imagine?"

I used both hands to rub my face. "I see your point, and I'll make sure to correct that mistake."

"So you won't let anyone else see or test Natura?"

"No, I won't."

"You promise?"

"Yes."

"Good!" Marco gave a satisfied smile. "I'm glad we could sort that out. There's just one other thing."

"What?"

"The recording of me and Natura. Could you erase it?"

"Why?"

"Because I don't want anyone seeing it."

"Don't worry, only a few authorized people have access to the recordings."

Marco tapped his fingers on the desk. "If you won't delete it, then at least give me a copy of it."

"Noooo," I exclaimed. "I can't."

"Why not?"

"I'm not allowed to."

"So you can watch it, but I can't?"

"Technically, I could watch it, but I don't intend to." I didn't tell him that I was the only person with access to that recording and that I'd already watched snippets from it three times.

Marco stretched his legs. "Look, you made the decision to send in Natura and you watched it. I think it's only fair if I get to watch it too."

My face had to be crimson red by now. "It's against company protocol to give it out. Natura is a secret project; we can't have recordings of her unaccounted for."

"Shelly, doesn't it bother you that someone could mistake Natura for you and think that you and I had sex together?"

Straightening up in my chair, I gave him a sharp look. "You sound like you'd be ashamed of having sex with me. Who's the snob now?" My eyes widened when I realized what his real issue was. "It's because of your wife, isn't it? You're afraid Gennie would see it."

"Gennie?" Marco scrunched up his face. "Who told you about Gennie?"

"I heard you got married years ago. But don't worry, you don't have to be afraid of Gennie finding out that you've been with me. I can assure you that any recordings are classified. She'll never see them."

"That I've been with *you*?" Marco's eyes narrowed and his nostrils expanded like a wolf picking up a scent of blood.

"Natura. I meant Natura."

"Yet that's not what you said. You were referring to yourself."

"Just wishful thinking," I joked and laughed. "I'm kidding, of course."

Marco looked skeptical. "Did someone tell you my wife's name was Gennie?"

"No, you did, when you tested Natura, remember?"

"Right." Marco stood up and, towering over me, he leaned down to be almost face to face. "Only, I'm not married and it's Storm who has an ex-wife named Gennie."

I tried to pull back, but I was stuck in the chair with Marco in front of me.

"But you *were* married, right?"

"No. I was never married. That day, I only went along with the Gennie thing because I was pretending to be Storm. Natura would be linked up to the system and in the system I was Storm."

My eyes widened as I realized my mistake.

"You, however, knew it was me in there."

I didn't breathe because the question was right there in his eyes and there was no way I could stop him from asking this.

"I should've known something wasn't right. A sex-bot would never ask me about my wife. Either you instructed Natura to ask that question or..." He narrowed his eyes. "Tell me the truth, Shelly. Was I with a sex-bot named Natura, or was I with you?"

CHAPTER 8
Reaction

Marco

When Shelly just stared at me, I repeated my question. "Was it you in that room with me?"

She licked her lips. Her breathing was shallow and her face flaming red.

"Was it?" I repeated for the third time, already knowing the answer in my soul.

"Of course not." Shelly was looking at my shoulder now. "That would just be crazy."

"Shelly, look at me." I waited until she did. "It's very simple. Show me Natura so I can see for myself that I tested a robot or tell me the truth right now."

Her shoulders sunk lower and she couldn't meet my eyes.

"You... we... but that can't..." I tried to make a coherent sentence, but I couldn't think straight. Pulling back to create distance between us, I stared at Shelly. "Why?" I finally managed to ask.

She offered no explanation but kept her face hidden from me by looking away.

"Why, Shelly?" Anger rose inside me. "Was this some kind of prank?"

"No." She shook her head and finally met my eyes.

"You lied to me."

"To an extent."

"To an extent? What the fuck is that suppose to mean. Are you the next-generation sex-bot?" The question was rhetorical at this point.

"No, but I do plan on building one. And in my defense, it was you who assumed I was a robot. I just went with it. And my skin *is* grown from human tissue."

"Christ, Shelly, you were always different, but I never took you for a liar."

"I'm not a liar," she protested. "Not usually anyway."

"*We had sex.*" The realization hit me hard and I scrunched up my face. "You fucking tricked me."

She wrung her hands, still sitting in her chair with her eyebrows drawn close enough to resemble the unibrow she'd once had.

"Why did you sleep with me?"

Her gaze was glued to her thighs now.

"Look at me," I demanded, and when she did, her eyes were moist.

"You used me, Shelly. You should have told me who you were."

"I'm sorry."

"That's not good enough. You owe me a fucking explanation."

She wrung her hands and spoke in a low voice that made me have to lean in to hear her. "I was curious."

"Curious?"

"I'm sorry."

I moved around her desk and back again. "This is why I never wanted to marry a Motlander. Everyone thinks you're kind and gentle people, but it doesn't run very deep, does it? How would you feel if I'd tricked you into having sex with me?"

Shelly looked devastated. "You're right, I wouldn't like that. I didn't like it when I tricked you either."

Something in that sentence bothered me. "Are you saying you didn't like tricking me or that you didn't like the sex?"

Getting up from her chair, Shelly moved around, uncoordinated and nervous. First, she rolled her chair back to the desk, then she began moving things aimlessly around. "It's probably best if you leave now."

I was still angry but nowhere out of questions.

"Leave? I don't think you understand the ramifications of what you've done."

"I've made you angry and I'm sorry."

I scoffed and walked over to turn her around. "I'm just fucking confused about why you did it, and I would have liked a choice."

"I understand."

"I doubt it." I hardened my jaws. "It means that we'll be marrying."

Shelly took a step back. "No."

I scrunched up my face. "Don't be stupid. When you slept with me you chose me. You can't sleep with a man and then not want to marry him. That's not how it works here in the Northlands. You're mine now."

Shelly gave a chuckle of disbelief. "Marco, you're angry and not thinking straight."

"Don't think so. I'm not the one pretending to be something I'm not. It's obvious that your genius pushed you toward insanity. I'd say I'm the one with the clearest mind here."

"I'll *never* marry you." Her eyes were wide open and she was staring at me.

I jerked my head back. "Wow. That's harsh, even for you."

There was a flash of regret on her face before she looked away. "I'm not trying to hurt you, I just don't believe in marriage. It would never work anyway, since I'm only here for a short while before I'm going back to the Motherlands."

"Then why the fuck did you sleep with me?"

She walked away from me and stopped in front of a large glass board with notes on it that made no sense to me. With her back to me, she repeated what she'd told me before, her voice back to being low and apologetic. "I was just curious."

My head was exploding with questions but I was too confused, upset, and humiliated to talk about this in a calm way. "And it never occurred to you to tell me who you were?" I hissed.

Shelly's head was bent down in shame and her tone of voice was defensive. "Yes, but then things just escalated. I didn't know you'd be this angry about it."

"I'm fucking furious."

"I can hear that." Her voice was thick and she nodded her head, still making sure to keep her back to me.

I watched how she moved over to stand in front of Mindy and fiddled with the robot's hands, making herself look busy and shutting me out at the same time. The small bobs of her shoulders told me how she was suppressing her tears. Her breathing was shallow and coming in fast inhalations, as if she was taking in air but not letting it back out. I had seen this behavior in Nboys many times when they were too proud to cry in front of others.

"You want me to go, don't you?"

"Yeesss." Her word broke and I could tell she was close to the last straw before she would be sobbing. It pulled at my soft core. Shelly was still sensitive and proud, as she had been ten years ago.

"We'll talk about this later then. This should teach *you* not to lie," I said, throwing her own words right back at her before I slammed the door behind me on my way out.

All the way home, I was in a state of shock and my initial anger turned to disbelief. I'd had sex with a real woman who had given herself to me freely. In what world did that happen?

Shelly was beautiful and smart, so why was I so bothered by what had happened between us?

Because it felt like she'd been laughing at me the whole time. She'd known what was going on, while I'd been the dumb fuck who was tricked.

But that was only half of it.

I kicked at Storm's shoes, lying in the middle of the entrance area, when I came home wondering again why I hadn't recognized her. Maybe because every time I'd thought about Shelly these past ten years, she'd been fifteen with a large mane of unruly hair just like the last time I saw her. Opening the top drawer in my bedroom, I picked up a small box and pulled out a seashell she had given me before she left the school. Memories took me back.

"A seashell is symbolic in a way," Shelly said while holding the small stone I'd given her as a joke. I had called it a portrait but only painted her gigantic brain on it.

"Symbolic of what?" I asked.

"Of you. The animal who lived inside that shell was soft and vulnerable on the inside and needed a hard shell too."

I laughed and insisted that I was as tough as they come, but Shelly knew better and just shrugged. "If you say so."

"I'll treasure this shell. If people ask me I'll tell them it's a wonderful reminder of a genius girl who was wicked smart but needed to learn to shut up once in a while. You know, like a clam or an oyster."

In her usual way Shelly retorted with ease. "And I'll show people your gift and say it's a reminder of a young man who had stones for brains."

I would have never made fun of her lack of a filter if I'd known that the one time I needed her to speak up, she'd quiet and not tell me who she really was.

The thought that I had been inside Shelly Summers had me plunking down on my bed, my arms spread over the top of my head, and my eyes fixed on the ceiling with memories from that day.

Shelly had always been like a fucking unicorn. So rare and special that everyone around her knew they should be honored to know her. She was the kind of person who would go down in history for making the world a better place with her goddamn genius. Kids would learn about her in school and talk about her contributions to the world. I just knew it!

If I'd known who she was that day in the testing facility, I would have treated her with the respect and care she deserved. Her sad face when she left me was back to haunt me and made me curse out loud. I had hurt her feelings and made insensitive comments about her body and her skills in bed. I had fucking talked about her imperfections and shoved my cock down her throat. *Jesus!*

Self-loathing made way for shame as details from that day stood out clearly in my mind's eye. She had been so beautiful, and I'd complained that I couldn't make her breasts bigger. What a moron I'd been.

By some miracle, a woman had taken an interest in me and I'd been given a chance to prove myself worthy of her.

What had I done with this once-in-a-lifetime opportunity? I had fucking blown it.

Not that I stood much of a chance to begin with. This was Shelly Summers, for fuck's sake. The genius.

I was mad at myself and mad at her for tricking me into thinking that she was a machine and nothing else. Fuck, I wish I had known. She should have told me!

My apartment was quiet and I sat on my sofa just thinking for a long time. When Storm came home, he went straight to the kitchen.

"Don't drink the last beer, it's mine," I said from the open living room.

"Shit, you scared me," he exclaimed. "I didn't see you. Why didn't you turn on some lights?"

"It was still light when I got home, and I guess I dozed off." It wasn't true. I'd been so deep in my thoughts that I hadn't paid attention to the sunset outside.

"You missed out on the best part. Why the hell did you leave so soon? Hunter and I got to ride in the winning drone with Tristan. It was only a few minutes, but still. You wouldn't believe how fast it accelerates. It's like your whole body gets smashed back into the seat and you can't move."

Storm was building a pile of food on a plate. He came in with it balanced in one hand while carrying a glass with the other. "Tristan said he was there with Shelly, and that you took her home." He took a seat on the couch next to me.

"Yeah, she had a headache."

"I remember Shelly. She was a quirky type."

"Still is," I said in a flat tone. "Definitely out of the ordinary."

"But I'm confused. If Shelly was the one sitting next to Tristan, then how come you thought she was a sex-bot?"

"I was wrong." I turned my head and looked at Storm. "She just looked similar, but once I got closer I could tell it wasn't her."

Storm began stuffing his mouth and made non-verbal sounds because of all the food in his mouth.

"I have no clue what you just said."

He swallowed. "I said, I can't believe that Shelly turned out this hot. She was butt-ugly when we knew her."

"Hey, I recall you with a fair portion of zits too. We all looked funny when we were teens. At least Shelly had more brainpower than all of us together."

Storm laughed. "True, but remember how she would always go off about random things no one cared about? Or how we all dreaded it when she had kitchen duty?"

I gave a lazy roll of my shoulders, the corners of my mouth curving upward. "I remember one time when she

81

and I had to do arts and crafts with you children. Shelly had this idea that we could all do something called knitting. She had studied the technique and could explain it perfectly, but she was so fumble-fingered that it was a big waste of time. I was laughing so hard because she refused to give up and kept at it long after the kids had left. It was ridiculous, but she had stamina, I'll give her that."

"I don't remember the knitting, but I remember she couldn't run or fight for shit." Storm peeled a banana. "Remember how she always got lost on the morning runs because she got distracted by some flower, tree, or animal that she had to get closer to?"

"It's the curse of smart people," I said. "They don't have much common sense."

Storm made grunts of agreements and I snatched some chips from his plate, adding to the conversation: "But when it came to the academic stuff Shelly was phenomenal."

"I can't argue that. But to be honest, I always found it a bit spooky," Storm mumbled.

"What do you mean, spooky?"

He lifted his shoulders in a shrug. "I don't know, it was just like she wasn't all human, you know."

A triangle formed between my eyebrows as I frowned. "No. I'm pretty sure Shelly's all human."

"She had that freaky photographic memory and she could read a page a second."

"She couldn't read a page a second." I threw a chip at him. "That's sick."

"Maybe not a second, but she would read a chapter in the time it took me to read a page, and we used to do quizzes on her to test how much she could remember. It was spooky."

"You mean impressive."

Storm ate his food for a few minutes and then he spoke again. "Hunter said that Willow might come visit soon. You know what would be fun?"

"What?"

"A reunion. We could invite all the first students from the school and have a summer party. I mean Shelly and Tristan are already here."

"Tristan didn't go to our school."

"No, but he was there a lot, so he counts."

"I don't know. It sounds like a lot of work to track down everyone. Especially the ones from the Motherlands."

"It's not that many when you think about it. Mila and Raven live on the West Coast with their families, and with Shelly living here and Willow visiting Hunter, it's only six others that we need to find. Rochelle is easy since she's Shelly's sister, and I'll bet being a Motlander she has contact info on the others too."

I lifted my hands in the air. "If you want to do it, be my guest. If you can pull it off, I'd love to go."

Storm drummed his fingers on the armrest and looked thoughtful. "I'll ask Hunter and Tristan to help. It'll be epic."

"That's great."

Storm leaned back in the sofa, brushing crumbs off his t-shirt. "Maybe we can do another test on Shelly. See if she's still sharp."

"Test her?" My neck began itching as it flamed up.

"Yeah, I'll bet she still has her photographic memory. Do you think she'll let us test her?"

I didn't answer because his words of testing Shelly brought back strong memories of being deep inside of her. The thought of any of the others being that close to her made anger flare up inside me.

"What's wrong?" Storm asked.

"Nothing."

"Then why do you look so pissed all of a sudden?"

"It's nothing."

Storm changed the subject and when all he got from me in return were grunts and one-word sentences, he soon disappeared into his room.

I, on the other hand, was left feeling shocked at the force of possessiveness that his talk about testing Shelly had caused in me. The last thing I needed was to develop feelings for her. She had made it clear that she wasn't interested in me and that she would be going back to the Motherlands soon. Besides, I would be going to a tournament and hopefully marrying Louisa.

Giving a small groan, I curled up on the sofa. This was all so fucked up!

CHAPTER 9
Tristan's Headache

Shelly

"You didn't eat much." Tristan nodded to the plate I'd pushed aside.

"That's because nothing tastes good here."

"The chicken pie is tasty." Tristan snatched at my plate and popped a piece of broccoli in his mouth.

"Yeah, they know how to cook meat. It's the greens and salads they mess up. Fried rice with vegetables shouldn't be that hard. Even I can do it and that says a lot, because I'm no culinary expert."

"True, my taste buds are still recovering from that awful cake you made."

"I didn't swap salt and sugar on purpose. Sometimes, I just get distracted."

"Which is why I'm happy you're not working in a lab with chemicals," Tristan pointed out with humor sparkling in his eyes. We were in one of his favorite places. To me the pub looked like a pre-war museum with all the wood panels on the walls and the benches and tables made of solid planks. A large sign above the bar said McGregor's Irish Pub and topless bar-bots were pouring out large-size beer glasses to the many patrons in the bar.

"Since you're not eating anyway, do you mind if we look at the plans?" Tristan made room in the middle of the table for a large paper with drawings on it.

I felt the paper. "Is this real paper made from trees?"

"Yes."

"Don't you have it in an electronic format?"

"It's just a draft. Why, what's wrong?"

"Sometimes it's like you've never lived in the Motherlands at all. You know that traditional paper hasn't been used for centuries. In fact, the amount of wood in this place would be offensive to most."

"I know, but I like it. It's cozy and this is the Northlands – we've got nothing but trees."

"Trees are living beings, Tristan. They communicate with other trees and if one is injured by lightning or under attack from insects the others will distribute water via their root net. As a Motlander you are raised to appreciate all living beings and acknowledge that their lives are meaningful and important too."

"Sure." Tristan leaned over the table. "But sometimes I'm a rebel and I use paper anyway. We did at the school, remember?"

"Yeah. But there are alternatives."

"Shelly, you never complained about it at the school, so don't get hung up on it now."

I shrugged. "Okay, I'm not exactly the typical Motlander, am I?"

"Good. So now that you got your little rant out of your system, can we focus on my promotion?"

Placing my forearms on the table I leaned in to look at the drawings. "Walk me through it."

Tristan was working on a public transportation system with the scope of supporting both the Northlands and part of the Motherlands. He didn't find it as glamorous as designing racing drones, but he was passionate about how many people the system would benefit.

"Pearl specified that speed and comfort are on the wish list but are secondary compared to durability and reliability," he explained.

"What will it run on?"

"Algae biofuel or electricity. I'm not sure. Pearl probably has an opinion on that."

"I thought you were the designer."

Tristan tapped his fingers on the table. "True, but as the ruler's wife, Pearl has a big say in everything. Besides, I value her input. She takes time to understand things, and she listens to others."

"She'll tell you to find a way to make the drones self-sufficient. You're using carbon fiber, right?"

"Of course, it's lightweight and strong."

"What if you incorporated modular sun panels? The carbon fibers could store the energy and the solar panels would charge them. It would be environmentally perfect."

Tristan raised an eyebrow. "That would be brilliant, but I'm foreseeing all sorts of issues."

"We're engineers. Coming up with solutions is the fun part."

"But I don't have modular solar panels that can withstand the pressure or the weather elements. This isn't like installing sun panels on a roof or a bike lane, Shelly. The wind resistance is significant, not to mention potential hail, rain, snow, and lightning. I don't even think they had something that advanced before the war."

"Then you'll have to build them."

Tristan gave me a look that said, *That's easier said than done.*

"I'll help you come up with ideas and you can have the engineers in the environmental department help you too. I bet they'd love this project." Tapping on the drawing, I added, "And is this the design?"

"Yes, it's just a rough sketch, but I was inspired by the military drones we have here in the Northlands. They can transport up to fifty people at a time and resemble large bumblebees."

I stared at him. "Why in the world would you go with something like that?"

"Because you always tell me to imitate nature."

"Yes, but when it comes to flying the bumblebee isn't the most refined specimen."

"I was focusing on the size of it."

Letting my fingers trail along the outlines of the large drone he had created, I shook my head. "I don't like it."

"You don't?" Disappointment dripped from Tristan's voice.

"No. Biomimicry is admiration for the perfection of nature. What do you want to imitate? Give me your top five features."

Tristan counted on his fingers. "I want it to be silent, fast, energy efficient, flexible, and solid."

I tapped my upper lip, thinking. "We already talked about the fuel, so let's make a shape that causes as little air resistance as possible. If we can get this bad boy to soar it would be perfect, wouldn't it?"

"Soaring is nice, but people have places to go. Like work." Tristan took another bite of his pie, and his upbringing in the Motherlands showed when he covered his mouth with his hand when he spoke while chewing. "It has to have some speed as well."

"Speed is your specialty. I trust you can do some magic there."

"Right, but racing drones aren't built to accommodate up to forty or fifty people."

Twirling a lock of my hair and thinking hard I sat for a while going over options in my head while listening to Tristan's challenges with his design.

"The Adélie penguin."

"The what?"

"The Adélie penguin."

Tristan scratched his head. "We're talking aerodynamics here, Shelly. Penguins don't fly."

I leaned forward. "That's right. But they swim and slide with perfection. It could give you the angle for your bottom."

"Penguins are so fascinating with their white and black colors." Tristan frowned. "If nature is such a genius, how come they have white and black colors when they live on ice? You would think they would be all white so they could camouflage themselves against ice to avoid predators."

"That's a good point." I tapped at my lip. "There must be a logical explanation."

"It doesn't matter, Shelly. It was just an observation. You know, because I'm so sharp." Tristan chuckled, but I wasn't listening to him. My mind was digging through everything I ever read about penguins.

"The Adélie penguins don't have many predators on land. They forage their food in the ocean, and the black color on their backs will blend in with the depths when viewed from above, while the white front will keep them from standing out against the bright sea surface when seals or other predators approach from below."

"Huh. Yes, that makes sense. So, you want me to use their shape for the bottom of the drone?"

Another thought occurred and I grabbed Tristan's forearm. "The kingfisher!" Excitement filled me from within. It was perfect.

"The kingfisher?"

"Yes, please tell me that you've learned about the kingfisher in school."

"Ehhm," Tristan scratched his neck. "If we did, I don't remember it."

"You can't learn about aerodynamics and not study the kingfisher." I pulled out images on my wristband, turning them around in the air, to see the bird from different angles. "The Adélie penguin is a torpedo in the water while the kingfisher dives from the sky into the water to catch fish. It goes down so fast and with such precision that it hardly leaves a ripple when it breaks the surface of the water. Notice the beak – see how sharp it is – and the way the bird's whole head is like an arrow?"

"Uh-huh." Tristan shifted in his chair, his eyes blinking as if taking pictures to memorize it. "Show me."

I found clips of the bird diving.

"Wow, I see what you mean."

"If you want silent and energy-efficient, you'll need the minimum of air resistance. This is nature's recipe. You should imitate this shape."

"But a drone can't be shaped like that."

I raised an eyebrow. "How do you know?"

"I don't think it would look good. Drones aren't rockets or birds; they're not supposed to have pointy fronts."

I got up, "Do as you want. It's your assignment, Tristan. If you want to adopt a set of limitations from how you *think* a drone is supposed to look like, then your job is easy. Just make another copy of drones from the past four centuries and give it a different color."

"Shelly, come on. I didn't mean it like that. I'm just saying there are rules in the field of aerodynamics that you're not aware of. I studied this, remember?"

I scoffed a little. "If you want to tell me that any of the drones that man has created are superior in aerodynamics compared to the kingfisher and other birds, then I have to question what they taught you in school."

"Maybe I'm just not visionary enough to see how you could implement it into a design that's useable." Tristan stood up too, handing me a pencil. "Please, Shelly, help me out."

I sighed and took the pencil. "How about if you do like this..." I'd never been good at drawing and was frustrated that the image in my head didn't transfer well to paper. In the background Nmen at the bar were growing louder and rowdier.

"You could scale it depending on the size needed. I suggest you do different versions of size and then combine them whenever you need to transport a large number of people at events. Otherwise you'll end up with oversized drones that fly around half empty or sit on the ground most of the time. Consider programming the drones to fly in formation, like real birds do. It will save energy with less wind resistance. Trust me, birds have perfected the formation for millennia.

Tristan and I sat in a bubble of ideas and creation, ignoring the drunken people at the bar. Only when the bar-bots began blinking the ceiling light did we look up.

"Shit." Tristan swore softly and I noticed that others were getting up from their seats.

"What's wrong?" I asked, still doodling on one of my ideas.

"They've called the police. Probably because someone is drunk and threatening. The light is a signal for people to get out."

"Oh." I spotted the group of Nmen arguing by the bar. "Maybe they need help reconciling. Should we offer to help?"

"No!" Tristan was already up, his hands folding the paper with hurried movements. Taking the hint, I finished my drink in a long slurp.

"We should mind our own business and get out of here." His eyes darted between the men at the bar and me. "Come on, Shelly, hurry."

We were on our way out when a police squad of two fully armed officers with four police-bots came rushing in. To avoid being trampled, we backed inside again and that's when the chaos began. The unruly group of Nmen were not open to leaving their drinks, and when the police-bot moved too close, warning the group to calm down or suffer arrest, a large angry-looking guy smashed a glass of beer into the bot, shouting, "Leave me the fuck alone."

Tristan covered me with his body, pushing me against the wall when things began flying through the air.

"Fuck, fuck, fuck," he muttered and protected his face with his hands when a steak knife came flying in our direction.

"We have to get out of here," I yelled in the noisy chaos and pulled at his shirt to get him to move with me toward the door again. Still covering our heads, we made it to the exit, where people were pushing to get out. "Hurry," I screamed in panic when I heard the first shot.

Tristan was pushing from behind me and I was stuck between large sweaty bodies on all sides.

Fear has a smell. I knew that from my training, and while being pushed and squeezed by men trying to save their lives, the analytical part of me was going over scientific facts about the olfactory bulb, which is the part of the brain that detects smell. It's located just above the nasal cavity and below the frontal lobe, and I fixated on all the details I could remember to keep from panicking from the lack of air in my lungs or the constant shots from inside the bar.

And then, finally, *finally*, we got pressed through and I could breathe again.

Taking Tristan's hand, I moved fast in the direction of his drone, but we'd only taken twenty or thirty steps when his hand slipped out of mine. I turned to see why, and gasped.

Blood was running down Tristan's face and he was staring at his fingertips, red from the blood as if he'd just touched his face.

"Tristan, what happened?" I exclaimed with concern. He was pale as a corpse, and I only just managed to support my friend before he fell to the ground, passed out.

With hands trembling from the sheer panic I was in, I searched his scalp to see where the bleeding was coming from and saw a large open wound.

Did he get shot?

No, it looked more like a large cut, like he'd been hit by an object sharp enough to break his skin and hard enough to cause him to pass out.

I needed something to stop his bleeding, but there was nothing close to us that I could use.

His shirt.

I tried pulling it off him, but he was too large and heavy for me to move around and get his t-shirt off.

Looking around in a panic, I shouted for some of the men back by the bar to lend me a shirt, but they were arguing among themselves and too far away to hear me.

Determined not to let my friend die from blood loss, I did the only thing I could. Pulling off my yellow summer dress, I pressed it against his wound and called for Tristan to wake up.

He was limp and lifeless and it scared me.

"Tristan, open your eyes," I coaxed and supported his head in my lap, while drying off blood with my dress.

The dark night was lit with flashing lights coming from inside the bar and the loud sound of the police drones ordering people to get on the ground and surrender without resistance. At least the shooting had stopped by now. Still holding my bundled-up dress to Tristan's wound, I looked around, hoping to make eye contact with someone who could help me. Seeing only large angry-looking men, many still holding glasses of beer in their hands, my better judgment told me they would be more dangerous than helpful.

Call for help. I raised my wristband but had no clue who to call. The people I knew were on the East Coast or in the Motherlands and I didn't know the number for medical emergencies in the Northlands.

Raising Tristan's wristband, I chose recent calls and Storm's name came up. When his face popped up in front of me, I almost cried with relief. I would have recognized Storm anywhere. He had been two years younger than me at the school, and often gotten in trouble for his impulsive behavior.

My voice was frantic. "Storm, it's me, Shelly. You have to help Tristan. He's hurt."

"What the fuck is going on? Where are you?"

"Outside a bar. They were shooting and we made it out, but then he fainted. I don't know what to do. He's unconscious."

"Is he breathing?" Storm asked.

"Yes, I think so."

"Good. I recognize where you are, I'm on my way."

"Hey, what happened to your clothes?" someone called from behind me and others chimed in. "She's only wearing underwear."

"Look, her protector got shot."

Men were gathering around me and my worry for Tristan grew to include fear for my own safety. I wanted to scream at them that Tristan wasn't shot, but I was too afraid to even look at them. Like predators sensing a weak prey they moved closer, and tears began dripping from my eyes. Most Nmen were protective of women, but drunken men in a group had been known to suspend their values and do things they later regretted. I was unprotected, and only wearing panties and a thin white camisole that went to my navel. This was definitely bad.

"Hurry," I begged Storm, who from the look of his picture was running.

"I'm not far from you. Stay with Tristan... and keep talking to me."

"Tristan needs medical attention," I said, focusing on Storm's image, and ignoring the large stranger who was now squatting down next to me, way too close.

"Hey, beautiful, looks like your protector isn't doing too well. You need a new one?" he whispered, his alcohol breath making me wrinkle my nose.

My body stiffened and I leaned away from him, my focus still on Storm, who was talking.

"You said there were gunshots – that means the paramedics will be on their way. Don't worry. Just stay with Tristan."

The stranger next to me didn't touch me but he was close enough for me to feel his warm breath on my skin. I closed my eyes to block him out.

"Three minutes, Shelly... Hold on, okay? Storm assured me.

Three minutes sounded like three decades. Tristan and I needed help *now!*

For a full minute I sat, counting seconds in my head, hearing drunken men make lewd comments about my curves and others telling them to shut up. A fight broke out, and one of the few men who had been protective of me limped away with a bloody nose and his hand to his jaw. I watched him leave with my heart in my throat, afraid that the men would attack me now.

"Storm," I said, needing to hear that he was still there on the line.

I saw him move his lips before a loud siren made me look back toward the bar. As Storm had predicted, paramedics arrived on the scene, but they ran straight into the bar and didn't see me or Tristan.

I kept counting the seconds, and when I got to one hundred and eighty seconds, Storm still hadn't arrived. The man next to me was breathing into my ear, talking about all the ways he could make me a happy woman. The eight men standing close to us chimed in with unwelcome offers of their own.

"Your protector is dead. You'll have to think about your future." One of them laughed. "I've got my own boat and I could pop some kids into that belly of yours real fast."

"We could make it easy for you to pick. Kiss each of us and have a little sample."

"Careful," one of them said when his friend stepped closer to me. "If you touch her without consent, they'll kill you for it."

"So what?" he said in a drunken slur. "Maybe the pretty woman is worth dying for. I reckon I could at least get a quickie in the alley before they take me out."

The other men encouraged him with laughter and pats on the shoulder. They were old and unattractive men. I wanted to tell them that women cared about hygiene and that they should too, but the situation was already tense and I was afraid of provoking them.

"We're landing, Shelly, be with you in ten seconds." Storm assured me.

"Hurry!" I begged, my hands keeping pressure on Tristan's wound, my head turned away from the man too close to me, and my heart racing from terror.

10, 9, 8, 7, 6, 5, 4, 3 I counted in my head before running footsteps were followed by a deep threatening voice giving a firm command. "Get away from her, right now!"

Marco stood between me and the group of men, his shoulders squared and his back straight. With a quick glance down at me and Tristan, he cursed, and pulled his black t-shirt off his ripped torso and handed it to me. "Put it on!" he ordered.

"I can't. I'm putting pressure on Tristan's wound. Where is Storm?"

"He's finding a paramedic." Marco narrowed his eyes at the man too close to me. "Get the fuck away from her."

"I was protecting her," the creepy guy defended himself. "I never touched her."

With a large palm on my shoulder, Marco bent down over me. "I'm her protector now, so fuck off!"

As if I were a child, Marco helped me dress in his t-shirt while I shifted between using my left and right hand to keep pressure on Tristan's bleeding.

It occurred to me that he could have just squatted down and taken over on Tristan. That would have freed my hands to put on the t-shirt, but for some reason he didn't.

"The show is over. I said, fuck off," Marco yelled at the last four men still remaining.

"Fuck you," the drunken men mumbled back at him, but Marco was too pumped up with adrenaline to care about their numbers. "Why are you here?" he asked me in a blameful tone.

"Tristan and I had dinner,"

"In a bar? What was he thinking?"

"It's his favorite pub."

Marco rolled his eyes. "You Motlanders are too goddamn naïve. Bringing a woman to a bar is stupid."

"I'm okay, Marco. It's Tristan who's hurt."

Marco lifted the dress to take a peek. "By all the Devil's demons, that's a lot of blood." He turned to look over his shoulder. "Where the fuck are the paramedics?"

We waited another minute before Storm came running with help. When the paramedic took over, Marco pulled me back to give some space. I stood close to him watching in slow motion how the paramedic examined Tristan.

"Did he hit his head when he passed out?" the paramedic asked Storm, who was kneeling next to Tristan.

"I don't know, I wasn't here." Storm looked to me. "Did he?"

I shook my head, my arms wrapped tight around my midsection. "No, he didn't hit his head."

"Was he drunk?"

"No."

"Does he suffer from any medical illnesses?"

"Not that I know of," Storm replied.

I took a step closer. "Is Tristan going to be okay?"

"This guy?" The paramedic was a skinny man with black circles under his eyes and a serious demeanor. "I doubt he'll make it."

I just stared at the man, too shocked to breathe, and a sob erupted from me. Marco was quick to pull me into his arms.

"I'm joking." The paramedic lifted one edge of his mouth in a sarcastic smile. "This wound is nothing. I don't see anything but a long cut. The blood makes it look worse than it is." He slapped Tristan's cheeks hard, shaking his shoulders. "Time to wake up now."

I sucked in a deep breath, my voice trembling. "Are you sure?"

Tristan stirred and blinked his eyes open.

"Welcome back," the paramedic said, and supported Tristan when he tried to sit up.

"My head."

Tristan lifted his hand, but the paramedic made sure he didn't touch the wound. "Don't touch, I'm almost done cleaning it."

"What happened?" Tristan looked up at me with confusion on his face.

"You got hit in the head," I explained in a soft voice full of sympathy.

"Have you ever fainted before?" the paramedic asked him.

"Yes, once."

"Was it related to seeing blood?"

Tristan gave a small nod and looked down. "I watched one of my younger sisters being born and I passed out."

"That explains it." The paramedic patted Tristan's shoulder. "Don't worry, you're not the only one." After doing a quick test to determine that there were no signs of a concussion, the paramedic closed his medical bag.

"You're good. As long as you don't aim to become a warrior or work in the medical field, you'll be fine."

"I design drones," Tristan said distractedly, still looking around to orient himself. His eyes fell on Storm and Marco before he spoke to me. "Why are they here and what happened to your dress?

"We're here because Shelly called for my help. You're lucky, because I was busy watching some good porn, I almost didn't answer. Good thing I did, though, because sitting outside a crowded bar with drunken men wasn't the best place for Shelly to flash." Storm offered Tristan a hand to pull him up from the ground. "There was also the part about her fearing that you were dying that made us hurry down here."

"Shit, I'm sorry, Shelly." Tristan pointed down to the dress on the ground, now more red than yellow. "You ruined your dress."

"I had to stop the bleeding."

When Tristan looked like he was losing balance again, Storm was quick to grab his arm for support. "Don't look at the dress. I'm taking you home. Where's your drone?"

Tristan raised an arm and pointed to the right.

"You take Tristan, and I'll take Shelly," Marco instructed. Storm lifted a hand to signal he had understood.

"I think I should go with Tristan and make sure he's safe," I insisted.

"Storm has him. Come on!" Marco picked up the dress. "You want to keep this?"

"No." I shook my head and picked up the rolled-up drawings that Tristan and I had been working on.

I was still shaking from the incident and followed Marco to his drone without a word.

"Are you okay?" he asked when the drone took off from the ground.

I nodded but felt anything but okay.

What if Tristan or I had been killed by a stray bullet?
What if Marco and Storm hadn't come to my rescue?
The severity of the danger I'd been in was sinking in. "Shelly, talk to me."

"I'm sorry about your t-shirt," I said because it seemed like the safest topic at the moment.

"Forget my t-shirt. I'm asking you if you're okay."

"Yes, I'm fine."

He studied me with deep lines on his forehead. "Liar. You're not fine, how could you be?"

Meeting his eyes, I admitted, "I was scared, that's all."

He didn't say anything, just waited for me to continue.

"I was scared that Tristan wasn't going to make it, and I was scared of that man sitting next to me, and the other men ogling me."

"Good." Marco gave a firm nod. "At least that shows you have *some* situational awareness."

"What's that supposed to mean?" I asked, a bit offended.

"Come on, Shelly, you don't want to open up the discussion about you having sex with me without my consent again, do you?"

"Just because I'm a Motlander doesn't mean you get to pick a fight with me. I'm not like the others. I'll fight back, you know."

"I'm not picking a fight with you, I'm just stating the facts," Marco muttered and looked straight ahead. "You practically raped me."

The fear from earlier, combined with the shame I felt, made me release all my emotional garbage on him. "Take that back!"

"No. If you can't see what you did was wrong, it's because you're lacking empathy."

That hurt. It was time to bring out the facts and put him in his place. "You were there to have sex, and I have a form signed by you that states you were a willing participant to a sexual act."

"Yes, but not with you."

"What's the difference? You asked for an old prototype because you were horny and wanted 'release'." I held up my fingers for quotation marks and spoke loud and fast.

"The difference is that I know you, Shelly."

I scoffed. "You don't know me. You didn't even recognize me."

"True, but that's because I was expecting a robot. I didn't ask to sleep with a human."

"And now you're scarred for life?" I flung the words at him with thick sarcasm. "Funny, since I remember you enjoying it."

"I'm not denying that I enjoyed it. That's not the point. The point is, Shelly, that you were this kid and I never..."

I swung my head to face him and interrupted. "I'm not a kid anymore. I'm a grown woman, a psychologist, biologist, engineer, and award-winning designer. I'm twenty-five years old. In case you haven't noticed, I haven't been a girl for a long time."

Marco's eyes stared at me. "I fucking noticed alright."

It was like all the air went out of me, and I just sat there spent and tired.

"Better?" he asked me after a pause.

I frowned at him.

"I do it to my students sometimes when they're scared. I anger them. It beats being afraid."

"You provoked me on purpose?"

"Uh-huh." He kept looking at me. "You're welcome."

"Oh, now I'm supposed to thank you for making me feel bad about myself?"

"You're calmer now, aren't you?"

I was too tired and miserable to care about politeness. "You accused me of *raping* you," I said in a blaming tone.

Marco remained calm. "Yeah, I knew that detail would get to you. A little far-fetched, but it did the job, didn't it?

"So now you're saying that I didn't rape you?"

He scoffed. "Of course, you didn't rape me. I wanted to fuck you, for sure. It just got weird when I learned your real identity."

My mouth opened and closed like a fish out of water.

"Come on, Shelly, you have to admit that you were shaking with fear and now you're not."

I shook my head, too confused by his strange logic to know what to say. The drone had landed on a rooftop that I didn't recognize, and because of our argument, I hadn't questioned what we were doing here. Now I turned my head and looked around. "Where are we?"

"My place."

"I thought you were taking me home."

"That was the plan, but you seem too upset for me to feel comfortable leaving you alone. It's better if I keep an eye on you."

"No thanks." I hugged myself and looked away.

"Come on, it'll be fine. We got off on the wrong foot, but this could give us a chance to get to know each other again."

I gave him a look of complete disbelief. "Why? All we ever do is argue."

Marco shrugged and exited the drone. "Are you coming?"

"Do I have a choice?"

"No."

I supposed I could have protested harder or refused to get out of the drone. But the prospect of going back to my office or to my room in the city didn't excite me either. For better or worse, I was still curious about Marco.

"Okay, but I can't stay long," I muttered and got out. "It's already late."

"I know." Marco waited for me to walk around the drone and get off the automatic parking lane before he pushed in a code on a key panel. I watched as the drone rolled to the parking area, allowing room for the next drone to land.

"I figured you'd be tired, which is why you're sleeping at my house tonight."

"I'm not sleeping here," I exclaimed and stopped walking.

Marco kept going at an unhurried pace, as if he had no care in the world. "Yup, you are, and tomorrow we'll talk." Opening the door, he held it open with his foot, and turned to me. When I still didn't move, he lowered his brows. "Shelly Summers, I'm done arguing with you for one day. You're staying with me tonight, and that's that!"

The stubborn part of my personality dug her heels in, refusing to be ordered around by him. And yet, my body moved forward, controlled by the curious, reckless, impulsive part of me that Marco had a talent for bringing out.

CHAPTER 10
Mutual Arrangement

Marco

Seeing Shelly vulnerable tonight had gotten to me.

Both her harsh rejection last week that she would never marry me, and my anger with her for tricking me by pretending to be a sex-bot, had evaporated the moment I understood she was in danger.

Shelly could have taken on any man at that bar and crushed him in an argument or an academic challenge, but it wouldn't matter. I'd seen the look in their eyes. They couldn't have cared less about her brains. To them she was tits, ass, and smooth skin. A live version of what they'd only seen in antique porn from the time men and females were equal in numbers.

"Sorry about the mess. It's Storm; he's annoying like that," I said as we walked into my apartment.

"Storm lives here?"

"Yes, he's my roommate. Helps pay the bills and all." I waved for her to follow me down the hallway.

"It's small, so you won't get lost." Pointing around, I said, "Kitchen, living room, bathroom, and down the hallway are the two bedrooms."

"Do you mind if we check up on Tristan? Maybe you could call Storm. I just want to be sure Tristan is alright."

I made a quick call to Storm, who told me he'd brought Tristan home and that they had just spoken to Tristan's father, Finn.

"He wants Tristan to be with someone for the next twenty-four hours, in case there's a concussion."

"Why? The paramedic checked him over. There were no signs of a concussion," I pointed out.

"I know, but Finn is a doctor and he said it wouldn't be the first time some overworked paramedic made a wrong assumption. He made me promise that I'd stay with Tristan tonight."

"Okay, I guess I'll see you tomorrow then."

"Yeah. Did you get Shelly home safely?"

"She's fine. Don't worry about it." I put on a t-shirt from my closet since Shelly was still wearing mine.

"What did you mean when you said it was a mess?" she asked when I was no longer speaking to Storm.

"Just the shoes lying around; didn't you see it when we walked in?"

She raised an eyebrow. "That's your definition of messy? What are you, some cleaning freak?"

"I like it tidy, that's all."

"Since when? I don't recall you being obsessed with tidiness at the school."

"I'm not obsessed. It's just that this place is small. Maybe if I could afford something bigger, I might be more relaxed about it."

"Do you still teach?"

"Yes."

"Then how come you don't live at the school? Isn't that the norm here in the Northlands?"

"Things have changed. I work at an integrated school where more than half of the children have families to go home to. The older ones came when their moms married an Nman while the younger ones have mixed parents. We call them Nomo children here."

"So do we." Shelly looked around my apartment. "The media came up with the term when Christina and Boulder had Indiana. He was the first mixed Northland and Motherland child to be born."

"That's not true. All of us Nmen are mixed."

105

Shelly drew her eyebrows close and moved to the window. "True, but you Nmen were taken from your Motlander moms and sent here when you were three years old. Nomo children don't suffer that trauma since they grow up with both their parents."

"You make us sound broken. We're not, you know."

Shelly didn't react to my comment but asked a question. "How many Nboys stay at your school?"

"Thirty-two. I have night shifts, but it's only twice a week. That's why I like to have my own apartment to go home to." I smiled. "We also have three sisters attending school, which I'm excited about. They are real Ngirls."

"Meaning both their parents are Northlanders?"

"Yes, their dad won their mom in a tournament and it's funny because there's less than a year between each of the three girls and they have a younger brother too. I guess some people are just lucky."

Shelly widened her eyes and I got the impression she didn't share my definition of luck.

"But of course, the sisters have their mother so they go home in the afternoons as well."

"Don't you feel sorry for the Nboys that don't have families?"

"Not really." I offered her something to drink. She settled on a glass of water. "In a way it was easier for my generation. We didn't have anything to compare it to. If you ask me, the Nomo children are often caught in the middle with parents who disagree on how to raise them."

Shelly swallowed a sip of her water. "Integration takes a lot of compromising."

"True. And with Nomo children soon being the new normal, we'd better get used to it. The number of Nboys we receive from the Motherlands has decreased by ninety-four percent this year compared to ten years ago."

"Ninety-four percent?"

"Yes. Around five hundred thousand women have moved here and we have a large growth in births. The Council in the Motherlands insists that newcomers of all ages will count instead of the Nboys we normally get. I suppose it's their way of keeping our numbers in check, but it will only last for so long. With the influx of women moving here to marry and start a family, our number of inhabitants will be exploding in the future. I predict that soon all Nboys will grow up in families."

"That's inevitable," Shelly agreed. "And good, right?"

"Maybe." I sighed and plunked down on the couch. "It changes our culture for sure. Teaching the Nomo children is different than teaching the Nboys. Last week I had a mother come and tell me I was too hard on her son."

"And were you?"

I snorted. "Her kid got punished because he deserved it. It wasn't anything personal, but she said I was a sadist for making him do forty push-ups in front of the others."

"Augh."

"Yeah, some of the moms stress me out with the way they pamper their children. They are worse than Kya ever was, and I remember how Archer and I used to laugh at all her talk about inclusion and kindness. These moms take that shit to new extremes."

"Give me an example." Shelly sat down on the couch and curled her feet up under her, but I could still see some of her creamy skin, and it made it hard to focus so I looked away.

"Ahh, mostly it's the way they are involved in everything we do as mentors. They have a lot of issues with the way we Northlanders teach and it's fucking annoying that I have to defend the way we've been doing things for generations. One of the moms demanded her boy be excused from fight training because he could get hurt. I refused but because he's a Motlander child, he's protected by certain rules and the female Motlander

107

teachers I work with allowed him to sit out. The next week the mom wanted to expand that to any type of physical exercise because apparently you can trip and fall while running. She also complained that we allow the children to climb in trees and play tag." I shook my head. "Tell me, Shelly, why the fuck would a woman like that come up here to marry a large strong man? I mean, did she think her husband became that fit by watching others exercise?"

"What does he say about it?"

"Same as me, of course. What dad wouldn't want his son to be strong and fit?" I shrugged. "That mom is just one example of how backward-thinking Motlander women can be. And then there's the *stop and think* application that the kids have on their wristbands. It's driving me fucking crazy."

She chuckled. "I know the lady who invented that. She was one of my professors when I studied to be a psychologist."

My face scrunched up in a grimace. "I would never hit a woman, but with her I might make an exception. Every time the children say something that the application deems rude or insensitive, a small hologram with an avatar pops up and gives a small lecture on how to stay balanced and create a peaceful environment for all. If I hear the word *inappropriate* one more time I will bang my head against the wall.

"Sounds like you've got a lot of drama at the school."

"Sometimes. Not always. I just wish Motlanders would be more open to how we deal with things here in the Northlands.

Shelly smiled at me. "Do you still like teaching?"

"I used to love it and there are still good days, but honestly it's not as much fun as it used to be. If I didn't need to pay bills I'd become a writer instead."

"A writer?"

"Yeah. I would love to write a book one day, but I don't have the time. That's why I need to win the million dollars in the tournament."

Shelly nodded slowly. "Right. And when is the next one?"

"In three weeks."

"Three weeks," she repeated before quickly looking away. "That's soon."

"Uh-huh."

"And the bride... what's her name?"

"Louisa."

Shelly picked at my t-shirt that she was still wearing. "I don't like tournaments."

"Few Motlanders do."

We were quiet for a few seconds, before Shelly spoke in a low voice. "At least now you know what to do on your wedding night."

My lips lifted a little. "True, thanks to you."

Shelly picked up her glass of water again and dried off water drops from the table with her hand. She must have taken my comments about being tidy a bit too seriously. I was just about to tell her to relax when she asked me a question that threw me off a bit.

"I wasn't your first, was I? There was that time in the Motherlands when we visited the beach. As I recall it, you got a lot of attention from women.

"Are you asking me if I had sex with any of them?"

"It's none of my business." Shelly looked down at her right hand rubbing her wet thumb and index finger together. "I just figured that the girl you were kissing with out in the water... well, I don't know, it looked very passionate, that's all."

"I can't believe you remember that."

Her tone was dry. "I have a good memory."

"Right. Well, some of the kids were playing too close and we couldn't go all the way."

Shelly's face was growing red and it was a boost to my male pride that the subject of me having sex with someone else seemed to upset her.

"I know that I was your first," I said.

She averted her eyes. "I already apologized for that."

"Don't apologize. It was just a shock, that's all. I mean, what if you're pregnant?" The question had been on my mind ever since I found out the truth.

She shook her head. "I'm not."

"You can't know that."

"It would be very unlikely. Did you know that a woman only ovulates once a month and that the sperm cell only has about twenty-four hours to find and penetrate the egg? Sperm can survive approximately five days, so in theory the sperm cells that are already inside her have a better chance."

"No, I didn't know that. Do you know when you're ovumating?"

"It's called ovulating," she corrected me and shook her head a little. "And the answer is that I don't know. I never worried about that sort of thing."

"Well *I* worry about it. I know you said that you'd never marry me, but if you're pregnant, Shelly, that would change things, right?"

Shelly turned her head away from me. "Marriage is only done here in the Northlands. The rest of the world ended that tradition hundreds of years ago."

"I don't care. If you're having my child, you'll marry me."

"I'm not pregnant and I'm not marrying you."

"For all I know, I might have super sperm and gotten you pregnant already." I felt a rush just saying the words, but Shelly didn't look like she believed it for one second.

"Statistically, getting pregnant the first time you have sex is unlikely. I've heard that in the olden days they had pills for men and women to prevent pregnancies." Shelly wrinkled her forehead. "It's sad how so many important inventions have been lost. Christina once told me that in the twenty-second century they had some kind of technology to stop women from having their menstruation. That was before the world went mad in that awful wave of the post-war naturalism that ruined it for all of us."

"What naturalism?"

"Oh, you don't know about it? Well, Modern Naturalism is believed to have started somewhere in the 2080s. There was a purge of all things artificial for your body. No hair coloring, body brandings, implants, or other beauty enhancements. Having your period was seen as something natural that shouldn't be tampered with." She sighed. "Those women were fools."

"Why?"

"Trust me, Marco. If you were a woman, you'd understand how unpleasant it is to have your period. Anyway, Modern Naturalism lasted almost a century and it wasn't until around 2170s that it became fashionable to color your hair and nails again. Sadly, by then it had been generations since women had known a life without menstruation and no effort was made to bring back the technology. To this day we still pay the price for Modern Naturalism to ruin it for all of us."

"How bad can it be to have your period?"

"It's different for every woman, but in general it hurts, and sometimes I get sad and emotional for no reason. I would give up my period in a heartbeat."

"Even if it meant you could never have children?"

Shelly played with a lock of her hair. "I'm not planning on having children anyway, so yes I would."

I widened my eyes. "Why the hell not?" It seemed like a colossal waste to have a woman not reproduce.

Shelly's only answer was a small shrug.

"No, seriously, why wouldn't you want to be a mother?"

"It would take time from my work."

"You wouldn't have to give up your work. Most of my friends are married and their wives still work while having children."

Shelly chewed on her lip. "It's not in the cards for me, I think. I'm not a family unit person and I would never sign up for the Matching Program."

"Me neither."

"Even if you don't win a tournament?"

"Most of the Motlander women who sign up to be married do it for the wrong reasons. I mean, there are happy couples, but I've seen too many failed marriages to be interested."

"And yet you were quick to offer to marry *me*."

I swung my hand in the air. "That's different."

"Why."

"Because I know you and you're nothing like the other women who sign up for the Matching Program."

"Interesting. If I'm not like them, then what am I?"

"You're different."

"In what way? Less woman?"

"No, you're more like the rational kind of woman, aren't you? And smart. I can see you winning the Nobel Prize and shit."

"I don't know about that, but you're right about one thing: I'm hoping to set my mark on the world and improve the quality of life for millions of people, Nmen included."

"By building better sex-bots?"

"And other things. I've got so many ideas that my head sometimes feels like it's exploding."

I lifted my arms in a yawn. "All I'm saying is that my friends' wives are working and having children at the same time. It's possible."

She raised her eyes to look straight at me. "I'm getting the feeling that you're hoping that I'm pregnant."

"No, of course not." It flew out of me a bit too loud, but after her repeated refusal to marry me, having a child with Shelly would be a recipe for disaster.

Shelly's face tightened. "Afraid your child would be a freak like me?"

"A freak? What are you talking about."

"Brainy, remember?" She was referring to my old nick name for her.

I gave a small eye roll. "Ah, come on, being a genius isn't the worst that can happen to a person."

"How would you know?"

"Hey, are you insinuating that I'm stupid?"

Shelly drew in a long breath and hid her face in her hands. "No, that's not what I meant. Why do we always have to argue?"

"Because you always assume the worst about me."

"I don't. With you it just feels like I constantly have to defend myself."

"That's bullshit. I always liked you."

"That's not true," she muttered, letting her hands fall down, and looking up at the ceiling. "Most of the time I was invisible to you and when you saw me, you teased me."

"How else was I going to bring balance between us?"

"What do you mean, balance?"

"My pride was under pressure from the beginning just from the fact that we were both assistant mentors yet you were five years younger and introduced as a genius. Shelly, I was trying to prove myself to Archer and you kept correcting me when I taught a lesson."

"I only corrected you when you got something wrong."

"Then I must have gotten a lot of things wrong according to you, because you fucking corrected me daily. It was humiliating."

Shelly moved on the sofa – showing more of that creamy skin before she tugged the t-shirt down to cover her thighs. "I'm sorry. I guess it's the empathy thing you talked about. I don't always sense when it's the right time to keep quiet."

I shook my head. "It wasn't that I didn't like you, Shelly. It's just that from the moment you arrived it was clear to everyone that being at the school was a short stop for you on your way to the moon."

"The moon?"

"Not literally. But you were always unique, and we all knew it." I held out my hand with the palm down. "There was us." I smiled at her and raised my hand way up. "And then there was you. I've already told you how jealous I was of you."

She looked like she was processing what I'd just said and finding it hard to believe that anyone would be jealous of her.

Moving closer, I placed my hand on top of hers. It was a bold move and I was nervous she would slap it away. Touching a woman from the Northlands like this would be dangerous, but Shelly was a Motlander and she just looked at my hand with interest. "Shelly, there's one thing that I still can't figure out. Why did you have sex with me?"

She sighed. "You can't let it go, can you?"

"No, it's a fucking big deal to me, and I don't understand what happened."

"I told you I was curious. I work on optimizing sex-bots for Nmen, and for weeks before you came in, I'd been studying Nmen testing out Mindy. Every time I watched them, questions popped into my mind. Some of them stayed in the room and cuddled with her as if they were pretending she was real. That confirmed to me that my idea of Natura had merit. People always say that men only care about the visual, and that's why the sex-bots have those unrealistic proportions. But I think Nmen long to feel a connection to a real woman."

"Of course we do."

Shelly, got up on her knees, her eyes shining with interest. "Be honest. If you could choose between Mindy or Natura, what would you pick?"

I smiled at her sudden enthusiasm and chuckled. "Nice try, but you're avoiding my question. Why me?"

With a sigh she bit her lower lip. "It wasn't something that I'd planned, Marco. It just happened."

"You could have stopped me. Why didn't you?"

She looked away with a troubled look in her brown eyes. "Maybe I should have, but I wanted to know what sex feels like. When you mistook me for a sex-bot, I just went with it." She rubbed her nose. "For research."

"For research?"

"Uh-huh."

"You had sex with me as research for your work?"

"Something like that."

"That sounds pretty cold."

Shelly shrugged. "What do you want me to say?"

"I don't know. That you felt attracted to me, maybe."

She looked thoughtful. "I knew you wouldn't hurt me and that I'd be safe with you."

I groaned. "At least there's that."

"And I always thought you had nice eyes," she added.

"Did you at least *enjoy* your research?"

She gave a small shrug. "It was different."

My jaw hardened. "Is that a no?"

"I liked the feeling of you sliding in and out of me, but I didn't like how I lost control." She fixated on her hands again, avoiding my eyes. "Or maybe I did. I'm still analyzing that part. It was a new side of me and I'm not sure I liked it."

I loved that side of you. My blood pumped a little faster, just from our talk about sex. She was damn right, she'd

115

shown a new side of herself, and I hadn't been able to get her sweet moans and kisses out of my mind since it happened. Wetting my lips, I asked the big, pressing question. "Do you need to do more research?"

"I'm not sure."

"Are you planning to sleep with other Nmen than me?"

Shelly blinked her eyes and lifted her hand to twirl a lock of her hair. "I hadn't thought about that. That's a good point. A scientist always needs a wide number of samples for comparison."

The sides of my neck tensed up and heat spread to my face as anger flared up inside of me. "Is that a joke? You're not going to sleep with a bunch of men for your research, are you?" The thought alone made me want to smash any other Nman who came close to her.

"It wasn't in my plan. I'll think about it."

"Look, if you need to do more research, I'll help you, okay?"

She arched a brow. "You'll find more Nmen for me?"

"No, of course not. You know what I meant, Shelly."

Her head fell to one side and the edge of her mouth lifted. "You said I shouldn't assume, so why don't you spell it out for me?"

"If you need to do more research on sex, you can experiment with me."

She straightened up a little and narrowed her eyes.

I cleared my throat, my pants feeling tighter, and my eyes noticing the curve of her breasts. "I'm serious, I wouldn't mind having sex with you again."

Shelly pulled back a little, like she wasn't sure I was serious, so I added, "Only if you want, of course. I told you I enjoyed it, and it would be different now that I know you're not a robot."

"But you said you would have never done it if you knew it was me."

"Right."

"Well, you know it's me now, so what changed?"

"For one, we already had sex and the fact that you're not fifteen anymore is finally sinking in. I would be lying if I didn't admit that I think about that day all the time. You're beautiful and I'd have to be dead not to want you."

Shelly took a few seconds before she answered. "In three weeks you're going to be in a tournament."

"True. So that gives us time to experiment all you want until then." I shifted in my seat. "I got the message loud and clear that you don't want to marry me and you're going back to the Motherlands soon anyway. In a way the timing is kind of perfect. I could help you with your research and you could..." I trailed off.

"I could help you practice so you're ready to impress Louisa in bed, is that it?" Shelly's voice was low and her stare was direct. This had sounded so much better in my head.

"I didn't mean it like that. Just forget that I asked." Getting up from the couch, I stood for a second, before I muttered, "You can take my bed tonight and I'll sleep here on the couch. Just give me a minute to change the sheets." Without waiting for Shelly's reply, I walked down the hallway, angry at myself for having brought up sex in the first place. What the hell had I been thinking?

My movements were rough as I made the bed ready for her. I had brought Shelly here to give her a safe space after the traumatizing events she'd been through tonight. So what had possessed me to jump on her with my suggestion for us to have sex again? It was a miracle she had done it the first time. To think she'd do it again was like hoping it could be summer all year round.

"Marco."

I pivoted around to see Shelly in my doorway. Her pretty features were molded into a serious expression and her hands formed into fists down by her side.

"I have conditions."

She had my full attention.

"If we have sex, you can't come inside me."

My Adam's apple bobbed in my throat. "Shelly, you don't have to, really..."

"Promise me," she said in a firm voice.

Putting down the pillow on the bed, I walked closer to her. "Shelly, I shouldn't have asked you. It's a bad idea. After everything that happened to you tonight."

Shelly lifted her face up toward me, and I was sucked into those brilliant eyes of hers. "If I say stop, you stop, and you can't hit or spank me."

I nodded.

"I mean it, Marco. You once said you really wanted to spank me but if you do, it'll be the last time you touch me."

Both my palms flew up in the air. "I won't spank you, I promise."

"You don't get to make demands of me or become possessive."

"Understood." Every nerve ending was on alert and I was struggling internally. I'd never heard of an Nman only having sex with a woman, but maybe setting ground rules from the beginning would make everything easier.

"No one can know about us."

I agreed. "Deal."

She raised an index finger. "And my last condition is that I can add more conditions if something pops up."

"Fair enough. I have a condition too," I said.

"What's that?"

My voice was deep and stern when I spoke. "Don't lie to me ever again."

"Are you sure you want to enforce that rule? Sometimes I lie to spare people's pride or emotions."

I raised an eyebrow. "And sometimes you pretend to be a sex-bot when you're not. Don't fucking lie to me, Shelly. It's that simple"

"Okay. I promise that I won't lie."

118

"Good." I watched her closely. "Were you serious about sleeping with other Nmen?"

"No." Because she let her eyes fall down she missed the small smile on my face.

"Shelly." Using my finger, I lifted her face again. "Will you take a shower with me? I've always wanted to try that."

Shelly tugged at the t-shirt, looking a little shy. "Naked?"

I grinned and stepped close enough for our bodies to touch. "Do you Motlanders wear clothes when you shower?"

"No."

"Then how about we shower naked together? For your research, you know. I can show you what men will want Natura to do in the shower."

"Okay," she muttered into my mouth when I bent down and kissed her.

CHAPTER 11
Research

Shelly

Marco's body seemed enormous in the small shower. He was a head taller than me, his shoulders were broad, and his chest hard and chiseled.

I had heard Motlanders refer to Nmen's visible muscles as vulgar, but his weren't too bulgy and they didn't bother me.

"Can I touch you?" he muttered against my neck.

"You already are." I smiled when his hands slid from my hips to my breasts.

"I want to wash you all over." There was such suppressed excitement in his voice that I laughed a little.

"Let me guess, you would like me to wash you all over too?"

He confirmed that with a boyish smile and began applying soap to my body, leaving no spot untouched.

"You're very thorough," I praised him when he lifted my arms and spun me around.

"Lean your head back." Marco was careful when he washed my hair. The intimacy of it was both strange and wonderful at the same time.

"Tell me if the water is too hot," he said and used his large hand to shield my eyes from the water as he rinsed out the shampoo from my hair.

"The temperature is fine."

When it was my turn, I watched his chest rise and fall when my hands slid around on his body. His eyes were watching my every move – his beautiful brown eyes shining with lust.

"Could you speed it up a little?" he asked and leaned in to kiss me. "There are about a million things I think would benefit your research."

I smiled. "Like what?"

"Like how happy a man looks when a woman blows him in the shower?"

Lifting my index finger, I raised an eyebrow. "Don't do that thing you did last time. I couldn't breathe."

Marco placed both hands behind his head. "I'll let you be in control."

Squatting down in front of him, I had the water falling on my back. "Your penis is one of the nicer ones."

"What?" Marco frowned down at me. "What did you just say?"

"I've seen a lot of penises in my research, and some of them have large veins or they're crooked. Yours is smooth and has a very good size without being enormous."

"Are you saying my cock is small?"

"No, you're among the top twenty percentage in the test group, but to be honest, the largest ones scare me."

"My cock was never measured. How would you know?"

"Oh, the test bots collect that sort of data for us. We measure how deep you get in. The average erect penis size of the testers here in the Northlands varies from 13 to 22 centimeters with an average of 16 centimeters and a circumference of..."

"Tell me in inches – you know we don't use the metric system."

I played with his shaft and calculated in my head. "The average Nman is 6.3 inches long compared to 5.2 in the Motherlands. I checked your stats and yours is 7.2 inches long with a circumference of 5.3."

Marco shook his head. "The fact that you know that is just weird."

I gave him a small smile and licked the length of him. "I was paying you a compliment. Yours is perfect."

"Thanks." He smiled back at me as I spread my lips and took him inside my warm mouth.

With a deep groan of pleasure, Marco closed his eyes and leaned his head back.

As a true scientist, I approached my research with great curiosity, testing out different approaches to oral sex, all the while paying attention to Marco's reactions. He liked it when my tongue played over his sensitive crown, he liked it when I licked him up and down his shaft, but he seemed to get the most pleasure when I massaged him up and down with my hand on the lower part of his erection, while at the same time sucking the top part with my mouth.

"Ohh, that feels fucking unreal," he moaned when I made suction with my mouth and increased the amount of saliva to use for lubrication.

"You're a genius at this too, Shelly."

Empowered by his praise, I continued and met his eyes, which were hazed with lust.

"Fuuck... stop, stop." Marco's voice sounded pained.

"Did I do something wrong?"

Marco pulled me up and hugged me. "No, you did everything right."

"Then why did you stop me?"

"Because I was going to come and I didn't want that."

"Oh."

Marco's hands were in my hair and he met me in a deep passionate kiss. "I want to get inside you." He was eager and almost shaking with desire when he picked me up and pressed me against the wall.

With his fingers, he warmed me up but it only took a few seconds before he smiled with hooded eyes. "You're nice and wet." With me sitting on his hips, the tip of his erection was pressing against my entrance. At the same time, Marco pinched my nipple between his fingers, sending powerful signals to my core that an intrusion was close. "Do you want me to fuck you?" he muttered in between the deep kissing and sucked on my lower lip, releasing it with a pop.

"Yees." The word came out in a long raspy drawl.

"Then say it."

"I want you."

"Say that you want me to fuck you."

We were nose to nose, looking deeply into each other's eyes when I spoke the naughtiest words in my life. "I want you to fuck me, Marco."

A deep guttural sound came from him before he pulled me down over his stone-hard erection, widening me, stretching me, and squeezing my cheeks with his large hands while holding me up against the wall.

My hands were around his neck, my eyes taking in how his mouth was open, his breathing heavy, his dark hair falling down his forehead in thick locks with water dripping from them. Lowering my eyes, I watched where our cores met and his smooth erection drew in and out of me. It was arousing and I could feel my own pulse speed as if I was running. An interesting detail, since I did nothing but let him take me. His deep thrusts were close to painful, but not quite. I wondered if there was such a thing as pleasurable pain since that was the best way I could describe it.

"Do you like it?" he muttered and stared into my eyes with his pupils dilated from arousal.

"Yes." I gave a small moan and began panting when he picked up his pace and took me hard and fast.

His six-pack stood out to me, and underneath the sexual haze that I was in, my analytic mind was wondering about all the strength it took for him to hold me up like that. I doubted a normal Motlander male would be able to do it and noted to myself that Natura would have to be on the lighter end of the scale.

"I want you from behind," Marco panted and put me down on the floor of the shower before turning me around. He had to bend his knees because I was shorter than him, but once he got a good grip around my hips he pushed in deep and swiveled his hips. I planted my palms on the wall to steady myself and was no longer able to think about research. Marco felt huge inside me and looking over my shoulder, I almost purred from the sight of my long-time crush looking like he wanted to eat me up. There was no man in this world that I wanted to do this with but him. I trusted Marco.

"Do you like it?" he asked with hooded eyes.

I bit my lower lip, the edges of my mouth tugging upward. "Can't you tell?"

"Talk dirty to me." He kept pushing in and out, his fingers boring into my skin.

"Marco, it feels so good when you take me from behind."

"Taking you feels fucking amazing. I could get used to this view of your gorgeous body." With a firm hand on my right breast he pulled me back against his chest and spoke low into my ear. "You might not want to marry me, but right now you're mine, do you understand?"

I pushed my body back to meet his every thrust and closed my eyes when he reached around my hips to stimulate my clitoris with his fingers.

"Yes." My legs felt wobbly, like all I wanted to do was fall in love and let him catch me.

He kept going, holding me up on my toes, and panting from the fast movements of his hips. Marco stretched and softened my insides as if he were a relentless blacksmith pounding iron to his will.

The overdose of oxytocin spreading in my body put a blissful smile on my face and I moaned with delight as I leaned my head back against his shoulder. Marco was so large and strong compared to me, but I felt at peace and my breath whooshed out: "I trust you."

My words undid Marco, who tightened his hold around me and bit into my neck without breaking the skin. "I can't hold it much longer," he warned.

"Yes, Marco... yes...." The rush of being taken by him with his arms holding me so tight, the sound of his deep breathing in my ear, and the slight pain from his bite on my neck had me tensing up in my body, my pelvic muscles tightening as my orgasm came rolling in, and made me whimper while he roared out his deep groans and intensified the pace in a short sprint of deep and fast pumps.

The release was powerful and for a minute we stood linked together with his body resting over mine, his head leaning down on my shoulder, and him still spearing me with his erection.

"That was out of this world," he mumbled and kissed my cheek.

"Marco." My brain had begun operating again.

"Uh-huh." He didn't move.

"Did you just come in me again?"

"Shit!" He straightened up and pulled out of me, his eyes large with regret. "I didn't think. I'm sorry."

"You promised."

"I know. I don't know what happened." His hands were in his hair. "Fuck."

I spread my legs and began pressing the semen out.

"Here, see if you can wash it out," he said and pulled down the showerhead.

"Wash it out?" I gave him an *are-you-serious* look. "How do you know the water won't push it further up?"

"Do you have any better ideas?"

"One. Don't come in me when I tell you not to."

125

He pushed the shower hose at me. "At least try washing it out," he encouraged.

With an annoyed sigh, I squatted down a bit and pressed the shower head to my opening,

"Do you want me to help?" Marco asked, shifting his weight from one foot to the other.

"I think you've done enough."

"Shelly, I swear I didn't mean to come inside you."

"Yet you did. Twice!"

"The first time wasn't my fault," he defended himself.

My eyes were on the water running out of me. "Let's hope you don't have super sperm as you talked about."

"And that you're not ovulating any time soon," he added.

When I'd done what I could to flush his semen out, we turned off the water and used the dryer function. Marco was apologetic and hugged me.

"Are you mad at me?"

"Yes" would have been the right answer but I was raised in a society of politeness and said, "What good would that do?"

"I'm sure you're not pregnant. You said it yourself, the chance is slim. Some of the couples I know had sex for many months before they got pregnant. Like eight months, and sometimes more than a year. It's rare to get pregnant right away."

I knew Marco was trying to calm himself down and went along with it. "You're right. We have nothing to worry about."

"Let me get you a clean t-shirt to sleep in," he said when we got out of the shower.

"No, it's fine." I picked up the t-shirt he'd lent me and didn't tell him that I liked how it smelled of him.

"All right. Suit yourself."

After cleaning our teeth, and Marco getting some clothes from his room, we stood in the hallway – me in his t-shirt, him naked, holding the clothes in front of his crotch.

"Then I guess I'll see you tomorrow."

"You could sleep with me in the bed, if you'd like. Maybe we could snuggle," I suggested.

Marco shook his head. "Nah, I'd better sleep on the couch in case Storm comes back early. I wouldn't want him to know what happened between us." He moved toward the living room.

"Right." Disappointment filled me as I watched him walk away.

"Sweet dreams," he said over his shoulder.

"Marco."

He stopped. "Yeah?"

"What do you think Storm would say if he found us in the same bed?"

"He would assume we were getting married. Since you don't want that, there's no need for him to know anything. He wouldn't understand."

I fiddled with the hem of his t-shirt, asking the painful question on my mind. "Are you ashamed of sleeping with me?"

Marco walked back at a slow pace, his forehead wrinkled in frown lines. "Shelly, we agreed that we didn't want anyone to know."

"Yes."

"You want me to tell Storm now?"

"No."

"Good, then let's just stick to the plan. I know it's unconventional, but if anyone can make it work, it's us."

I didn't respond, but just stood there and watched him give me a small smile and walk away again, his naked behind firm and round.

"Why?"

Marco turned for the second time, this time with a sigh. "Why what?"

"Why can we make it work better than anyone?"

He lifted a hand. "Because we were never in love and we never made any promises. You asked me not to get possessive and I won't."

"Nmen typically are possessive by nature."

"True. But you made it clear that you're not interested in me as a mate."

"I only said that I wouldn't marry you and that I have work in the Motherlands."

"Exactly."

An inner voice shouted that I wanted nothing more than to be Marco's mate, but I wasn't a fifteen-year-old girl with juvenile dreams anymore. I understood that culturally we were too different and that we could never make each other happy.

"Will you be possessive of Louisa?" It just slipped out.

"That's different. If I win her, she'll be my wife."

"I see." Intellectually his words made perfect sense but they still hurt. I might not want to marry Marco, but I wanted to be with him. Laugh with him. Explore sex with him. If only there was a way that didn't include children and marriage.

I hurried into bed, holding back the pain in my heart.

The blanket was pulled up high and my back was to the door when Marco suddenly spoke from the doorway.

"Hey, Shelly?"

I didn't turn around but made a sound to let him know I was still awake.

"You're not going to tell anyone, are you?"

"No."

"Good, 'cause people wouldn't understand and it could blow my chances with Louisa if she hears that I was sleeping with a Motlander. She might think I'm in love with you and pick another champion because of it."

Why did he have to drill it in that he wasn't in love with me? It was the second time he said it within a few minutes.

"I understand." My voice sounded deceivingly unaffected, and Marco left with a small whistle while I ignored the tear running over the bridge of my nose and landing without a sound on the pillow.

CHAPTER 12
Reunion Plans

Marco

Tristan couldn't take his eyes off Willow, and I didn't blame him. Willow had been the prettiest girl at the school ten years ago, and now at twenty-two she lit up the whole room when she walked into Tristan's apartment with Hunter and me.

"I heard you fainted," Willow said with concern and sat down on the armrest of the sofa where Tristan was occupying half of it with his feet up. "How are you feeling?"

"Willow?" Tristan pushed himself up, his smile growing. "I didn't know you were in town."

She gave him a blinding smile and pushed her long shiny hair back over her shoulder. "I'm trying to get Hunter to move to the Motherlands so we can be closer, but so far I'm the one who has to travel up here to see my brother."

Hunter, who had the same spectacular green eyes as his sister, crossed his arms. "We swung by Storm's place, but he wasn't home, and Marco told us what happened so we came by to check up on you."

"Thank you. I'm doing a lot better." Tristan reached for a glass of water on the table next to him. "If only my head would stop hurting."

I was angry at Tristan for having been so reckless the day before and gave him a hard time. "You deserve to be in pain after putting Shelly in danger like that. What were you thinking, taking a woman to a bar? Do you realize what could have happened to her?"

"What happened to Shelly?" Willow asked with a frown.

I told the story of finding Shelly half naked and surrounded by a group of drunken males.

"Oh no, poor Shelly, she must have been so frightened," Willow exclaimed. "I would have gone into hysteria."

"Shelly isn't like that." Storm tucked his shoulder-length hair back behind his ears. "She was scared, but she didn't panic or cry like other women would have."

"I saw tears in her eyes," I added. "Not a lot, but she was terrified."

Willow scratched her collarbone and Tristan's eyes followed her every movement. "Shelly was always tough. I remember thinking of her as an adult back when we went to school, even though she is only – what? – three years older than me."

"That's because she's so different from the rest of us." Hunter pulled a chair over to sit close to the couch. "I mean with the way her brain works."

"I wish I had a photographic memory." Storm sighed and then he lit up. "You know what? Since we're all here, you can help me plan the reunion party."

"What reunion party?" Willow asked.

"We were the first students to be mixed together from each side of the border. I thought it would be fun to get everyone together again and celebrate that it's been ten years."

Willow's eyes flew to Hunter and back to Storm. "Are you going to invite *everybody*?"

"That was the plan."

Hunter rose up to his full height. "You're not inviting Solo."

"Ah, come on, it's been years," Storm argued and looked to Willow for help. "Don't you think it's time to move on and forgive him?"

Willow and Solomon had been a couple back at the school, but they had been only twelve and fourteen and too young for me to ever take it seriously.

"Are you still in contact with Solo?" Willow asked me.

"No. He just kind of fell off the radar. I'm not sure what happened to him."

Tristan spoke up. "He trained with Magni until he left the school. I know he hoped to join the Huntsmen, but I don't know if he ever did. I tried connecting with him, but after what happened, he cut me off."

Storm turned to Hunter. "Look, I know that Solo messed up, but he used to be our friend and I want everyone to be at the reunion."

Hunter's jaw was set and he didn't look forgiving at all. "If you invite Solo, Willow and I won't be there."

Willow's lips disappeared in a thin line.

Throwing his hands in the air, Storm sighed. "Fine, but at least think about it. For all we know, Solo might be married by now and have kids. Maybe you could drink a beer with him and laugh at what happened back then."

Hunter snorted, lifting the edge of his upper lip. "Not fucking likely."

Willow's hands were playing with her hair and her eyes glazed over as she looked out the window, no doubt long gone in memories from her time with Solo.

"What happened exactly?" I asked because only vague memories of hearing about a falling out between Hunter and Solo came to mind.

"I don't want to talk about it." Hunter's tone was dismissive and he walked over to stroke Willow's back in a soothing manner.

Storm crossed his arms. "Alright, then forget about Solo, but what about the rest? Do we invite the old people or just us young ones? I mean, Archer and Kya are a must, but what about Boulder and Christina? They kind of built the school so I want to invite them too."

"You invite everyone, of course," I said, as to me it was a no-brainer.

"Even Lord Khan and Pearl?"

"*Especially* Pearl and Lord Khan. They came up with the idea to create the school to begin with and the school is named after Pearl."

Hunter nodded. "I agree, but there's no way they'll come. I mean Lord Khan is our ruler. I doubt he has time for us."

I leaned against the wall, my arms folded. "The school was always important to him and Pearl. If they have time, they'll come."

Storm's eyes widened as if he'd just thought of something worthy of a genius. He spoke with excitement. "What about Magni? You think we could get him to come? It would be the biggest scoop ever to have him there."

I angled my head. "How is it a bigger scoop to have Magni come than his brother, the ruler?"

Storm scrunched up his face. "It's fucking *Magni Aurelius* – the man is a living legend. He's my hero."

I narrowed my eyes. "Do I need to remind you that he almost killed me that time when he thought I'd slept with Laura?"

Storm and Hunter burst into grins and spoke at the same time. "It was epic. He almost crashed his drone when he came for you."

"I thought Magni was going to kill you for real. He looked like an avenging demon coming straight out of hell to kill you."

I spoke in a dry tone. "I'm glad you two were entertained."

Storm rocked back and forth with sounds of suppressed excitement.

"What is it?" I asked.

"I just remembered something hilarious." Storm grinned. "Never mind, though, it's about Solo, so I probably shouldn't say it."

"What?" Willow asked. "What about Solo?"

"Don't you remember that Magni knocked him out?" Storm lifted his arm and made a right hook in the air. "Boom – good night, Solo, sleep tight."

Willow tensed up. "It wasn't funny then and it's not funny now."

Storm was still grinning. "Oh, it's funny." He pointed at me. "But at least Solo was standing up to Magni. You fucking ran like a girl."

I scoffed. "I had no problem with Magni and didn't want to fight him, that's all."

"You were terrified of him." Storm clapped his thighs with laughter while Tristan came to my defense.

"Shut up, Storm. We were all terrified of him, you included. I would like to see what you'd do if Magni stormed after you with murder in his eyes."

Hunter crossed his arms and snorted. "We all know the answer to that question. Storm would be begging for Magni's autograph."

"Have you decided on a day for the reunion?" Willow asked and brought us back on track.

"No, not yet, but I was thinking late July or early August, before the new school year starts. That way there will be fewer children at the school."

"You want to have the party at the school?"

"Of course. We can bring tents and make it a fun weekend."

Willow picked up a bowl of nuts and offered it to Storm, who was trying to reach. "And how far are you with the planning?"

"I spoke to Kya about it and she loved the idea. She said she would talk to Archer about a date. When it comes to invites, the adults should be easy enough, and from the kids I already have us four plus Nero, Mila, Raven, and Shelly."

I frowned. "Wait a minute, why are you counting me as a kid? I was an adult."

Storm leaned his head from side to side as if not quite sure. "You and Shelly were kind of in between."

"We were assistant mentors. Not students."

"True, but Shelly was only fifteen."

"So? I was twenty." I raised an eyebrow, speaking slowly and clearly. "I was *not* a kid."

"Okay, fine, Marco, then you can sit at the grown-up table."

"Do you need help finding the Motlanders?" Willow asked.

"Actually, I was planning to ask Shelly to get her sister Rochelle to track down the rest of the Motlander students. Isn't Shelly and Rochelle's mom a member of the Motherland Council?"

"Yes, she is," Willow confirmed.

Storm nodded with satisfaction. "Then she'll have the connections to find them."

"And how are you going to track down the last students from the Northlands?" I asked.

Storm gave me a sly smile. "Actually, I was hoping Tristan could help me with that."

Tristan pushed further up on the couch. "Me?"

"Uh-huh, you talk to Mila sometimes and being Magni's daughter, she's bound to have connections too."

"Sure, I can ask her," Tristan offered.

"Good." Storm clapped his hands together. "Tell you what. I'll call Kya right now and ask her if she's got a date yet while you call Mila and get her on board." He turned and pointed to me. "Can you call Shelly, and fill her in? Tell her we need her to enroll her sister Rochelle."

We all stared at him, not used to Storm's being so organized.

"Go…" he said with impatience, gesturing with his hands for us to spread out.

Ten minutes later we were all back in the living room surrounding Tristan, who was still on the couch.

"Kya and Archer are excited. We're doing it the first weekend of August," Storm reported and looked at me. Did you get a hold of Shelly?"

"Yes, she said. "Rochelle will be happy to help. According to Shelly, Rochelle is already in contact with the other Motlander students anyway."

"I knew it!" Storm gave a satisfied nod. "And what did Mila say?"

Tristan and Willow had talked to Mila, and they exchanged a glance before Tristan spoke. "The good news is that Mila is more than willing to help."

"That's great."

"Yeah, but there's just one problem."

"And what's that?" Storm asked.

"It's just that Mila is a true Motlander at heart. She's a strong believer in second chances, and inclusiveness."

Hunter stiffened next to me. "I think I fucking know where this is going."

Tristan pushed higher up on the sofa. "Mila didn't like the idea of inviting everyone and leaving Solo out. She says that she'll help, but only if everyone is invited."

"I doubt that he'd come anyway," Willow said in a low voice. "He's too proud for that."

I really wished that someone would tell me what had happened between her and Solomon back then, but with the tension emanating from Hunter, I wasn't going to ask again.

"Did you tell Mila that Willow and I won't come if Solo comes?" Hunter asked.

Willow's bright green eyes locked on her brother. "No."

"Why not?"

136

"Maybe it'll be good for me."

"Are you fucking serious?"

"He wouldn't hurt me, Hunter. You know that."

Hunter paced the floor. "You're damn right he wouldn't hurt you. I wouldn't let him get close enough to *touch* you."

"The chance of Solo coming to the reunion is very low. If he does, maybe it can give me some closure."

"You don't need closure, you're over him." Hunter said it like it was an order and underlined it with his hand cutting through the air.

With her chest rising in a deep intake of air, Willow gave a slow shake of her head. "I have so much anger when I think of him. So much deep resentment. Maybe if I found answers to some of my unanswered questions, I could finally find peace."

"How about Mila invites everyone and then we take it from there," Tristan suggested. "If Solo comes and you want him to stay away from Willow, we could always tell him that Willow and I are a couple now."

Hunter stopped pacing and his hand flew to the back of his head, his face turning toward Tristan. "What did you say?"

Tristan paled. "You know, to make Solo stay away from her."

"Ahh, yes, that's not a bad idea. That would work on every male there, not just Solo."

"Hey, don't talk about me like I'm not here, and for the record: I don't lie," Willow protested.

"It's just a little white lie for your safety," Tristan pointed out. "After I failed Shelly yesterday, I would like to help you if possible."

Willow got up from the couch and walked to the window overlooking the city. "Why don't we wait and see if Solo is even interested in participating?" Her hands played with a necklace around her throat. "Storm has a point. There's a big chance Solo is married with children now. He probably doesn't think much about us anymore."

"Wonderful. Then I'll get the invites rolling," Storm exclaimed. "It's going to be the wildest party ever. You'll see!"

CHAPTER 13
Pragmatist

Shelly

Does being a pragmatist make you less emotional?

It was a question I pondered over as I analyzed my relationship with Marco. For as long as I could remember, I'd been told I lacked a filter and needed to develop more sensitivity.

I'd taken a psychology degree and learned to compensate for my so-called lack of empathy by analyzing body language, non-verbal sounds, and making sense of it all.

Now that Marco was back in my life, dormant feelings had surfaced from the time I was a teenager with a crush, and I'd concluded two things.

One: Maybe I didn't express my feelings as openly as normal Motlanders, but I still had strong emotions. Marco brought out a wide range of feelings in me, strong enough to cause physical reactions and sleepless nights.

Two: I *did* have a filter. Not once had I told anyone, including Marco, about the way he made me feel. Declaring my love would only complicate things between us when it was really very simple. We shared chemistry but had vastly different ideas of what our futures looked like. I planned to travel, explore, and develop things to improve life for all humans. Marco dreamed of a life in the Northlands with a sweet wife, children, and material wealth.

I was rational enough to understand that we would never be able to make each other happy. The realization that I had not just a filter, but a strong one, made me think that maybe I wasn't lacking empathy either. Maybe I was just less attached to outcomes than others and therefore less impacted by emotions.

Like the time my sister didn't get into the school she wanted and she cried for a week. I didn't understand why she was so upset when there were other schools to pick from. It wasn't that I didn't see how disappointed and sad Rochelle was. I just didn't see the sense in sharing it and feeling sad myself. That would only make it harder to cheer her up.

Charlie called me and because I'd just been deep in thought, pondering the subject of empathy and how I could apply it to Natura, I asked him, "Charlie, would you say empathy is important?"

My boss tilted his head. "Very much so."

"And would you say that I have empathy?"

Unlike Nmen, Charlie had no facial hair, and wore a bit of make-up. "Why do you ask, Shelly?"

"I spoke to my sister Rochelle a few days ago and she accused me of being selfish because I didn't sympathize with her complaints."

"Why didn't you?"

"What would be the point? How would it help her?"

"Well, it can be nice to feel like someone else cares."

"Rochelle said that I haven't developed empathy because no one expects me to show it. According to her, everyone thinks I'm quirky and emotionally limited."

"And you disagree?"

"I know I'm quirky, but to call me limited... I don't know, Charlie. The thing is that I've observed an interesting pattern. When my sister is sad, she'll fall apart around her friends or my mother. But when she's with me, she'll collect herself and suck it up."

"Maybe it's because she doesn't think you understand anyway," Charlie commented.

"Exactly. But from a practical standpoint isn't it better to compose yourself than to fall apart? Meaning, am I not doing her a favor compared to the others who make her feel worse by asking endless questions about her pain?"

"It's not that simple, Shelly."

"Why not? I would think I'm doing a sad person a favor by not sharing in their misery. I'm almost forcing them to move on, am I not?"

"It's not always about moving on so much as it is about venting."

I picked up a robotic hand that was lying on my desk and played with it. "By venting you mean complaining about what is wrong?"

"More like reflecting on it. It's a helpful exercise to feel relief. People often feel lighter after discussing what burdens them. It you try to suppress bad experiences, they'll only come back as memories or bad dreams, and if you have enough unresolved issues in your system, it can cause depression. That's why it's better to discuss it with someone who cares enough to show sympathy."

I tilted my head and gave him a thoughtful expression. "But who has time for all that venting?"

"People *take* the time."

I scoffed. "Some people have too much time then. Not me, though. I'm much too busy working on solutions."

"Yes, that you are." Charlie smiled. "So give me an update on the work you've done."

Charlie and I discussed the research program, the data, and my improvements on Mindy before he changed the subject again. "That's all very impressive, but how come you're not telling me about the mail that you've been receiving?"

My hands rearranged a few things on my desk. "Why would I?"

"I wish you'd told me about it. I had to find out via personnel."

"It's nothing."

"It's not nothing. Internal systems alerted the personnel department. They told me that you've been on the receiving end of some vicious hate mail with strong wording that is unacceptable and mean in nature."

"It's not that bad."

Charlie looked upset. "How can you say that, Shelly? I was deeply shocked when I read some of these harsh and cruel letters. Like this one." He began reading aloud. "What a waste to give a genius brain to a traitor and Nman lover. I dislike you, Shelly Summers, and I wish that you'll trip and get hurt." Charlie's expression when he looked up was stern and severe. "To think that someone here in the Motherlands would use such explicit language and wish harm on you."

I shrugged. "I have spent too much time in the Northlands to be offended by that."

"But why haven't you told me about these harsh attacks on your person?" Charlie asked.

I shook my head, not having a satisfying answer for him.

"Shelly. I want to help you, but I'm not sure how."

"Don't. They're not saying anything I haven't heard before. People are just angry at me living and working here when they think I should be performing miracles in the Motherlands."

"One of them called you a *big-brained romantic*. That must have hurt." Charlie looked like it pained him to say it. "I suppose it's a reaction from people who have seen you on the news. You are aware that the media has mentioned that you're working in the Northlands, right?"

I sighed. "People need to leave me alone."

"Shelly, you're the daughter of a prominent councilwoman and the biggest genius we have. If you didn't want people to care about you, you shouldn't have said yes to all the articles or that documentary they did last year. You're a celebrity now and that means people have high hopes for you."

I scratched my arm, looking away.

"I'm your boss, and even I have a hard time understanding why this area has your interest. Why sex-bots for Nmen? It makes no sense. You're not going to win any design awards for your work here; I hope you understand that.

"I'm not in it to win awards and it doesn't have to make sense. It was something I was interested in and that's why I'm here. When I'm done, I'll move on and work on something else. I have a project in mind."

Charlie lit up. "Interesting. Tell me."

"I want to reinvent pregnancy prevention and the technology to keep women from getting their period."

Charlie looked like I'd just told him I wanted to go to Saturn. "We already produce pregnancy prevention. There's a sperm-killing spray on the market but it's not selling well."

"I know. I had some of it shipped here, and did you know that it's only ninety percent effective? It says so on the spray."

"No, I didn't."

"It also leaves a sticky residue on the penis and the taste is awful."

"Why would the taste matter?" Charlie asked with a line between his eyebrows.

"In case the couple wants to enjoy oral sex."

Charlie was pulling at his earlobe. "That sounds absolutely disgusting."

"Exactly, you should taste it yourself and you'll know what I mean. So you see there's a need for pregnancy prevention that is more practical."

"Hmm."

"Now that the Northlanders are marrying Motlanders they have sex, and there's going to be a need to control when and how often the women get pregnant."

"If they don't want children, they should simply cease to have intercourse. We don't need a device or a pill for that."

"You're missing the point, Charlie. The couples have sex for pleasure, not just to have children."

Charlie shook his head. "I don't think I'll ever understand the fascination with sex between people when we're producing such excellent robots for that very purpose. Either way, Shelly, the market for a product like that would be minuscule. You can't throw away your genius for a tiny niche."

I ignored his protest. "And like I said, I also want to set women free from their monthly periods. No more cramps and bleeding. I guarantee there's a *large* market for that."

"I doubt it. Women have had their period for thousands of years and they've been fine. No need to change that."

"Easy for you to say. You're a man, so you wouldn't understand. I'm going to improve the quality of life for millions of women around the world."

"Shelly, Shelly... every department is asking for your help and this is what you want to spend your time on? Sex and menstruation?"

"Yes."

Charlie sighed. "What a shame, but I suppose there's nothing I can do about it." His eyes searched the office. "Where is Mindy?"

"Over there. I fixed her."

"And how is your natural robot project going? Did you interview more Nmen?"

"Yes."

"And?"

"I still feel there is a large market for it. Ultimately it depends on how real we can make Natura seem, and how cheaply we can produce her."

"You named her Natura?"

"Yes. Do you like it?"

Charlie lifted one edge of his mouth in a forlorn smile. "Hmm, yes, it's a fine name... just remember to run all your plans by me."

"Of course."

Charlie fiddled with the collar of his yellow sweater. "You know I don't like confrontation, which is why this is very hard for me to say."

"Charlie, are you all right? What's wrong?"

"I have to be honest with you, Shelly. There's a rumor that you already produced the robot. That's not true, is it?"

I lowered my brow. "No, of course not."

"That's what I thought, but apparently Tristan has some friends who know a man who said that he tested it. Tristan mentioned it as a side note and thought it was funny, but it had me worried."

I let my tongue run over my teeth, suddenly feeling dry in the mouth. "Charlie, there is no prototype of Natura. Where would I even get the resources to produce one?"

He lowered his brow and scratched his ear. "You would tell me if you are working with someone else, wouldn't you? I'm not stupid. I know there are people in the Northlands with a lot of money who would offer you material benefits if you were to work for them. We would be devastated to lose you."

"Charlie..." I began but he continued talking.

"You know that you can pick any project to work on. There is a very interesting ocean farming project taking place in the Yellow Zone. You could live on a beach and enjoy the sun and sea."

I gave Charlie a soft smile. "That sounds wonderful. I'll think about it."

"Of course. Oh, and by the way, did you hear Tristan was attacked?"

I stiffened. "Who told you that?"

"Tristan did. It happened last Saturday. Makes me worry about you staying in the Northlands, Shelly. Nmen are violent and unscrupulous."

It was clear that Tristan hadn't told Charlie that I'd been with him that night. It was for the better.

"I'll make sure to check in with him and see if he feels better," I assured Charlie.

"Good. Let's talk in a few days. I'll send you more information on the ocean farming project. They could really use your help." His eyes continued roaming around the office as if looking for the rumored sex-bot.

"Sounds good, Charlie."

"Be careful and go in peace," he said politely. "And remember to do something else than just work."

"Don't worry, I will," I promised before I ended the call

As I looked at the time, a smile grew on my face. Marco would be here in ten minutes. He was coming by with lunch for the third time this week, and this researcher's job was about to get very hands-on.

CHAPTER 14
Checking Off the List

Shelly

Half an hour after my call with Charlie, I stood bent over my work desk, Marco driving in and out of me like I was his meal and he couldn't get enough. The food that he'd brought was spread around my table: a salad with a fork full of cucumber and red beets that hadn't reached my mouth before Marco had initiated sex.

His burger was close to the edge of the table, half eaten and moving closer and closer to the edge with the rocking movement of the desk.

I thought about moving it but found a strange satisfaction in Marco caring more about being with me than saving his burger.

Being obsessed with details, I knew that this was our ninth time having sex together. Marco had taken his offer of helping me with my research very seriously. He'd even introduced me to the archives on the old Internet with pre-war porn, something I knew existed but didn't have access to in the Motherlands.

Some of it was arousing; other parts were disturbing and raised a lot of questions on my part. Marco had answered, giving me his perspective as a man, and we'd discussed the differences between female and male sexuality.

He also suggested we pick out five things we each wanted to try and include them in the experiment. So far, we'd tried sex in the shower, in a bed, on a couch, in a drone, and we had done it in twelve different positions.

Marco had taught me how he loved it when I looked up at him during oral sex.

In return, I had taught him to be patient and not go too deep at the beginning when he penetrated me. He had learned how to give me time to stretch and adjust to his size.

"You're so fucking hot," Marco panted behind me. "Tight and wet for me."

I moaned, enjoying the feel of his fingers playing with my nipples.

"Please can I try it?" he asked and I knew exactly what he was asking.

"No."

"I'll be careful, I promise."

"No, Marco."

"Don't you trust me?"

I turned my head. "It's an exit only."

"But it's on my list and you saw it yourself in the porn movies. Anal sex used to be as common as standard sex. They *all* did it back in the day."

"Okay, but go slow."

Marco pulled out of me and used lubrication from my first hole to wet the second one while my face tightened in tension.

"Just relax," he instructed and pressed against my back entrance. I squeezed instead.

"Shelly, you're not relaxing," he said and placed kisses along my spine.

"I don't care what they did in the old days. It hurts."

"How can it hurt when I'm not inside you yet? It's in your mind, and it's because you're too tense. Just relax and let it happen."

I shook my head. "No, it feels weird. I don't like it."

Without seeing his face, I knew Marco was disappointed but he turned me around.

"It's okay, we can always do it some other time when you're more comfortable." He kissed me, lifting me up to sit on the table before pressing inside me. "This morning I was jerking off thinking about you, and you know what I thought about?"

I smiled a little. "What?"

"The other day when you let me come in your mouth. That was..." He groaned with pleasure. "I swear, Shelly, that way you opened your mouth and showed me the cum on your tongue. I'll be thinking about that till the day I die."

It had been one of the five things on Marco's list. Despite my initial reluctance to let him come in my mouth it hadn't been half as bad as I feared. It was the same when he had used my breasts to slide his erection between. He'd been sitting on top of me, his muscles ripped and his eyes fixed on the way he squeezed my breasts together. It hadn't done much for me, except make me feel desired and wanted, which I concluded was arousing in itself.

Marco still had two things left on his list, but those were the things I'd been reluctant about. The anal had failed and I wasn't keen on letting him tie me up and blindfold me either.

"Lie back," Marco said and raised my legs to his shoulders. "What's wrong?"

"Something is poking me in the back." I moved on my desk to be more comfortable and enjoyed the sight of Marco between my legs, his lips parted, his eyes roaming over my breasts and face with lust shining from his hooded eyes.

For a while there was no talking, just groans, moans, and the sound of him slapping against me in a steady pace. With his thumb, he circled my clit, my moans grew longer and my voice rose in volume.

"It feels so good, Marco. Harder. More."

His ears were red, his breathing fast, his body emanating heat, and I loved the determined expression on his face as he kept pushing in and out of me, harder and faster just like I'd asked for.

"I can't hold it much longer," he groaned with his hands boring into my hips to keep me in place.

Pushing up on my elbows, I reached for him, wanting to feel him – the intensity of emotions washing over me as he grabbed a fistful of my hair, pressing his face into my temple and saying my name over and over.

"Yes, Marco, yes." My pulse fluttered at my wrists and throbbed at my throat. I leaned my head back, closing my eyes and giving in to the powerful volcano erupting inside of me. Marco intertwined our fingers and as I panted out his name, I squeezed his hand tightly. "Oh, yes.... yes, Marco, yes. I'm coming."

He moved his hips in fast aggressive movements and forced out his words. "I. Can't. Get. Enough. Of. You."

"Ahh, yes, Marco, that's right..." My body was still in that blissful orgasmic state with my inside fluttering and my muscles twitching with tiny aftershocks. I was high on the wonderful feeling of connection between us.

"I'm coming." Marco's warning came a split second before he pulled out and used his hand to ejaculate on my belly.

Dazed from the sex haze and fascinated with the clear semen landing on my creamy skin, my eyes went from the cum to Marco's face. I watched him pant with his mouth open and his eyes closed.

"You're so..." The word beautiful was on my tongue.

"What?"

"Sweaty."

He gave me a small grin and lowered his face to the crook of my neck, his warm breath on my skin. "Yeah, that's because I'm doing all the hard work. You're just lying there looking gorgeous."

I used my right hand to nuzzle his brown curls, taking time for us to catch our breaths while I caressed his back with my left hand.

"Can I ask you a question, Marco?"

"You're always asking me questions." Marco chuckled and leaned back to watch me. "Oh-oh, I have a feeling this is going to be one of the more awkward ones. What do you want to know?"

"If you marry Louisa, will you ask her to do the things on your list?"

He reached around me, picking up some napkins, and began drying me off. "Probably not."

I waited for him to elaborate.

"What you and I have is different. You said it yourself, it's an experiment and I'm enjoying trying different things with you. Why do you want to talk about Louisa now?"

"I'm sorry. It just boggles my mind that you would risk your life fighting in a tournament for a woman you don't love. Is it really just because of the money?"

Marco didn't meet my eyes but pulled away from me and bent down to pull up his pants. "I'm tired of being poor. Why shouldn't I have nice things like other men?"

"What other men?"

"Hunter, Tristan, Boulder, Magni, and the others who have fast drones and large apartments.

"Tristan isn't rich."

"He's not poor like me."

"See, that's why the fairness principle in the Motherlands is so much better than the capitalistic system you Nmen have. We all contribute with our unique talents and we should be paid the same."

"I'm not a fan of the fairness principle." Marco helped me down from the table. "All your system does is keep everyone equally comfortable. At least here we have a chance to live in abundance."

"If you win a tournament, that is?"

151

"Yes." He walked into the bathroom and washed his hands while talking to me. "There's also the prestige that comes with being one of the fiercest warriors and having your own family."

"Yeah, but that last part can't have as much status as it used to, I mean, with all the Motlander women coming." I arranged my clothes while Marco walked over to pick up his burger and take a big bite.

When he was done chewing, I was the one washing my hands. "So does it?"

"Does it what?"

"Does winning a tournament bring as much status as it used to?"

"I would say so. Northlander women are special, you know."

I stiffened. "In what way?"

"They're the real thing."

"You mean in contrast to us fake women?" My lips pressed into a thin line.

"No, you don't get it."

"Then why don't you explain it?"

"Northlander women are rare and precious. They know and understand our culture. They respect their husbands and are obedient by nature."

I pushed my chair back in place and picked up a book that had fallen down. "Have you met Laura?" My tone was sarcastic. "Why don't you ask Magni how obedient she is?"

"Laura is an anomaly."

I gave him a sideways glance. "And you'd rather have a wife who bows her head and says yes than one who challenges you?"

He shrugged. "I told you. I've seen too many unhappy marriages between my friends and their Motlander wives. I'm not signing up for the Matching Program. Not that any of them would pick me anyway. I don't have much to offer a woman if I don't win the million dollars."

152

"Motlander women aren't materialistic."

Marco scoffed. "Bullshit. Men with money have a ninety-two percent bigger chance of being picked by a Motlander woman through the Matching Program. That's a fact!"

I sighed because, sadly, he was right.

"Not everyone in the Motherlands is like that, and I don't believe you'll be happier just because you have a faster drone and a bigger house."

"I do," Marco stated. "It would help a lot."

Shaking my head, I sat on top of my desk and reached for my salad just as Marco plunked down in my chair. "You think we Nmen are strange."

"Because you are."

Marco smiled at me. "But we know how to fuck."

"You do. I can't speak for the rest of your countrymen."

"If anyone is an expert, it would be you, what with all your research."

"Good point, but I meant that I can't speak from personal experience."

We ate in silence for a minute or two before Marco spoke again. "Why don't you want children, Shelly?"

"I told you, it's not something I've thought about."

"You haven't gotten your period yet."

I hesitated before answering. "No, I haven't."

Marco lifted his foot and placed his right ankle over his left knee. "Do you think you'll get it soon?"

"Probably."

"Look, I know you've told me several times that you're not interested in being a wife and mother, but if you're pregnant with my child, we need to figure ou…"

"I'm not, Marco." I cut him off in a firm tone.

"Shelly, I don't have much to offer, I know that, but I would love our child."

"There's no child, Marco."

"But if there was, what would you do? I know you don't want to live in the Northlands permanently, but you'd still let me see my kid, right?"

I got up. "I don't want to speculate about hypothetical problems. I'm a pragmatist, I like to relate to facts only, and so far, nothing suggests that I'm pregnant."

CHAPTER 15
Alcohol and Weed

Marco

"Sure, you can mix alcohol and weed," Storm said with an authority that rubbed me the wrong way.

We were all hanging out in my apartment, and Storm had convinced Willow it was time to embrace the culture of the Northlands and get drunk.

"Go easy," Hunter instructed his sister, who was wrinkling her nose up at the smell of whiskey. "You're not used to alcohol, so you won't need much to get drunk."

"Are you with me, Shelly?" she asked with a playful smile. "I'll do it, if you do it."

Taking a small sip from the glass Storm had given her, Shelly gave a grimace. "That tastes awful."

I was on a chair, facing the sofa where Shelly sat in the middle with Willow and Storm on each side of her. Hunter was sitting on the armrest next to Willow with a glass of whiskey of his own. Tristan was on a chair next to me.

"If you don't like the whiskey, you can mix it with soda or take this instead." Tristan held out a weed inhaler.

My nostrils flared a bit when Shelly reached for it and turned it around in the air. I wasn't her protector and couldn't tell her what to do, but I didn't like her getting high or drunk. One of my friends had once confessed that when he got his Motlander wife drunk she became horny. Shelly was already too curious for her own good. I didn't need her to develop the same type of scientific interest in Hunter, Storm, or Tristan that she had for me. If she did, this whole secrecy thing between us would be off. She might not be mine, but she wouldn't be theirs either. Not tonight anyway.

"Did you know that archeologists now think that cannabis seeds were used as a food source in China eight or nine thousand years ago? People still use it in the Motherlands for medical purposes, but it won't give you a high. It's actually a chemical called tetrhydrocannabinol that causes the high."

"Shelly, shut the fuck up and inhale the damn thing." Storm was pushing her with his shoulder and grinning. I clenched my teeth wanting to ask him not to touch her.

While Willow clinked her glass with her twin brother and got some of the whiskey down, Shelly inhaled the weed, and handed the inhaler back to Tristan.

"Do you feel it?" he asked with eagerness.

"I think I do." She had the cutest expression on her pretty face. Her eyes and mouth widening in a silent "Whoa."

"Let me try," Willow said. Tristan was quick to give her the inhaler and watched with interest when Willow took a deep huff and coughed before speaking. "You and Archer used to smoke these sometimes at the school, didn't you, Marco. I recognize the fragrance."

"It was rare," I said and took another sip of my beer.

"We had so much fun at that school." Willow's voice sounded wistful. "And that first year when you and Shelly were there was the best part." She pointed to me and Shelly. "You were always bantering over something stupid and we kids would pick sides and be on team Marco or team Shelly."

"That's awful." Shelly coughed.

"I was on team Marco, but there were a few times when you almost won me over." Hunter nodded to Shelly. "One time you and Marco were discussing something and you told him in a polite way to go fuck himself."

"I would never use such words!"

156

Hunter smiled. "It was in such a subtle way that he didn't even pick up on it. But we boys did and we thought it was hilarious."

"What didn't I pick up on?" I asked with a frown.

"Shelly had you under pressure discussing something and when you ran out of arguments, you pulled the age card saying that you were right because you were *many* years older than her." Hunter was grinning as he told the story. "Shelly didn't buy it and challenged whether five years qualified as many, which of course you insisted it did, telling her that five years was a third of her age." Hunter pointed to Shelly. "The best part was when you just looked at Marco all cool and collected and said in the driest voice, 'Thank you for explaining the word many to me, it means a lot,' and then you walked away."

Willow grinned. "Hunter always tells that story."

"Because it was hysterical. I just knew I wanted to grow up and be like you, Shelly."

Shelly arched an eyebrow. "What, involuntarily funny and socially awkward?"

Willow raised her hand up in the air. "I was always on team Shelly and I loved it when you would tell jokes while teaching."

"Oh, no, those jokes were awful," Storm interjected.

Willow grinned. "What made them funny was that Shelly laughed at her own jokes. Don't you remember how she would sometimes grunt like a pig and all us kids would laugh with her?"

"You mean *at* her," Storm looked at Shelly and gave her an apologetic shrug. "I'm sorry, but you were a bit quirky."

"I still am," Shelly admitted without shame.

"Storm, don't be an ass," I muttered to him.

"I'm not, I'm just being honest. If I could remember one of her jokes you'd understand how lame they were."

"My jokes are funny." Shelly sat up a bit straighter, her eyes sparkling with humor. "I remember one I used when I taught you geometry. Wanna hear it?"

"Yes," Willow said and was already laughing.

"Okay, what did the triangle say to the circle?"

"What?"

"'You're pointless.' And then the circle responded, 'That's how I roll.'" The way Shelly's shoulders were bobbing in infectious laughter had everyone laughing too. "Told you it's still funny."

"The only thing funny about that joke is that it's you telling it," Storm pointed out.

"You should take that as a compliment," Willow told her in a bubbly voice.

Storm leaned in. "Speaking of compliments, did I tell you that Marco and I think that you are hot as hell?"

"I'm not," Shelly objected and looked to me.

"Don't be shy about it." Storm grinned. "I can't wait to see the other men when they see you at the reunion."

Tapping my hand on my thigh, I asked a question and tried to make it sound casual. "Do you think they're going to come on to her?"

If all went according to plan, I would be married to Louisa by then, but the thought that Shelly would be the target of other men's attention didn't sit well with me at all.

"If they drink enough liquid courage, they might."

"Storm, that's an awful thing to say," Willow complained. "You make it sound like no sober man will want her."

"Oh, they'll *want* her all right. But just like the rest of us, they'll be intimidated by Shelly's brains."

"I didn't think Nmen got intimidated," Shelly retorted.

"Aren't you supposed to be fearless?" Willow asked with her brows raised and a smile on her face.

"There is a difference between being fearless and being foolish. Let's be honest, you would never be interested in any of us, would you? I mean, we were your students and none of us can match your intelligence."

Shelly didn't get a chance to answer him before Storm pointed to Willow. "You, however, that's a different story."

"Why? Because I'm not as smart as Shelly?"

"You're more approachable, that's all."

"I'm approachable," Shelly insisted and looked to me. "Right?"

I almost choked on my beer. "Uh-huh."

"See," she said to Storm. "Marco isn't intimidated by me."

"That's because Marco is older and wise enough to not be interested in a Motlander. He thinks you're all too sensitive and crazy," Storm explained, swinging his hand toward me. "With the wife I ended up with, I can't blame you."

"That's not true, is it, Marco?" Willow asked with her green eyes wide. "Some of us are nice – you know that, don't you?"

"Sure," I muttered. "But I would never sign up for the Matching Program."

"That's a shame. Did you know that some of the girls had a secret crush on you back when we were in school?"

I scoffed. "Yeah, right."

"It's true. Archer was always the serious one but you were fun and you would play games with us kids. Sometimes you'd help us girls when the boys were being mean to us."

I looked over at Hunter and Storm. "It's the job of an Nman to be protective of females. They were just too young to understand that."

"Oh, come on, we were just having a little fun; it was innocent," Storm exclaimed.

Willow held out her hand to silence him. "You put spiders and frogs in our beds, and you kept turning the lights on and off to annoy us, not to mention that you blocked our door so we couldn't get out. It was traumatic."

"I don't remember any of that," Tristan said.

"That's because you only came to the school after Solo became my boyfriend. He made sure no one messed with me." Willow bit her lip and frowned before she returned to her rant. "But before that, Marco was our hero. One night you put your mattress on the floor outside our room and told the boys that you'd beat them up if they messed with us again."

"It wasn't a big deal," I insisted.

Willow laughed and flashed her white teeth. "Marco, we loved you for it. Just like we loved you the time you helped us out at that survival camp in the forest where we were freezing and starving."

"What about it?" Tristan asked. "What happened?"

"We couldn't get a fire going and ended up sleeping together in one big bundle of sleeping bags to keep warm. We were miserable and a lot of the girls were crying because of the cold and the fear that wolves or bears would come and eat us. When we woke up the next morning someone had made a fire for us." Willow looked at me. "That was you, wasn't it?"

I smiled. "No comment."

"I don't believe you. There were footsteps and Nicki said she recognized your pattern."

"She must have been wrong."

"Admit it, Marco. We were your girls and you didn't want us to be freezing."

I laughed. "I'll admit that you girls were never as alone in that forest as you thought you were. But it wasn't just me. Magni, Archer, Boulder, and I all patrolled the area and made sure you were safe.

"Did you make the fire?"

"I can't remember."

She grinned up at me. "You did, I know you did. You were always kind to us, Marco. It was a sad day when you left."

"Thank you." I raised my glass to Willow. "It's nice to be appreciated."

Willow took another sip of the whiskey and gave a grimace again. "We should go to a dance bar. I have a friend who lives around here; she knows a bar that's safe."

"We're not going to a bar," I said firmly. "It's a pain going anywhere with Hunter to begin with and with you and Shelly, the chance of us men getting into fights is too big."

"I'm with Marco," Tristan exclaimed. "I don't need to be caught in another bar fight."

"But I want to dance." Willow pouted and moved to the edge of her seat.

"I'll dance with you," Tristan offered and the two of them began discussing what music to put on.

"The Butterflies made this upbeat song called 'Dance with your Eyes.'"

"The Butterflies?" I asked. "You mean those three guys we saw perform when we went on a field trip to the Motherlands?"

"Yes. They were so good. Remember?"

I laughed. "You can't be serious."

"I love their music."

"I'll find something better for you." I put on The Fuckheads, one of our most famous bands, and hard tones began to play.

"Turn it off." Willow shouted over the music. "I can't dance to that."

"Well then, you'll have to find something else – I'm not playing the fucking Butterflies in my apartment. What if the neighbors heard it? They might think I'm suicidal and take it as a cry for help or something."

"Fine, how about this number then?" Willow found something else that'd I never heard before.

"What is this?"

"It's a remake of pre-war music. What do you think?"

My foot began bobbing up and down to the rhythm. "Not bad. I like the singer."

Willow got up from the sofa, took Tristan's hand, and began dancing. Storm and I stared at them because we'd never seen dancing like that.

My eyes went to Hunter, who I was sure would attack Tristan for dancing that close to his sister, but Hunter just took another sip of his whiskey.

"Is that how people dance in the Motherlands now?" I asked Shelly, who had the weed inhaler in her mouth again.

"Yes. Well, not many are as good as Willow, but she's a professional dancer so it's not fair to compare her to others." She handed the weed to me. I took it because I could use the help in relaxing.

"We're definitely *not* going to any bars," I said to Hunter, knowing full well that any Nman who saw Willow move the way she did would lose his fucking mind.

Storm stood up, leaned his head back, and emptied his whiskey. "Time to dance, Shelly," he said and she took his hand.

Shelly was laughing and telling him that she couldn't dance, but he didn't care and soon the two of them were imitating Willow and Tristan.

I hated it!

Storm was too close to Shelly. He whispered in her ear and they were laughing together. His darker skin contrasted with her creamy skin, which was too pale for summer and a testament to how much time she spent working inside. My eyes were burning holes in his head from my chair, but Storm didn't seem to notice.

Hunter brought me a beer that I drank in two large gulps. I had promised Shelly that I wouldn't be possessive, but it was easier said than done when she was swinging her hips and smiling at another man.

It didn't get any better when Hunter asked Shelly to dance next. Being a star athlete playing for the best soccer team in the Northlands, he had enough money to buy her anything she wanted. At least, Hunter kept a bit more distance than Storm had. Still, I kept my eyes on them. According to Storm, his wife Gennie had been all over Hunter, and one would have to be blind not to acknowledge that Hunter was handsome. I kept looking at Shelly trying to read her. Was she attracted to Hunter?

Willow distracted my attention when she came and pulled me up from the chair. "Your turn," she said with a wide smile and began dancing around me like a fairy, light on her feet. In comparison, I resembled a big oak, swaying a little from side to side.

"What's wrong? You don't like to dance?" Willow asked me and took my hands and moved closer.

My eyes were on Shelly, who was laughing with Hunter.

When Willow placed her hands around my waist and swayed from side to side with me, I stiffened and almost didn't breathe. "It's okay, Marco. Hunter isn't going to be angry. This is dancing and my brother understands that."

I still kept my hands away from her body. My heart was racing from the unusual closeness to Willow and the fear that anytime now someone would accuse me of overstepping my boundaries.

Willow was beautiful with her long brown hair and pretty features, but I wasn't attracted to her the way I was to Shelly.

"I love your curls, Marco."

When she raised her hands to feel my hair, I leaned away, trying to create more distance between us.

163

Willow pouted. "Why can't I touch your curls?"

"I need something to drink," I said and left her to dance with Hunter and Shelly.

Standing in my kitchen with a cold beer in my hand, I watched how Tristan and Storm joined the others and the five of them were dancing and laughing.

When Shelly flung her arms around Storm's shoulders I squeezed my beer harder and counted to ten in my head. She didn't look at me or invite me to dance with her. It was like there was nothing between us. None of the others had any idea that this past week, we'd had sex several times. I knew exactly what hid underneath Shelly's white pants and purple shirt. How her breasts felt and tasted, and what sounds she made when I was inside her.

Storm spun her around and beamed at her with a charming smile. My knuckles turned white from squeezing my beer so hard.

"Shelly, can I talk to you?" I asked when they were done dancing and Storm was pressuring Willow and Shelly to drink more whiskey.

"What's wrong?" she asked.

My eyes bulged with silent urgency. "Nothing. I just want to show you something one of my students made. You'll like it."

She followed me down the hallway and when we got out of ears reach, I turned around confronting her. "Can you turn it down a bit?"

"Turn what down?"

"The weed and the drinking." I wanted to say dancing but knew that was overstepping the line.

"Why? I'm having fun." She narrowed her eyes. "You're drinking, so why can't I?"

"Because you're not used to it, and it's a bad idea."

After a few seconds of silence, Shelly opened the door to my empty bedroom and pointed inside. "Do you see what I see, Marco?"

"What do you mean?"

"That's a room full of all the people who think you should decide how I live my life."

I frowned my forehead and she blinked her eyes, her pupils expanded from the weed.

"Do you get it?" She gave a small snicker. "You know, because it's empty..."

"Yeah, I get it." I pulled back from her. "I was trying to look out for you."

"Aww, that's sweet, but I'm an adult." She was swaying slightly when she lifted her hand and counted on her fingers. "I'm a biologist, an engineer, a psychologist, and a *real* adult, Marco."

"You told me several times." I rolled my eyes and took a step toward the living room.

"That's right. I can drink and take weed if I want, and I can have sex with whomever I want, because I'm a free woman."

Her words made me stop and turn around. Keeping as cool as possible I stepped back into her personal space, grateful that the others were still listening to loud music.

"Did you get your period yet?"

"No."

"As long as you're sleeping with me, there will be no one else, do you understand?" My intensity made Shelly take a step back.

"You're possessive," she breathed.

"No."

She blinked a few times. "Yes, you are."

"I'm leaving for the tournament in four days. Do you think you can keep faithful for that long?" My tone was blameful, as if she'd done something wrong.

"Faithful would imply we were in a relationship," Shelly pointed out and tilted her head, her beautiful brown eyes looking up at me.

My body was shaking with emotions that I didn't want. Stepping even closer, I pressed my body against hers and spoke into her ear. "I accept that you don't want to marry me, but either you're with me exclusively until the tournament, or we won't have sex again."

Shelly didn't kiss me or assure me she liked only me. She broke free from my hold and walked away from me, her back straight and her head high.

I already regretted giving her an ultimatum. It had been a mistake that had backfired. If I had magical powers, I would have made the others disappear so I could talk to her, but they were having a party and Storm pushed a glass of whiskey into Shelly's hand, telling her he'd mixed it with a sweet soda to make it easier for her to drink. In a juvenile act of rebellion, Shelly looked straight at me when she forced down a large sip of whiskey.

In return I picked up my beer and emptied it, hoping that the alcohol would numb my desire for the headstrong, infuriating genius who would never find me more than entertaining.

"I still can't believe how pretty you are now," Storm complimented Shelly.

She chuckled. "It's because of my CBC machine or what Tristan likes to call my Troll Transformer."

"That's right." Tristan took over. "Every night Shelly has to hook up to this machine that files her claws and plucks out her beard so she can look like a princess."

The others laughed.

"It's true. I designed the machine to clean my skin and do my nails while I sleep. It's called Convenient Beauty Care or CBC for short."

"What? *You* invented that?" Willow shrieked. "I love my CBC."

"You have one?"

"Of course. So do all my friends. It's the best machine ever invented."

"Not true, but thank you anyway." Shelly smiled when Willow gave her a tipsy kiss on her cheek.

"How come I didn't know you had designed it? I love you, Shelly, you're the smartest, most badass woman I ever met."

Shelly looked confused. "How much did she drink?" she asked Tristan.

"Don't be modest," Tristan replied and slapped Shelly's back. "You've made some remarkable things already, and we're all just waiting to see what you've got up your sleeve next."

"Oh, can I make a wish?" Willow blurted out and sat up straight. "Could you please invent some kind of calorie condenser? Something that removes bad fat, sugar, and carbs from food we love but leaves behind flavor, nutrition, and satisfaction?"

Shelly tilted her head. "That's an interesting thought, but I have another project that I'm passionate about."

"What's that?" Storm asked.

"Pregnancy prevention."

Her announcement was met with complete silence.

"When I'm done with my current project, I'm going to make sure that any woman who wants to have sex doesn't have to worry about getting pregnant. It's going to change the world."

"What are you talking about?" Hunter leaned forward. "Why wouldn't a woman want to have children with her husband?"

"Maybe they aren't married. Maybe they're just lovers."

"Lovers?" Storm laughed and held up a hand. "That's it. No more weed or drinks for you, Shelly, you're babbling."

"I'm not babbling. What if Willow and I were the type of women who didn't want children and marriage, for instance? We could still want sex."

167

"But Motlander women don't like sex," Tristan pointed out.

"Gennie did," Storm argued. "She didn't like me, but she liked the sex."

"I want the whole package with children and a husband," Willow said and pushed her hair back. "I know I'm a freak like that, but I don't care. And I want it with a large Nman."

"I'm at your service." Tristan winked at her.

"You don't count. You're too sweet. It's because you grew up in the Motherlands."

"I'm not sweet." Tristan objected. "I'm tall, strong, the son of a Northlander, and I curse, eat meat, and get drunk on occasion."

Willow tilted her head and smiled at him. "Tristan, you're the sweetest Nman I know."

His shoulders sank. "I can be tough for you."

Willow leaned in and placed her hand on top of his. "You're my friend, Tristan, but it's never going to be you and me as a couple."

"You sure?"

Willow nodded. "I'm conditioned to like large brooding guys. I can't help it."

Hunter rubbed his forehead. "Can we talk about something else?"

"I could tell you some fascinating facts about what happens when we drink alcohol. Would you like to know?"

"No, Shelly," Tristan said and waved a hand in the air to stop her, but Willow gave her all the encouragement she needed when she sat back in the couch and looked at Shelly with admiration. "Yes, tell us. God, you just know everything, don't you?"

"Of course not, but I do know that our liver can only metabolize fifteen milligrams per deciliter per hour, which means that if you drink more than one drink in an hour it will lead to alcohol accumulation in the bloodstream, which will lead to intoxication." Shelly spoke a little slowly, concentrating on pronouncing all the words correctly.

"I had three drinks, does that mean I'm drunk?" Willow asked with a snicker and ruffled Storm's hair, with a grin. "I feel great."

Shelly intertwined her fingers and continued her small lecture. "Me too. That's because the alcohol will decrease activity in certain areas of our brains, one of them being our prefrontal cortex where our inhibitions and self-control are located. Alcohol also increases our production of dopamine, which is our feel-good neurotransmitter."

"Whoa, slow down, Professor." Hunter laughed. "I wish I could swap brains with you for one day and experience what it's like to be a walking library."

"No, go on, Shelly. What happens if I swallow this drink? It's my fourth." Willow poured herself a mix of whiskey and soda and held it up to her mouth.

"Well, side effects would start to show such as problems with your balance or coordination, slurred speech, and if you continue to drink the symptoms will be vomiting, nausea, and blackouts. Of course, alcohol is poison, so if you drink enough you would eventually pass out and die."

"Die?" Willow's smile turned downward.

"Don't worry, sis." Hunter touched Willow's shoulder. "I've seen a lot of men drunk, but so far none have died."

"That's not true. Ronaldo died a few years back, remember," Storm said.

Hunter scrunched up his face. "Because he fell asleep in a pile of snow. He died of hypothermia."

"Yeah, but he passed out because he was drunk."

Willow put down her drink on the table. "Maybe I should stick with the weed instead."

"Sorry, but we're out of weed." Tristan held up both hands.

"Then maybe we can do some of the party games we play in the Motherlands," Willow suggested.

"I'm not doing a fucking love circle," I said. "I have enough of those at work."

"A love circle isn't a party game, silly." Willow grinned at me. "We could do the connection game or the 'secrets are better shared' game."

"I'm not sharing my secrets." Hunter leaned back. "That's a stupid name for a game."

"Then let's do the connection game."

"What is it?"

"Okay, so two people have to sit and stare into each other's eyes for two full minutes. One of them has to focus on a message he or she wants the other to know, while the other person has to receive the message. When the two minutes are up the receiver has to guess what it was."

"I'm game," I said. "Let's see if Brainy can read my mind."

Maybe it was the fact that I used my old nickname for Shelly that provoked her to accept the challenge, but we pulled the chairs close together and sat knee to knee.

Hunter and Willow did the same, joking that their twin connection would give them an advantage over Storm and Tristan, who couldn't stop laughing about the funny faces they were making at each other.

"Wait, shouldn't the person with the message write it down before we start?" Hunter asked. "I mean as proof in the end. Otherwise the couples could cheat."

"You're always so competitive," Willow teased him. "It's a party game, you can't win anything."

"Then why call it a game in the first place?"

"Shhh, just look into my eyes, and read my mind."

"The timer is set for two minutes," Tristan informed us. "Starting.... Now."

Shelly grew serious as she locked eyes with me.

I love having sex with you.

I love having sex with you.

I love having sex with you.

I love having sex with you.

I kept thinking the same thought over and over while pouring my regret for making the stupid ultimatum into my message.

I love being close to you.

I love being close to you.

I love being close to you.

The intensity of looking into her eyes and seeing every speck of light reflected in her dilated pupils made my heart race. I'd seen her pupils dilated like that when she was aroused, but it was probably the weed that was doing it now.

I smiled a little, and Shelly mirrored me with a small smile of her own. My stomach did a somersault and I wet my lips fighting my desire to lean in and kiss her.

I love.... There were so many things I loved about Shelly.

I love... I couldn't remember what message I'd started out with, only that it started with "I love."

I love...

Her smile widened and I took a deep breath in to steady my heart.

I love... your smile.

I love your eyes.

I love your hair and your sharp brain.

I love... I love... Releasing the air in my lungs, I finally knew what my message was.

I love everything about you.

I love everything about you.

I love everything about you.

I love...

171

My smile grew as the thought crystallized and filled every part of my being. *...you...*

I love you.

"Time's up." Tristan called but Shelly and I kept looking into each other's eyes, just smiling.

"I have nothing," Storm said. "I'm clearly not a mind reader."

"What are you talking about? You were supposed to send me a message and I was going to read *your* mind."

"Fuck." Storm laughed. "That explains why I didn't get anything. I was worried that you didn't have any brain activity at all, my friend."

"What was my message?" I asked Shelly and stroked her knee discreetly with my thumb.

"You like me."

My smile grew. "I do."

"Was that the message?" she asked.

"Yes."

"Did you guess it?" Willow asked Shelly.

"I did. Marco was being very friendly and said that he likes me."

"Aww, that's sweet."

"What about you, Hunter, did you guess Willow's mind?"

"Not even close. But she's a woman, so it's no surprise. It would be a fucking miracle if any man could figure out what's going on inside a woman's head."

"You're right about that," I agreed and truly wished I knew what was going on inside Shelly's head. Did she feel anything close to how I felt about her? And if she did, would she move to the Northlands and be with me?

"Hey, Tristan," Willow called out and distracted me. "Hunter was talking about the drone you designed. Will you take me flying in it one day?"

"Sure, I can arrange that. You like fast drones?"

She smiled. "Who doesn't?"

172

Willow's words hit me hard. I had an old, crabby drone that couldn't fly fast for shit. I was grateful when it chose to start in the morning and take me to work. Shelly deserved the best of everything, and without the million dollars I could win in a tournament, I couldn't give her that. But if I won the million dollars, I couldn't have her.

I want to be with Shelly.

I love Shelly.

Loving a woman so far out of my league was depressing. She'd already made it clear that she'd never marry me, and still I was falling hard for her.

Get your shit together, I scolded myself. *It's never going to happen, so stop fucking dreaming.*

"So Marco, if Shelly could read your mind, does that mean there's a special connection between you two?" Willow teased.

I could feel Shelly's eyes on me when I answered with an overwhelming powerlessness pressing in my chest. "I doubt it. Shelly would probably be able to read your mind too. It's her super brain. No special connection here."

"You wanna try, Shelly?" Willow asked and soon the two of them were staring into each other's eyes. I felt a prick of jealousy at Willow. My minutes with Shelly had been wonderful. To have her undivided attention like that had made me feel like I was special to her. For two full minutes, I'd fooled myself into thinking that she loved me too.

CHAPTER 16
The List

Shelly

A real genius should be able to come up with a solution to just about anything.

I had nothing!

For two minutes, I had stared into the eyes of Marco. And during those precious one hundred and twenty seconds I had known that he was as important to me as eating, sleeping, or breathing.

When I was fifteen, I had been infatuated with Marco.

Now that I was twenty-five and we were lovers, my infatuation had grown into something deeper.

I loved his beautiful smile, the way the edges of his eyes crinkled when he grinned. The way he argued about things that mattered to him. His love for children. I loved the way he smelled after we'd had sex. The groans and moans he made.

Marco was the only man I could ever imagine being with. But his biggest wish was a marriage to a Northlander and I couldn't give him that. Nor could I give him the million dollars he could win in a tournament, fighting for his Northlander bride.

Lying in my bed, regret kept me awake.

Maybe it would've been better for me if I hadn't entered into a sexual relationship with him. At least then I wouldn't know what I'd be missing out on when he married soon.

He might not make it to be one of the five champions. And even if he does, Louisa might not pick him, I reminded myself. *After all, despite Marco being an amazing fighter and making it to be one of the five champions in the last two tournaments, he's still unmarried.*

It should have calmed me, but just the thought that Marco would have to fight, and could potentially get hurt or die, made me toss and turn. I came up with creative ways to sabotage the tournament to prevent him from putting himself in danger. But if this was what he wanted, who was I to take it away from him?

I imagined seeing him with his bride. The visions made me curl up with excruciating pain in my stomach.

Marco and I have never spoken about love between us. It had been understood from the beginning that our relationship would end when he left for the tournament.

Once, I had asked him what would happen if he didn't win, and he had dismissed my question, saying he was going to think positively.

What if I was willing to marry him?

I sighed with the realization that it wouldn't be enough to make him happy. I didn't have a million dollars lying around. The times he'd asked me to marry him I'd never felt love was a part of his reason for asking.

It's for the best. How would I explain to my friends and family at home that I love an Nman? Most people I knew were intellectuals and many of them were part of the groups of concerned citizens who protested the integration with the Northlands.

So what? I've never cared what others said. Marco is the only man that makes me feel truly alive when I'm with him. My love for him is what makes my days colorful.

Groaning out loud, I rubbed my forehead, hating that my thoughts were those of a hopeless romantic, and wondering how shocked Marco would be if he knew that I was in love with him. So far, I'd managed to keep it well hidden and focus on how incompatible we were.

It's better if I let him go.

175

A strong push of resistance inside me refused. *No, I can't let him marry Louisa. Maybe he doesn't love me, but he doesn't love her either.*

I was awkward, quirky, and unsure about my future, but the only thing that made sense to me was having Marco in my life.

If I don't at least tell him how I feel about him, I'll blame myself when he marries another woman.

Turning on some light, I sat up in my bed, pulled out my notepad, and began making a list of reasons why he should be with me.

1: Sexual compatibility.
2: Stimulating conversations.
3: Shared humor.
4: I love him.
5:

I stared at the electronic pad, wanting to put down at least ten things but all that came to me were reasons that made staying apart the most logical solution.

1: He wants children, I don't think I do.
2: He wants marriage, I don't see the need.
3: He is materialistic, I'm not.
4: He wants to live in the Northlands. I prefer the Motherlands.
5: He has never been in love with me. I've been in love with him since I was fifteen.
6: Northmen are possessive and controlling by nature. I'm too independent and need my freedom.

More things were on my mind, but I put down my pad and pushed it away. Curling up in a fetal position, I admitted defeat. If I truly loved Marco, I would have to let him marry Louisa, who could give him marriage, children, money, and the obedient wife he was born to dream of.

Telling him about my love for him would only confuse him and make things awkward between us. My time with Marco was running out. In three days he would leave. In six days Louisa would choose her husband and Marco might share his wedding night with her.

The same imagination that helped me come up with ideas for inventions now tortured me with images of Marco making love to another woman. In my mind Louisa was perfect and he would whisper all the little things that he had practiced on me – telling her that she was his and that he would never get enough of making love to her.

The heaviness in my chest felt like I was sinking to the bottom of the ocean, pressure building to a painful sense of suffocation that had me struggling to breathe. I couldn't see, what with all the tears filling my eyes, and pulled in oxygen in little gasps of hyperventilation. Suddenly, unable to release the air in my lungs, my chest was cramping and my eyes opening wide with fear that my body was literally shutting down in grief.

I couldn't speak, I couldn't breathe. All there was left was a heartbeat loud enough to hear it in my ears, dark spots in front of my eyes, and gut-wrenching pain in my chest at the realization that soon I would never touch Marco again.

Grateful... be grateful. It was my mother's mantra that saved me as I began thinking about all the other things in my life I had to live for. I saw my sister hugging me, my mother laughing in her kitchen, Tristan teasing me about the CBC or the troll machine as he called it, Charlie wrinkling his nose at the talk of sex, and Willow kissing me on my cheek. I wasn't alone – there were people who needed me to breathe.

As if I were pushing burning lava through my nostrils, I exhaled a little, forcing my cramped lungs to relax. It felt like a desperate need for survival, but one small breath at a time my lungs began to cooperate and breathe again. Scared from my anxiety attack, I curled up in a fetal position and sobbed for hours, reminding myself over and over again that I should be grateful for the time I'd spent with Marco, and that I'd always have the memories.

By four in the morning, I still hadn't slept, but I'd come to terms with my decision to sacrifice my own happiness for his. Wasn't that the true essence of love anyway? I would act as normal as possible and find it in me to be happy for him when he left. In three days it would all be over. That was seventy-two hours of hiding my feelings from the man I loved.

When Marco called me in the morning, I was confused and sleep-deprived.

"What time is it?" I asked with a large yawn.

"Nine. How's your head feeling? Do you have a hangover?"

I yawned again and stretched my arms. "I feel like I've been doing intense fight training for a week. My body is sore all over."

"Everyone has a different reaction to alcohol."

I tried to move but moaned from the pain in my stomach muscles. This wasn't alcohol. This was the result of sobbing for hours. My body was exhausted and I could hardly lift my arms.

"Can I see you?"

"You are seeing me."

"In person." He sounded more eager than normal.

"Is something wrong?"

"No, I just thought we could spend some time together today. I have a training session at twelve, but it should only take about two hours. We could meet up for a late lunch."

"You want to take me out for lunch?" My tone was incredulous, since that had never happened.

178

Marco hesitated. "If you want... or I could bring some takeout to your office like the other times."

"Right." I rubbed my eyes, remembering his words: that he didn't want to be seen in public with me. I was his dirty secret who could ruin his chances with Louisa.

"What do you say, your office around two thirty?"

I yawned again and rolled on my side. "I need some more sleep."

Marco smiled. "Where is the troll machine?"

"I only use it twice a week now."

"More a princess than a troll then, are you?"

"Neither." I cleared my throat feeling that familiar pressure in my chest from last night, but I managed a small smile. "Just the same quirky Shelly that I've always been."

"Talking about that... Did you really ask Hunter and Storm if they wake up with morning wood? Storm told me before we went to bed. You should have seen him –he was laughing so hard about it, saying that he'd never seen Hunter look so awkward in his life."

I wrinkled my forehead. "Hunter was the one bringing up aging and future health concerns. I was just pointing out that for men morning wood is one of the indications that they are healthy."

"Shelly. You can't ask a man that sort of thing. That shit is like... personal."

"I see." It was classic Shelly to either share too much information or ask questions that were too personal. "In that case give Storm my apologies, and I'm sorry if I embarrassed you." I pulled my blanket higher.

"Storm doesn't know that anything is going on between us. He just thinks you're hilarious."

"Right." My tone was flat. It was one more thing I could add to my long list of why Marco was better off without me. My lack of social finesse. More tears were pressing behind my eyes and feeling heavy as a house; it suddenly felt impossible for me to keep up a charade. "Actually, Marco, I can't do lunch today. I'm kind of busy finishing off my research project."

"Oh, okay, can I see you later then?"

"I'm sorry, but today won't work."

Marco ran his hands through his hair. "Shelly, what's going on? Did I offend you?"

I gave a small shake of my head, the tightness in my jaw and throat making it hard to speak. "No. I'm just busy and besides, you have to prepare for the tournament."

"Tomorrow then?"

I had to end the çall or he'd see me break down. "Not sure. I'll get back to you on that."

Marco's voice grew in volume. "Shelly, what's going on?"

Tears were pressing, and turning the camera away from my face I spoke fast. "Nothing. I have to pee, so we'll talk later." I ended the conversation knowing that Marco had to be sitting back in confusion about what had just happened.

It had been a month since I pretended to be a sex-bot and since then we'd enjoyed sex together numerous times. There was nothing I'd rather do than be close to him again, but my heart couldn't take it anymore. Like in a jigsaw puzzle, pieces of what had happened between us at the party yesterday began to fall into place.

Marco had acted almost jealous and told me not to drink or smoke weed. He'd denied that it was possessiveness, and I had been so disappointed. At least if he was possessive it would have meant that I mattered to him.

The minutes we shared with deep eye contact had made me feel like a thousand butterflies were playing tag inside my body. I had felt such a deep connection between us, but the mind will show you what you want to see. Marco's denial that there was a special connection between us, when Willow asked him, suddenly rang truer than it had yesterday when I'd convinced myself that he was lying. Now that Marco had just pointed out to me how awkward I was and how his friends were laughing at me, it all made sense. How could I not have seen that the reason he didn't want me to get drunk or high yesterday was that he was embarrassed by me? That's why he wouldn't take me out to lunch either. Sure, he didn't want me to mess up his chances with Louisa, but he didn't want to be embarrassed by me either.

With an angry movement, I dried away a tear. I might be embarrassing and quirky, but I still had pride.

Unrequited love is for masochists. I had read it somewhere, and my photographic memory fetched it back like a well-trained dog trying to be helpful.

I wish I could throw my feelings for Marco away or bury them like a bone, deep enough to forget about. But my brain didn't work like that. I had clear memories from my early childhood, and I would remember my love for Marco to the day I died.

Inhaling deeply, I forced air down lungs that felt like an iron band was squeezing them. Never again would I let anyone tell me that I didn't have emotions. I had too many and they hurt.

I should have known that a bit of clean skin and bigger breasts didn't make much difference. I was still Brainy and Marco was still my secret crush.

A message popped in. "Please can I see you tomorrow?"

I knew what this was about. Marco wanted to have sex with me as many times as possible before he left to get married. The experiments and dirty talk would stop with me. Louisa was precious and clean. As one in less than a hundred women born in the Northlands, she was what he called the *real thing*. A rare pearl compared to one of us one point three billion Motlander women on the other side of the border. No wonder Marco would cherish her. She would become the mother of the children he so longed to have.

I read the message again. "Please can I see you tomorrow?"

It was so tempting to say yes, and I almost did before I stopped myself. *You're a psychologist. Apply what you've learned. There is only one person who can stop your suffering. You've been obsessing over Marco and conditioned your brain to think of him all the time. What you need in order to heal is a clean cut.*

My heart was screaming for him, but my brain kept arguing. *The pain is real, so distract yourself and don't think about him. Don't drag out the suffering and wait for him to leave.*

Before my heart could justify one last day in his arms, I changed my answer and stared at the words that were so opposite to how I felt.

"Marco, get ready for your tournament. I have the research I need. Take care and good luck with everything."

A new message popped in. "Wow, that's cold."

It was followed by another message. "Just tell me one thing at least. Did you get your period?"

Closing my eyes, I took a deep breath before I wrote a last big lie in a single small word. "Yes."

With my tears falling and my heart breaking, I looked at the picture of Marco from our last chat and whispered a last "Goodbye."

CHAPTER 17
The Tournament

Marco

This was madness.

I was risking my life to marry a woman whom I didn't love or feel attracted to?

Not even the million dollars Louisa came with made me truly want to win this fight.

My opponent shouldn't have been hard to take. The kid was twenty-two and too pumped and eager in his movements. Yet he'd gotten some good blows in on me and I was annoyed with myself.

It didn't help that I'd spotted Lord Khan and Magni among the spectators just a second ago. As a former champion in previous tournaments, I was fighting in the main arena with a large audience that had to be wondering what the hell I was doing prolonging this fight when it should have been a walkover.

It's because part of you doesn't want to win, my subconscious whispered.

I want to be rich and respected.

My opponent jumped from foot to foot in front of me, his ebony-colored skin glistening with sweat and his chapped lips pursed in a confident smirk.

"You tired, old man?" he provoked me.

I was thirty years old. Strong, virile, and fast. My response to his disrespect was a clean uppercut. That should teach his bloated ego to keep up his arms to block.

Stumbling back, he narrowed his eyes before attacking me with uncoordinated fury.

This fight should have been over by now. The guy had such a weak defense and had given me ample opportunities to knock him out.

So why haven't I?

It was almost like my fight was less against him and more against myself.

If only I knew for sure. There was a gnawing feeling in me that Shelly might have lied to me about her period.

What if she's pregnant?

She's not. She said she wasn't.

But how do I know for sure?

"That million dollars is *my* money," my opponent hissed at me as we danced around each other. "I'll send you a thought tomorrow night when I pump my seed into *my* bride."

I snorted but didn't reply.

With a million dollars I wouldn't have to work again. I would have the money to write a book. Nice drones, clothes, and other material things would all be within my reach. Men would envy me, and there was a lot of prestige in being a tournament winner.

So why wasn't I really fighting for it?

Because I'd rather be with Shelly.

The answer increased the pain I'd felt these last three days. After the party, I'd been ready to declare my feelings for Shelly. It was that damn party game of looking into her eyes that had made me dream. The small chance of her loving me back had kept me up all night thinking about all the ways that I would convince her we could be right for each other. But before I got a chance to embarrass myself it was over. Shelly had made it clear we were done. She'd had her fun and I'd been entertaining to her for a while, but that was it. It was almost comical that I'd thought I could make her change her mind and want to marry me when she had already rejected me several times.

For Shelly, all it had taken was one text to tell me she didn't have a use for me anymore.

We might be over in her world, but to me it was a big guessing game as I tried to understand what had made her discard me in such a cold and sudden manner.

Maybe she was bored with me.

Maybe it had truly been a matter of research for her.

Maybe she just never liked me that much.

My head had been spinning nonstop to think of reasons, but in the end it was a fool's game. I should have known from the beginning that Shelly Summers wasn't a woman any man could tie down. She was meant for greater things. It had been my life's biggest mistake when I pretended to be Storm and went to test out that sex-bot. No matter who I married now, I would be settling for someone less than perfect. Without wanting to, I would compare any woman to Shelly – which was unfair, since no one could compete with someone as extraordinary as her.

Boom, my opponent's shin connected with my ribcage. The wind was knocked out of me, and the fucker saw his chance and let hits and kicks rain down on me. It almost felt like a relief when the emotional pain I was in was overshadowed by his physical blows to my body.

Protecting my face and ribs, I took it, and understood for the first time why some people sought out fights in bars. There was a quiet place in the pain – a bubble of disconnectedness where the boos from the audience, their shouts of profanities, and their cheering for the underdog to beat me registered but didn't affect me. Not even the rejection from the woman I loved mattered in this vacuum of pain. It was like a few seconds of an insane high that I didn't want to come out of.

"Marco..." Magni's voice broke through to me and as if someone had turned the radio from silent to full volume, the shouting and screaming from the crowd was back with a vengeance.

"Marco." From the way Magni's voice overpowered the others, I knew he had moved down close to the edge of the arena. "Get the fuck up and finish this already."

I was mortified that the best warrior in the world was watching me take a beating when I'd always wanted Magni to respect me. The motivation to impress Magni got me up, and I focused all my energy on proving to him what a great fighter I was.

My inexperienced opponent was so convinced that he had the upper hand that he was grinning to some of his friends. With his attention distracted, I moved in, placing a strong knee in his stomach and pushing him back to create the distance I needed for a roundhouse kick. He wasn't grinning anymore when he stumbled back, his eyes wide with disbelief.

"That's it, Marco, now fucking finish it so we can have some beers," Magni shouted from the sidelines.

My opponent, who had been so cocky before, was retreating now, shaken from the roundhouse kick to his chest that made it hard for him to breathe. With my hands up in front of me I moved forward step by insistent step with him backing away, trying to avoid my punches by moving his head.

"That's it, Marco," Magni shouted. "Show him who's the champion."

Empowered by Magni's words, I used the force of my body to give a high kick. With my opponent turning his head, the impact of my foot was right on his temple.

Like a robot with a breakdown, all the lights went out in his eyes. Knocked out, he fell forward, landing face first on the ground.

Still pumped with adrenaline, I kept my eyes on him, waiting to see if he would get up.

When he didn't, the announcer finally boomed over the wild cheering from the audience. "And we have a winner."

Medics rushed to my opponent on the ground as my right arm was being raised in the air by Magni, who had stepped into the arena, patting my shoulder and grinning at me. "Took you long enough, you lazy bastard."

I swiped at my forehead, brushing away sweat.

"Come on, I'm sure your friends want to congratulate you." Magni led me out of the arena and I was instantly surrounded by people with smiling faces.

Hunter, Storm, Nero, and four of my other friends were patting my shoulders, and from all around me comments were hailing down on me, giving me shit about this being my worst fight ever.

"What the hell happened?

"Were you too bored to fight, or were you toying with him?"

"I was close to rooting for the other guy. At least he looked like he wanted to win."

Using a towel to dry off sweat, I laughed at my friends' comments and smiled when I looked up to see Mila, my former student and Magni's daughter.

"I didn't know you were here." I stepped away from my friends to the young woman who stood out among all the men. Her adoptive mother, Laura, stood by her side and looked like an older sister to Mila since there were only ten years between them in age.

"I'm sorry you got hurt, Marco." Mila reached out both her hands to me. "May peace surround you."

It surprised me that she still used that formal Motlander greeting after having lived here in the Northlands for so many years. Mila would be twenty now but she still had those cute dimples that I remembered.

"May peace surround you too," I said politely and waited for a nod from Magni before I took her hands.

"When is your next fight?" she asked with concern. "I'll come and watch."

I smiled. "I thought you hated violence."

"I do. My parents say that I'm too sensitive and that it'll be good for me to toughen up before my own tournament."

"So you are having one?"

She nodded. "Some time next year. I didn't want to at first, but my dad insisted and then I did something foolish." She looked back to Magni, who stood behind her. "I told him that if he would wear a bead in his beard for a year, I'd do it."

"Huh. That explains the fashion trend."

Mila's large blue eyes looked up at me. "I never thought he'd do it or that it would spread the way it has. Maybe if I'd specified that it had to be more than one bead and in different colors... but I didn't think that far ahead."

The sole blue bead in Magni's beard looked good on him and he had a smug smile on his face.

"Listen, Marco." Mila lowered her voice. "I know you must have been very disappointed when you weren't picked by the bride the last two times, but I'm certain Louisa will pick you this time. She came to see your fight and I saw her smile when you were announced the winner. Just be sure to smile at her when you stand with the other four champions. You have a warm and beautiful smile. She'll pick you for sure."

My jaws stiffened, the thought making me tense up.

"Oh no." Her face tilted to one side with a sympathetic glance. "I can see how afraid you are of being rejected again." Mila was misreading my reaction as fear. "Don't be scared. If Louisa doesn't pick you tomorrow, I'll pick you for my champion next year, if you want me to."

Laura moved closer. "Mila, please don't make a promise like that. It wouldn't be fair to the other competitors in your tournament."

"I know, but Marco has a good heart and he would treat me well. How is it different from you promising Dad that you would pick him? You did it out of pity too." Her eyes flew to me. "I'm sorry, Marco, I probably shouldn't have said that."

"It's okay, Mila. I know you're only trying to be nice, but I would never fight in your tournament."

"Why not?"

"Because I was your mentor. It would be weird."

"Right." She nodded, with her kind blue eyes expressing sympathy. "Then let's hope that Louisa picks you tomorrow."

I was grateful for Mila's kindness and the way Laura and Magni helped distract me from my misery by discussing the fights with me. Yet, something urgent was pressing inside of me. I needed to talk to Shelly and be a hundred percent sure she wasn't pregnant before I fought my next fight. Excusing myself, I found a quiet place and called her up.

CHAPTER 18
Proof

Shelly

I had never felt inclined to throw things around.

Until now.

A tournament was a huge event in the Northlands and sent out live for all to see. Right now, there wouldn't be a bar in the country that wasn't tuned in, and more people were following the tournament from their homes.

I was in my office, watching Marco's fight – hating how the two commentators were bashing him.

"Looks like the underdog is showing up the champion in this fight. Such a disappointment for many to see Marco Polo look so lost."

The other commentator laughed. "Good one, but you're right, physically he looks to be in great shape, but mentally he doesn't seem prepared. I wonder if he's still battling the disappointment of being rejected in the last two tournaments."

"Yes, this champion has been close a few times. Could be that he was so sure of himself against this underdog that he's a bit rattled by the hits young Neil Jefferson has gotten on him so far."

"Oh, here we go again. Fuck, look at that energy Jefferson is attacking with. He really wants to win, doesn't he? Son of the Devil, that had to hurt. Did you see the punch to Marco Polo's face?"

For someone who had always claimed that I wasn't attached to a certain outcome, watching Marco fight was a rude awakening.

I was scared to my bones that Marco would be injured and I had already decided that if he got paralyzed, I'd dedicate my genius to finding a way to make him mobile again.

"Would you look at the way Marco is protecting himself? Why doesn't he fight back?"

"That's a good question. It's hard to watch, knowing that this is the same warrior who defeated great champions like Danielson and Zillinger just a few years ago."

"You're right. I would like to see him use the fighting skills we know he has."

My fingers covered my eyes when Marco took punch after punch. I couldn't watch it, and turned my head away.

"And if you look to the right corner you'll notice Magni Aurelius is shouting at the contestants. He looks like he wants to go in and fight himself, doesn't he?"

"I wish he would; this fight hasn't been as entertaining as we'd hoped it would be."

"No, but look at that..." one of the commentators gave a loud outburst. "Dancing demons... what a comeback." The commentators were laughing and it made me dare to look again. "Such a perfect roundhouse kick, and yes... look at that, Marco Polo just followed up with a classic high kick that knocked Neil to the ground."

"I think that's it. Neil isn't coming back up, is he?"

"No, he's not. Now, you might not be able to hear this at home, but people in the audience are cheering for the kill."

"That's not his style, is it?"

"No. Marco isn't that kind of fighter; we know that from previous years. So far he has spared the life of each of his opponents."

"I have to say that as an old-school fighter I think it's a shame that it's becoming the norm. There used to be a much bigger risk involved and that was what made these games so exciting."

"I have to agree with you on that. So far we've only had two deaths in this tournament, which has to be the lowest number in history." He chuckled, low. "Soon they'll accept safety gear as well."

"We shouldn't joke about something like that; they might hear us and think it's an excellent idea... oh, and here comes Commander Magni Aurelius. He just entered the arena and he's calling out Marco as the winner."

The two men were laughing. "Looks like Marco Polo found his way back after all. Let's see the last part in slow motion again."

My mouth gaped when Marco jumped up, spun in the air, and kicked the guy with brutal force. I'd seen Marco fight before, but it had always been for training purposes and this was for real – the concentration on his face, his eyes closing and opening, and the way every muscle on his body was working as a weapon. They zoomed in on Neil's face when he landed on the ground, his head bouncing a few times with his lips and cheeks vibrating because of the slow-motion effect.

All the talk about fights and deaths made me turn off the show. Marco might be the winner of this fight, but in a few hours he'd be at it again, putting his life at risk.

Picking up a small tool, I threw it against the door. It made a thumping sound before it fell on the floor, mocking me by not making a dent in the door or a difference to anything.

I should find something heavier to throw, I concluded, but the practical part of me didn't see the point. *Breaking a door won't mend your broken heart.*

It would be easier if I could attain some detachment and not care.

If we were meant to be together, he would have fallen in love with me by now.

We'd shared a month together and rationally, I understood that Marco was too attached to his goal of winning a tournament to being open to anything else.

If I were a bigger person, I would find satisfaction in Marco's being happy, even if it's with another woman.

My head was in my hands, my elbows on my desk in front of me. Maybe I would be a bigger person in time. Right now, all I could feel was sorry for myself.

I'd been deep in my own self-pity for a while when the sound of an incoming call made me jump a little.

A picture of Marco, with his amazing curls and charming smile, popped up in front of me, making my heart hammer away.

Don't answer, a warning sounded in my head, but my shaking hands accepted the call before I could stop myself.

"Shelly." Marco's face was serious.

Brushing my hair back, I put on a brave face. "Hi, Marco. Congratulations on your first win."

"You saw the fight?"

"Some of it."

"How much?"

I bit my lip. "Most of it."

"Hmm, it wasn't my best fight."

"You won."

"Yeah, I did." He frowned. "Look, I think one of the reasons that I couldn't focus in this fight is that I need proof."

"Proof of what?"

"My next fight is in less than three hours but I need to have my head on straight. Did you really get your period?"

"Yes, I told you." My already racing heart was beating so fast I could feel it pumping in my ears. With all the energy pouring into my blood, I couldn't sit still and got up from my chair.

"Good. Then it should be no problem for you to show me."

I lowered my brows. "What do you mean?"

"Show me." Marco looked dead serious.

I gave a sound somewhere between a gasp and a laugh. "Show you?"

"Yes. You've pulled down your pants for me before. I need to see that you're having your period."

"You want to see the blood in my panties?"

"Yes."

"That's gross."

"Believe me, I can handle some blood. I just need to be sure that you're not carrying my child."

My hands were scratching my neck, suddenly feeling like the room temperature had gone up to that of a sauna.

"Shelly?"

"Mmm."

"Show me."

"I don't want to."

Marco angled his head. "Shelly, look at me and tell me again that you're having your period."

I hesitated, my fingers fiddling, my feet moving around.

"Shellyyyy."

"Marco, I…" My voice failed me, and I blew out air and looked up at the ceiling. "I can't."

"Why?"

When I didn't answer, Marco drew the logical conclusion. "You aren't having your period, are you?"

"No." It came out as a whisper.

"Then why the fuck am I here?" he exclaimed in a deep voice.

"I'm *not* pregnant. My period is just late, that's all."

"You keep saying that, but it's been over a month since we had sex the first time and when I asked you when you last had your period, you said it had been a few weeks before we were together the first time. That means that you are more than two weeks late. I've looked it up, Shelly, and you should have gotten it by now."

"Marco, even if I am pregnant, it shouldn't stop you from following your dream."

"My dream?" He was frowning. "Shelly, you're carrying my child. That changes everything."

"You don't know that I am for sure."

"I'm coming home." There was such decisiveness in his words, but it was freaking me out.

"Marco, what if I'm *not* pregnant? Don't throw away your chance to win the money and your Northlander bride. You're going to resent me forever."

"I'm leaving now and I'm coming straight to you. Don't go anywhere. I'll be there tonight and then we'll find a doctor."

"Don't be foolish," I objected. "If you want proof, I can go to a doctor myself and call you with the result."

Marco shook his head. "No. You already lied to me about this twice."

"Because I don't want to come between you and your dream."

He looked like he wanted to scream at me but turned his head and collected himself before he spoke. "Promise me that you'll be there when I get back. If you take off to the Motherlands, I don't know what I'll do to you, Shelly."

"Is that a threat?"

"More like a warning. I fucking told you not to lie to me, and you did it again."

"It was a white lie," I defended myself.

"No, it was a huge, fucking, life-altering lie, and if you can't see that then you're not as smart as everyone thinks."

"I didn't mean to lie, it just happened."

"Just be there when I get back. Do you understand?"

"Yes," I breathed.

Marco stared at me, not talking for some seconds.

"I promise," I added before we ended the call.

For three hours I walked around in a haze waiting for Marco to arrive. At least seven times I checked to see if I'd gotten my period, but there wasn't even a bit of spotting in my panties.

With my late period ruining his dream, it was no wonder that Marco was serious when he arrived. The first thing he said when I met him outside my office building was, "From now on there can be no more lying, Shelly."

I nodded and looked down as I followed him to his drone. For the first five minutes we didn't talk and the atmosphere between us was loaded with all the things unsaid.

"I don't normally lie, you know," I whispered in a low voice. "In fact, people have often accused me of being too honest."

Marco gave me a sideways glance but didn't speak.

"I get that you're disappointed with me." I studied his profile when he looked ahead again. His beard was shorter than when I last saw him a week ago, and it made him look more like the Marco I'd fallen in love with all those years ago when I was just a teenage girl. Except back then he'd been smiling and cracking jokes.

"I should have been honest with you. I know that the timing of this is… umm… very unfortunate."

"You think?"

"If I had been honest with you last Sunday, I could have done a test before the tournament and you'd know that I'm not pregnant."

"Stop saying that." It came through gritted teeth.

"Why? I thought we were both hoping that I'm not pregnant."

Marco turned his head in a slow movement and gazed straight at me.

"What?" I asked with some confusion. "You're hoping that I'm pregnant?"

"Unlike you, I always wanted children."

196

"Yeah, but with someone like Louisa," I burst out.

"You'll marry me," he said in a matter-of-fact way that left me cold.

Shaking my head, I gave him an answer in the same flat tone. "No, Marco. I won't."

He didn't look surprised but said, "Then you'll sign a contract."

"What contract?"

"That I can see our child."

"What are you talking about?"

"If you're serious about living in the Motherlands I want a guarantee that I'll be able to see our child and be a father to my kid."

"This is silly. I'm telling you that I'm not pregnant."

"We'll know tomorrow morning. I found a doctor who can see you then. He's a friend of a friend, and when we go there we'll pretend to be married. Do you understand?"

"Yes."

"Good." Marco still looked very serious. "We're staying at my apartment tonight."

"Why couldn't you just pick me up tomorrow morning then?" I asked.

"Because I would worry all night that you'd be going to the Motherlands."

"I see."

We were quiet the rest of the way to Marco's apartment and when we got there, he moved around his kitchen and living room, leaving me to wonder what he was thinking about.

"Do you hate me?" I asked when the pressure inside me became too much to bear.

Marco, who stood by a mirror taking in the bruises on his face from the fight, answered in a hoarse voice. "No, I don't hate you."

"But you aren't talking to me."

197

With a slow turn of his body, he looked at me. "My head is so fucked up right now, I don't know what to say."

"What did you give as an excuse to leave the tournament?"

"I didn't, I just left."

"They'll be wondering, though."

Marco looked away. "I'll have to make up a lie. I guess being around you, that shit is infectious."

That stung. "I'm not trying to destroy your life. You know that, right? I mean, I'm not asking anything of you."

Marco sighed and gave a small nod before coming to sit down beside me. "I know, Shelly, and that's what worries me. You don't need me the way I need you."

"You need me?" My eyes widened.

With his eyes fixed on my knee, he radiated tension. "I'm well aware you can go back and join some family unit with our child, but I would be left out and it scares me. I checked in with some friends on my way back from the tournament and it looks like I'm pretty screwed. As an Nman I have no rights if you go back to the Motherlands to have our child. I would need a visa to visit and even if I was willing to move there, I couldn't without your consent."

"Marco, you're overthinking this. My only concern at the moment is how mad you're going to be at me when there's no child and you realize you left the tournament for nothing."

"Yeah, well, I guess we'll know in ten hours." He got up from the sofa. "I'm sore from the fight and I could use a shower. You're welcome to sleep in my bed. I can take the couch if you need me to."

"No, it's fine. We can share the bed." I bit my lip. "I promise I won't touch you."

Marco moved away from me too fast for me to see the expression on his face. "We have an appointment with the doctor at eight a.m. sharp," he said over his shoulder. "He should be able to determine if we're having a child or not."

CHAPTER 19
Taking the Test

Shelly

Marco tossed and turned a lot that night. I know, because I didn't sleep much either.

At eight o'clock we met with a doctor who was in his early thirties and clean-shaven.

"Don't look so shocked," he said and smiled. "It was my wife's birthday yesterday and at the top of her wish list was a week with me clean-shaven. I know I look stupid, but my wife really wanted to see what I looked like without my beard, so we had a good laugh about it."

"You must really love her," Marco replied with a smile and nudged me a little forward. "This is my wife. And of course, you know why we're here."

The doctor smiled. "Yes, and being newlywed myself, I understand the excitement. It can be hard to wait for the answer when we all so urgently want to start a family."

I raised an eyebrow, looking at Marco. He stepped closer to me, placing his arm around my shoulder.

"That's right; it's just come a little sooner than we expected, so we don't have all the practical details figured out yet."

"I understand," the kind doctor said and gave me a smile. "My name is Robert and I'm honored to have you as my patient."

"Thank you. I'm Shelly. Shelly Summers."

His eyes expanded. "Like the genius?"

"Yeah, but my wife isn't actually her. They just share the same name," Marco said before I had a chance to talk.

"Don't worry, I didn't actually think you were her. I've seen interviews and documentaries with the real Shelly Summers." The doctor chuckled. "Not that you're not real, of course. It's just so impressive to see someone so gifted."

"I'm sure you're more gifted than her in many areas," I said. "I've met her and she's not that special."

"You've met her?" His smile grew. "What I wouldn't give to spend an hour in her company. I was blown away by her inventions giving photographic memory to ordinary people. Of course, brain implants have been considered risky since so many had their implants hacked during the war. But Shelly's contribution to the modern implants is extraordinary. If it were legal here in the Northlands I would consider it. Imagine having your eyes being your camera and to have access to everything you'd ever seen. It changes photography, doesn't it?"

Marco gave me a nod of recognition. "Sounds both scary and brilliant to me."

"Yes, I can't wait to see what else we're going to be seeing from Shelly Summers." Robert was moving around his office. "Anyway, I'm sure you hear about her all the time because of your name."

I shrugged. "It happens."

"Well..." The doctor gave me another genuine smile. "You might not be a genius like her, but you're much prettier and if it makes you feel better, I'm sure all the Nmen would pick you over her any day."

"Why?" My polite smile stiffened.

Robert squatted down in front of a shelf to locate something. "Oh, just because no Nman would enjoy feeling inferior to his woman. We're proud men."

Marco avoided eye contact with me and even the doctor picked up on how tense he was when he stood back up. "Relax, Marco, we'll have an answer for you in no time. Let's start with a urine test and a blood test, shall we?"

"Yes."

201

"After the tests I can examine you if you'd like." Roberts eyes darted between Marco and me. "Of course, Marco will stay in the room and make sure nothing inappropriate happens."

"How many female patients do you have?" I asked.

"Four." The doctor sounded proud. "I'm very curious about women and I'm hoping to get more patients. It brings variety to my job and new challenges." While talking he was collecting what he needed and handed me an oval-shaped cup. "If you can urinate in this one, please."

"Where?"

"Ehm, wherever you'd like." Both men were looking at me as if I was supposed to pull my dress up and pee in front of them.

"Do you have a bathroom?"

"Of course, just outside the room and to the left."

Marco followed me and only stopped when I asked him to stay outside. "I don't need you to help me pee."

He was still standing guard outside the door when I was done. "You okay?" he asked.

"Yes, I'm fine."

"Good." Marco was tense and kept close to me. "Do you want me to take it?" he asked with a nod to the cup.

"No, I can carry my own pee."

The doctor was smiling and took the cup with both hands like it was precious. "Have a seat. It'll just take a few minutes before we have a result."

I sat down as instructed while Marco paced the floor.

Robert turned back to us, took off his gloves, and gave us a smile. "I did the test. Now we'll have to wait two minutes for the result.

The atmosphere in the room was heavy from Marco's pacing and I didn't know what to do about it.

"What are the most common causes of death in the Northlands?" I asked Robert to make some light conversation.

Robert raised both eyebrows. "I don't think anyone has ever asked me that. Are you worried about your safety here?"

"No, I'm just curious."

"Okay. Well, I suppose you Motlanders think that Nmen die violent deaths and I would say that it used to be that way with all the wars and rebellions our country has suffered through, but not any longer. Now, people die from disease and accidents mostly."

"What kind of accidents?"

"Oh, there's a long list of hunting accidents that involves falling from great heights and getting shot. Many are active outside and think they're immortals; last week I had a patient who died because he insisted on rock climbing without the right safety gear."

"Are the two minutes up yet?" Marco asked with impatience.

Robert turned to the test, lowering his head to see.

"Accidents related to sports, you say?" I said in a desperate attempt to prolong the time before the doctor could give the answer that I was afraid of getting. "What else?"

"Oh, you know. Suicide happens too often up here. The dark winters are the worst."

"Just tell me what the test says!" Marco exclaimed, his voice high-pitched.

"Be patient, Marco." Robert waited the five seconds until the timer made a sound and then he picked up the test. "Congratulations, it's positive."

My whole body stiffened, the world going into slow motion and my eyes fixed on Marco.

"You sure?" he asked the doctor and looked like he wasn't breathing.

"Yes, you're going to be a father."

"Are you *completely* sure?" Marco asked.

"These tests are very accurate. Of course, we should still do a blood test and an exam but yes, Marco, I feel confident that your wife is pregnant like you suspected."

"Fuuuck." Marco leaned his head back, looking up at the ceiling before his eyes closed.

Robert laughed. "I know it's a huge thing. I can't wait for it to be my turn. My wife and I have been trying for almost a year now." The doctor was patting Marco's shoulder. "You're a lucky man."

Marco nodded and the doctor turned to me. "Congratulations to you too of course. It's must be so exciting."

My eyes were tearing up, and I whispered a low "I'm sorry" to Marco but the doctor misunderstood.

"There's no need to apologize for being emotional. I know we Nmen have a reputation of being tough, but I suspect I might tear up a bit myself when it's my time to get great news like this."

After doing a blood test and promising us an answer the next day, the doctor again offered to do a pelvic examination on me. He looked deeply disappointed when I told him I'd get one in the Motherlands on my next visit.

"Are you sure? I've studied the female anatomy very carefully and it really would be a great honor to perform my first pelvic examination."

"What exactly is a pelvic examination?" Marco asked.

When I explained he narrowed his eyes at Robert.

"Maybe some other time," I said with a forced smile to the doctor as we walked out the door that Robert was holding open for us.

"Just let me know. And again, congratulations to you both on the good news. Now you can go home and talk about what to name your baby."

CHAPTER 20
Alternative Ways

Marco

Everything had changed within the last twenty-four hours.

I was supposed to be fighting for Louisa today. And chances were that she would have picked me and we would have been starting a family together.

Instead, I'd already started one with Shelly.

"I'm sorry," Shelly repeated for the third time since we'd gotten the result. I'd taken her to one of my favorite places outside the city and we were sitting on a large rock with our feet dangling. The lush meadow was full of wildflowers and the calming sound of water running in the small creek below us. We'd taken off our shoes and walked upstream to sit on the rock, so far tiptoeing around the inevitable subject of the child growing inside her.

I didn't comment on her apology; instead I was trying to digest that I was going to be a father. This could be the best thing that ever happened to me or it could be the worst – it all depended on whether or not I could convince her to let me be part of the child's life.

This place was tranquil, and sudden visions of seeing my kid play with the water like I had as a child made my heart race faster.

"I used to come here a lot as a boy." I threw a small stone into the stream and pointed to the right. "My school was less than a mile that way."

"I'll bet you were a cute kid."

"Who knows? As I remember it, I was a troublemaker."

"Why?"

"Too curious for my own good and convinced that I was smarter than our mentors." I smiled a little. "I was the master of pranks. That skill has served me well, though. I'm always a step ahead of my students when they try to pull a prank on me."

Shelly smiled. "Remember that time you told me to check my bed before crawling into it?"

"No."

"We had the night shift and you told me that the boys had acted funny and that you suspected they were up to something." Pulling her legs up, Shelly wrapped her arms around her knees. "You offered to check my room for me, but we'd been bantering that day and I was too proud to let you. I wanted you to see me as an equal."

Vague memories came back. "What happened again?"

"I found a snake in my bed and I freaked out."

"Why didn't you ask me to remove it?"

"Because I didn't want to look weak or childish. For a long time, I stood in the corner of the room, terrified that the snake would move, but it stayed curled up in the middle of the bed. After I overcame the worst of the fear, I found a way to move the snake without touching it or getting too close by gathering the four corners of the sheet." Shelly demonstrated with her hands. "I twisted the sheet until the snake was trapped. After that it was easy to hold it out of the window and release it from a safe distance."

"You could have just picked up the snake and thrown it out the window. Or better yet, put it in one of the boys' beds for revenge. You know they did it, right?"

"To be honest, I wondered if it might be you."

"Me?" I pointed a finger to my chest. "You just said that I was the one who warned you to check your bed."

"And if I'd said yes and you'd found the snake, I would have been indebted to you, wouldn't I? Could have been an easy plot on your part."

That had me laughing. "Lady, you have trust issues."

"Look me in the eye and tell me it wasn't you."

Cupping Shelly's chin with my left hand I looked deep into her beautiful eyes. "I swear that I didn't put that snake in your bed."

Her eyes squinted and she held my gaze. "Did you have someone else do it?"

"Nooo."

"Hmm…" She sounded skeptical.

Holding up my palms, I grinned. "All right, I'll admit that I had forgotten about the snake thing, but the truth is that I knew it was there."

"Aha!" Shelly poked her finger into my chest. "It *was* you."

"I spotted William and Plato leave your room snickering, so obviously I went in to check. At first, I was going to remove it, but then the idea of you asking for my help grew on me. That's why I warned you instead."

"And when I didn't ask for your help?"

I released her chin and pulled back. "I was disappointed of course."

"Why would William and Plato try to hurt me? I always thought they liked me."

Turning my head, I threw another small rock into the water. "They weren't trying to hurt you. That snake was harmless. If it's any consolation, I made sure they got their punishment."

"I thought they liked me," I repeated.

"Hey, you really shouldn't take it personally. The boys messed with all us mentors from time to time. To them it was nothing but a fun prank, and I assure you that I did stupid things like that all the time when I was a kid."

Shelly sat for a while, her head leaning on her knees, which were still pulled to her chest. "Would you describe your childhood as a happy one?"

"Yeah, I would say so. I mean, I've taken my share of spankings and physical punishments, but it shaped me to be resilient and strong."

"Violence is wrong."

"So you Motlanders say, but in the Northlands it's been that way for centuries and growing up I didn't know it could be different." I cleared my throat. "Things were simpler when I was a child. With the impenetrable wall between our countries there wasn't a matchmaking program or integrated schools. All we had was the Northlands with ten million men and what?... a hundred females or so. Being named after role models from the past, we were raised to dream of greatness and taught to fight so we could become champions. I grew up surrounded by friends and we all wanted the same ultimate prize, a wife."

"Statistically, few of you could achieve that dream if you really only had a hundred women."

Pushing my chest out, I reminded her, "I'm a champion."

"Sure, but for every five champions, only one gets married."

"True."

Shelly found the same lock of hair that she always twisted when thinking hard. Rolling the strands of hair around her finger seemed to somehow sooth her. "Marco, I feel guilty for coming between you and your dream."

"Stop saying that you're sorry. I'm tired of hearing it. What I need you to say is that you'll marry me." It came out in the clumsiest of ways and I rubbed my forehead with a sigh.

Shelly was unnervingly quiet while I battled my fear of being alone up here if she took our child out of my reach in the Motherlands. When she finally spoke, she sounded casual, like it wasn't my whole goddamn future on the line. "You know what makes a genius?"

"Yeah, a high IQ."

"You would think that, but it's not true. Throughout history there were people with high IQ's who contributed nothing of significance to the world. It's not about that."

"So what defines a genius then?"

"It's a hard thing to define, but my definition is that it's someone who is original in his or her thoughts and achieves something that hasn't been done before. They see connections where others don't." She leaned back on the rock, placing her hands behind her as support. "Geniuses are often considered crazy for their wild ideas at first, but then when they turn out to be right, we call those ideas revolutionary. I wonder how many revolutionary ideas have been shot down by small-minded people because the idea didn't fit the norm."

"A lot," I guessed.

"One thing that's generally true about geniuses is that they are productive people who are blessed or cursed, depending on how you see it, with a mind that is spinning constantly. You know the saying, 'The key to having a great idea is to have many ideas'?"

"Uh-huh."

"Being productive is a component, but so is stamina and discipline. You can't be lazy and go with the first solution to a problem you have. There's always other options, you just have to explore them."

"Not sure about that. Sometimes you're bound and have no options."

Shelly frowned. "Don't be an elephant, Marco."

"A what?"

"An elephant. You know, the giant animal with the long trunk."

"Yes, I've heard of them."

"There was a shameful time in human history where people would enslave animals and keep them for entertaining. You would think an animal that large and powerful would be impossible to contain, but humans enslaved their minds."

"How?"

"By tying them up to a pole when they were babies. In the beginning they would try to get free but eventually they gave up and accepted that a rope around their neck meant they couldn't move."

"You lost me, Shelly."

"You said that sometimes people are bound and I referred to the elephants because the restriction was all in their minds. There're always more options, even though some of them seem crazy. Maybe what defines a genius is their bravery in thinking crazy thoughts and seeing connections between ordinary things that, when connected, become revolutionary. That's what I did with the photographic brain implant. I didn't come up with brain implants, photography, or the technology to control things with your eyes. All those things were already invented. All I did was figure out a way to combine them in a way that makes it easier for humankind."

"So you're admitting you're a genius? You used to hate it when I called you Brainy."

"I prefer to be called a skilled thinker."

I smiled. "A skilled thinker who's a great tinkerer."

"Funny, but do you get my point?"

Moving up a little higher on the large rock to be closer to her, I admitted, "I have no fucking clue. To be honest, I thought this was just another of your random lectures. *Is* there a point?"

"Of course, there's a point." Shelly shifted her position, pulling a foot up under her. "Your constant go-to solution is for us to marry. It's like you can't see other options, but marriage is only *one* solution, Marco. Let's explore what other options we have."

"Shelly, I wanna be a part of my child's life."

"I understand that." Shelly placed her hand on mine. "I'm not trying to take that away from you, I just want to find the best solution for *us*. We don't need to copy other people when there might be an alternative that suits us better."

"So you'll let me see our child?"

"Why wouldn't I? People raise children together in the Motherlands without being married. If we go back in history there are plenty of examples of unmarried parents."

I groaned. "The shitty thing is that Storm is moving out soon, but I'll find another roommate, and I promise that I'll work two jobs and do whatever it takes to make sure our child has everything he or she needs."

"Storm is moving?"

"Yes. He was only supposed to stay for a month or two and it's been almost five so it's time, but I could use the rent money."

Shelly smiled. "This could work for us."

"How?"

"I'm renting a room with a couple. If Storm moves out I could rent a room at your place instead."

I was so eager that I took both her hands and spoke in a high-pitched voice: "You would move in with me?"

"I'll have to spend some time in the Motherlands, but it would be practical to have a base here in the Northlands that I could return to when I'm here."

"How often will that be?"

"I don't know. It depends on what projects I'm working on. If I can work from here, I'll do it, but it might not always be the case."

I wanted to tell her to stay with me, but this was Shelly and limiting her would be selfish, so instead I muttered a low, "I understand."

"Are you serious about working two jobs?"

211

I nodded and released her hands, my eyes following a leaf that was floating down the stream of water.

"Then I have a job for you."

I raised my gaze and met hers. "What kind of job? If you're going to offer me money to help you with your research, don't! I'm not taking money for sex."

She laughed. "That's not what I was going to suggest."

"Good, because that would have been fucking offensive."

"Advanced Technologies pay an Nman to be my protector. He's always on stand-by for whenever I need him, which isn't very often since I stay at the office most nights. I could ask Charlie to hire you for that job instead."

"Shelly, no..." I held up both hands. "You're carrying my child. Of course, I'll protect you. What kind of man do you take me for?"

"Someone who is smart enough to let Advanced Technologies pay him for something he would do for free."

"But what if I'm at the school and you need to go somewhere?"

"We'll figure it out. I'm sure you have friends who could step in if there was an emergency, but I don't think it'll be an issue."

"They would really pay me to protect you?" The concept was so strange to me that I needed her to confirm it again.

"Yes."

"How much are we talking about?"

"I don't know, but anything helps, right?"

"Yes, of course."

"How much does Storm pay for the room now?"

"Two hundred a month, but you wouldn't have to pay anything. I would be delirious if you'd move in and let me be close to you and our child."

212

"Two hundred?" Shelly angled her head. "I'm no expert on Northland money, but that sounds very cheap. Is it because he's your friend?"

"No, it's the normal rate."

"It can't be. I'm paying six hundred for my room and that's only a bit bigger."

"Do you have your own bathroom?"

"No."

"Do you have a view?"

"Yes, but it's nothing special."

"Is the location exceptional?"

"No. I don't think so."

My face split in a grin and I elbowed her. "Some genius you are. You're paying triple the rent and you had no idea."

"I was told it was a reasonable price to pay."

"By whom?"

"By personnel."

"Who's that?"

"That's our human resource department. They set it up for me. One of the ladies working there is the sister of the woman I'm renting a room from." Shelly closed her eyes the minute she said it and spoke on an exhalation: "Which of course explains the high price."

"What about the hired protector? Is he connected to that same sister you live with?"

"Yes, he's a friend of her husband."

I kept laughing. "Let's hope he's getting paid triple too."

Shelly frowned. "Stop laughing. It's not very nice of them to trick us like that."

"Hey, people do what they have to as long as it serves their agenda. You tricked me too and that's how we ended up in this mess to begin with." I held up a hand when she got that frown line between her eyebrows again. "I'm gonna stop you before you apologize again. It's getting old."

"Okay." Shelly licked her lips and looked down. "It'll take some getting used to. The idea that I'm going to be someone's mom."

"I get that," I said and tucked my hands under my thighs. "How do you feel about me being the father of your child?"

A shy smile flashed across her face and it instantly soothed my soul. "I never thought about having children or being roommates with a man, but if it had to happen, I would want it to be with you."

My eyebrows rose up. "Yeah?"

She nodded. "Maybe then my child will be athletic and socially competent."

I gave her a bright smile and she returned it with humor playing across her face.

"Plus, you'll bring some balance to the IQ, which is good."

"Hey." I bumped her shoulder with my arm. "Keep telling yourself that you're the smart one. I'm not the one paying triple rent here."

We laughed together and for a minute we sat dangling our feet and smiled.

"Somehow, I think we're going to make this work," Shelly pondered out loud. "We'll find our own version of a family unit."

"Does that unit include sex between the parents?" I asked her with hope in my chest.

Shelly squinted one eye closed when a sunbeam hit her face. "Would you like it to?"

"Is that a trick question?"

"I don't know. I had the impression you were done with me."

I opened my eyes and mouth wider in a look of complete bewilderment. "What the hell gave you that impression?"

"You always said that it would end when you went to the tournament."

"That was then."

"But you went."

"And I came back."

"Because of the pregnancy. Not because of me."

"What? You're the one who is pregnant. You can't separate the two."

"Yes, I can. You wouldn't be here if it wasn't because of the baby."

I pushed off the rock and jumped down to stand in front of her with my bare feet in the water. "Shelly, you were the one who told me you had all the research you needed. You were done with me before I left. You never gave me a chance to tell you that..."

She looked down and cut me off. "Can we not talk about this right now? I'm trying to take in that I'm pregnant. It's enough for one day."

"All right. I'll talk to Storm and see when he can move out. You talk to your work and ask them about making me your protector."

Shelly tried to get down but was unsure how to, so I held out my arms to her. "Careful," she warned. "Don't drop me or we'll both get wet."

"When can we tell people about the baby?" I asked with suppressed excitement.

"Can we wait some months at least? I'll have to tell my family before anyone finds out."

"What do you think they're going to say?"

Shelly leaned her head back and looked up at the white clouds. "They'll say I've lost my mind."

Her words worried me. "You'll still move in with me, right?"

With a tired smile she gave a small nod. "If you think I'll let others' opinion of me dictate how I live my life, then you underestimate me. I'm used to people seeing me as crazy, eccentric, odd, awkward –take your pick."

"My pick would be a unicorn."

Her eyebrows rose with a look of surprise. "Isn't that a horse?"

"Yes, but the most rare and beautiful one there is. It's magical."

"I don't believe in magic." Shelly yawned. She probably hadn't slept much last night either.

"You're tired. Do you want to go back to my place?" I asked, hoping to spend more time with her.

"I'm just overwhelmed by the whole thing. This wasn't in my plans and I don't think I've fully understood it yet."

We were still standing in the stream letting the water run over our bare feet. "Yeah, me too. Once your belly starts growing it'll be easier to understand and maybe then you'll be more excited about it."

"Yeah, maybe when the initial shock subsides. It's different for you. At least you always knew you wanted children. I hadn't thought about it until you came in me five weeks ago."

"But you'll love our child, won't you?"

"Of course I will." She reached up on her toes and touched my face. "And I'll love you."

I was so stunned by Shelly's unexpected words that she had started walking back the way we'd come before I kicked into gear.

"Do you mean you'll love me because I'm the father of your child or will you love me for real?"

Shelly kept walking. "The two are the same."

"No, they're not. Would you love me if there was no child?"

She cast a glance over her shoulder. "Ah, so we are asking each other the same question. I asked you if you'd be here if not for the child and now you want to know if I would love you if not for the child."

"So what is your answer?" I asked.

Shelly climbed up a group of stones to where we had placed our shoes.

"Shelly, do you love me?" My arms were spread out and my head leaned back to look up at her.

"I do." It felt a little flat since she was putting on her sandals and didn't look at me.

Unsatisfied, I climbed up to her, brushed my hands off on my pants, and rose to my full height in front of her. "Why do I sense there's a 'but' in that sentence?"

"Marco, I've always liked you."

I stepped closer. "Just tell me if…"

With a hand to my mouth she silenced me. "Please, Marco, I'm exhausted and need some time to digest this whole thing."

I stood back watching her walk to the drone while I put on my shoes. She said she loved me but there was no indication that it was a romantic kind of love. More like she'd just realized that we were related and now she felt obligated to love me as her kin.

Make her fall in love with you.

Never had I craved anything as much as this. I would find a way to convince her to accept me as more than her roommate. She was carrying my child. Whether Shelly understood it or not, that made her my mate.

CHAPTER 21
Promises

Shelly

"Mom, if people knew how you live they wouldn't take you so seriously," I said and took a look around her kitchen, where colorful furniture were mounted on the wall in ways that the people who built them had never intended. A dresser hung on its side, the drawers converted to narrow pull-out shelves and its legs horizontal with pans and pots dangling from them. Next to it a beautiful glass cabinet hung upside down with plates stacked on what had been intended as the underside of the shelves.

My mom smiled at me, her dark hair flat against her forehead and just long enough that she could tuck it behind her ear. "Shelly, life is supposed to be fun – you never understood that, did you?"

"I'm fun."

"You're quirky, that's not the same thing."

Stabbing my fork around my salad I wrinkled my forehead. "How could I not be quirky? I grew up in a house with shoes and chairs glued to the ceiling."

My mom looked up. "It's an art installation."

"Hmm."

"People are too limited in their thinking. That's why I'm so proud of you, my dear." My mom leaned forward and cupped my cheek. "You've never been afraid to think outside the box."

I gave her a small smile. "True, but what if I'm so occupied by everything that's outside the box that I miss the good stuff inside the box?"

"What do you mean?"

"I've never been normal."

My mom pulled back and scoffed a little. "Normal. What is that anyway? Certainly not something to strive for."

I sighed. "You always say that, but with being normal comes invisibility and for someone like me it sounds like a superpower."

"You lost me."

"I'm Shelly Summers, *the genius*."

"So, I'm Sheana Rene Summers, the councilwoman. We all have an identity."

"But don't you ever wish you could walk around and have no one expect anything of you?"

My mom dusted crumbs from the table into her hand and put them on an empty plate. "No. I'm proud of who I am and the role I serve."

"Yeah, but that's because you're awesome. I've only got this explosion of thoughts in my head and half of it sounds idiotic even to me."

"Who cares? No genius ever came up with only brilliant ideas." Sheana gave me a soft smile and squeezed my hand. "I'm beginning to worry about you, honey – where is this new self-doubt coming from and since when do you care what other people think?"

"I don't." Turning my head, I searched for a way to tell her that the only approval I cared about was Marco's.

"Are you sure? Something is different about you. It's not those letters that Charlie told me about, is it? I was so shocked to hear you've been getting hate mail. You know, I told him not to worry about you because you never cared about such things, but seeing you like this, I wonder."

"It's fine, Mom, those letters are irrelevant."

She was watching me with her interest, as if I was a riddle to solve. "Maybe you're developing a social interest? Heaven knows you've always been liked by people. I would welcome it if you let some of them in."

"I have friends," I said a bit defensive.

"Sure, but do you ever see them?"

"I saw Tristan not so long ago."

"That's one person, Shelly. What about Rochelle? She's your sister and she said that she never hears from you."

"I get caught up in my work and then I forget time. It is what it is."

"All your life I've seen people circle you and try to become your friend. I wish you'd prioritize that part of your life, honey. Social connections are important."

"I know, but I'm fine."

"You promise?"

"Yes." I looked down for a second. "Mom, I'm thinking about extending my stay in the Northlands."

Her head jerked back, "Why?"

"Because I'm on to something with this project and I'm getting a ton done."

"You could get a ton done here."

"It's more isolated up there."

My mom folded her arms across her chest. "If you want 'isolated' then go to Granny's village. You love it there."

She was right. My grandmother lived down south in a small village overlooking a beautiful bay where all the houses were tucked into the hillside. It was a brilliant way to let the earth keep the dwellings cool in the summer. Not only did the houses have a magnificent view through the panorama windows facing the sea, but the overhead windows nestled in between the wildflowers on the hillside provided natural daylight to the rooms positioned in the back of the house.

"It's not a bad idea," I said in a polite manner, "but I have everything I need in the Northlands and I already spoke to Charlie about it."

"What did he say?"

"That he wants me to be happy."

My mom chewed on her lips. "Yes, of course he would say that."

"He should. My inventions can benefit a lot of people."

"Creating advanced sex-toys for Nmen isn't on the top ten list of what this world needs." Her tone was hard for a Motlander.

"Maybe not, but my robot would be the best-made robot in history and the technology could be applied to all other robots after that."

"Robots are already amazing. The sex-bots I use look very authentic."

"Only until you look closer." I paused and waited for her to meet my eyes. "Mom, mine would be a companion and not just a sex-toy. She'll be able to converse, share humor, and if the man doesn't treat her nicely, she'll be grumpy like a normal woman."

"That's all very fine, Shelly, but just because you can replicate a human doesn't mean you should."

I opened my mouth to reply, but nothing came out.

My mom got up, taking her cup of tea to the sink. "We lost billions of people once because humankind was blinded by optimizing the human experience. All those brain implants making people speak different languages and having access to endless data. What good did it do them?"

"Mom, that was a long time ago. We're wiser now."

"Are we?" She swung around, leaning against the sink and pinning me with her eyes. "Brain implants are back. I heard you even helped improve them. Now you want to create the perfect woman for Nmen. Why this obsession about perfecting what is already perfect?"

"You misunderstand. I'm doing the opposite. Sex-bots are a mockery of real women, with their fake curves. I'm bringing back the focus to the beauty of the natural woman. That's my motivation."

My mom looked thoughtful and drew a sigh before she spoke. "There's something you're not telling me. Why do you care what sex-bots the Nmen play with? The rest of us couldn't care less and it's none of our business anyway. If the men of the North want sex-bots with four breasts and two vaginas then we should give it to them. As long as it makes them happy who are we to judge?"

"I care."

"But why, Shelly?" Sheana was throwing her hands in the air, frustration showing on her face. "Why?"

Her question served as a trigger and the reason spilled out of me. "Because when I was an assistant teacher at the experimental school, we went on a fieldtrip to the Motherlands and we visited Advanced Technologies. There were sex-bots, and the boys and male teachers talked about them with such excitement."

"So?"

Popping my eyes, I squeezed my hands. "I was right there, Mom."

"Yes?"

"And none of them had ever shown any interest in me. They would rather have sex with a dead thing than..." I couldn't say it.

"Than you." My mom finished the sentence for me.

I looked away, my shoulders drooping and my mind racing to the obvious conclusion that I'd never been brave enough to admit to myself. This project had always been about Marco. He had hurt my pride that day when he had praised the sex-bots and at the same time seen right past me. I wanted to create a natural sex-bot to prove that men would prefer a real woman over a fake one.

"Shelly?"

Slouching over the table, I hid my face by placing my hands on my forehead.

222

"Shelly, are you okay?" My mom sat down next to me and stroked my back. "You were a teenager back then. We are all self-absorbed and concerned about what others think of us in those years of our lives. But now that you're older you can laugh about it, can't you? It's not like you'd want to have sex with an Nman anyway. It was just a prick to your pride."

In a slow movement, I turned my head and looked at my mom. "I have had sex with an Nman."

Her eyes grew wide.

"Not just once but several times."

"Honeyyy…" Her face fell in a look of deep pity.

"You don't have to look at me like that. I'm not sick."

My mom wasn't stroking my back anymore. "I didn't say you were sick, but clearly you're stressed. I want you to go to a place of reflection. This isn't you."

"That's where you're wrong." My voice was low but my tone firm.

"Shelly, I'm concerned for you."

I swung my hands around the kitchen. "You always taught me that different is good. You were right, Mom. Sex is different and at the same time it's amazing."

"Is that why you want to stay in the Northlands? So you can have *sex*?" The way her upper lip lifted when she said the last word made me shake my head. I had come here to tell her that I was pregnant and that I'd be moving in with Marco, but she wasn't ready to hear it.

"Shelly, please don't go back to the Northlands." My mom's voice broke and tears welled up in her eyes as she squeezed my hand. "Please."

"I'm going, Mom. It's the right thing for me and I'll be okay." I moved over to comfort her.

Sheana cried in my arms. "What if one of them hurts you while having sex?"

"Mom, I'm not having sex with random men. Only one, and I trust him."

223

Using the heels of her hands, Sheana dried away tears. "Just promise me one thing."

"What is that?"

"Don't *marry* an Nman like all those other women have. I know that you're smarter than that, but I want you to promise me, Shelly." Her tears kept falling.

I loved my mom, and I wanted to take away the pain that I'd caused her. Kissing her on the cheek and hugging her tight, I whispered the words that would calm her: "I promise I won't marry him."

CHAPTER 22
Welcome

Marco

My apartment had never been this clean.

It had been a month since we'd found out Shelly was pregnant. Storm had finally moved out and Shelly was back from a two-week visit with her family and friends. We hadn't had much time together because she'd been busy working and I had sensed she needed some space to come to terms with the new situation.

"Stop feeling bad about it," Shelly insisted after I'd shown her what Advance Technologies were paying me to protect her.

"It has to be a mistake, though, right?"

"You're being paid to be on stand-by even when you're not working."

"But they are basically paying me two times what I make in a month as a mentor."

"You should see that as a good thing."

"It's ridiculous is what it is."

Shelly brushed her hair back and picked up a slice of the orange that I'd cut out for her. "Why aren't you happy about it?"

"Because it feels dishonest to take that much money for so little, especially when they're paying me rent too."

She shrugged. "Money is just fictive numbers changing hands."

"No it's not. Only a Motlander would say that. Money isn't fictive. It's very real. With this kind of income, I could put down a deposit for a new drone in two months."

Shelly smiled. "Then why don't you?"

"Because when something is too good to be true it usually is." I placed a large glass of water in front of her and studied her closely. Shelly still looked as beautiful as when I last saw her, and every part of me wanted to kiss her. Over the past two weeks, I'd thought of this moment a million times, aware that I had to do this the right way or I might scare her. I wanted her to move in with me for real. Not in the guest bedroom as a roommate, but in my bed, as my woman.

"Don't be pessimistic," she said and sucked on a grape. It was all it took for me to grow hard. Trying to distract myself, I focused on the subject we were discussing.

"Advanced Technologies will realize they're overpaying and ask to have their money back."

"I doubt it." Shelly smiled and nodded to the plate with fruit in front of her. "Are you going to cater to me like this all the time? Did you do that for Storm too?"

"No, but I figured I should be good to you on your first night here."

"Thank you."

"You had me worried. I was starting to think that you were going to stay in the Motherlands."

Shelly frowned a little, placing her elbow on the table and resting one chin in her palm. "I thought about it."

I stiffened and stared at her, waiting for her to continue. When she didn't I asked a burning question. "Did you tell your family about me?"

"Only my mom."

My face fell. "Not Rochelle?"

"She was away at school and had finals. I want to tell her in person. Don't worry, I'll see her in a few days at the reunion weekend. Then I'll tell her."

"All right. What did your mom say when you told her about the baby?"

"I didn't tell her that part."

"Why not?"

"Because I'm only two months pregnant and it'll take a while before it shows. I told her I'll be living here for a while longer, and she didn't take that well. My mother knows I've had sex and she was crying about it."

The sadness on Shelly's face told me how much she cared about her family.

"I had to make her a promise."

"Who, your mom?"

"Yes."

"What promise?" I leaned closer, afraid to breathe. What if she had promised that she'd only stay for a minimum of time?

Shelly sighed. "I promised my mom that I wouldn't marry an Nman."

"You did *what*?" I exclaimed in a loud outburst. "Why the fuck would you promise her that?"

"Because she was devastated and you and I agreed that we weren't going to marry anyway. It doesn't matter, Marco, we can still raise our child together and be a family of sorts."

"Of sorts?" Pushing my chair back, I moved around the table to stand in front of her. All my careful planning about wooing her was forgotten. "It might not matter to you if we're married or not, but it fucking matters to me."

Looking baffled by my strong reaction, Shelly asked, "Where is this coming from? We agreed that we didn't need to copy other people and that we could find our own way of doing this. We're living together, isn't that what you wanted?" She took my hand. "Marco, we talked about it that day by the creek, remember?"

"I only agreed to that solution because it was a big fucking step up from you going to the Motherlands and leaving me here to never see our child."

"What are you saying?"

"I want to marry you, make love to you, and have a ton of babies with you. I want you to be mine and I want the whole fucking world to know it."

Shelly gaped, her eyes big and expressing what her words didn't – she was shocked.

"I love you Shelly." There, I'd said what I wanted to say for so long.

"It's because of the sex, isn't it?" she asked and began ranting. "I'm not opposed to it, and you don't have to say that you love me to get me to sleep with you again. I figure that as long as I'm pregnant we don't have to worry about you coming inside me or not."

Cupping her face with both my hands I kissed her, deep and with insistence. "There's something I should have told you from the beginning."

"What is that?"

"I know that you're like a unique specimen of mankind and way out of my league, but I love you and I loved you before I knew about the baby."

"You mean humankind. To say mankind would imply we're all men, and as you know women outweigh men in numbers, so to dismiss us in the description of..."

With a smile I tucked a strand of her hair behind her ear before I interrupted her by leaning in and kissing her again. "I fucking missed you, Brainy. This is so typical of you."

"What is?"

I chuckled low, chewing softly on her lower lip. "To get hung up on the most insignificant details of an important message. Did you even hear what I just told you?" I whispered into her mouth. "I loved you before I knew about the baby."

She gave a sweet sound of delight and met my gaze. The edges of her eyes crinkled as her smile lit up every corner of my soul. "I missed you too, Marco."

Those words were all I needed and without waiting for more, I picked her up and carried her to my bedroom.

"You ripped it."

My impatience to get her naked had me ripping her shirt to get it off her. "I'll buy you a new one," I muttered and kept undressing my woman. The need to merge with her was giving me tunnel vision. I could see only Shelly's creamy skin and beautiful face.

"I want you so fucking bad." Even my voice held a tremor from the state I was in.

"Slow down, Marco," Shelly urged, but I couldn't.

"I need you."

She helped me undress by pulling my t-shirt over my head while I was kicking off my shoes and pants.

"It tickles." She laughed when I buried my head between her legs and nibbled at the soft skin on her inner thighs. When I moved my tongue to her clitoris and bored my fingers into her skin to keep her in place her laughter changed to sweet moans. I had never been as hard or aroused as I was in that moment. Shelly was moving into my apartment and I was claiming her. She knew I loved her, there were no more secrets between us, and we were having a child together. I didn't want to stop to think about things that could go wrong. Right now, I wanted only one thing, and that was her.

"Oh, Marco."

Shelly was arching a little, her head bent back and her eyes closed.

I kept using my tongue and felt like coming myself when she kept calling my name.

"Marco it feels so good, yees…"

As I moved up her body, the slightly salty taste from her creamy soft skin worked as an aphrodisiac and I couldn't wait any longer.

Lifting her legs, I pushed inside her wet pussy, my movements eager and demanding. She held her hand on my hip as if to hold me back a little, but I was too horny and pushed deep inside her.

"Ohhh," she moaned, grimacing in pain.

"Shelly, I fucking need you," I panted and kept pushing in and out with so much force that I was moving her body up the mattress.

I knew I wouldn't last long like this, but I had finally told her that I loved her, and the animalistic need to fill her with my semen and claim her was driving me to this crazy ride.

"Marco, slow down. We have time."

"I love you." Locking eyes with her, I forced myself to turn it down a bit. Letting the head of my cock slide up and down her folds, I bit her shin, which was leaning on my shoulder.

"Augh." Her smile was seductive.

"I could just eat you up."

"You're different today. What's gotten into you?"

"You have. That's why I need to be inside you too."

Shelly pushed me back on my haunches and climbed on top of me. Wrapping her arms around my shoulders, she whispered, "I like this position."

"I like any position. As long as it's with you."

Shelly silenced me with more kissing, using her hips to rotate on top of me in the most delicious way. My hands were firmly planted on her behind as I closed my eyes and groaned. "Fuck yes, this is good."

I could tell that Shelly wanted to control the pace and enjoy me longer, but I still had that pressing urge to fuck her hard.

If she knew how difficult it was for me not to go full speed, she would know how deep my love for her was.

My hands played with her nipples while I enjoyed the full shape of her delicious round tits hovering over my open mouth. I let my tongue flicker out, tasting one of her

230

tight little pink nubs and bringing her body closer to suck her nipple into my mouth.

The sweet sounds of pleasure that came from Shelly had my ball sack tighten, ready to fire.

Not yet, not yet, not yet, I chanted in my head, forcing myself to lie still and let her ride me.

Shelly was no longer the shy virgin but a woman growing confident in her sexuality. Working her core up and down the length of my cock she whispered into my ear. "I missed you. I missed having you inside me."

I felt deprived when she pulled back and I could no longer taste her nipple. In compensation she gave me a glorious sight of her beauty when she kept rotating her hips on top of me while raising her hands to interlace them in her hair. Holy fuck, my woman was gorgeous and sexy as something out of a dream. If I kept watching her perky tits bounce in the rhythm of her fucking me for one more second, I'd lose control, so I closed my eyes.

When her moaning picked up in intensity, so did my eagerness.

"Yes, Marco, I'm so close... more, give me more."

Like a racehorse having been forced to walk I was finally given free rein, and I lifted her up enough that I could hammer in and out of her at full speed, making her screams grow louder and my groans deeper.

"Fuck yes... Fuck yes..." I panted and squeezed my eyes closed while enjoying the symphony of my woman coming hard on my cock.

"Marco, yes... oh, Mother Nature, yeeesss..."

The release was mind-numbing with my orgasm nailing me in the back of my spine and making me clench my teeth together to keep from roaring out like a fucking lion. Shelly was already pregnant with my child, but I still felt such satisfaction filling her up, like I was depositing some of me inside her to strengthen our connection.

After rolling down on the bed to catch our breaths, we lay for minutes, merging our fingers and enjoying the high of the best sex we'd ever had.

"I love you so much," I muttered and kissed her on her hair.

Shelly looked up at me from her position nuzzled up against me. "I told you that you don't have to say it."

"It's the truth. I'm not the one telling white lies. Trust me. I love you, Shelly."

She gave me a skeptical glance.

"Remember the party game we played where you had to guess what I was thinking?"

"Yeah."

"You guessed that my message was that I liked you. My real message was that I loved you."

"Really?"

"Yes, I love you very much."

Shelly licked her lips, her eyebrows drawn together. "When did that happen?"

"That night at my apartment. You were right when you accused me of being possessive. I was falling in love with you. I would have told you if you hadn't been so quick to cut me off the next day."

Shelly tilted her head, a small smile on her pretty face. "It hurts, doesn't it?"

"What?"

"To be in love."

Her words were like a gigantic blow and I pulled away from her. With my legs over the edge of the bed, I bent forward, fisting both hands through my hair. She had told me she loved me but it had been a polite kind of love, and here I had bared myself to her. Swallowing my pride, I spoke in a low voice. "Shelly, all I'm asking for is time. Maybe you can learn to love me."

The gentle laughter behind me made me turn to see Shelly propped up on an elbow, facing me. Her hair was a mess and her cheeks flushed from our intense lovemaking.

"Why are you laughing?"

"The reason I know how much it hurts to love someone who doesn't love you back is because I've been in love with you since I was fifteen years old."

I lowered my brow. "You're not serious."

"I'm very serious."

"But you were so young."

She smiled. "Feelings have no age. I fell in love with you back then and when I saw you again, all my feelings came back."

My brain was sending out celebratory jolts of electricity that ran from the top of my spine all the way down, creating a sizzle of warm excitement in my body.

"And what are those feelings exactly?" I asked and rolled back on top of her, my eyes locked with hers. "Tell me."

"You want to know how I feel about you?"

"Uh-huh." I trapped her with my large body, making sure she wasn't going anywhere until she had shared what was in her heart.

"It's simple. I love you too."

"Say it again." My eyes were searching for any sort of deceit in her eyes.

"I love you, Marco."

"And this isn't one of your white lies to make me feel better, is it?"

She shook her head.

"Why didn't you tell me sooner?"

"You know me; I've never been good at expressing my feelings. That's why when you mistook me for a robot, it was a chance to experience sex with the only man I've ever been attracted to without making a fool of myself. Or at least that was my intention."

"Fuuuck..." My head fell down to nuzzle against the crook of her neck. "You *are* serious."

"Marco... are you hard again?" Shelly's question had a tone of surprise in it.

"Hell yeah, I'm hard. Your words have to be the biggest turn-on I've ever experienced. You handpicked me because you were attracted to me. Not because I was the only male available."

Shelly laughed and it sounded sweeter than sugar tastes. "Marco, come on, you know that you're attractive. You saw it when you went to the Motherlands; the women were all over you."

"That was ten years ago. I haven't experienced that since then."

"Until I came back into your life, that is."

I tightened my hold around her. "Just so you know, Brainy, that rule about me not being allowed to be possessive is off the table now. I'm not giving you up or letting other men near you. Do you understand?"

Shelly's smile grew when I kissed her. "You don't have to feel threatened. I've only ever wanted to be with you."

"Then you'll marry me?"

Her hands were nuzzling the hair in my nape. "I can't."

"Why not? We love each other and we're starting a family. It's a complete no-brainer. We *are* getting married."

"I can't marry you, Marco. I made a promise to my mom, remember?"

Pressing my head against her neck, I muttered in frustration. "I love that you want to honor a promise, but I won't stop asking until you say yes."

Shelly didn't look fazed by it, but just pulled me in for another kiss.

CHAPTER 23
Reunion

Shelly

We left for the West Coast on Friday, only three days after I came back from the Motherlands.

Marco was frustrated with me. He wanted to tell everyone that we were together and that we were having a baby, but most of all he still insisted that we should marry.

I had gone so far as to tell him that I would consider it, but in reality, I still didn't see the need.

Hunter and Willow picked us up around noon in the luxurious large drone that had been especially designed for Hunter.

"Where's Storm and Tristan?" Marco asked. "I thought we were all flying together."

"I changed my mind," Hunter said. "In case Willow and I have to leave, you two can fly home with Tristan and Storm."

"Nothing is going to happen," Willow insisted. "Mila said that he hasn't even responded to her invitation."

I didn't have to ask whom we were talking about; it was obvious that Hunter was nervous about Solomon coming to the reunion.

"Do you want to talk about what happened between you and Solo?" I asked Willow, but Hunter shut us down by taking off with such speed that we were pressed back in our seats. Willow and I exchanged a glance and she mouthed a "later."

It took a little over three hours to get to the island on the west coast where the school was located. It had grown with more buildings and a proper soccer field.

"I thought there weren't supposed to be any students at the school?" Willow said when two handfuls of children stood ready to welcome us. "Oh, look at them – how cute."

"They're not students. At least not all of them. They look too young," Marco pointed out and then the door swung open.

Marco had told me about Hunter's fame, but it was something else to see how the kids surrounded him and screamed his name. A few of them were talking so fast that I couldn't understand a thing.

"Finally, you are here." Female voices made us look up to see Pearl, Laura, and Christina walking toward us.

"Kids, give Hunter some space. He just arrived," Laura instructed.

"Will you play soccer with us?" a boy who looked to be around ten asked Hunter while pulling at his sleeve.

"You must be Indiana," Hunter replied. "The last time I saw you, you were around six; do you remember?"

The boy shook his head before Christina hugged him from behind and gave Hunter an apologetic shrug. "Sorry about that. The kids have been waiting for hours for you to arrive."

Laura laughed. "That's right. You were supposed to be here three hours ago. I thought that drone of yours was one of the fastest in the country."

"It is. Problem was that I had a mandatory practice session that I had to go to," Hunter explained. "We came as fast as we could.

"So will you play with us?" a boy in front of Laura asked, and with his impressive height and his hair color being the same rich one as Laura's, I figured he had to be her and Magni's son.

236

"Patience, Mason." Laura patted the boy's shoulder. "Hunter can beat you in soccer later – right now I want you to help carry the luggage and show our guests to the campsite."

Three of the boys argued about who should have the honor of carrying Hunter's bag.

"Those two are mine too," he said and pointed to Marco's two bags. The problem was solved when the three children carried one bag each, with proud expressions on their faces.

Willow and I hugged all three women and walked with them up to the school.

"Our children have been allowed to stay for a few hours to meet you all," Pearl explained to me and Willow as the three of us were walking behind the others. "I figured they would help ease some of Hunter's tension about coming back here." Pearl smiled a little and hooked her arm under Willow's. "And yours too of course."

"Thank you, the children are wonderful and sweet."

Pearl chuckled. "Don't let the boys hear that you called them sweet. Things haven't changed *that* much up here in the Northlands."

"Is Khan here too?" I asked.

"He and Magni will be here later." Pearl placed her free hand around me. "Shelly, I'm so excited to catch up with you. Tristan told me that you have been a great inspiration for his public transportation project."

I smiled back at her. "And here I thought he dismissed my ideas as crazy."

Before we could talk further old friends started calling out to us, and Willow was picked up and twirled in the air by Raven, who had a large grin on her face. It looked funny because Raven was shorter than Willow.

"It's about time you people showed up. We were starting to think that you had gotten cold feet."

Willow grinned back at Raven "Of course not, I wouldn't miss it for the world."

"That's the spirit," Raven exclaimed and turned to me. "Long time no see, Shelly Summers. Come get a big hug."

"Can I get your attention?" Kya was standing on a chair and clapping her hands. Her dark curls, chocolate-colored eyes, and caramel skin made her look as pretty now as she had been ten years ago. Only now, she was even curvier, and Archer stood close to her with his hand on the small of her back, sending a not so subtle signal to his former male students, who were all grown men now, letting them know that Kya was still his woman.

"Thank you so much for coming. It's so much fun to see you all back here to celebrate the ten-year anniversary of the Pearl Pilotti School of Inclusion."

Half of the group began clapping but Kya continued. "I would like to give the floor to our founder, Pearl Pilotti."

Pearl didn't step up on the chair; instead she signaled for us to form a large half circle and addressed us with a soft smile.

"Lord Khan sends his greetings. He wanted to be here to officially welcome you all, but unfortunately something urgent has delayed him. He asked that I welcome you instead, and that I tell you that he and Magni are very much looking forward to joining us as soon as they can. Now, there are a few practical things that Lord Khan asked me to make clear to you." Pearl held up a note in front of her and as her eyes ran over it, she tugged at her lip. "Maybe it's easier if I read it out loud. That way you will know that the profanities are his and not mine."

People laughed.

"Okay, here we go." Pearl took a deep breath, which allowed for a pause. "Tell them that every woman attending the reunion is under my protection, and that any fucker who thinks he can touch them because they used to be friends will be dealt with swiftly." Pearl lifted

238

her gaze from the note and looked to us men. "In other words, the same rule applies here as it does everywhere else in the Northlands. You cannot touch a woman without her consent."

"Understood," Storm piped up.

Pearl read on. "Also tell my Nmen to collectively behave as protectors to all the women present. That means stepping in if they see any sort of troubling behavior from a peer. Other than that, just tell them to have fun and save some beer for me and Magni."

Marco leaned in and whispered in my ear. "If anyone misbehaves you'll come to me."

I dipped my head. "Of course."

His eyes fell to my lips and he leaned in a little. It instinctively made me pull back. I wasn't ready for everyone to know about us. Widening my eyes and moving my eyeballs toward the others, I told him without words that now wasn't the right time or place to kiss.

Marco's face tightened before he walked away to join the other Nmen, who seemed to have taken to heart the stern warning about not touching us women. They kept to themselves, drinking and laughing out loud.

"I thought this might happen," Mila said, her eyes darting between the divided group of men and women. "But don't worry. I planned all sorts of fun games for us."

Looking on, I followed Mila's failed attempt to organize a party game.

"Sorry, Mila, we promised to play soccer with the kids." The men excused themselves and headed to the soccer field.

I mingled with the former students as well as Kya, Pearl, and Athena, whose two sons came complaining to her that there wasn't room for them on Hunter's team.

"It's because all the grown-ups want to be on his team too," the older one said, while the younger brother stood with his arms crossed and kicked at the ground with a pout on his face.

"Finn," Athena called out. "The boys want to play with their idol."

Finn just waved back, looking like a kid himself and shouted, "Me too."

"Boys, go tell Dad and Tristan that they can play for ten minutes and then you'll take their places," Athena instructed her sons, who ran full speed back to the soccer field.

I waved to my sister, Rochelle, who looked to be in a passionate discussion with William; he had been the youngest boy when the school first started out.

"You don't kill humans just because they can't talk or answer academic questions. So why animals? They still have emotions, dreams, loyalty, and a right to a full life too," she argued. "Killing animals is inhumane."

William spread out his arms. "That's the fucking point, isn't it? It's inhumane because they're not human."

I changed my course as I wasn't in the mood to hear another argument on that subject. Killing animals for food was illegal in the Motherlands but here it was considered normal, and I didn't see that changing anytime soon.

"Hey, Shelly."

I recognized Nero right away. He had that same bead in his beard that I had seen so many men wearing when Tristan took me to the drone race. "Hi, Nero, how are you?"

"Good."

"Why aren't you playing soccer with the other men?"

He looked over to the soccer field. "I'll play later, when there are no kids."

"You don't like kids?"

"Sure, but I get so competitive and I don't want to hurt one of them by accident."

"Raven doesn't look like she's holding anything back."

We both took a second to look at the game, where Raven was the only woman playing with the men and the children.

"Did you talk to her yet?" I asked him. "You two were always fighting. Hopefully you can laugh about it now."

"Nah, it was mostly in the beginning. It got better after you left." He turned to face me. "I read some of your articles. The one about using fish to grow plants was very interesting.

"Yes, I'm very passionate about finding ways to grow food with a minimum amount of water waste. I'm in regular contact with some of my friends that I got to know while studying to be a biologist. One of them is working on a very interesting project down in the Yellow Zone."

"One of the articles said that you did your dissertation on the subject of awkwardness. Is that true?"

"Yes, but not while studying to be a biologist. That was my psychology degree."

Nero tucked his hands in his pockets and rocked back on his heels. "I figured as much."

"Right." I smiled. "Awkwardness seemed like a fitting subject for me to dive into and understand better at the time."

"Are you admitting that you're a perfect research subject yourself?" There was humor in his voice.

I kept my face straight. "No, but back then I came straight from the Northlands and had been with enough of you Nmen to know awkward behavior."

His brow rose and he pointed to his chest. "Are you saying *we're* the awkward ones?"

"Some of you more than others."

Nero looked a bit confused and it was hard not to laugh at my own joke, but his next question made me tingle with excitement. "And what did you find out? Is there a formula for awkwardness?"

"Well, I discovered that every society has a set of rules and limitations that we operate within. First there are laws of science and biology that tell us basic things like we can't go without sleep, we can't spread our arms and fly, or jump back in time to correct a mistake. You get the point, right?"

"Yeah."

"Then there are human-made laws that we submit to, and those vary between the Motherlands and the Northlands, of course. In some cases, what is legal here is illegal there and vice versa."

Nero nodded. "Like hunting."

"Exactly. And after the criminal laws comes etiquette, and that's a different beast since it's not written down per se. It requires training and social awareness to read a situation and know what is expected of you. What makes it even more tricky is that etiquette varies across the world. Breaking the etiquette could get you shunned or ostracized socially, which is a high price to pay because it means isolation and loneliness."

"So what? A little isolation can be nice. I have a cabin that I sometimes go to when I need some peace and quiet."

"Sure, but long-term loneliness affects your immune system and can cause depression, which makes it a big deal, Nero," I emphasized and continued my little lecture. "Of course, breaking etiquette can vary depending on who judges. It takes a lot more to be rude here than in the Motherlands but generally speaking we're dealing with categories from rudeness, to mean and disgusting behavior, followed by the subtlest of all, which is *awkwardness*." My voice was a bit eager because it always gave me a buzz when someone showed an interest in something I was passionate about.

"I find this so interesting," I continued, "because awkwardness is connected to awareness and is used to adjust the finer details of social behavior that etiquette doesn't define. It's not a violation of the laws of physics to laugh too loud, over-share personal information, or congratulate someone on being pregnant when they're not. There's no law against it either. It's just very awkward."

"True," Nero agreed. "You know what else is awkward? Coming back to see your old classmates and realizing that the girls that you used to make fun of have turned into beautiful women and now you wish you'd been nicer to them." He laughed.

"Anyone specific?"

"It goes for all the women. You included."

"Me?"

"Yes, you're very beautiful, Shelly."

I looked down. "Thank you."

"We need people on the food team!" Kya shouted from the doorway to the school.

Raising my hand, I offered my help. "I'm happy to give a hand."

"Have you learned how to cook?" Nero asked with a skeptical expression on his face.

"I wouldn't say it's my biggest strength, but I can peel and cut some vegetables if that's what you mean."

"It's okay, Shelly, I got it," my sister Rochelle called out.

Kya placed her hands on her hips and smiled. "That's great, Rochelle, but I need two more people."

"I'll do it," Nero declared and smiled at Nicki when he walked past her. "You wanna help out?"

When Nicki hesitated, Nero added, "Shelly is threatening to go into the kitchen, so we could really use your help."

Nicki's eyes flew to me and then back to him. "Sure, I'll help."

"I'm not that bad of a cook," I defended myself.

Nero grinned back at me over his shoulder. "Why don't you invent time traveling while we go make dinner? I think those physical laws you talked about only apply to us normal people. I'm sure you could find a way around them if you wanted to."

With Nero and the others inside, I walked over to watch the soccer game. Mila and some of the others were sitting on the grass cheering so I joined them.

"This is just like old times," Mila said and smiled at me while at the same time helping two little girls braid a crown of flowers.

I was staring at Marco, who had a small girl on his shoulders with his hands wrapped around her ankles to hold her in place.

"That's Dina," Mila explained. "She's my youngest sister and she was crying just now because she couldn't play with the others."

"How old is she?"

"Three." She tilted her head. "It was so sweet of Marco to include her."

"Yeah, it was, but he loves children. I'm sure he doesn't think it's a big deal."

Mila tilted her head watching him. "Marco is going to be the best dad ever."

I widened my eyes, wondering if Mila somehow knew about the baby.

"I offered to marry him." She said it as if it were the most natural thing in the world.

"You did what?"

"I said that I would pick him as my champion next year when I have my tournament."

I wanted to talk to her about the tournament but for now I was just stunned that Marco hadn't told me about this.

"And what did Marco say to your offer?" I asked, trying not to reveal how much my heart was beating at this moment.

"That's it, Mason, nice goal," Mila cheered and pointed to one of the boys that we had seen when we first arrived. "You're making your sister proud."

I clapped my hands to show my support while repeating my question to Mila. "What did Marco say to your offer?"

"Oh, he said it was nice of me, but he wouldn't fight in my tournament." She sighed. "It's a shame, because he would have made a wonderful father and I really like him."

"You like Marco?"

"Yes, he's very strong and fit and also kind and funny."

"But he's ten years older than you."

"That doesn't bother me. My dad is nine years older than my mom and they are very happy together."

"But do you love him?"

"Who, Marco?" Mila had such an innocent look in her blue eyes. "No. I've never been in love, but I'm told that those feelings can often grow within a marriage." ·

"Did Marco tell you why he wouldn't fight for you?"

"Yes. It's because I used to be his student. He said that would be weird."

"He's right." My pulse was starting to come down again. "It would be just as weird as me marrying Hunter."

"Nonsense. You and Hunter would make a great couple. So would you and Tristan. He really likes and admires you."

"Mila, Tristan and I are just friends."

"That's good. A strong friendship is the best foundation for a marriage anyway."

"Why do you even want to get married, Mila? You wouldn't even be thinking about it if you were in the Motherlands. It's outdated and serves no purpose."

"I disagree." Mila's words were soft but firm. "There is something beautiful about two people uniting."

"There's no need. Not everyone finds the love that your parents have. Look at all the couples from the

Matchmaking Program. Many of them are getting divorced."

"I blame it on the Motlanders."

"Why?"

"Because they want to change the Nmen."

"I think that goes both ways, though."

We sat for a while, watching the game and cheering every time someone scored. When they were done playing, Hunter showed off, keeping the ball bouncing in the air using his foot, knee, shoulders, and head.

"Khan and my dad are hoping that this weekend will result in some new couples," Mila said out of the blue. "Who do you think would be likely to end up together?"

"I don't know."

"Make a guess, then."

"You and Tristan."

Mila laughed. "I don't think he would go through the trouble of fighting in a tournament. Do you?"

"No, but if you fell in love he wouldn't have to, would he?"

Mila plucked some grass. "My parents wouldn't like it if I married someone who hadn't fought for me. They are old-fashioned that way."

Just when I was about to go into a discussion about being an independent woman, Marco came over and put down Dina on the ground. "Thank you so much for letting me borrow your sister. She was a great help," he said with a large smile.

"You're welcome." Mila got up and brushed off her long flowery skirt. "Did you have fun, honey?"

The little girl nodded and began telling Mila about the game.

"I'm thirsty. Wanna grab something to drink?" Marco asked me.

"Sure." I lifted my hand and he pulled me up from the grass.

"I could use a drink; how about you, Mila?"

"Sure, I'm just going to send off the kids. They are going back to the Gray Mansion where Grandma Isobel is hosting a party for them."

"That sounds like fun." Marco smiled and bowed down. "Hey, Dina."

"Yes?"

"If there's a party, make sure you dance for me, will you?"

"Uh-huh." She gave him a shy smile.

"I'm a real good dancer, so you gotta show me how you're going to dance."

Encouraged by Mila, Dina gave us a small performance, swaying her hips and swinging her arms in front of her. We all clapped and laughed.

"I should've known you would be a much better dancer than me," Marco complimented Dina. "I think I'm going to steal some of your moves. Would that be okay?"

She agreed with pride before Marco and I split up from them. As soon as we were out of earshot, Marco said, "I saw you talking to Nero."

"Yes, he was asking about my work."

"You two were laughing a lot."

"Were we?" I shrugged. "He was making fun of my cooking."

"He's single, you know."

I frowned a little. "What does that have to do with anything?"

"Just keep your distance, okay?"

"Marco, I'm not here to pick up a man."

"That's right, because you already have me. But it doesn't change the fact that every single Nman who came here will be hoping that maybe he has a chance with one of you women."

"I doubt it."

"Oh yeah? How many chances do you think we Nmen have to be around single women? I'll bet you that most of these men have signed up for the Matchmaking Program, but that still leaves a small chance of success."

"But they are all so young. Solo was the oldest student and he's not even here. The others aren't even twenty-four years old."

Marco rolled his eyes. "Just because *you* don't want to marry, doesn't mean the rest of us feel that way. I don't like the idea of any of the men coming on to you."

"They wouldn't, I was their assistant teach..." I didn't get a chance to finish my sentence because Marco pulled me behind a tree and began kissing me.

"They fucking would, and that's why I need to tell every one of them that you're mine."

"Don't. At least not until I've told my sister," I breathed.

Marco had me pushed up against the tree, lifting my leg and grinding against me while kissing my neck and jaw. It occurred to me that his behavior was almost animalistic in nature and a way for him to put his scent on me. If I didn't stop him, I had a strong suspicion that Marco would take me against the tree.

"Not here. People will hear us."

"I need you."

"There are children around."

Marco's breathing was heavy against my neck. "Tonight then."

"It's better if we wait until we get back home."

Pulling back a little to look into my eyes, Marco raised an eyebrow. "I don't fucking think so. I'm already bursting to have you."

"You're not being rational. It's only two days."

"I don't care. You knew what you were getting into. If you wanted a nonsexual man you should have chosen a Motlander."

"Marco, you're being ridiculous. Stop acting like a caveman high on testosterone who feels threatened by all those single men. You already impregnated me, so you can relax now."

"Oh, so I'm a caveman now?"

"No, but you're behaving like one."

He took a step back, his jaw tightening. "Then you'd better run back to the civilized people. I hear them calling."

He was right; I recognized Raven's voice calling out for us to gather.

When we walked back to the school, Marco looked straight ahead avoiding my attempts to soften him up with small talk about how hungry I was. He was angry at me for my comment about him being a caveman, and my refusal to let him make our relationship public.

I didn't understand why he was in such a rush when I needed time to get used to the idea without adding other people's opinion to the mix.

Being that it was a beautiful summer day, we grabbed plates with food from the dining table when it was time to eat and sat on benches and chairs outside. Some people were standing, some were sitting, but everyone was catching up with old friends and there was a lot of laughter.

Marco took the last seat at one of the picnic tables where Hunter, Boulder, Finn, Archer, and Nero were already sitting. It was a tight squeeze with their broad shoulders.

"Are you starting some kind of brotherhood?" Raven called out to them. "How come you are not mixing with women?"

"Because you talk too much." Boulder winked at Raven, his adoptive daughter.

"Nonsense." With a big grin, she waved a dismissive hand at him before turning to me. "Come sit with me,

Shelly. I heard you're designing sex-bots and I'm curious to learn more about it."

At least ten people turned around giving me a strange look, but Raven couldn't be bothered and just pulled two chairs together and signaled for me to sit down.

"What is it you do exactly?" she asked and put her drink down on the ground while balancing her plate.

"You just said it. I design sex-bots."

Raven's black hair reflected the sun with her curls popping out in all directions. As a child she had always looked a lot like Kya, who had brown skin too, but now that Raven was an adult, her features were more pronounced with high cheekbones, full lips, and eyes full of life and fire.

"You've gotta give me more than that, Shelly. I'm sensing a juicy story here."

"I don't know what to tell you." I crossed my legs and smiled. "It's a fun project because it challenges my skills as an engineer and at the same time I'm using psychology to make the robots more realistic."

"Are the robots male or female?"

"At the moment I only work with female robots. I have a dream about making a natural-looking robot for the Nmen."

"Interesting." Raven nodded her head and chewed on a stick of celery.

"When you look at the specifications for the sex-bots here in the Northlands they are based on old-fashioned evolutionary psychology. For instance, the robots have long legs and high-heeled shoes on. The reason for that is that men recognize that a female with long legs is no longer a child and therefore able to bear children."

"But she's a robot, she can't bear any children."

"No, of course not. But that doesn't change that men are attracted to an imitation of a childbearing female. The high heels elevate her behind and make it puff out by twenty-five percent and that's a big hit with men too."

"Why?"

I sighed. "It's the same with breasts. Curves are sexy to men because it's a visual sign of health and that a woman has enough fat to go through a pregnancy. Of course everything has to be perky and firm to signal youth as well."

"But none of those things should matter, since it's a sex toy."

"I can't argue with that. My conclusion is that sexual arousal trumps rational thinking. People do really stupid things when they are horny."

Raven nodded her head and used the celery stick to underline her words when she stabbed it through the air, "I've read about that. My parents have a lot of antique books and some of them are quite steamy."

"You've read them?"

"Uh-huh. They're very entertaining, and some of the books are making me curious to see if I could lose my head like that."

"You probably could. You're very spontaneous and adventurous by nature."

"Thank you." Raven gave me a lopsided smile and popped the last piece of celery in her mouth.

"I didn't mean it as a compliment. I just meant that it can happen to the best of people."

"Except you. You could never lose your head like the people in those books, could you?"

It was tempting to tell her the truth and see how shocked she would be, but instead I picked up a piece of broccoli pie, making my response sound as casual as possible. "I would like to say no, but in reality, none of us are safe from our biological dispositions."

"What does that mean?"

"Just that intelligence is no armor against arousal and attraction." Tilting my head, I gave her a sharp look. "And neither is being a fierce fighter, by the way."

"That's a shame, because I'm a pretty badass fighter."

"I know you are, but if the day ever comes when you get physically attracted to someone, you can't punch your way out of it."

"Are you sure about that?" Raven reached down for her drink and looked around with a mischievous smile. "Too bad I'm not attracted to anyone here or we could put it to the test. There are a few of the boys that I wouldn't mind punching a little over what they did to us back when we were kids."

"Violence never solved anything."

Raven looked amused and stood up. "Hey, boys, who wants to go for a few rounds and have your ass kicked by a Motlander woman?"

All the men turned to look at her. "Did she just call us *boys*?" Nero asked.

"I did. So how about you prove to me that you've turned into a man?"

"I don't fight women."

"No, I could see why you'd be afraid of fighting me." She looked at the others. "Maybe one of you guys is braver than Nero?"

"I'm not afraid of fighting you," Nero defended himself. "I'm afraid Boulder is gonna tear me apart for hurting you."

"Ha! What do you say, Dad, would you be okay with me kicking Nero's ass?"

Boulder nodded. "Sure. As long as you use protective gear."

"Are you sure you want to do this?" I asked, as I remembered Nero was a good fighter when he was a student.

Raven just grinned down at me. "I've been training for this moment for ten years."

CHAPTER 24
The Fight

Marco

There will be no fighting tonight!"

I had never seen Mila so serious. She almost looked like her father, Magni, with the way she stood and stared the whole group down, her legs slightly spread and her hands firmly planted on her hips.

"Raven and Nero, if you must be physical, let's put on some music and dance."

"Isn't dancing and fighting in the same category?" someone joked and laughter spread.

Laura walked over to stand next to Mila. "We are all adults here; if people want some healthy fighting, I don't see the problem."

"That's right. A bit of fighting won't harm anyone," I chimed in. "I wouldn't mind going a few rounds myself."

Not ten minutes ago I'd overheard some of the men comment on Shelly's transformation and I was vibrating with frustration. I'd wanted so badly to tell them all that she was mine.

Mila threw her hands up in the air. "But I have all these amazing party games planned for tonight."

"Mila, I think the Northlander version of party games *is* fighting," someone called out.

"Can't we just have fun for one night?" Mila begged.

"What could be more fun than seeing Nero get his ass kicked by Raven?" Tristan asked and grinned.

Nero made a loud "tsk" sound. "Not even if I had both arms tied behind my back would she win against me."

Boulder, who was sitting next to Nero, laughed and patted his shoulder. "You have no idea."

"I wouldn't mind going up against Marco," Nikola called out. He had been one of the older students at the school and like the rest of the Nmen here, he was an excellent fighter. "I saw your fight against Neil Jefferson last weekend and I can't say that I was impressed."

I was already annoyed with Nikola for making comments on how gorgeous Shelly looked so I pushed out my chest and spoke in a deep voice. "I was distracted."

"Sounds like an excuse to me. Maybe you just don't have it anymore. Is that why you pulled out of the tournament? I could never take you as a kid, but now..." He gave a cocky smile. "I think it would be easy."

In a slow graceful movement, I rose up to my full height. "Challenge accepted."

Raven, Laura, and all the men of the North broke into excited chatter.

Nikola stood up too. "Let's do it."

Pearl and Mila were insisting on safety gear, but I was so provoked by Nikola's calling me out in front of everyone that I wanted to do it the raw way. His grin wouldn't be so cocky if he lost a tooth or two.

Boulder made us take the fight to the soccer field where there was no chance of our destroying furniture or injuring other people.

Despite the Motlanders' aversion to violence, they all came along to see the fight. Unlike my fight with Neil, I was pumped and focused from the beginning.

Nikola was fit and had packed on a lot of muscle since he was a kid, but I had seven more years of experience than he did and my pride on the line.

The fight was messy from the beginning, and the drama only intensified when one of my punches gave him a bloody nose.

With his right hand, Nikola tried to dry the blood off his face but only managed to smear it over his cheek and forehead.

"Please don't kill each other," Mila shouted with her hands to her face and Laura holding an arm around her.

Never had I been sharper in a fight. Shelly, the person I most wanted to impress in this world, was watching and I needed her to see that I was a strong mate.

"Upfhh..." Nikola took a hard blow to his solar plexus and bent over.

"You want more?" I asked and moved around him.

With a face as red as an overripe tomato, he growled and took a swing at me.

I blocked, and swept him off his feet, getting on top of him and pressing his cheek to the ground.

He bucked and groaned from the weight of my body on top of him.

"Tap your hand," I demanded and spoke in a low tone. "You don't want to miss out on the rest of the weekend because you're injured, do you?"

Nikola refused to give up and with the energy of a bull on steroids, he bucked me off him and we both got up again.

"And here I was trying to go easy on you," I muttered.

Our audience was cheering and commenting when Nikola gave some impressive kicks that had me move back and block.

"Careful, Marco," Shelly shouted to me and it gave me a surge of energy for my fierce and aggressive counterattack. This time I didn't go easy on him, and with my signature roundhouse kick, I knocked him back with such force that he fell into the circle of our audience. Oscar, Tristan, and Plato picked him up and pushed Nikola back to face me for another round of kicks and hits.

When I knocked him down for the third time, he was smart enough to stay down.

Mila ran to Nikola, worried that he was injured and calling for Finn to provide medical assistance.

"I'm fine," Nikola muttered and slid his thumb over his teeth to check that they were all there.

"Marco, you didn't have to beat him up like this. He's bleeding." Mila's tone was blameful and then her eyes fell upon Raven. "There will be no more fighting tonight. You and Nero will have to wait until tomorrow."

"I don't know." Raven tilted her head and gave a mischievous smile to Nero. "I worry he might not be able to sleep tonight from fear."

"That's sweet, Raven. You think I'm intimidated by you." Nero shook his head. "Sorry to disappoint you, but I'll be sleeping like a baby looking forward to our fight tomorrow."

"Dancing demons, you've got moves, my friend," Hunter came to give me a manly hug. "Fuck, that last kick was cold."

The Nmen were all high on the adrenaline of the fight and chatting in loud voices. My eyes searched for Shelly's but she and most of the other Motlander women were already walking back to the school. Looking over her shoulder, Shelly's eyes met mine and disappointment filled me. She wasn't impressed.

It hurt my pride and without thinking, I called out. "Hey, Shelly, aren't you glad you have a strong protector?"

Several of the women gave me strange looks and Rochelle, her sister, asked Shelly out loud. "What does he mean by that? Is Marco your protector?"

There was a moment of uncertainty in Shelly's eyes as they darted to the other people around her. I wanted her so badly to tell the truth.

"Yes, he is."

Rochelle stopped and lifted her hands, with a puzzled expression. "Since when?"

My heart beat fast, waiting for Shelly to finally tell her sister that she and I were together.

"It's a recent thing," Shelly began, her posture tense. "Advanced Technologies is paying Marco to be on stand by when I need to go somewhere."

"Oh, I see." Rochelle nodded before she walked on.

I stared after the two sisters. *What the fuck?*

"Great fight." Storm pulled at my arm to congratulate me and I turned to face him with fire in my eyes. "Holy shit, the fight is over. You look like you're ready to go another round."

I was furious with Shelly for reducing me to a paid bodyguard instead of acknowledging that I was her mate. Her rejection of me sexually earlier, combined with her dismissal of my role in her life and the adrenaline from the fight, had me on edge.

"Are you okay?" Storm asked.

"I'm fine. I just need to get wasted."

Storm lit up. "Now you're talking. Hey, let's get our fighters some beers. Nikola can use the bottle to ice his bruises and Marco can drink it to celebrate that he's still a kick-ass fighter." Laughter broke out as we headed back.

"Need a hand?" I asked Nikola, who was being supported by Finn.

"Not from you."

"Don't be a sore loser. At least I let you keep all your teeth and you don't have any black eyes."

Nikolas held a hand to his face. "I think my nose is broken."

"That's an easy fix," Finn comforted him. "With a bit of bone accelerator and beer, you'll be ready to fight again in a few days."

An hour and a half later, I was on my fifth beer when people started dancing. The Motlanders' style was very different from ours and their taste in music was enough to give a man a headache.

"Look at them." Nero was scratching his head. "They look like fairies with the way they twirl and swing their arms and move their heads."

On purpose I'd positioned myself so I could keep an eye on Shelly. I was mad at her, but her safety was still my highest priority. At the moment she was in deep conversation with Pearl.

"When are Magni and Khan coming?" I asked Finn.

He took a swig of his beer and dried his mouth with the back of his hand. "They won't make it back tonight, something urgent came up."

"What?"

Finn exchanged a glance with Boulder before he answered. "Some trouble up north."

"Rebels?"

"No. More like a very serious domestic violence case."

At the same time, Storm, Hunter, and I leaned closer. "What does that mean?"

"We don't know the details. Just that a woman was killed."

"Fuuuck," I breathed. "Someone killed his wife?"

"Yes."

"Why?" Hunter had his hands in his hair. "That makes no sense."

"Maybe she cheated on him," Storm suggested. "That sort of thing can make a man snap."

Boulder spoke in a deep low voice. "At this point we can only guess. Maybe he pushed her back and she fell and hit her head. Maybe he panicked when she threatened to leave him. We really don't know."

"Khan will have to find a way to calm the Council in the Motherlands or they will surely close down the Matching Program."

"Does Pearl know about this?"

A few of the men turned their heads to look at Pearl, who had been a member of the Motherland Council before she married Khan.

"Yes," Finn said. "Pearl supported Khan's decision to go and get all the details for himself."

"And the Council, have they been informed?"

"Uh-huh. They have asked for a meeting next week."

"Fuck, this is really bad, isn't it?" Hunter's eyes darted between Boulder and Finn. "I hope they understand that just because one Nman fucks up, doesn't mean that we're all violent psychopaths."

"They *have* to know that," Storm insisted. "I mean, some of us are pure saints for dealing with the crazy Motlanders they send us."

"You married?" Finn asked with surprise.

"Yes, and we divorced too. The bitch was a nutcase."

Boulder's fist slammed down on the table and his eyes were shooting daggers at Storm. "We did not raise you to be disrespectful of women."

For a second Storm looked like a schoolboy who had been scolded. With his raised shoulders he resembled a turtle retracting into its shell for protection.

Finn was quick to ease the tension. "Let's not ruin a perfectly good night when we're supposed to be celebrating."

"That's right." I raised my glass. "Cheers."

"Cheers," the others chimed in and we all emptied our glasses and smacked them down on the table again.

Finn stood up and grinned down at us. "Now, let's put on some real music and go show the fairies how we dance here in the Northlands."

CHAPTER 25
The Law of the Nmen

Shelly

I had just come out of the bathroom when Marco pulled me aside. "Meet me by the trees," he whispered with beer on his breath.

"That's a bad idea," I protested and looked around us to make sure no one saw how close we were.

He gave me a charming smile. "It's an excellent idea."

"Marco, don't," I said but still allowed him to pull me by my hand. "Someone is going to see us."

"We'll be quiet and quick."

Once he got me behind the teacher's cabins he pressed me against the wall and kissed me hungrily. "I want you, Shelly."

My hands were in his hair and my head leaning back. "Marco, you're crazy. I don't want someone to walk up on us. We should wait. I told you earlier."

"I don't want to wait. I fucking want my woman."

"You're drunk."

"Not compared to some of the others. William is hammered." Marco snickered and I shushed him.

"Quiet or they'll hear us."

"With the loud music they won't hear shit." Marco's hands were pulling my dress up and nibbling at my earlobe. "Don't you want me?"

"That's the problem. I always wanted you and I still do."

He was leaning into me, his forehead against my hair. "I'm yours, Shelly," he whispered in my ear and pushed my panties to the side, inserting a finger inside of me.

"Ohh." A moan escaped me but my hand tried to hold him back. "Marco, please, not here."

"Yes, right here." He spoke in a raspy voice. "They don't know you like I do. I see sides of you that no one else does. You need me just as much as I need you."

I bit my lip, my eyes closed and my insides on fire from the arousal he brought out in me. "This is a bad idea."

"We're a family."

"I know, but..."

"I'm the only man you'll ever allow inside of you, isn't that right?"

"Uh-huh..." My vocabulary had never been smaller but that was the thing with Marco. He made me unable to think straight.

My mind was trying to break through the haze of lust but my hands were clinging to Marco for more.

Lifting me up, he positioned me on his hips, grinding against me. "Shelly, tell me you want me inside of you."

"Marco, don't – no, we shouldn't..."

He swallowed my words with a deep kiss, my back against the wall, his fingers tugging at my panties to get them down.

In a last attempt from my brain to warn about the dangers, I pushed at his chest and turned my face away.

"Marco, stop it. Please stop."

"I need you so fucking bad." His hands were demanding, and with a jerk he moved me so he could use both hands and rip my panties apart.

"Marco, don't," I protested but he just threw the fabric to the ground and ground against me.

Had we been alone his intense desire would have been the biggest turn-on, but unlike him, I was sober and too aware that someone might find us here.

"Marco, please stop." I pushed at his shoulders.

He groaned with need. "Don't fight it, you want it too."

He was right, but not here. "Marco, no... please stop."

"Get away from her." The command was icy and spoken in a deep threatening voice.

Marco and I both stiffened for a split second before he was brutally jerked back, leaving me to fall to the ground.

I watched in horror as Boulder beat on Marco in pure rage. We were too far from the others to be seen and with the music they wouldn't hear us, but I needed to do something or Boulder would kill Marco.

Picking up a large stone from the ground, Boulder used it as a weapon; he raised it above Marco's head.

"No," I screamed when Boulder's right arm smashed the stone down and only missed Marco's skull by the width of a hair. "Stop it!"

The two large men were rolling around on the ground, growling like bears, and fighting with an intensity I'd never seen in practice. Boulder wasn't trying to get hits in or use impressive kicks. His eyes were crazed and he was trying to get his arm around Marco's neck.

"Boulder, stop it," I cried out again and screamed when Boulder hammered his elbow into Marco's stomach.

They were both intoxicated; there was no way I would get Boulder's attention by shouting. Running back and getting the others to help would take too long, and I wasn't sure how long Marco could hold up against Boulder without one of them getting killed.

"Boulder, no." I made a last attempt to shout at him when I saw Marco's face growing purple as Boulder was strangling him.

We Motlanders are peaceful people, but in desperation I bent down and picked up a large stick to swing with.

"Stop strangling him," I cried out and brought the stick down hard on Boulder's shin to get his attention.

With one hand, Marco got a hold of Boulder's hair and tore hard.

"Arrgghh..." Boulder was growling but pulled back enough for Marco to breathe in a violent fit of coughing, his hands to his throat.

"Boulder, it's not what it looks like," I screamed and clung to the stick as a weapon.

Boulder got up from the ground, his chest rising and falling as he panted, and with a last hard kick at Marco's leg he roared at him, "What part of not touching didn't you understand?"

Marco was still struggling to breathe and couldn't answer. His eyes were bulging and he kept coughing.

"I'll fucking kill you for what you did." Boulder's face was flaming red and twisted in anger as he stood with his legs spread and his hands folded into fists.

My heart was racing with fear and adrenaline. Being stunned about the violence and rage had me momentarily speechless. Faced with violence, my body was setting priorities, and right now all the blood was pumping into my legs, which needed to run for safety, leaving nothing behind for my brain to think with.

"Christina saw you drag Shelly away and I came just in time to hear her say 'no.'" Boulder's scowl was fixed on Marco. "You know what we do to men who can't keep their hands to themselves."

"Marco and I are together." I pushed the words out in a high-pitched hoarse voice.

Boulder stiffened and his eyes shifted to me. "Come again?"

"We're together." My head bobbed up and down to emphasize that it was true. I rambled on: "I live with Marco and I'm expecting his child."

Boulder took a step back, his eyebrows drawn in as his gaze darted between Marco and me. "Why didn't you tell us you married?"

"Technically, we didn't." I walked in between Boulder and Marco, holding up both my palms in a placating manner. "Marco has been asking me to, but I didn't see the need."

"Are you out of your fucking mind?" Boulder's hands fell to his hips and he angled his head. "I almost killed Marco for touching you."

Boulder's rage was lifting and he walked over to offer Marco a hand. "You should have told me what was going on."

Getting up from the ground, Marco brushed himself off. "I wanted to but Shelly wants to tell her sister before we make it official."

Boulder dragged his hands through his hair. "This is no joke. You need to tell everyone before you get Marco killed."

The danger of the two men killing each other was over and my brain was beginning to work again. "Attacking Marco like that was wrong. You could have asked us what we were doing."

"Why? I have eyes in my head. I could see what he was doing and you were clearly saying no."

Boulder squatted down to pick up some moss and handed it to Marco. "Here, for your bloody nose."

Marco didn't say much but took the moss in Boulder's outstretched hand. "Thanks."

"I misread the situation." Boulder looked from me to Marco and back again. "Did I hear you right? Did you say you were pregnant?"

"Yes. Promise that you won't tell anyone until I've had a chance to tell Rochelle myself."

"My lips are sealed." Boulder used his finger to indicate an imaginary zipping of his lips.

"Thank you."

"Are we okay?" Boulder patted Marco's shoulder.

"I wish you would have given me a chance to explain myself."

Boulder brushed some moss from Marco's shoulder. "I took a vow to protect the girls. Shelly is one of them and I take that responsibility very seriously."

"Me too, but you can't always trust what you see. You've got to ask questions before you kill a man."

A corner of Boulder's lips lifted. "No need to get dramatic. You're still here, aren't you?"

With a hand to his throat, Marco spoke in a hoarse voice. "Barely.

"Yeah, you sound a little rusty. You might wanna put some lotion on those vocal cords."

I stepped forward. "You can't put lotion on vocal cords," I informed them. From the look they gave me it was clear that they knew that already.

"Are you two coming back to the party?" Boulder asked Marco.

"Yes, in a minute."

"I'll tell people that you had a private discussion if they ask."

"Thank you."

When Alexander Boulder walked away, Marco turned his head to me. "Now, do you see why being married makes a big fucking difference?"

CHAPTER 26
Drunken Memories

Marco

Shelly went to bed around one a.m., at the same time as most of the Motlander women.

The eight women who had once been students were excited about sleeping in their old beds. Pearl and Shelly joined them inside but took the teachers' rooms.

Only eleven out of the twelve men who had once shared two rooms inside the school were here, and most of them preferred to sleep in tents they had brought from home.

Hunter had a tent large enough for both of us and had offered to share it with me.

I was sore from Boulder's attack but didn't let it stop me from staying up with the rest of the men. It was three in the morning before we were done drinking and telling exaggerated tales from our time at the school.

"I have to take a piss," Hunter said in a slurred voice and got up from the log he'd been sitting on around the bonfire.

"Take one for me too, I'm too tired to do any heavy lifting," I teased and laughed at my own joke.

Hunter grinned and walked toward the line of trees.

"At least try to walk in a straight line, you drunken bastard," Tristan called after him.

Without a word, Hunter looked over his shoulder before pulling down his pants and mooning Tristan and the rest of us.

Nero, Storm, and Tristan got up to moon him back and we all howled with laughter.

Even in my drunken state, I was aware that our level of jokes had sunk to a very low level and that it was time to go to bed. "I'm calling it a night," I said and slowly rose up.

"Yeah, we should probably close down this party," Tristan agreed and pulled his pants back up. "Archer threatened to have us all go running in the morning like in the old days." He looked toward the large log cabin where Archer and Kya lived with their children now. "I'll bet that's why he went to bed at midnight. You know, so he can look sharp tomorrow."

Pointing my finger at them in a slow drunken movement, I gave a hiccup. "I can still outrun any of you," Two more hiccups followed. "I just need to sleep for an hour first."

"Deal." Tristan raised his wristband close to his eyes. "It's seven minutes past three. We can sleep for almost four hours." His words were slow and slurred.

"Sounds like a plan." I nodded my head to William, who had fallen asleep an hour ago in his chair. "What do we do about Willy?"

Storm walked over and pulled William's head back, slapping his right cheek a little. "Go to bed, William."

Without opening his eyes, William pushed at Storm's hands and groaned.

"Just let him sleep. It's not that cold; he'll be fine." Boulder instructed. "If it starts to rain, he'll find his way to bed."

The other men said their good nights, and Boulder and Finn walked to the cabins while the rest of us spread out to find our tents.

"Careful," I said when Hunter stumbled into the tent.

He gave a small laugh. "I'm so fucking drunk."

"Yeah, me too."

"How about we take a morning dip in the lake tomorrow when we wake up. I'll bet that will sober us up real quick," Hunter suggested.

"Yeah, it's a solid plan. Very solid."

Like me, Hunter was too tall to stand upright in the tent. "Where the fuck are my tooth cleaners?" he asked while digging through his bag. "Oh, here they are."

"So you're Shelly's protector now," Hunter asked when he finally lay down.

"Yeah. We're having a child together." It flew out of me without a filter.

Hunter laughed. "Now you're dreaming, my friend. Not all women marry their protector."

"It's not a dream." I propped myself up on my elbow and focused my blurry eyesight. "Shelly is really pregnant with my child."

Hunter gaped. "For real?"

"Yeah, for real."

He sat up. "Wait, I'm confused."

"Shelly and I began having sex together and she got pregnant."

"But you're not married," he said and rubbed his chin.

"Not yet. But we will be soon if I can convince her. Boulder found us making out tonight and he was close to killing me for it."

"Shit. That's bad." Hunter pulled his knees to his chest and leaned on them with his head in his hand. "Hang on – I'm very drunk so I have to make sure I get this right. Are you saying that you're going to be a father?"

"Yup." I nodded my head with drunken exaggeration. "That's exactly what I'm saying."

"And Shelly Summers is the mother?"

"Yup, the genius herself."

"Jesus Christ, congratulations." He lit up. "That's fucking phenomenal. I'm so happy for you."

"Thank you."

"Do you love her?"

I broke into a wide grin. "You have no idea. I'm so fucking screwed, that's how crazy I am about her."

"And you're going to marry her?"

"I would have already, but Shelly doesn't see the point."

Hunter's expression changed to a serious and more guarded one. "Hmm, that does sound like something a Motlander would say."

"The good thing is that she has moved into my apartment, and she says that she loves me."

"Hmm." Lying back down, Hunter stared up at the ceiling of the tent. "This could get ugly. If it was me I would go crazy with jealousy. I mean, your woman is among single men here and they don't know she's taken."

"I *am* going crazy."

"How can she say that she loves you and not want to marry you?"

"Because despite her being a genius, sometimes she's not very bright."

Hunter nodded. "This is why I'm staying away from women in general. They break your fucking heart."

"Who broke your heart?"

"It doesn't matter. Let's just say that you're not the only one who's had his marriage proposal rejected."

"What happened?"

"I don't want to talk about it."

"Is that why you're so protective of Willow? Because you know what it's like to have your heart broken?" I asked.

Hunter sighed again. "Could be. And because I would be a fucking lousy protector if I allowed Solo to get anywhere close to her again."

"What happened between Willow and Solo?"

Hunter kept gazing at the ceiling. "He hurt her."

"Physically or did he break her heart?"

"Both."

My eyes widened. "No way. Did Solo hit Willow?"

Hunter turned his head to look at me. "Don't be stupid. Solo isn't like that."

"I was just going to say that. He was always so protective of her."

Rubbing his forehead, Hunter began to talk. "Remember how much in love they were? It was like they were magnets or something; they always took enormous risks to touch or kiss when it wasn't allowed. Magni almost killed Solo once because they got caught kissing."

"Yeah, I remember that."

"Willow and Solo made some stupid pact that as soon as she turned eighteen they would marry. Of course, Solo had to leave the school that year when he turned fifteen and after that contact between them was only sporadic."

"Let me guess – he got mad when she wanted to break the pact."

"I wish, but no, that's not what happened. When Willow turned fifteen and it was her time to leave the school, the contact between them intensified. Two weeks before she was scheduled to return to the Motherlands, Solo panicked and convinced her to run away with him."

I lowered my brow. "What? That's not possible – where would they live?"

"The woods." Hunter's chest rose in a deep intake of air. "It was a stupid plan, but he managed to convince her anyway."

"She ran away with him?"

"Yes, and it took us eight miserable days to track them down."

"You helped?"

"At first the mentors wouldn't let me, but I threw a major fit." There was pain in Hunter's eyes. "Willow is my twin and he had stolen her from me."

I nodded in understanding. "But how could it take eight days? This island isn't very big."

"He took Willow off the island. The first two days, the search party consisted of me, Archer, Boulder, Magni, and the two ranchers that live on this island with their hunting dogs. Initially, the men all thought it would be easy since it was basically two kids on a small island. But Solo has always been fucking phenomenal in the wilderness and he managed to trick us several times."

"Eight days is a long time."

"On day two, Magni realized they weren't on the island and he brought in three of his Huntsmen; still we didn't find them. On day five he brought in ten more of his Huntsmen, and it took the sixteen of us three more days to find them."

"How is that even possible?"

"It shouldn't be." Hunter yawned. "When we found them, Willow was injured. Her hand was broken; she had a concussion, and scratches from a bad fall. She could have died."

"I'm surprised Magni didn't kill Solo on the spot when he found them."

"I think he would have, but he wasn't the one to find them. Three of the Huntsmen did, and Willow threatened to kill herself if anything happened to Solo, so they spared his life."

"Now I understand why you are angry with him."

Hunter turned on his side, using his hands as pillows. "We used to be friends, Solo and me."

"I remember."

"On my good days I remind myself that he was just eighteen and madly in love. But there are days when I want to kill him for putting my sister in danger like that. She and I never talked much about what happened to her in those eight days, but I know they must have been traumatic to her. She cried for weeks and fumed that we'd

272

separated them. It wasn't until they sent her to a place of reflection in the Motherlands that she began to see that Solo had been asking her to abandon her friends and family for him. She understands now that it was a selfish plan on his part and that they would've both been miserable living in the woods."

"Does she still love him?"

"She hates him."

"Are you sure?"

"Yes, she's completely over him by now. It's taken many years, though."

"Wow." I yawned and rubbed my eyes. "I had no idea about this part. All I heard was something about you and Solo being in a fight."

Hunter gave a loud yawn too. "That's because things were hushed up. The fight happened here when I saw Solo after he and Willow had been found. I was so furious that I attacked him."

"I don't blame you. What Solo did was rotten."

For a few minutes I was quiet while reflecting on what Hunter had just told me.

"Hey, Hunter."

Hunter's eyes were closed and his breathing heavy. "Mmm?" he muttered.

"Did the students find out about what happened?

"No, the adults kept it a secret."

"Everything?"

His speech had turned into a drowsy muttering. "They said Willow had been called back to the Motherlands to a dying relative or something. They didn't want any of the other kids to get inspired to run away."

"I see. But why would the kids try to run away? It's fucking paradise here."

A light snore revealed that Hunter had fallen asleep.

Comparing myself to Solo, I concluded that I was the lucky one. He could've never married Willow in the woods, but he would've been happy living with her in exile. I was already living with my woman and she was carrying my child. Maybe Shelly had a point that those were the things that mattered the most anyway.

CHAPTER 27
Illusions

Shelly

Nero was swearing out loud and spitting on the ground after Raven got a kick to his ribs. At least with this fight, Raven and Nero were wearing safety gear. I didn't understand why Marco had fought yesterday without protection. To me that was stupidity.

"Whoa!" Some of the men gave impressive cheers when Raven followed up with another kick that looked painful. Nero resembled a wild boar when he made his counterattack: red face, fury in his eyes, and his head down.

"Can I talk to you?" I touched my sister's arm.

Rochelle turned her head to me. "Sure."

"In private." I signaled for us to walk away from the fight, where Raven and Nero were now wrestling on the ground while giving groans and growls.

We moved around the school building, out of earshot, before I began talking. "Rochelle, there's something I need to tell you."

Rochelle had both our mother's height and her black hair. We didn't look much alike, which wasn't uncommon in the Motherlands. With women being impregnated in fertility clinics using anonymous sperm donors, we all had different fathers than our siblings.

"I'm not sure how to tell you this, so I'm just going to come out with it."

"You slept with Marco?"

It took me by surprise and I blinked a few times. "Ehm, yes, how did you know?"

"Mom told me about your conversation with her."

"But I never mentioned Marco's name."

A curious smile tipped the corner of Rochelle's mouth. "Ahh, so I was right."

"Yes, but how did you know? I've been careful not to show anything around you."

"I'm your sister; of course, I would pick up on the heated looks between you two. Plus, I did a test on Marco yesterday to be sure."

"What test?"

"Showed him a lot of interest, laughed at his jokes, and sat close to him. He got so flustered that he got up and left. And then later when he was fighting, the first person he looked to was you. He was trying to impress *you*, Shelly."

"Was it really that obvious that something was going on between us?"

"Maybe not to the others, but after the fight you told me that he was your protector, and then I knew."

"Does Mom know?"

Her smile was gone. "That it's Marco? No, I spoke to Mom yesterday and I said that I had an idea about who it was, but she didn't want details."

"If you knew, then why haven't you come and talked to me about it?"

Rochelle lifted her shoulders in a small shrug. "I was waiting for you to come to me. To be honest I've been a little bit offended that it's taken you this long."

"It's not an easy thing to tell your family that you have fallen in love with an Nman."

Rochelle's expression did not change; it merely seemed to tighten, so shadows now appeared beneath her cheekbones. "Didn't Marco just fight in a tournament to win a bride?"

"Yes. But he pulled out of the tournament and came back to be with me."

"Be with you?" Her eyes grew bigger. "What does that mean?"

"Marco and I..." I paused and licked my lips. "We're not just sleeping together. We are a couple."

"You *married* Marco?" Her words came out loud and shrill. I hurried to hush her voice.

"No, we're not married."

"But if you slept with Marco, he's going to demand that you marry him. You know how territorial and possessive Nmen get."

"Rochelle, I didn't come to the Northlands to marry."

She threw her hands up in the air. "Then you shouldn't have slept with him. You could have gotten pregnant."

Taking a deep breath, I spoke in a soft voice. "I did."

Rochelle's reaction was so delayed that I wondered if she had heard me at all, but then her eyes fell to my belly.

"It's only been two months, so it'll take a while for it to show, but I'm pregnant, Rochelle."

"I don't know what to say." She was visibly shaken and fiddled with a ring on her finger, a classic variation of calming behavior that told me Rochelle was thrown off balance. "Mom is going to freak out when she hears that."

"That's what I'm afraid of. She was terribly upset about me having sex with a man."

Rochelle leaned against the façade of the school, as if she needed support to stay on her feet. "I can't believe you put yourself in this situation. What were you thinking?"

I lifted my shoulders and let them fall down with a sigh. "I wasn't thinking, it just kind of happened."

Rochelle's eyes were fixed on the ground and for a while neither of us spoke.

"This changes things," Rochelle said in a low voice.

I gave a nod in agreement and looked up to meet her eyes when she broke into quiet laughter.

"What's so funny?" I asked.

"I just realized that for the first time ever, I might be Mom's favorite daughter for a while."

"Don't say that. I'm not her favorite," I protested.

"Tsk." Rochelle made a sound similar to that of a bike tire getting a flat. "She brags about you all the time, but one thing is for sure: she's not going to be bragging about you getting pregnant with an Nman."

"I guess not."

"If I were you, I'd call her right now and tell her about the pregnancy. Just get it over with."

"Maybe now isn't the right time," I said, trying to delay the inevitable.

"There's never going to be a right time to tell Mom that you are pregnant and in love with an Nman. It's not fair that other people know about it and she doesn't."

I kicked at some dirt on the ground, looking down.

Rochelle took my hand. "If you want me to, I'll stay for support."

"Maybe she won't be upset," I said in a hopeful tone.

Rochelle tilted her head, giving me a *don't fool yourself* look. "Prepare for her to freak out. You know Mom. She likes plans and this isn't part of the plan, is it?"

"I think everybody needs to calm down and remember that every child is a miracle."

"Mom isn't going to mind you having a child, Shelly. It's Marco that will freak her out. She's hoping that you working up here the Northlands is some sort of unfortunate phase that we can soon put behind us. It's going to break her heart that you're choosing him."

An idea struck me. "Maybe not."

"Oh, I'm one hundred percent certain that it will crush her."

My eyes were darting around, my mind spinning to find a way to tell my mom in a way that would make it easier for her to accept it.

278

"You're twirling your hair again. I know what that means but you can't solve this with some advanced mathematical equation."

"I can fix this."

"How?"

"Would you do me a favor?"

"Shelly, what are you up to?"

I explained my simple plan to Rochelle and it left her with an expression of horror.

"I can't do that."

"Yes, you can."

"Mom might die of shock."

"Don't be silly. Mom has a perfectly healthy heart, she won't die of shock."

"If I tell her what you just told me to say, she will." Rochelle hardened her jaw. "I once heard about a woman who got so shocked that she died."

"That woman probably died of fear, which isn't the same thing." I began to explain. "What happens with fear is that if you get scared enough, the reaction can release too large a dose of adrenaline, which will numb the heart and cause it to stop beating."

"I don't need a lecture. Just know that if Mom's heart stops beating, I'm blaming you." Rochelle was pointing her finger at my face.

"Just tell her exactly what I told you."

Rochelle was reluctant, and it took a bit more coaxing until she agreed and called our mother. I made sure I wouldn't be in the picture but kept close enough to hear her say the words that I knew would make my mother react strongly.

"It's done," Rochelle said afterward. "Your plan is crazy, Shelly. I hope you know that."

"It'll work. Give her a few minutes and Mom will call me."

"I don't want to be here when she calls."

"I understand."

"Promise that you'll be gentle with her," Rochelle said and hurried away when our mother called me.

"Shelly, I just spoke to your sister," my mom began as soon as her hologram appeared. "I'm shaken to my core. Look at my hands, do you see how much they're trembling?"

"Yes, I can see that you're upset."

My mother's face held a flustered expression, and she spoke at a fast pace. "Upset isn't the word. You sat here in my kitchen and gave me a solemn promise, and then I learn that you're throwing everything away. I won't allow it." It was very rare for a Motlander to raise their voice, and my mother was almost screaming.

"Mom, calm down."

"No. Why would you quit your job at Advanced Technologies without consulting me about it? Do you have another job lined up?"

"No."

"You are a genius, Shelly. And with that comes a responsibility. I refused to believe it when Rochelle told me you're planning to take a break from working to spend more time with an Nman. *An Nman, Shelly*. How can you throw away your dreams like that?"

"Mom, his name is Marco and I love him. We're having a child together."

She gasped. "Rochelle told me, but it's not true, is it?"

"It's true, I'm pregnant."

My mom looked like she was about to cry. "How did this happen?"

"Well, as women we release an egg about once a month and if we have unprotected sex with a fertile male, chances are that…"

My mom cut me off. "That's not what I meant. How could you let this happen? You are a modern woman. You don't need a man in your life. I've raised both you and

Rochelle to be strong and independent women, so why would you do something this reckless? Where is this absurd attraction to Nmen coming from? You're not one of those romantics without a speck of common sense. You're too smart for this."

When she ran out of air, I took my chance to get a word in. "Mom, the truth is that I've always been attracted to Marco. He was the other assistant teacher when I taught here at the school. You've seen him."

"When?"

"Remember when we went on a week-long field trip to the Motherlands, and you came to meet us at that beach hotel?"

"Yes."

"Do you remember the young man who climbed the flagpole?"

"Vaguely."

"That was Marco."

My mom closed her eyes. "I blame myself. It was a mistake to allow you and Rochelle to go to that school in the first place. Look at the mess it's gotten you into."

"Mom, I'm very happy with Marco."

"Women haven't needed men to be happy in centuries. It's a phase, and I promise you one thing; you're not going to be happy when you are bored out of your mind from not working."

"But the child will keep me busy. Maybe it would be good for me to take a break," I said with my best poker face on.

"No, it wouldn't. I know you, Shelly, and you would be miserable if you didn't work."

She was right about that. But I didn't admit to it.

"Some people would thrive with being home with a baby all day, but you're not like that. Don't give up on everything you care about just because you're having a child. I had you and Rochelle, and I still lived my passion and contributed to society. You can too. Please don't give up on your dreams when you've worked so hard for them."

"I understand that you're disappointed, but at least I kept my promise. I haven't married him, even though Marco has asked me several times."

"That's good. Marriage is redundant."

"Yes. I've told him that it doesn't matter. I mean it's just a title anyway. The important thing is that we live together and raise our child together. Marco is such a warm and wonderful person, Mom. You're going to love him. He said that he would work two jobs to support me and the baby."

"Shelly, listen... listen..." My mother, who was normally always calm and articulate, was out of words. Pulling at her collar, she waved a hand in front of her face as if to cool herself off.

"Are you okay, Mom? You're not having one of those hot flashes again that you talked about, are you?"

"Stop talking about hot flashes. I'm trying to think of a way to solve this awful situation you've put yourself in, Shelly. I can't believe you would even consider giving up your career."

This was exactly what I had been planning for. Ever since I was a toddler, my mom had been invested in my academic brilliance.

"Did you say he would work two jobs?"

"Yes."

"But honey, why would you let him work two jobs instead of contributing yourself? How is that teamwork?"

"It's complicated. The thing is that I would be the only pregnant woman who isn't married in this country, Mom. Marco is taking it pretty hard and once the other Nmen find out, he's going to be under a lot of pressure and ridicule."

My mother tucked her hair behind her ear. "What does that have to do with you working?"

"I just thought it was a way for me to show Marco how committed I am to him and our child. He knows how much I love my work and that it's a huge thing for me to give up."

"No. I won't let you. You can't give up your work." My mom sounded frantic. "Shelly, listen to me, darling. Maybe it would be better if you came back and took some time to reflect on the whole thing."

"Sorry, Mom, but this isn't a rash decision. I've taken time to think about it. Marco was against my giving up my job."

"He was? Then you should listen to him."

"He understands that it's my way of compensating for not being able to marry him."

"Then marry him. As I see it, it's the lesser of two evils. Just please don't give up your career."

"You don't mean that!"

"I do. You can work and have a child at the same time. I did."

"You think so?"

"I know it."

I placed my hand on my collarbone. "Maybe I will. It's just that I never imagined having children."

My mom seemed calmer now. "Oh, don't worry, honey, you're going to be an amazing mother. I'll be here to give you all the advice you'll need. Just promise you won't give up on your work. It's important."

My plan had succeeded. My mother had been so distracted by talking me out of giving up work, that she hadn't had time to freak out about the pregnancy.

"I'm going to need a lot of advice."

"That's what I'm here for." My mother gave me a stiff smile. "Maybe you could convince Mando to come and live here in the Motherlands."

"Marco."

"Yes. Marco. You should bring him."

"I don't think he'd like that."

"Why not?"

"Because he would miss the Northlands too much. All his friends live here and it's where his work is."

"Tell him that I will be happy to assist in getting him resident status here if he's willing to move."

"Mom, you're the best. I love you so much and I promise to try and convince him."

"I love you too, honey." She sighed. "I'll need a strong cup of tea after this. You truly scared me with your talk about giving up work. Good thing Rochelle called me and had me talk some sense into you."

"Yes, I'm happy we talked."

It was almost too good to be true, the way she had accepted the baby and Marco. "Are you okay now? It must be a shock to you that I am pregnant and in love with an Nman."

Sheana played with her necklace. "After you told me that you had sex with an Nman I was preparing myself that something like this might happen."

"So, you're not surprised?"

"Charlie told me that you were renting a room with a single man who is now your protector, so no, I'm not that surprised. Of course, I was hoping it was just a phase and that you would soon be home again."

After ending the call with my mother, I found Rochelle close to the school. She was on her knees in the vegetable garden, digging up potatoes for dinner.

"How did it go?" she asked in an eager tone.

"Mom took it a lot better than I thought she would."

Rochelle dried her forehead and got a bit of dirt across her eyebrow. "Really?"

"Yes, the plan worked. Thank you for helping me set it up."

"I hate that we lied to her."

284

"Why? Instead of being devastated, Mom is now relieved that she made a difference and talked me out of giving up my career. I gave her a victory."

"It was an illusion. A manipulation of the truth at best. You never intended to give up working."

"I don't see the problem."

"That's because you are *you*, Shelly."

"Who else would I be?"

"No, I mean, you're insensitive that way."

Jerking my head back, I gave her a sharp look. "Insensitive? I did everything I could to break the news to Mom in a way that wouldn't leave her heartbroken. That should qualify as being sensitive to others' feelings."

Rochelle scrunched up her face in an expression of pity. "You just don't get it, Shelly."

I had heard those words from her a million times; I turned my back on her, walking away.

I'd only taken a few steps when Rochelle called out to me. "Don't get mad. Like you said – end of the day, a child is always a miracle, even if I don't understand why you would submit yourself to producing it the way you did."

I turned to look at her and spoke in a flat tone. "Having sex is the natural way to produce a child."

"That might've been true in the past, but we humans have progressed since then."

I gave a small laugh. "You wouldn't see it that way if you knew how good sex can feel with the right man."

Rochelle wrinkled her nose up. "I'm not tempted."

"That's your loss."

"But if I were to pick one of the Nmen, it would be Hunter for sure. Or maybe Tristan; he's very charming."

I suppressed a smile and looked to the soccer field. "I can't believe they're still fighting," I muttered. Raven and Nero were sitting on the grass with the others while William and Plato were now going at it.

Rochelle got up and looked in that direction too. "I hope your child gets Marco's curls."

"And his eyes," I added. "He has really nice eyes."

"He does." She smiled at me. "And he's sharp too."

"That's why I like him so much. He's challenges me because he's intelligent like me."

"Let's not push it. No one is like you," Rochelle teased and tilted her head.

"Rochelle and Shelly, over here," Mila called out from the doorway to the school. We waved back and walked over to her.

"Do you want to help me prepare for a fun game that we can all play?" Mila asked.

"Sure, what kind of game is it?"

"It's a memory game. We have to remember things about each other."

"That shouldn't be too hard." I lit up in a smile. "Sounds like my kind of game."

"I know, but you can't participate." Mila smiled at me. "It wouldn't be fair to the others."

Crossing my arms, I frowned. "What kind of backward logic is that?"

"You're too good, Shelly."

"Are you going to tell the best fighter that he can't fight because it's not fair to the others?"

"No."

"Are you going to tell the best runner that he can't run because he's too fast for the others?"

"No." Mila shook her head.

"Will you tell the person who cooks the best that they can't be in the kitchen because they make people like me look bad?"

"No, of course not, but it's not the same thing."

"It's exactly the same thing."

"But you're a genius," Mila said with an apologetic shrug.

"I hate that word." I groaned and walked outside, where Willow sat against the wall of the school, her eyes closed and her face turned from the sun.

"Can I sit with you?" I asked.

She lifted a hand to shield herself from the bright light and smiled. "You don't have to ask, Shelly. I'd be honored. In fact, I could use a second opinion on something."

I slid down next to her. "I'm listening."

"Pearl and Khan have invited me to be part of a planned tour here in the Northlands. It's a cultural exchange."

"You mean with your dancing?"

"Yes. I would be part of a group of performers from the Motherlands who will be touring for the next four months. Salma Rose will be there."

"The name sounds familiar. Is she a singer?"

"More like a phenomenon. You hear her songs played all the time."

"That's exciting."

"So you think I should say yes?"

"Why wouldn't you? Sounds like an adventure to me."

"It's just so last-minute. Lily White was supposed to go but she canceled. She's one of the best dancers in the Motherlands."

"I don't know her name. Why did she cancel?"

"Pressure from her family. Pearl told me that it's been difficult to find artists who are willing to perform here in the Northlands. They fear for their safety."

"And you don't?"

Willow gave me a funny look. "Do you?"

"There's been a few situations where I didn't feel safe. Things have changed a lot since we were children but having a protector by your side is still a good idea when you're a woman in the Northlands."

"Khan said that he would have his best men in charge of our safety."

287

"Then what's your worry?"

"I don't know. The commitments I have at home wouldn't stop me. I teach dance classes for children and perform with the theater, but we are in between productions right now, and they would be so delighted for me to get a chance like this."

"Sounds like you want to go."

"Yeah, I think I do." Willow smiled and looked up to the sky, where a drone was flying in. From the size and look of it, I had a good idea who it might be.

"I think Khan and Magni are here," I guessed.

Willow stiffened next to me. "Do you think they brought Solo?" she asked and paled.

CHAPTER 28
Body Language

Marco

The new arrivals caused a stir.

As our ruler, Lord Khan carried himself with authority, while his brother, Magni, was a brooding giant admired by all Nmen for his extraordinary fighting skills.

Last time I had seen them had been at Louisa's tournament, where they had both been wearing regal outfits and looked elegant. Today, the two tall brothers wore combat boots and uniforms. Magni had a smear of blood across his chest and his hair was anything but combed.

Mila came running to hug her adoptive father and spoke in a worried tone of voice. "Did you sleep at all? You look exhausted."

"No, I didn't sleep. We came straight here."

Pearl came to hug Khan and they spoke in hushed voices before he turned to the rest of us. "It's good to see all of you and I can't wait to hear how you're all doing. As you can see, Magni and I will need to shower before we sit down to eat with you tonight. We just stopped by to tell you that we haven't forgotten about the celebrations and that we'll join you in a few hours."

Pearl and Laura walked their husbands back to the large drone and Shelly came to stand next to me. "Something's wrong," she muttered low. "See how serious they look."

I agreed with her but I didn't want her to worry. "They're just sleep-deprived."

289

"True, but something troubles them and they are in disagreement about how to handle it."

"How do you know?"

"See how Pearl is using her hands to cut through the air. She obviously feels strongly about whatever they are discussing since she's underlining her words with her gestures. It's clear that Magni doesn't like what she's saying because he's exhibiting eye-blocking behavior."

"Eye-blocking behavior?"

"Yes, when we're exposed to something that we don't like, it's normal to close or rub our eyes, to look down or to the side.

"You're reading their body language, aren't you?"

"I am. Did you know that females are believed to be three to five times better at reading body language than men? Traditionally, women needed the skill in order to read babies that had no verbal language."

"They're calling for reinforcement," I said to prove that I could read body language too. Not that it was difficult, since Magni used his wristband to send a message and waved at Finn to come over.

Shelly and I tried not to make it too obvious that we were following the situation closely when Finn, Boulder, and Hunter all joined the four others by the drone.

"I get that Boulder and Finn have been called in since they've always been the advisers of Lord Khan, but why Hunter?" The minute I said it Shelly and I looked at each other.

"Solo." Her eyes widened. "This has to be about Solo."

When Laura looked over at us, we turned our faces away.

"Pretend that we're talking about something unrelated and laugh," Shelly instructed me.

I gave a small laugh that made her arch an eyebrow. "I'm funnier than that."

"Just keep your back to them and I'll look over your shoulder."

"What's happening?"

"Lord Khan is speaking to Hunter."

"And?"

"And nothing. I can't see his face."

"Did he stiffen, lower his shoulders, angle his head, or maybe form his hands into fists? Look for signs."

"How about you look and I keep my back to them?"

Pretending to be annoyed by the sun, Shelly swapped places with me.

"What do you see?" I asked.

"They are discussing. Hunter is agitated. He's moving his feet, shifting his balance; now he's pointing at Magni. This has to be about Solo."

"Fuck, you know what I just thought of?"

"What?"

"Yesterday, Boulder and Finn told me that the reason Lord Khan and Magni weren't here was because an Nman had murdered his wife."

Shelly gasped out loud. "No!"

"Yes. I don't know who he was or the motive for doing so, but why would they come straight here except to warn Hunter that Willow might be in danger again?"

"You think Solo is the murderer?"

Squinting my eyes, I wrinkled my nose up. "What else would it be?"

"But Solo was always so protective of women, remember?"

"He was also jealous and possessive."

"All you Nmen are. I refuse to believe that Solomon would do something like that."

"That doesn't change the fact that a woman is dead and her husband was the one who killed her."

I didn't like the strange look that Shelly was giving me. "You don't think I could do that, do you?"

291

"No, of course not."

"Good, for a second you had me worried. Killing your wife isn't normal behavior, you know."

"I wish I could read lips or get close enough to hear what they're saying," she mumbled.

"Me too."

"Lord Khan has his hand on Hunter's shoulder. He's leaning in and speaking with a serious expression on his face. Hunter has his arms crossed; he does not like what he's being told."

"What is he being told?" I asked.

"That's the mystery, isn't it?"

"Okay, quick, laugh. They're breaking up the meeting and Hunter is coming this way. He's looking pissed."

I didn't laugh, but I did follow Hunter into the woods.

From the way he was stomping and moving fast, his mood was easy to read. When I stepped on a branch that broke and made a loud sound, Hunter turned to see who was following him.

"What do you want?"

"Hunter, what's going on? They told you something about Solo, didn't they?"

"Yeah."

"I know I was drunk last night, but I still remember what you told me about Willow and Solo. You can trust me. If Willow is in danger we can leave now."

Hunter waited for me to catch up to him before he spoke. "They came to warn me that Solo might show up."

"Here?"

"Yes, he was invited so he has every right to participate."

"Not if he killed his wife."

"What?" Hunter's face twisted into a big question mark. "What the fuck are you talking about?"

"Remember yesterday when they told us about that domestic violence case where the man killed his wife?"

292

"Yeah?"

"They came straight from that to warn you, so Shelly and I figured that maybe Solo was the husband."

"That's ridiculous."

"He's not the husband?"

"No!" Hunter threw his hands up in the air. "Solo is on the Doom Squad."

"No way." The Domestic Violence Team, also known as the Doom Squad, was a specialized unit under Magni who investigated claims and dealt with offenders. Lord Khan stuck to the century-old policy of zero tolerance for violence against women.

"Those guys are brutal. You sure Solo is part of that?"

"Magni said it himself."

"Then why were they warning you?"

"Because he talked about coming?"

"Here?"

"Where the fuck else would he be coming?"

"Did they say when?"

"Could be tonight or tomorrow. They don't know if he'll show at all."

"What are you going to do?"

Hunter threw his hands in the air. "I don't know."

"You'll need to talk to Willow about it. Let her decide if she wants to stay or go."

Leaning his head back, Hunter ran his hands through his hair. "I can't!"

"You have to."

"Pearl and Lord Khan want me to keep it to myself."

"Then why did they tell you?"

It was like Hunter couldn't come to rest. He squatted down, picked up a twig, and used it to poke at the ground with jerky stabs. "Because they don't want a repeat of the last fight we had. They asked me to promise not to attack Solo if he arrives."

"That's a big thing to ask."

293

Hunter got up and spat on the ground. "You wanna know the worst part?"

He didn't wait for me to answer.

"They said that they were trying to protect me. That my soccer career could be in danger if I got injured. Like I can't fucking fight. I'm a top athlete and a formidable fighter."

"They know that. All you students were selected because you each were the strongest and fiercest warrior for your age."

"That's right. I'm lethal and I'm not afraid of Solo. If he comes close to Willow, I'll take him out."

I took a step closer and placed my hand on Hunter's shoulder. "Look, you're angry and worried about Willow. I get it. But I have to agree with them. Getting into a physical fight with Solo won't be a good move. He was the best fighter back then and being an elite soldier probably hasn't slowed him down."

Hunter narrowed his eyes. "You don't think I could take him?"

"Hell, I don't think *I* could take him, Hunter."

Hunter spread out his arms. "What's that supposed to mean? I could take you any day of the week."

"Sure, if we were playing soccer."

"Fuck you."

I laughed. "Fuck yourself."

"Are you trying to make me fight you?"

"If that's what it takes to make you calm down,"

With his jaw tense and his nostrils flaring, Hunter scoffed. "I'm calm."

My lips twitched in a grin. "The calmest I've ever seen you."

His humor was still suppressed by anger but he threw away the twig he'd held onto and walked back toward the school. "If he hurts Willow, I'll kill him."

"Deal. I'll help you."

"I don't need no fucking help. I'm strong enough."

I followed him. "Can I at least help dig the hole?"

Hunter gave me a sideways glance. "That's too much work."

"Then let's throw him in the lake for the fishes to feed on."

Hunter kept walking.

"Or maybe it's better to leave his body to rot in the forest until the animals tear his flesh apart one piece at a time."

"That's right. If he hurts my sister the wolves can have him." Hunter looked straight ahead walking fast. "And the birds can feast on his fucking eyeballs."

"Hell yeah," I said, letting him vent.

We had only walked another ten steps when Hunter turned his head to me. "You realize we're talking about someone who used to be our friend?"

"You mean he was *your* friend. I was his teacher. Different thing. I'd leave all my students to rot in the forest if I could."

The edge of Hunter's lip lifted a bit. "You *talk* a big game."

"No, I'm serious. You don't know how annoying I thought you all were."

"Bullshit, you loved us."

With a grin I flung my arm around his shoulder. "I'll never admit to that, and if you start spreading nasty rumors about it, the birds will be feasting on your handsome eyes before this weekend is over."

CHAPTER 29
Party Games

Shelly

I was dying to have a real conversation with Marco, but we were being pulled in different directions all afternoon. Five of the Nmen had gone hunting for old time's sake and carried back a deer with pride.

Paysey, Nicki, and Rochelle broke into something close to hysteria, accusing the men of murder.

"You want to help us skin it?" Oscar asked with a grin.

"Oscar," Archer called out as if he was still his teacher. "What did I always tell you about teasing the girls?"

Oscar gave a crooked grin. "They're not girls anymore."

"I know, but that doesn't change anything. If you're going to be a smartass, be sure you're smart because otherwise you're just an ass."

"You got to admit it's a fucking good catch. The steaks are going to be juicy and..."

Kya, who came to stand next to Archer, stopped Oscar. "You've had your fun upsetting the women, now take that deer away from here."

"We were going to eat it for dinner."

"Fine, but the rules haven't changed. Take it to the butcher's house and fill up the fridge with what you don't need for tonight."

My sister shot the men a disgusted look. "I don't understand how you can live with yourself. You just killed an innocent being that had feelings and you're laughing about it."

"Rochelle, that's not necessary." Kya faced her. "The cultural differences between our countries won't magically disappear in only ten years. You don't need to understand or condone their customs, but you do need to tolerate them and not judge."

"But did you see the poor deer?"

"Yes, and like you I'm a vegan. I understand your opinion, but I'm asking you to remember that respect goes both ways."

As if Rochelle was back to being a student, she bowed her head. "Yes, Kya."

Kya pointed to Marco. "Would you mind keeping an eye on the men? Make sure they know what they're doing."

"Sure." Marco gave me a quick smile before he jogged after them.

It ruined my plan of getting him to myself. I wanted to tell him that my mother had agreed to release me from my promise not to marry him. After the episode with Boulder yesterday, I'd come to the conclusion that keeping Marco safe trumped my resistance to marriage.

Willow was teaching a group of women dance moves. "No, you have to turn left, sway your hips, and then let your hand fall down."

"Looking good, ladies," Tristan called out from his seat on a picnic table where he, Nero, Storm, and Nathan were playing a card game.

I sat down with them. "Who's winning?"

"We all are." Storm grinned. "We aren't really playing. We're enjoying the show."

"You like dancing?"

He smirked. "Sure. As long as it involves women moving their bodies in a sexy way." Leaning in a bit, he lowered his voice. "Personally, I prefer voluptuous women with big tits and a generous ass."

"Like my sister?" I asked since Rochelle was on the heavier side.

He looked over to Rochelle, who had joined the dance lesson. "I wouldn't mind if she packed on a bit more, but yes, she's got a significant effect on my midsection."

The other men laughed.

"Are you laughing at our dancing?" Rochelle called out to them with a pout.

"No, they're admiring your moves," I shouted back.

Raven came from the side with leaves in her hair. "Hey, I wanna dance too," she said and put down a bow and arrow. "Plato and I almost got a squirrel, but it was too quick."

The men playing cards looked up. "I've never met a squirrel too fast for my gun," Nathan said. "Why are you messing around with a bow and arrow? This is fucking 2447, not the medieval ages."

"You went hunting too?" Rochelle gave Raven a pointed look that Raven missed because she was pulling off her shirt, leaving her in only a tank top.

"Geez, it's hot," she said and wiped her forehead.

Willow waved her hand to Raven. "Come join us if you want."

"Hey, Raven," Nero grinned at her. "If it's so hot, why don't you slip out of the rest of your clothes?"

Raven gave him an exaggerated smile and with a sway in her hips, she moved closer to him. "Let's make a deal, Nero. If I slip out of my clothes, you'll slip into something more comfortable too?"

His smug smile grew and his voice deepened. "Now you're talking. What would you like me to slip into? You?"

Raven gave a mischievous grin. "Nah, I was thinking you could slip into something relaxing like... well, I don't know, maybe a coma."

The men exploded in laughter. "First she kicks your ass this morning and then she whips you again. When are you going to learn not to mess with Raven?"

Nero crossed his arms. "I had to let her win. She's a woman and women have sensitive feelings."

Raven had already moved away and was now following the directions of Willow when Mila came carrying a basket.

"Who wants to play some party games?"

"Sorry, Mila, we're in the middle of an intense card game – maybe later," Storm lied. "Why don't you join Willow's dance class? I'm sure they could use another fairy."

Mila's shoulder sank. "Oh, okay. I guess I can do that."

It wasn't until three hours later, when Lord Khan and Magni had returned, that Mila had her chance again.

"Now that we're all here and dinner is over, I thought it would be fun to play some of the party games that I've prepared for us," she said and looked around for support.

"I'll play." Nicki and a few other Motlander women volunteered.

"How about you?" she asked Hunter and it occurred to me that she was taking a big risk. If Hunter said yes, the other men would most likely go along. But if he said no, there was no chance they'd play.

"Hunter will play," Marco said and got up. "And so will I."

Like ten birds taking off from a branch at the same time, my stomach was all aflutter. This was one of the reasons I loved Marco. He was willing to ridicule himself to save the face of someone else. I'd seen him let boys win against him when they needed a confidence boost, and now he was seeing Mila's struggle to get the Nmen onboard with her party games and gallantly coming to her rescue.

299

Hunter rose from his seat so slowly that it looked like he was lifting not only himself but a heavy pile of internal resistance to party games as well.

"We need four men and four women for this game," Mila instructed.

"I'll help," I said, inspired by Marco's good deed.

"What about you, Dad, will you play?" Mila blinked her eyes at Magni, who stiffened.

"Ehh... I think this is a game for younger men." Magni pointed to Plato and Sultan, but they got busy drinking beer.

"Please, Dad."

He sighed. "Okay, I guess Boulder and I can do it."

Boulder, who was sitting next to Magni, slammed down his glass of beer. "Why do I have to suffer just because you can't say no to her?"

"Fuck you. If I'm doing it, you are too."

People were laughing as the two large warriors made their way to the center of the outside area where we had enjoyed dinner.

"Okay, so first of all I think we should give our eight volunteers a big hand," Mila began and we all clapped.

"This is an improv game and we'll have two teams competing. Each team will have two men and two women."

"Why not men versus women?" Storm shouted.

"Because this is a school of inclusion and we don't want to pit the genders against each other."

Storm grinned. "You're afraid of us crushing you."

"Bring it on," Raven said and lifted her chin.

Mila's eyes flickered to Pearl and Athena, who were both wise and kind Motlander women. "I guess we could vote on it."

The men and Raven all voted for a gender vs. gender game.

"You've got this," Finn called out to Hunter, Boulder, Magni, and Marco, who stood shoulder to shoulder with serious expressions on their faces. The stakes had been raised and there was now pressure to defend the male honor.

Raven convinced Paysey to switch with her because she couldn't pass up a chance to compete.

"Now which team wants to begin?" Mila asked and picked up two baskets.

"We do. We do." Raven raised her hand.

"Raven, why don't we let the men show us how this game is played?" I said knowing that we would have a strategic advantage if we could learn from their mistakes.

"Need us to go first, do you?" Boulder grinned.

"Who is the leader of your group?" Mila asked and four hands flew in the air.

"Right," Mila licked her lips. "Ehm... Dad, why don't you close your eyes and pick a note from the basket? It will be a few lines describing a situation that once happened here at the school. Your job is to remind the men in the audience without using words. If they can guess it you get five points."

"Hmm." Magni stuck his hand down and pulled out a note that he and the other men studied for a minute.

"Easy," Marco said with confidence.

"Yes, but to complicate it a bit, you have to pull props from this basket, and I have to warn you that they are random and may be a distraction from the story."

Marco pulled out a pair of sunglasses, Boulder a yellow cape, Hunter an apple, and Magni a pink scarf with purple stripes that he held between two fingers as if it was a soiled diaper. That alone had all the men screaming with laughter.

The women's team moved back to give them space and the four men began moving around, unsure how to portray the situation.

301

Putting on the sunglasses, Marco pulled off his shirt and pants until he was in his briefs. It didn't escape me that like me most of the women were smiling.

Taking the cape from Boulder, Marco placed it on the ground like a towel and lay down, a hand shielding his eyes from an imaginary sun.

"Beach... he's on the beach," someone yelled.

Marco jumped up again and nodded eagerly, pointing to Magni ,who rolled his eyes and put on the pink scarf. It looked funny, and the audience were in stitches.

"He's a woman," Raven called out.

"Stop it, you're helping them," I scolded her.

"Sorry, I just get so competitive."

Hunter was laughing at Magni too while eating the apple that was supposed to be a prop. When Marco pulled him over and tapped Hunter on his shoulders, he seemed to understand. Squatting down a little he spread his legs in a strong stance.

The audience were cheering when Marco climbed up and balanced on Hunter's shoulders. It was an impressive feat and a testament to Hunter's strength. With his six foot three, Marco was only a few inches shorter than Hunter.

"It's that time when Marco climbed the flag pole in the Motherlands," Raven whispered to me.

Looking hilarious with his pink scarf on, Commander Magni pretended to write something down and handed the imaginary note to Boulder. Marco did the same after jumping down to the ground again.

"It's the time we beat the girls in the Motherlands," Nero finally shouted.

"Yes!" Marco turned to the male audience. "What the fuck took you so long?"

Khan and Finn were smacking their hands on the table and crying with laughter. "Oh, we knew from the moment Marco stripped out of his clothes. But seeing you four up there was fucking priceless," Finn said in a voice broken up by laughter.

"Next time you and Khan can get up here and we'll laugh at you," Magni retorted.

Like most people, Tristan's shoulders were bobbing up and down with laughter too. "I didn't see Marco climb the flagpole ten years ago, but I'm so happy I saw this epic moment. At the next reunion in ten years we'll be up there portraying the time Mila had us playing party games, and she got Magni to dress up as a woman and Marco to climb on top of Hunter."

"Yeah, yeah, very funny." Magni walked over to put the pink scarf on Finn's head, and the doctor stood up and made a funny impression of being a woman smitten with him and sending him air kisses.

Once the laughter had died down enough for Mila to be heard she spoke up again. "It took the male audience three minutes to guess the situation. Let's see if the women can do it faster." Mila waved us women to the center.

Less than three minutes and a lot of laughter later, we had won with our theatrical production of the time Archer and Kya got married.

Competitive to the bone, Raven made a triumphant fist in the air.

"That's not fair," Hunter objected. "We would have won if our audience had known they had to guess it on time."

"Nope." Finn shook his head. "Seeing Magni with a pink scarf was more satisfying than beating the women in some silly party game."

Mila's face fell and he hurried to explain. "Not that your games aren't great. I mean I haven't laughed so much in a long time."

Khan stood up. "Thank you, Mila, for bringing us such entertainment. I would like to remind all the single

303

women here that just because you weren't born in the Northlands doesn't mean that you can't have a tournament and experience the rush of men fighting over you. We've had more than seven women from the Motherlands find a worthy husband that way."

"How about you, Rochelle, you're old enough to have a tournament – would you like me to fight for you?" Storm called out.

She looked a bit flustered but when she didn't answer he continued, "If I could win you and a million dollars, I'd risk my life in a heartbeat."

My eyes searched Marco's but he had his head down, staring at his glass of beer.

Khan swung his arm. "These are some of the finest men of the Northlands; why not embrace our culture and let them fight for you?"

Marco looked up just in time to see me perform the most impulsive and insane act of love when I lifted my arm to volunteer.

CHAPTER 30
No and Yes

Marco

I was all over Shelly so fast that she didn't have a chance to say a word. "No," I hissed.

"But..."

Aware of all the eyes on us, I spoke in a strained tone. "Can I talk to you alone?"

"Do you need a chaperone?" Khan asked Shelly.

Boulder stepped forward. "It's okay, Marco won't hurt her." He gave me a nod of understanding when I pulled Shelly with me. I didn't care how it looked. There was no way I was letting her do something as risky as volunteer for a tournament.

We walked away at a fast pace, heading for the wraparound deck up by the teachers' cabins where we could talk out of sight.

"What the hell was that about?" I asked in an incredulous tone, my hands shaking from shock that she'd do something that crazy.

Shelly swung her hands out. "I thought you'd be happy."

"Happy? Have you lost your mind?"

"No. Don't worry, it's a given that I'd pick you for my champion. I thought you'd be excited that I'm willing to marry you. And with the tournament you could get that million dollars you always dreamed of." She had that expression that told me she was convinced she was right, but this time we weren't discussing math or science. I was the expert on Northland traditions and I wasn't backing down.

305

"You don't understand, Shelly. Nmen have to raise a lot of money to participate in a tournament, not to mention train to be the best warriors. It's no fucking joke. There are so many holes in your plan."

She shrank into herself and looked down.

"Don't you get that you couldn't possibly be a candidate for a tournament when you're already pregnant and have a mate?"

She blinked her eyes but didn't speak.

"The moment you chose to sleep with me, I became yours and you became mine. Do you understand?"

"I didn't mean to make you angry. It's just that I know how much you long for that million dollars."

She wasn't listening to me, so I raised my voice and squeezed her arms to get through to her. "I don't give a shit about money at this point. I'm already richer than most men because I have the woman that I love."

"But then why are you always complaining about your lack of money?"

I stepped closer, my hands sliding down to lock around her waist. "If it was just me I could live in a cabin and be happy. The money is only important because I want a family and I want to provide well for that family."

"You should know me well enough to understand that money never interested me in the first place."

"That's because you've never lacked anything."

"That's the Motlander way. We may not live in mansions but we have enough."

I rested my forehead against hers, my heart finally calming down. "Babe, you can't do impulsive shit like that. When you raised your hand, I aged five years in ten seconds. We're a team now, a family. Why don't you get that?"

Shelly lifted her hand to cup my cheek. "I'm sorry. I shouldn't have done it."

"Here, feel how my heart is racing." I placed her hand on my chest.

"Sorry," she repeated and bit her lip. "Maybe now isn't the best time, but I got a call from Charlie and I wanted to talk to you about it."

"Charlie, the owner of Advanced Technologies?" I didn't like the serious expression on her face.

"He's been trying to get me to work on a project down south. It sounds intriguing and I really think I could make a difference."

The hair on the back on my neck stood up. "You're moving back to the Motherlands?"

"It's a sustainable farming project. Marco, it has enormous potential and will do so much good for the planet." She spoke fast. "Life is relaxed down there, with beaches where the water is warm all year round."

I let go of her, my throat tightening and my chest in physical pain. "Talk about mixed signals. Five minutes ago you were willing to let me fight for you in a tournament so we could marry and now you're planning to leave me."

Shelly lowered her brows. "Not leave you. When did I say that I wanted to leave you? I'm asking you if you want to come and live on a beach with me in the Motherlands."

"You want me to come with you?"

She planted both hands on her belly and tilted her head. "How else will we be a family?"

In a deep exhalation I released the anger and anxiety that had been building inside me, and crouched down.

"What's wrong? Couldn't you at least give it a chance? Think of the positives: you wouldn't have to work two jobs and you would finally have time to write that book you talked about."

I rose up to my full height again. "What about the robots you've been working on?"

"I've been dragging it out, but I could wrap it up within a month if you'd come with me."

"How long would we live in the Motherlands?"

"I don't know. How about we stay until we get tired of walking barefoot in the sand and wearing shorts all year?"

"You're not talking a few weeks or months, are you?"

"No, probably not."

"Wait – so we would have the baby there?"

Shelly interlaced our hands. "Yes, and you'll have all the time in the world to be a dad."

Images of lying in a hammock with my son or daughter taking a nap on my chest made me interested. "I'm not joining some family unit. It would still be you, me, and *our kids*, right?"

"Kids? You said that in the plural."

I squeezed her hands and moved nose to nose. "Because I'm hoping we'll have more than one."

"You're hoping we're having twins?"

Placing a soft kiss on her lips, I whispered, "I'm hoping you'll want to have more children with me after this one. I love you, Shelly, and I'm serious about wanting everything with you."

Shelly kissed me back when I intensified my lips' pressing against hers.

"I want nothing more than to go up there and ask Khan to wed us. If I had a million dollars, I'd pay it all for that moment of seeing their faces when they realize that we're a couple." My excitement was radiating from me and made her smile.

Without losing eye contact, I kneeled down in front of her. "Shelly Brainy Summers, I know I'm asking you to break a promise to your mom, but will you please, please, please, do me the honor of becoming my wife tonight?"

This wasn't the first time I'd asked her to marry me, but it was the first time I'd done it right; and after her impulsive plan to volunteer for a tournament, I knew she had to be open to marriage.

"I want to say yes." Shelly lowered herself to settle across from me, on her knees as well.

"But?"

"But I'm scared."

"Why?"

"I'm not going to be easy to live with. I'm quirky, impulsive, and people say I lack social filters."

"Shelly, you don't have to explain."

"And working is everything to me. I want my children to come along on adventures to different parts of the world and explore cultures and different ways of living."

I had a soft smile on my face. She wasn't saying no and that was a good sign. "We'll figure it out."

"I might be distracted sometimes."

"Then I'll pull you back to earth. I'm good at that."

"We can come back here and visit if you want, Marco, if you get tired of the heat or miss your friends."

"I can live in a cabin by the beach."

"It's not a cabin, it's a house."

"That'll work too."

"So you'll marry me then," Shelly asked. "Despite all the things that come with it."

"That's a big fucking yes." I stopped breathing, hope making my chest swell up. "Did you just say yes to my proposal?"

Shelly's pretty face softened and her eyes teared up. "Yes, Marco, I'll marry you." Her voice broke a little, and a rush of euphoria made me scream with joy.

"You mean it?"

"Yes."

Cupping her face with both hands, I stared deep into her eyes. "Right now? Can we do it tonight in front of everyone here?"

Shelly's sweet chuckle made me let go of her face. "Yes, Marco, we can marry tonight."

Ever since I was a boy my biggest goal had been to become one of the few Nmen to share his life with a woman and enjoy the rare privilege of fatherhood.

I held Shelly's hand and felt eight feet tall when we walked back to the others, my insides bursting with the news.

As soon as we joined the party the white noise of talk went silent.

"Is everything all right?" Khan asked and got up from his seat. "I got the impression Shelly was interested in a tournament."

"She's not," I said in a firm voice, loud enough for everyone to hear. "Shelly is only interested in marrying *me*."

Gasps and mumbling were heard and I let my eyes scan the group of men that I'd once taught. "Shelly is *mine*."

"Is this true?" Pearl stepped forward looking straight at Shelly, her eyes falling to our linked hands.

"Yes. Marco and I have been seeing each other for a while now. We're starting a family together."

A fist slammed down on a table and I looked over to see Nero stand up. "You lucky bastard, Marco. How did you swing that one? As I recall it, you two used to bicker all the time."

I gave a lopsided grin. "That gives hope for you and Raven, doesn't it?"

Raven wrinkled her nose up at Nero, who was looking at her. "Whatever you're thinking, stop! It's not going to happen in a million years. I'd rather sit in a tree for a year than kiss you."

"How about me? Would you kiss me?" Plato called out with a sparkle of humor in his eyes.

"Does that mean you'll be moving to the Northlands on a permanent basis, Shelly?" Khan asked.

"Not right now. Marco has agreed to move down south with me. There's a wonderful village by the sea where the water is warm all year round,"

"Not fair." Nero sat down again and several of the Nmen muttered about beaches with warm water being a fucking dream.

I couldn't hide the big smug grin on my face. I would be just as envious if I were them, but this was my time to win the big prize and Shelly was it.

"Lord Khan, Marco and I would like for you to perform the marriage ceremony tonight," Shelly said and squeezed my hand.

"Are you sure about this?" my sister Rochelle asked.

"Yes, I've thought a lot about it and Marco has asked me several times."

"You didn't have to tell them that," I whispered.

"I just meant that it's not a rash decision," she clarified for Rochelle.

"No, I can't imagine you doing anything without analyzing the situation," Khan said.

I stared at him. Had he forgotten how she almost volunteered for a tournament ten minutes ago? Why were people so blinded by Shelly's brain that they didn't see the spontaneous and adventurous woman she really was? His words made me cough. If only he knew how we'd met.

As if Pearl had read my thoughts, she tilted her head and asked. "You said that you've been seeing each other for months now. How did you reconnect? Was it random?"

"Ehhm, yes, you could say that."

Shelly elbowed me, and I got the warning.

"Wait a minute." Storm stood up. "Tristan brought Shelly to the drone race and you mistook her for a sex-bot." He exchanged a look with Hunter and Tristan. "Does that mean..."

311

Shelly interrupted him. "It's a long story. No need to talk about that now."

"I would like to hear it," Khan said but received a sharp look from Pearl that made him clear his throat. "But then again, who has time for long stories when we have a wedding to perform?"

"You can't do it right now," Mila objected. "At least let us find a white dress for Shelly and some flowers. A wedding should be magical. Maybe we could postpone it until tomorrow and have some flower girls and a cake."

I shifted my balance, not wanting to wait another second out of fear that tomorrow Shelly might have gotten cold feet.

"Do you want to wait?" I asked, my inner voice screaming, *Please say no*.

"Flower girls and a cake sounds wonderful, Mila," Shelly said and my heart sank. "But it's not necessary and I think we'd prefer to do it as informally as possible."

Mila lifted her hands. "But a wedding should be special. It's a memory for life."

"It *is* special. We are surrounded by all of you, and what is more magical than marrying here at the school where we first met? This is where I fell in love with Marco so many years ago."

I gave Shelly a thankful smile and wrapped my arm around her waist. "I agree. It's perfect this way."

Laura and Mila made sure everyone stood up and formed a half circle around Khan and us.

Standing shoulder to shoulder, they were all smiling as Khan began the ceremony.

"When Pearl first suggested a school of inclusion, I made sure we handpicked the brightest, and fiercest Nboys in the country. My hope was that one day it would lead to couples formed of you Nmen and Motlander women. For some reason, that hasn't happened, *yet*." Khan smiled.

312

"Maybe they should have handpicked the girls better," one of the Nmen mumbled and it caused dampened laughter that were quickly shushed by the others.

"What I didn't expect was for the mentors to fall in love, but Kya and Archer did and so far, it has resulted in three beautiful children." We all looked over to Kya and Archer, who stood glued together with soft smiles on their faces. "Tonight, I'm honored to have the two assistant mentors follow suit and form a strong bond of marriage. You have both done outstanding work since you left the school and I'm speaking from experience when I say that with the support of a loving spouse, there's nothing you can't do."

I was lost in Shelly's eyes when Khan asked her the question, "Shelly Summers, will you marry Marco Polo?"

Shelly's eyes shone bright when she answered, "Yes."

"And you Marco, will you take Shelly to be your wife?"

"There's nothing I want more." My voice was loud and bubbly from happiness and pride.

"Then I declare you husband and wife."

Applause and cheers surrounded us as I picked up Shelly and kissed my new wife for the first time.

"I love you."

"I love you too, Marco."

We were hugged and congratulated from every angle, and Rochelle laughed at me when I stiffened as she flung her arms around me.

"Marco, we're family now. You can hug me."

"You're not mad at me?"

"No, Shelly is an adult. She makes her own decisions."

"Your mom is going to be angry, though. She made Shelly promise not to marry me."

Rochelle waved a dismissive hand. "Don't worry about it. Shelly found a way to get our mom's approval before she married you."

"How? That's impossible; she only just agreed to marry me tonight."

"She spoke to our mom hours ago. Let's just say that she manipulated the truth a bit."

"It wouldn't be the first time," I said and wondered why she hadn't told me about her conversation with her mother. I couldn't be angry at Shelly, because whatever she had done, she'd done it for us.

Hunter picked me up from the ground and squeezed me in a bear hug. "Fuck, you're a lucky dog. I'll never understand how you managed to convince someone like Shelly to marry you, except you did say that for a genius she isn't very bright."

I laughed. "Love is blind, my friend."

"Oh, so we're friends now? I though you just tolerated me."

"That depends on if you're willing to find another place to sleep so Shelly and I can have the tent tonight."

Hunter smacked my shoulder. "I don't think so. You would keep us all awake and make us men hate our lives if we have to listen to you two fornicate all night. Boulder suggested that you sleep in the gym. He says you can be as loud as you want in there."

"Thank you. I need it. We haven't been together for the last two days and I'm dying."

Hunter lowered his brow in an *are-you-kidding-me* expression. "Yeah, two days sounds like a real test."

"Sorry, it's just that once you've been with a woman, it's kind of addictive."

"I know." A ghost of sadness flew over his face but was quickly replaced by a bright smile.

"It's time for the wedding dance." Mila was pushing at me from behind and before I knew it, Shelly and I were pressed together and music was playing.

"How do you dance to this kind of music?"

Shelly grinned up at me. "I have no idea. Maybe we can just sway from side to side."

"This is epic. Dancing with you and letting the whole world see that I'm your man."

"You weren't that interested in me when I had pimples and a monobrow."

"I was twenty and interested in women. You were a girl, Shelly."

"If only I could have told that young girl suffering from your lack of interest that ten years later she'd be dancing with you under the stars with a new life growing inside of her."

I kissed her on her nose. "If only I could have told that young man to be less of a jerk to the girl he would one day be obsessing about."

We kissed, smiled, and laughed as we moved our feet while still holding on to each other.

Leaning her head on my shoulder, Shelly sighed. "I never want this song to end."

"I do. Otherwise we can't get to the best part," I teased.

"What part is that?"

"Our wedding night, of course."

"I don't know, Marco, I'm kind of tired," Shelly gave a yawn. "Would you mind if we wait until we get home tomorrow night?"

Pulling back to look at her, I opened my mouth to convince her that there was no way we were spending our wedding night apart.

"I'm joking, Marco."

"Fuck, for a second I thought you meant it. I was about to go bang my head against the biggest tree in the woods."

Shelly beamed at me. "That would be a waste of time when you can bang me instead."

We laughed and I whispered in her ear. "You know what's good about weddings in the Northlands?" I asked, my breathing picking up from the images in my head.

315

"What?"

"No one expects the newlyweds to stay long."

CHAPTER 31
Sex at the Gym

Shelly

I woke up when the door to the gym closed and Marco came in wearing only his briefs.

"Where did you go?" I asked.

"I had to take a piss." He hurried back under the covers.

"Argh, your feet are like ice cubes."

He laughed and nuzzled his head against mine. "That's why I need you to warm them with yours. It's chilly outside and there's still dew on the grass."

"What time is it?"

"Around seven. The others are still sleeping."

"You smell of peppermint."

"It's the teeth cleaner, you want one?"

I held out my hand and Marco turned to search for his packet in his bag.

"I prefer cherry taste, but they are seasonal. Do you have any of those?"

Marco handed me the cleaner and wrinkled his nose up. "I'm not a fruity kind of guy. I once tried mango but that was just nasty."

I laughed. "You're weird."

"Good weird?"

I let my chin point to the trampoline in the corner. "The sex on that thing was good weird."

Marco's eyes lit up and he let his finger trail over my jaw. "It was, wasn't it?"

"Uh-huh, I liked the second round on the weight-lifting bench too."

Propping himself up on one elbow, Marco looked over. "Maybe we should get one of those for home – it has the perfect height for me to take you while I'm on my knees."

"Which of the times was your favorite?" I asked and splayed my hand over his chest.

"Do I have to pick?"

"Uh-huh."

"The third, I think." He twirled a lock of my hair lazily around his finger. "Making love right here and falling asleep knowing that we're married now."

Marco's soft curls were irresistible to me; I had a blissful smile on my face when I slid my hands through them.

"I'm going to be bald soon with the way you constantly tug at my hair."

"Sorry, I think it's my favorite part."

"Wow, that's harsh."

I laughed. "No, I love *you* of course, but you don't understand how many times I've watched you and longed to touch your hair.

"You did once, didn't you?" Marco's grin widened. "You sat behind me the night before you left school and when I caught you touching my hair you said there was a spider."

"There *was* a spider."

He tickled me. "Admit it, you needed an excuse to touch me."

"You can't prove that." I laughed because of his tickling me, remembering all too well how my hands had needed to know what those amazing curls felt like. I should have known then that I couldn't trust myself around Marco.

"I have no impulse control around you."

"I'm sure the psychologist in you can explain that."

I smiled. "It's not something I've studied. It would be hard to find people who are in love back in the Motherlands, but theoretically, the neurotransmitters norepinephrine and phenylethylamine lead to focused attention, and that…"

Marco shut me up by kissing me and whispered into my mouth, "I love how smart you are, but now isn't the time for a lecture on love. I'm more a hands-on type of learner."

For the fourth time since last night's wedding ceremony, Marco and I made love. We had always been adventurous in our sex life with our list of five things, and yesterday had been fun using the different items in the large gym. This time he was spooning me, lifting my right thigh and drawing fully out of me then thrusting deep up into my belly.

"Fuck, you feel so wet and slick," he whispered and bit my earlobe. "I love how beautiful you look in the morning light, your hair all messed up from me fucking you all night. Makes me think about all the plans I have for you and me in the future."

Instinctively, I arched my back, feeling each thrust and how Marco slid out and ground himself into my clit, delivering delicious tingles.

He groaned low close to my ear. I moaned in return, surrendering my body to him.

With our other three times of having sex within the last nine hours, Marco had no problem holding on, and for long minutes he kept thrusting deeper and deeper inside me, my orgasm slowly building.

"You're mine now." He rolled on top, weighing down on me, his elbows on either side of my head keeping me in place as a sign of dominance, pushing me closer and closer to the edge.

"Yees," I moaned and lost myself in the pleasure of his pounding against my cervix while my nails clutched at his shoulders in a symbolic way of saying that he was mine too.

"Tell me you like it," he demanded, changing the rhythm of his strokes.

"More, give me more," I begged and panted from the speed of my heartbeat. "That's it, yeees, Marco, harder, yees."

He took complete control of my body, his hands moving down to grab my behind to hold me in place while pushing harder, deeper, and faster in and out. When I screamed out my orgasm, Marco covered my mouth, and groaned out his own release.

We stayed connected like that, both of our cores throbbing from the intense lovemaking.

After a minute or two, Marco gave a sigh of contentment and rolled onto his back. "I really don't care where we live in the world as long as we do this every morning."

"I don't know if I'm up for that when my belly grows big or we have three kids who need our attention."

"How can you say that? Morning sex is rejuvenating."

Nuzzling my head up against him, I teased, "I can make you a copy of me with retractable teeth and adjustable breasts. Would you like that?"

Marco held me closer. "No, I want the real deal. I could never settle for a robot again."

We lay close for a few minutes until a knock on the door had us sitting up.

"Come in," Marco called out.

Storm popped his head in. "Are you up?"

"No. Why?"

His voice was vibrating with eagerness. "Because I don't think you want to miss this."

"What happened?" I asked. "Is it another party game of Mila's?"

"No, Solo just showed up and we can't find Willow.

CHAPTER 32
Solo

Marco

Shelly and I dressed in a hurry.

"Are you coming?" I asked, already halfway to the door while putting on my t-shirt.

"Hang on, I just need to put on shoes."

"Bring the shoes, you can put them on later." My voice was eager and I had my hands on the door handle.

"What did Storm mean when he said that they couldn't find Willow?"

"I don't know. Hurry up already."

Shelly swung her hair back and used her fingers to gather it in a ponytail.

"You look cute, now hurry."

Hand in hand we jogged to the main building and when we turned the corner I stopped in my tracks.

The place outside the school showed that there had been a party last night. Plates, bottles, and bowls were scattered around on top of the five large picnic tables. The chains of lights that made the outside area cozy at night were still lit.

Most people had to be still sleeping, since only a small handful were there. Next to Archer, Tristan, Nero, and Storm stood a giant of man.

"Oh, Mother Nature," Shelly exclaimed next to me and squeezed my hand.

I hadn't seen Solomon in ten years and blinked a few times to take him in. Ten years ago, his status as the oldest boy at school had made him the alpha among the boys, outranked only by us mentors.

"What the fuck did you eat?" I asked in awe and walked closer.

"Nice to see you too." Solomon lifted his chin in a nod.

"Yeah." I shook my head. "I'm sorry, but I didn't expect this."

"Hey, Solo." Shelly stepped closer too and looked tiny compared to him when she leaned her head back. "Is it a medical condition?"

With a quick glance down at Shelly's hand in mine, Solomon spoke in a polite voice. "You must be Marco's wife."

He didn't recognize her.

"It's Shelly Summers," Nero exclaimed. "Our old mentor, remember? She changed a lot too."

Solomon shook his head in disbelief. "Wow, you grew up fine."

"Yeah, yeah," Shelly waved a dismissive hand. "Now answer my question. Is it a medical condition?"

"What do you mean?"

"Your size. Is it hyperpituitarism?"

"No." Solomon shifted his weight and lowered his brows. "I'm just slightly taller than average, but it's not that bad."

"He says he only seven-foot-two, but I think he's taller," Tristan told us.

"It's probably because of all his muscles," Storm chimed in. "He looks freakishly large, doesn't he?"

"Stop talking about me like that."

None of us Nmen were small men, but we were all looking up at Solomon.

Tristan put a hand on his arm. "It's impressive, but if you were an inflatable I would suggest you stop blowing now." Tristan laughed. "I mean, fuck, Solo, it's crazy to see you again after all these years."

"Ten years, huh?" Solomon smiled.

322

"Enough time for your hair to grow out again," Nero teased and let his hands run over his own hair. "Remember that time when Archer cut your hair short?"

"Sure, one of my favorite memories." The sarcasm in Solo's voice was thick.

Taking a step back to appreciate the full size of him, I said, "I always knew that you would be tall, what with your height and strength back then, but this is... something."

"Is every part of you this large?" Shelly asked in a matter-of-fact tone that made all of us stare at her.

Tristan broke into a deep belly laugh. "Did you just ask Solo if he has a huge dick?"

Shelly looked unfazed and once again proved that situational awareness wasn't her strongest suit when she locked eyes with Solomon. "Well, do you?"

Solomon's eyebrows rose up and he looked to me for help. "What am I supposed to answer to that?"

I grinned and planted a kiss on Shelly's cheek. "You can't ask a man that question. At least not with me standing right here."

"Why not?" Shelly's eyes wandered over Tristan, Nero, Storm, and me. "Admit it. You're just as curious as I am."

"Absolutely." Tristan couldn't stop laughing. "I say we ask Solo to pull down his pants and let us see the beast for ourselves," he joked. "Otherwise we'll all be wondering forever."

Solo fired back. "It's better that you don't know than living your lives feeling inadequate."

The friendly banter continued with loud laughter. It woke up others who had been sleeping in tents nearby.

"What the hell, is that you, Solo?" William asked when he popped his head out of a tent. "I was going to beat up the ones making noise this early, but on second glance, I might skip that plan."

"No, come out and challenge Solo," Tristan encouraged William. "It would make for great morning entertainment for the rest of us."

"Shut up, Tristan. I have a nasty hangover." William yawned loudly and stretched his arms.

"Solo."

The sound of a female voice made us all turn our heads to the school building from where Mila came running. "You came. I'm so happy. That means we're all here." She reached out her hands to him but he didn't take them. Instead he took a small step back.

"Good to see you, Mila. You look as cute as you did when you were ten."

"Did you hear the good news?" She smiled up at him. "Marco and Shelly got married yesterday."

"Yesterday?" Solomon looked to us. "Congratulations. I'm sorry that I missed out on your wedding. Work has been intense these past weeks and I couldn't..." He trailed off, distracted by something behind us that made his eyes narrow and his stance grow more rigid with his shoulders squared.

I turned my head to see Hunter and Archer returning from a morning run. They were talking and it took a few seconds until Hunter spotted Solo and the rest of us. The second he did, he stopped and stared.

Putting his hand on Hunter's elbow, Archer said a few words and they walked toward us in a steady pace with tense expressions on their faces.

"You came," Archer said when they were closer. "I'll give you a hug later when I'm not as sweaty."

"I'll look forward to it." Solomon turned his head from Archer to Hunter. The tension between them was tangible.

The rest of us men exchanged glances, silently alerting each other that a fight was in the air and that we might need to intervene.

"What do you want?" Hunter's voice was low and cold.

"I'm here to celebrate, just like the rest of you."

With a sideways glance, Hunter looked to me. "Where's Willow?"

"I don't know."

"She's not in the dorm," Storm added. "Tristan and I looked but we couldn't find her."

Mila, who was following the meeting between Hunter and Solomon with a concerned expression on her face, spoke up. "I think Willow and Raven went to swim in the lake."

Solomon turned his head in the direction of the forest trail that led to the small lake. "I'm going to go and talk to her. It's time to clear the air between us."

Hunter stepped in his way. "There's nothing to clear. It's been years and she never talks about you. I doubt she remembers much about you."

Solomon folded his hands into fists but didn't respond.

"Me, on the other hand," Hunter said and tilted his head, "I remember *everything.*"

Solomon's jaw tightened. "Me too."

"I'll let Willow decide if she wants to talk to you. My guess is she'll want to leave the minute she hears that you're here."

Solomon looked down, his chest lifting and falling. "I can't force her."

"That's fucking right." Hunter stepped closer, his voice threatening. "If you as much as look at her the wrong way, I'll kill you."

The two men stared at each other – Hunter with protective rage that made his nostrils flare, Solomon with suppressed emotions that had to take a lot of discipline not to show.

"I'm not here to fight you," Solomon muttered like a warning, his skin drawn tight over his cheekbones, his eyes haunted.

"And I'm not here to kill you, but I will if you get too close to my sister." Hunter backed up four steps before turning his back on us and walking toward the lake. I had no doubt that he was heading to give Willow a heads-up that Solomon had arrived.

"He doesn't like you." Shelly spoke the obvious and it somehow lightened the heavy atmosphere.

"Fuck, thank you for pointing that out, Shelly. I did get some vibes but wasn't sure how to read them," Tristan said.

Punching Tristan on the shoulder, I warned him. "Don't mess with my wife."

Tristan held up both his palms.

"Are you two the only old people here?" Solomon asked Archer and me.

"Old? In what universe is thirty old?" I asked in a tone that sounded offended.

"A child would think that you're old," Shelly speculated. "I think."

Archer pointed to Solomon. "Just because you've grown up to be bigger than a mountain doesn't mean Marco and I can't still crush you."

Solo snorted and flashed his teeth in a smile that didn't reach his eyes. "Sure you could. Granted, I would have to be drunk or half asleep and both of you would have to come at me at the same time using heavy weapons and a small army."

"One thing that hasn't changed is your confidence and arrogance." Archer patted Solomon's shoulder. "You hungry?"

"Starving."

"Good, then let's make breakfast and you can update us on what you've been up to."

I gave Shelly a kiss and told her to relax while I helped make breakfast. "You could pack our things in case we need to leave with Willow and Hunter in a hurry," I whispered in her ear.

"Can I be on the breakfast team too?" Storm asked.

"You can set the table," Archer instructed him and turned to Mila. "Mila Vanilla, will you do me a favor?"

"Of course."

"Boulder should be on his way, but get the message to him, Finn, Magni, and Khan that Solomon has arrived. They are at the Gray Mansion with all the women to spend the morning with the kids."

"No problem. I'll tell them to bring some of the puppies. Pets always have a way of calming people down; maybe it'll help Hunter. He seemed a bit stressed out."

"Fine, just don't bring the crazy frizzy one you brought last time. That thing pissed on the carpet in the school room."

"Egypt is young. He can't help it."

Archer gave me a sideway glance when we left Mila. "Don't let her pressure you into adopting one of her puppies. Mila has a whole litter of troublemakers in her room at the mansion. It's rare to see her without animals by her side."

"Thank you for the heads-up."

Ten minutes later I was stirring a large pot of oatmeal, Storm was setting up the breakfast buffet in the dining room, while Archer and Solomon were working on getting fruit, bread, jam, and a variety of nuts and vegetables ready.

"What happened to the bacon or steaks?" Solomon asked with one hand holding the door to the fridge open. "It looks like a fucking greenhouse in here."

"Don't worry. There's a large fridge up at the butcher's house with all the meat." Archer gave an apologetic shrug. "Kya wanted it that way; when she was pregnant the smell of meat made her sick."

"So? She's not pregnant anymore, is she?"

"No. But we struck a compromise."

"Okay. She got meat out of the fridge, but what did you get?"

"I get four days with her alone in a cabin twice a year." Archer held up the knife he was cutting with. "Don't give me that look. I share her with our kids and the students every day. Four days alone with my woman is a big deal."

Tasting the oatmeal, I added a bit of salt. "I get that, but the butcher's house is a five minutes hike. Sounds like a pain in the wintertime."

"It's worth it."

Solomon walked to the door. "I'll go and get the meat then."

"Hey, wait up, I'll come with you. In case you run into Hunter."

Solomon turned. "Don't worry. I'm not going to hurt him."

"Not intentionally." I turned off the oatmeal and put on the lid. "But you're both hungry, which always makes things worse."

"Good point." Archer pushed Solomon back into the kitchen and called to Storm in the dining room. "Hey, Storm, fetch bacon, sausages, and some steaks in the butcher's house, will you?"

"I'm not some fucking errand boy," Storm protested but still went out the door.

"Tell me about you and Shelly," Solomon asked and went back to cutting a large cucumber. "How did you get her to marry you?"

"I knocked her up."

Solomon put the knife down, turned, and sat on the edge of the corner of the sink. "She let you have sex with her without being married?"

"Yes, in fact she was the one who initiated it the first time. Took me a while to convince her that marriage was the right thing to do."

"Fuck." Solomon looked from me to Archer and back again. "That's like something from an antique novel or something. A woman chasing a man."

"I wouldn't call it chasing exactly. I mean I didn't make it hard for her."

"Well, no, of course not, you're not an idiot."

"Right." I cleared my throat. "No, but seriously, it's not just that I'm flattered that a woman wants to be with me. I would never do the Matching Program or anything. It's because Shelly is *special*… like a whole different gender in herself."

"What the fuck are you saying?" Archer's eyes widened. "Does she lack her lady parts or what?"

"No of course not – I just told you she's pregnant." I laughed. "I meant that Shelly is somehow *more*."

"More what?"

"More than most people. Smarter, sharper, better… it's hard to explain."

Archer shook his head and laughed. "You're in love. It'll pass."

"You don't understand."

"Oh, I understand. I've been obsessed with Kya myself. Nothing that a healthy dose of time together can't cure."

I frowned.

"You're blinded by her and it's understandable. Hey, I still get flustered sometimes when Kya smiles at me with those eyes."

"What eyes?" Solomon asked.

"She has a certain expression in her eyes when she's horny."

"Whoa, whoa, I don't need to hear that about Kya." Solomon held up a hand. "She was my mentor."

"She's also a woman."

"I know that, but still."

"What are you gonna say to Willow?" The question had been burning on my tongue.

329

Solomon scratched his short beard. "Magni told me the best thing to do is apologize and ask for forgiveness."

"I'm surprised. I didn't think that man knew what the word meant."

"Magni knows what it means, he just hardly ever uses it."

"Willow might not want to talk to you."

"I don't blame her."

Archer stiffened and I followed his gaze out the window to Willow, who was walking between Raven and Hunter, a small towel wrapped around her body doing nothing to hide her long gorgeous brown legs or the straps from her bikini top. Her hair was wet and pulled away from her face, which looked serious.

"What is it?" Solomon came to the window and froze to the spot. I watched his mouth open and then close as his Adam's apple bobbed in his throat. He didn't verbalize a thought, but the pain in his eyes said it all. "I need to talk to her," he muttered.

"Now isn't the time." Archer stopped him with a firm hand to his shoulder. "Let Willow come to you. If you're lucky she'll wait until we've had breakfast."

"I don't sit around and wait for things to happen."

"This time you will. Trust me on this. I've been married for ten years and one thing I've learned is that there are two ways of arguing with a woman. She'll initiate the most arguments when she's hungry or cranky from her period, but those arguments are impossible to win because they're not about changing your mind in the first place. Then there are the other arguments which are more practical and takes place somewhere between dinner and bedtime when there are no kids around."

"And they work better?" Solomon asked.

Archer chuckled. "None of them work."

"But you said there were two ways of arguing with a woman. Now you're saying that neither of them works?"

330

"That's right. Don't expect to better a Motlander in an argument. They look sweet and polite, but I'm warning you: they're relentless and stubborn beyond anything you can imagine." He held up an index finger. "And they use dirty tricks."

"Like what?"

"Like asking you to agree on something they know you don't want to do at the one time your brain is malfunctioning."

Solomon shook his head. "You lost me."

"Just after sex. When you're high on endorphins and shit, she'll ask something that sounds like a minor thing compared to the bliss of having just orgasmed inside her and then the next day you'll see your male students participating in fucking *honesty sessions*."

"You didn't," I breathed with my eyes wide in shock.

"What's honesty sessions?" Solomon asked.

Archer looked down and his shoulders lifted in a heavy sigh. "It's a thing they use in the Motherlands to build a bond between the students and teachers. Something that Kya wanted from the beginning and we refused to engage in."

"How long has this been going on?" I asked in a blameful tone.

"For about a year."

"Christ, Archer. We said that we'd never do that."

"I still don't understand what an honesty session is."

Turning to Solomon, I explained. "Motlanders believe in strengthening children's ability to not only verbalize their feelings and emotions, but also to detect what's going on inside them to begin with. You know how they do all that meditation?"

"Yeah. I kind of like meditation."

"Kya had a different word for honesty sessions – she called them exploration sessions and we shielded you Nboys from it."

331

"Why? What was so dangerous about it? If it's just talking, I mean."

"You don't get it, do you? Have you looked at males from the Motherlands? They are indoctrinated to suppress their nature and be gentle and kind. We wanted you boys to run, fight, climb, swear, and be *real* Nmen. She wanted you to calm down, be safe, and dive deep to find your inner voice."

Archer lifted his hands. "I have to say, though, it's not been as bad as I thought it would be. There's less uncontrolled fighting now that the boys are better at communicating their feelings."

"Don't tell me they hug it out?" Solomon snorted.

Archer bit his lip. "Look, the point is that Motlanders have learned how to express their feelings since they were little and arguing with them is a sure way to lose a discussion. Take my advice and at least wait until Willow and you have eaten. People who are hungry get unreasonable in arguments."

Solomon kept his eyes on Willow, who was close to the school building now. "But I just want to have it over with."

"Bullshit, Solo. You want her to forgive you, so be patient and let her come to you."

"I don't think I can do that. It's not in my nature to be patie..."

Solomon stopped talking when the kitchen door was flung open and Willow stood in the doorway with Raven and Hunter right behind her.

Willow was tall for a Motlander woman. She looked straight at Solomon with her green eyes darker than usual. For a long second they just stared at each other.

"I'm taking a shower and then we'll talk." It wasn't a question but an order, and Solomon blinked his eyes and parted his lips with a look of surprise.

"You should both eat first," Archer suggested.

Willow ignored him. Her gaze was burning with intensity and locked with Solomon's. As if a time bomb was ticking, I was waiting for an argument to explode with apologies, tears, loud voices, and accusations. Instead we all stood caught in a silent exhibition of raw emotions accompanied by loaded tension from unsaid things.

Solomon finally cleared his throat. "I'm ready to talk when you are."

"Meet me by the lake in twenty minutes."

Hunter pushed his way forward, grabbing Willow's arm. "You're not going anywhere with *him*."

Jerking her hand back, Willow ignored Hunter's comment, gave Solomon a last hard stare, and walked away.

"Be there," she said over her shoulder before the door to the shower room closed behind her.

"Hey, Raven," Archer called out.

"Yeah." Like Willow, Raven was wearing only a swimsuit. Her towel wasn't wrapped around her body but hung across her shoulder.

"Make sure Willow eats after the shower."

Raven's eyes fell on Solomon. "My guess is that she's lost her appetite."

"I don't care. Make sure she eats." Archer's order was clear, and then he turned to Solomon. "Don't even think about touching her or asking her to go anywhere with you. Do you understand?"

"Yes."

Hunter stepped closer. "This is not one of those gray area things. If you touch her you're dead. Magni gave me his word that you wouldn't touch her and that he'd let me kill you if you do."

Solomon's face tightened. "You really hate me, huh?"

"You stole my sister and *you fucking hurt her*." The four last words came out as a hiss, Hunter filling up the entire doorway and looking large and intimidating.

"I won't hurt her again." Solomon reached for an apple and a bun. "I'll go to the lake and wait for her. "

At first Hunter didn't move from the doorway.

"What are you going to do? Trap me in this kitchen forever?" Solomon waited for three seconds and all the time I held my breath hoping that he wouldn't physically push his way out. Hunter's behavior was an invitation to a fight.

Luckily Solomon didn't take the bait. "Would you mind moving so I can get out?" he asked in a calm voice.

Archer and I exchanged a glance, aware that Hunter had put both men in a predicament. If Hunter backed down and moved it would be a win for Solomon. They were both proud men, and we needed to intervene before Solomon had no other choice than to push Hunter out of the way.

"Hunter, can you put this on the breakfast buffet?" I asked and handed him a breadbasket.

It worked. With a last cold stare at Solomon, Hunter took the bread and moved to the side.

Solo stepped through the doorway and had only taken a few steps toward the exit of the school when Hunter's words made him stop cold.

"Willow is with Tristan now."

None of us saw Solomon's expression because he had his back to us, but from the way his shoulders tensed up it was clear that he'd understood.

"That's right, the two are in love, so keep your fucking distance."

If Solomon had seen the surprise on Archer's and Raven's faces, maybe he would have seen through Hunter's lie, but Solomon didn't turn around to confirm that he'd heard right. He was already moving away from the school in long strides.

"I didn't know Willow and Tristan were a couple," Archer said when it was just the two of us in the kitchen.

"They're not. I'm sure Tristan would love it, but Willow doesn't like him that way."

"Hunter is playing a dangerous game."

"I know, but Tristan volunteered to play the role."

"Brave fool." Archer sighed. "Do you think Willow will forgive Solo?" The question hung in the air as we watched the giant of a man duck his head under a branch hanging high over the path leading down to the lake.

"Even if she wanted to forgive Solo, she couldn't." I exhaled noisily. "We all know Hunter would never forgive her if she did."

CHAPTER 33
Love Declarations

Shelly

It was close to noon, and Marco and I were on the grass soaking up sunshine.

Others were sitting around in groups enjoying the last hours with their old friends before we would all split up and go back to our normal lives again.

"Marco, I haven't seen Hunter for a while. Do you know where he went?"

Marco was flat on his back, his eyes closed.

"I asked you a question."

His voice was low and drowsy when he answered, "Magni, Archer, and Hunter are keeping an eye on the situation by the lake."

"They're spying on Willow and Solomon?"

"Shh... keep your voice down. You didn't expect them to let Willow be unprotected, did you?"

"It's been hours. Do you think everything is all right?"

"I don't know. They must have a lot to talk about. Solo said that he was going to apologize to her, that's all I know."

I nuzzled my body into the crook of his shoulder and rested my head on his chest. "Willow told me about what happened before she left the school. It's sad, because there used to be so much love between them."

"Please." I snorted. "They were just kids."

"Don't say that. He was seventeen and she was fifteen when they ran away together."

"My point exactly. Fifteen is still a child, Shelly."

"I remember being fifteen and having strong feelings too. May I remind you that in this country women used to marry at the age of fifteen?"

Marco squeezed an eye open. "We fixed that. Now women have to be twenty-one."

"You're changing the subject. You might have been twenty when I was fifteen but I was way more mature than you."

"Ha! Not even close. I was an adult."

"Were you really? I remember you as being juvenile, with you and the boys competing about who could eat the most disgusting things, make the longest yellow line in the snow in the wintertime, and make the smelliest farts."

Marco laughed. "Okay, so I was a little immature."

"Solomon was more mature than you were. He knew he wanted Willow from the first moment he saw her and he was willing to risk paying the ultimate price for his love for her."

Marco shrugged. "Putting your life at stake is stupid."

"Says the man who has competed in at least three tournaments."

Marco rolled his eyes. "Don't make Solo sound like a fucking hero. He was nothing but a horny teenager."

"He loved Willow."

"Need I remind you that he's down by the lake asking for her forgiveness because he fucked up?"

I threw up my hands. "I'm just saying it's a shame it didn't work out between them. I thought they had something special together.

"Not every love story has a happy ending like ours."

I lifted my head to look at him. "How do you know ours has a happy ending? We've only been married for a day."

"Because I'm planning to make sure you never introduce yourself as a sex-bot to another man."

I gave a deep sigh. "When will you let that go?"

"Never. It's the best story ever and now that you're finally mine, I can even begin to laugh about it."

"As long as you're not laughing at me."

"Oh, I will." Rolling onto his side, Marco propped himself up on his elbow. "You say the most outrageous things, Shelly. Humor is key here."

I mirrored Marco's position, propping myself up too. "I'm pleased that I can be of entertainment to you."

A line formed between Marco's eyebrows and he looked down.

"What's wrong?"

Marco picked at the grass. "I used to think that was all I was to you: entertainment."

"And now you don't?"

"Not after you said that you loved me."

"Yeah, but I love mushroom risotto too."

Marco's eyes narrowed. "Did you just compare me to food?"

I smiled and kissed him again. "It's a good comparison when you think about it. Food is a source of survival while a husband isn't, so in a way I'm elevating you to a higher level of importance."

Marco raised his eyebrows. "Wow, so you're saying mushroom risotto has a higher ranking in your life than I do?"

"I couldn't eat you for survival." I grinned. "Well, I guess technically I could, but that would be disgusting."

"So, I'm your entertainment and your back-up plan in case you need food for survival, is that it?"

My laughter was bubbly as I cupped his face. "Isn't it wonderful to have a purpose in life?"

"It's offensive is what it is." Marco's lips were twitching with his own laugh. "You're supposed to be declaring your deep and eternal love for me and say romantic things like, I can't live without you."

"Oh, Marco, my truest and most eternal love," I said in an exaggerated way with my free arm swinging in the air. "You are the sun above my head, and the foundation under my feet. Without you my life wouldn't be worth living. I would wither and die out of boredom and starvation."

Marco pushed out his chest and flashed a big smile. "Go on. You're on to something."

"Marco, without you I would get a whole night's sleep and wake up rejuvenated and rested, but what woman needs that when she can have a large virile man keeping her up all night with endless orgasms and sweaty bodies?"

"You're welcome." He pulled me close and planted greedy kisses down my neck.

I laughed out loud and giggled while pushing him away. "Stop it, we're not alone."

"Not my problem. I have every right to kiss my wife."

"You're just trying to rub it in their faces."

"I might."

We smiled at each other, enjoying the connection between us.

"Do you think we should go down to the lake and see what's going on with Willow and Solo?"

"No. Archer already sent Mila down there with some lunch an hour ago."

I looked over to see Mila playing cards by a picnic table with three others. "I'll go ask Mila what she saw."

"You were born curious and it gets you in trouble." Marco pulled me down again. "Willow and Solo are grown-ups and unless he hurts her, it's none of our business what happens between them. I'm much more interested in what will happen between us and if there's a hammock in our new house by the beach."

"I'm sure we can figure something out."

"Good. I'm planning to write my book while we're there."

"What genre?"

339

"Sci-fi, I think. Something in the future where men and women are even in numbers and live as husbands and wives."

"Sounds like something from the past, not the future."

"Ah, but the past has a way of repeating itself. My book would be full of intrigues and drama." He lit up. "And it would have these futuristic details with space ships and aliens."

"Sounds very entertaining."

"Maybe there will be some love too." Marco angled his head. "Or at least some steamy sex scenes."

"Just don't write a book about a woman who pretends to be a sex-bot."

Marco's deep laughter attracted attention. "What's going on?" Tristan shouted to us and got up from the group he was sitting with.

"Shelly just came up with the best idea ever."

"You did? Is it something that's going to benefit the world?" Tristan asked her with excitement.

"No," she said. "It's nothing."

"She came up with the beginning to my new book. It's guaranteed to make people smile. Does that count as benefiting the world?"

Tristan gave a whistle. "You're going to write a book?"

"Yeah. I'll have time now that we're moving to the Motherlands. What else am I going to do all day by the beach?"

"What's the title."

"I don't know." Marco tapped his chin. "How about *Brainy and the Pole Climber*?"

Tristan wrinkled his nose. "Not very catchy, is it?"

Marco laughed. "Then we'll have to come up with something better."

"Is the book about you and Shelly?"

"Noooo... of course not. Just inspired by us, a little."

"I can't wait to read it."

340

"Tristan, please don't encourage him." Shelly gave me an exasperated glance. "Marco can find a thousand other more interesting things to write about. We're not that special."

"You could write a story about me," Tristan suggested. "It could be an action book with fast drones and women throwing themselves at me."

"See, that plot would fit right into the fiction category," I pointed out.

Tristan made a sound of mock offense. "I'll have you know that your sister has invited me to visit her, and Nicki asked if I wanted to stay in touch."

I chuckled. "Wow, I take it back then. The women are literally throwing themselves at you. How will you choose from the hordes?"

"I'm not sure. Nicki is quiet and your sister can be very bossy."

"It runs in the family," Marco teased.

There was no apology in my tone of voice. "We're strong women."

Marco took my hand and kissed the back of it. "Which is why you need a strong Nman."

"Hey, I'm an Nman too," Tristan exclaimed. "That doesn't mean I like being bossed around."

"You're a crossover, Tristan." Still holding my hand, Marco let his thumb trail back and forth over my knuckles. "You were fifteen before you discovered the Nman side of you. I'm afraid the damage was already done."

"What damage? I can deal with strong women; I grew up surrounded by them."

Marco looked at Tristan. "Yeah, and I'll bet you aren't attracted to a single one of them."

Tristan looked away and I followed his eyes to the lake trail, my heart sinking a bit when I verbalized what I'd suspected for a while. "You like Willow."

341

He squatted down, touching the grass. "It's hard not to."

I frowned. "But she doesn't like you that way – she said so herself, remember?"

"Maybe she will in time. Sometimes love can grow out of a strong friendship."

"It's not impossible," Marco agreed.

"Willow isn't like other Motlanders," Tristan argued. "You heard her. She wants to marry and have children. Do you know how rare that is?"

"That's because Solo filled her head with talk about it since she was twelve."

Tristan had a determined expression on his face. "I want to be that man for her."

"It's not enough that you want to be that man. She has to want it too."

"Why are you being so negative?" Tristan rose back up again.

"I'm not. I just don't want to see you get hurt. You're my friend."

"Don't worry about me."

"It's a little hard not to worry when you've gotten yourself entangled in the whole Willow and Solo drama. Did you see how big Solo has become?"

"How could I not? He was blocking the fucking sun." Tristan chewed on his lip.

"What if he decides to come after you? Did you stop to think about that?"

"Shelly, I already have a mom, I don't need you to fuss over me. Solo isn't some irrational lunatic who will come after me. I'm pretty sure he understands that he blew his chance with Willow seven years ago."

My eyes strayed in the direction of the lake again. "I wish we knew what was going on down there."

"Me too." Tristan walked off, throwing a last comment over his shoulder, "All I know is that there are more ways to win a woman than in a tournament."

"He's right about that." Marco looked after Tristan. "What did you think about Mila's suggestion to have these gatherings once a year?"

"I'd come. I've had fun and it would be a wonderful reminder of the most magical wedding I could have imagined."

Marco's smile was warm. "Really? You don't mind that it was informal?"

"Not at all."

"Do you think your family will be upset that they weren't there?"

"Rochelle was here." I trailed a finger along the bridge of Marco's nose. "I'm sure my mother prefers to pretend there was no wedding."

"You will tell her, though, right? I don't want it to be a secret."

"Oh." I laughed. "I don't think we could keep it a secret even if we wanted to. I bet there are already rumors spreading and soon the media will be asking for a comment. You're going to be in newspapers around the world as the Nman crazy enough to marry Shelly Summers."

"You mean lucky enough."

"Now you're just sucking up to me." I grinned and leaned down to nuzzle my nose against his. "Some people in the Motherlands will adore you like they did when you climbed that flagpole. Others won't like you no matter what you do."

"I don't care, Shelly. All I want is to be with you and for us to raise our kids together." His hand rested on my belly, his face soft with the crinkles at the corners of his eyes.

My hands played with his curls. "I say the wrong thing often, so I want to get this right." My eyes grew moist and

343

my voice a little wobbly. "Marco, I truly admire and respect you. You're funny, warm, generous, and patient with me, even when I'm insensitive, obstinate, and lecture you on things you don't care about. I've known for ten years that if I ever were to be with a man it would be you."

Marco stared at me with wonder. "I don't know what to say. That was a real declaration of love. I'm impressed."

I licked my lips and remained serious. "Maybe I'm not good with declarations of love, but I needed you to know how I feel."

Marco brushed his thumb across my lips and kissed me. "Shelly, I feel it. It's there in your kisses and your touch. When we make love you give me everything, and I feel so fucking blessed that you picked me."

Our hands intertwined and we sat up with Marco hugging me from behind.

It was the sudden silence around us that alerted me that something was happening.

"Shit," Marco whispered. "I guess that means they are done talking. He doesn't look too happy, does he?"

Solomon was walking fast, his head down, his stare fixed to the trail in front of him, and his hands folding and stretching, giving an impression of a heated internal dialogue.

A minute later Willow appeared from the woods with Hunter next to her. The two siblings walked without talking.

"Solomon," Mila ran after the giant man, who was aiming straight for his drone.

I was pushing up from the ground.

"Shelly, I mean it. Don't meddle," Marco warned.

"I just want to know how it went."

"It's obvious how it went, wouldn't you say?"

"Maybe they just need a mediator. Athena and Pearl are up by the school. I bet one of them could smooth things out."

"Shelly." Marco got up too. "We all want what's best for Willow and Solo, but maybe a friendship is too much to ask with their history and all."

"I just want to help."

"I know you do." Marco pulled me into a hug. "I think people are getting ready to leave anyway, so why don't we go ask Hunter if he and Willow are ready to fly home? I know I am."

CHAPTER 34
Four Months Later

Marco

Reading the words over in my head, I smiled. "I think I have a beginning for my book."

Shelly, who was tinkering with something inside the house, called out to me, "What did you say?"

Raising my voice for her to hear me better, I repeated, "I think I have the beginning for my book."

"That's great. What is it?"

"You want to hear it?"

My beautiful wife came to the doorway and leaned against the frame while unconsciously supporting her belly bump. "It's a good place to come up with creative ideas, isn't it?"

"The hammock?"

"Yeah, yesterday I got a brilliant idea. You know how we have brain implants here in the Motherlands?"

"Uh-huh."

"I think we could make one for animals as well. There has to be a way for us to enable them to communicate with us."

"You want to make animals talk?"

"Not all animals. I'd start with dogs."

I broke into easy laughter. "You're not serious, are you?"

"Why not? We're already using technology to help people with speech impairments. We could develop a system to give non-verbal beings like monkeys and dogs a voice." Shelly's eyes lit up. "Maybe even babies."

I held up a hand. "Remember that deal we struck that I'd tell you when an idea was more than just normal Shelly-crazy?"

"Yes."

"This is one of them. If you can make pets talk, fine. But you're not messing around with implants in babies' brains."

"But think about how practical it would be if a baby could speak."

"Practical? Did you ever wonder if it's a blessing that they can't speak? I doubt they'd have anything interesting to say except demanding things of you the whole day."

"I see your point. Then maybe not babies."

"Definitely not babies."

Shelly tapped her lips. "But dogs. I'll bet dogs would have something interesting to say."

"Like what? When is dinner ready? Can we go for a walk? Have you seen my ball? Stop blaming me for farting?" I grinned. "There, I just gave you the whole breakdown of a dog's world."

Shelly was biting the inside of her cheeks, her face in that thinking expression I'd come to know so well. "I'll think about it," she said and walked back into the house.

"Hey, Brainy, come back here," I called from my hammock. "I was going to read you the beginning of my story."

"That's right. Sorry, I got distracted." Shelly came back and this time she walked over to sit in the foot end of the hammock, her right foot still on the ground to keep her balanced.

Looking down at my text, I began to read aloud. "Of all the tall alien women, the one in the middle caught his interest first. She had humanoid features but her dark red skin color, yellow eyes, and green hair gave her an exotic look compared to the women he knew from Earth."

I looked to Shelly. "What do you think?"

"Ehm... why does she have red skin and yellow eyes?"

"Because she's an alien."

"You said she's tall. How tall is that?"

"Don't dissect what I wrote, just tell me what you think."

"I think it gave me questions more than answers."

"It was two lines. You're not supposed to get answers. You're supposed to understand that this is sci-fi and that there's a man and woman involved. Did you get that part?"

"Of course."

"And did you feel hooked? Like you wanted to hear more."

"Sure, like what planet is she from and how did the other aliens look if they weren't humanoid. Were any one of them dangerous in terms of bacteria unknown to humankind?"

I laughed. "I thought about giving her three breasts but maybe that would be a bit much."

Shelly raised her eyebrows and her tone turned sour. "Why not five while you're at it? She's *your* dream woman."

"She's *not*."

Shelly walked away and I used swearwords while getting myself untangled from the hammock to run after her. "Don't get jealous of a fictional alien. That's silly." Moving up on her from behind, I rested my head on her shoulders and placed both hands on her belly. "You didn't want me to write about you, so I have to come up with a fictional character who is just as hot."

"With three breasts?"

Shelly couldn't see my smile. "It's kind of cute that you get jealous."

"I'm not jealous, it's just hormones."

"I know. But it feels like jealousy so I'm going to enjoy it while it lasts."

"Well, it might last for a long time if that neighbor girl doesn't stop flirting with you."

"Ah, come on, she's just a teenager."

Shelly turned around in my arms and pointed a finger to my chest. "Do you think it's a coincidence that she sits on the beach every morning when you go swimming?"

"She's a sweet kid. That's all."

"She's nineteen and has a crush on you."

"I doubt it."

"And what about my doctor? Don't think I haven't noticed how she giggles every time we come in for a checkup."

I lowered my head to look into her eyes. "I don't care if a million women giggled when they were close to me. No one compares to you. I'm so fucking proud to be your husband."

Shelly looked down. "You mean that?"

"Yes, and I will tell you every day if you need me to. If you could feel what I feel when I see you walking around barefoot with your pregnant belly. It's pure bliss to me."

Her eyes widened and she grabbed both my shoulders. "Marco, that's brilliant."

"What is?"

"If I could feel what you feel..." Her thinking face was back on. "Maybe we don't need to put an implant in babies' brains. Wouldn't it be cool, though, if we could pick up on sensations that others were experiencing? Like during sex. I've always been curious to know what it feels like for you. You could feel what an orgasm is like for me and vice versa."

"What about your farming project?" I asked but Shelly broke free to pace the room, her finger twisting her lock of hair.

"You're not done with this project, are you?" I asked, a bit unnerved. "I like our beach life."

"What?" She blinked her eyes as if coming out of a trance.

"I don't want to move."

"Why would you move?"

"Just promise me we can stay here."

Shelly planted a distracted kiss on my lips. "We're staying for now. I just have to jot down some ideas for future projects. There are other nice beaches in the world."

"All right. Then I'll go back to writing my best-seller." I smiled as I walked back to my hammock feeling the warm sand between my toes, a sense of peace and tranquility filling me.

Later that night Shelly fell asleep early: exhausted from the pregnancy, the thousand thoughts in her head, and our intense lovemaking. I got up to get something to drink and stopped in her study, taking in the walls already plastered with big and small ideas. To the soundtrack of the waves outside, washing up on the beach in a slow steady rhythm, pure awe washed over me in that room. It was incredible that inside my small woman lived a giant imagination.

The thought of how my life had changed these past six months made my throat tighten and I swallowed hard, fighting the tears that formed in my eyes.

I didn't know a single Nman who lived a life as rich as mine. No one who had access to a beach with warm water or the chance to travel and experience different parts of the world. What did it matter that we traveled in community planes and drones or that we didn't own the house we lived in? We were free and happy.

Using the back of my hand, I brushed my happy tears away and got back into bed with the love of my life.

"Where did you go?" Shelly muttered, half asleep.

"There was an alien delegation outside who wanted to discuss my portrayal of them in the book."

Shelly yawned and curled up against me. "Did you tell them to come back tomorrow?"

"Uh-huh. They took it well."

"Good aliens."

"I know, right? Go to sleep, darling." I kissed her forehead. "I love you."

"I love you too. Most of the time."

Brushing her hair to the side, I whispered, "What do you mean 'most of the time'?"

Shelly didn't open her eyes, but she smiled a little. "When you aren't trying to get me to eat fish."

"It was *one* time."

She cracked an eye open. "You should know better."

"Okay, I won't offer to share my fish with you again." I squeezed her closer, my cheek to her hair.

"Good. Then I'll love you all the time," she whispered.

"All the time and forever?"

"Yes." Her eyes closed again, her breathing slow. She was falling asleep.

"Shelly Summers, I'll love you all the time and forever too."

The small smile on her lips told me she had heard my words, and it filled me with pride. My woman was happy, sated, and loved. I was sure of the fact that we were the luckiest people on earth and fell asleep with a last thought for my friends back home, hoping that, somehow, they would find their own happy endings.

This concludes Men of the North #6 – The Genius

A message from Elin Peer:
My goal is to entertain and reach as many readers as possible to put a smile on their faces. You can help me do that by leaving a review on Amazon.

ELIN PEER

MEN OF THE
N #7 ORTH

THE DANCER

The Dancer – Men of the North # 7

Sometimes the purest love can turn to the deepest hate.

I was twelve when I promised Solo that I would one day marry him. Maybe I would have if he hadn't gotten impatient and ruined everything that summer when I was fifteen. For the last seven years I've replaced the love I once felt for him with anger over his almost getting me killed.

Willow, a talented Motlander dancer, goes on tour in the Northlands. What should have been a chance for a new beginning brings her face to face with her traumatic past when Solo, a mountain of a man and the fiercest warrior of his generation, is put in charge of her safety against her will. If she can't get rid of him at least she can return the favor and make his job a nightmare too.

The Dancer is the 7th book in Elin Peer's wildly successful *Men of the North* series that has readers gushing over the Nmen, unusual plotlines, and the strong set of characters.

If you like large alpha men, strong women, humor, and a lot of depth, then this romantic sci-fi is for you.
Get it on Amazon today!

Check out my website elinpeer.com for an overview of my other books and make sure you sign up for my newsletter to be alerted when I release new books.

Want to connect with me? Great – I LOVE to hear from my readers.
Find me on facebook.com/AuthorElinPeer
Or connect with me on Goodreads, Amazon, Bookbub or simply send an email to elin@elinpeer.com.

ABOUT THE AUTHOR

Elin is curious by nature. She likes to explore and can tell you about riding elephants through the Asian jungle, watching the sunset in the Sahara Desert from the back of a camel, sailing down the Nile in Egypt, kayaking in Alaska, and flying over Greenland in helicopters.

She can also testify that the most interesting people aren't always kings, queens, presidents, and celebrities, because she has met many of them in person.

After traveling the world and living in different countries, Elin is currently residing outside Seattle in the US with her husband, daughters, and her black Labrador, Lucky, which follows her everywhere.

Elin is the kind of person you end up telling your darkest and deepest secrets to, even though you never intended to. Maybe that's where she gets her inspiration for her books. One thing is for sure: Elin is not afraid to provoke, shock, touch, and excite you when she writes about unwanted desire, forbidden passion, and all those damn emotions in between.

Want to connect with Elin? Great – she loves to hear from her readers.

Find her on Facebook: facebook.com/AuthorElinPeer
Or look her up on Goodreads, Amazon, Bookbub or simply go to www.elinpeer.com.

Made in the USA
Lexington, KY
27 June 2018